Praise for

THE DEFY THE STARS SERIES

★ "**Nuanced** philosophical discussions of religion, terrorism, and morality advise and direct the **high-stakes** action, informing the **beautiful**, realistic ending. Intelligent and thoughtful, a highly relevant far-off speculative adventure."

—*Kirkus Reviews* (starred review)

★ "**Poignant and profound**...a tale that examines the ethics of war and tackles questions of consciousness, love, and free will. Gray's characters are nuanced, her world-building is intelligent, and the book's conclusion **thrills and satisfies while defying expectations**."

—*Publishers Weekly* (starred review)

"Replete with rebels, bots, and battles, this **top-notch space adventure** features a well-developed plot and an unexpected, satisfying ending. This is a complex and well-told tale about loyalty, love, and the meaning of life. **A must-buy for sci-fi readers**." —*SLJ*

"*Defy the Stars* is a **unique** and masterful sci-fi space opera that will take readers across the galaxy on a fast-paced thrill ride....**Brilliantly done**." —*Romantic Times*

"With a love story that sweeps across the galaxy and a heart-racing high-action plot, *Defy the Stars* brilliantly explores what it means to be human. **This book shines like the stars.**"

—Beth Revis, *New York Times* bestselling author of the Across the Universe series

"**Startlingly original and achingly romantic,** Abel and Noemi's adventure will linger in my imagination—and my heart—for aeons. *Defy the Stars* is **nothing short of masterful.**"

—Kass Morgan, *New York Times* bestselling author of The 100 series

"The action **raises the stakes,** for individuals and entire worlds, and the romance satisfies without overwhelming, right up to a huge cliffhanger ending. **A fast, fun follow-up.**"

—*Kirkus Reviews*

"The story involves nearly **constant adventure** and suspense along with a complicated slow-burn romance that is sure to delight teen readers. **A thrilling science fiction adventure.**"

—*SLC*

"The **taut writing,** engaging characters, unique universe, **abundant plot twists,** and a cliff-hanger finale in this sequel will keep readers on the edge of their seats and wanting more....**A must-read.**"

—*SLJ*

DEFY
THE
FATES

DEFY THE FATES

CLAUDIA GRAY

L B

LITTLE, BROWN AND COMPANY

New York Boston

Little, Brown and Company
Hachette Book Group
1290 Avenue of the Americas, New York, NY 10104
Visit us at LBYR.com

First Edition: April 2019

Little, Brown and Company is a division of Hachette Book Group, Inc. The Little, Brown name and logo are trademarks of Hachette Book Group, Inc.

Library of Congress Cataloging-in-Publication Data
Names: Gray, Claudia, author.
Title: Defy the fates / Claudia Gray.
Description: First edition. | New York ; Boston : Little, Brown and Company, 2019. | Series: [Defy the stars ; 3] | Summary: "Abel, the most advanced robot in the galaxy, must save teenaged soldier Noemi by resurrecting her into a human-mech hybrid, a decision which will have consequences throughout the galaxy and may just turn the tide in the war between Genesis and Earth"—Provided by publisher.
Identifiers: LCCN 2018036970| ISBN 9780316440752 (hardcover) | ISBN 9780316440745 (library edition ebook) | ISBN 9780316440721 (ebook)
Subjects: | CYAC: Soldiers—Fiction. | Robots—Fiction. | Cyborgs—Fiction. | Interstellar travel—Fiction. | Orphans—Fiction. | Science fiction.
Classification: LCC PZ7.G77625 Dec 2019 | DDC [Fic]—dc23
LC record available at https://lccn.loc.gov/2018036970

ISBNs: 978-0-316-44075-2 (hardcover), 978-0-316-44072-1 (ebook)

Printed in the United States of America

LSC-C

10 9 8 7 6 5 4 3 2 1

For everyone who ever gave me concrit for my X-Files fanfic back in the day

1

DEAD SPACESHIPS DRIFT IN ZERO GRAVITY BY THE DOZEN, rudderless and dark. They range from tiny one-person vehicles to freighters, from sleek military starfighters to vibrantly painted Vagabond craft. Demolished mechs speckle the void around these ships—some with splintered metal jutting from their twisted limbs, others indistinguishable from human corpses. Some human bodies float in the chaos, too. Beyond it all shines the enormous silver ring of the Genesis Gate.

This is what the Battle of Genesis has left behind.

Most of the surviving ships have fled, but one of them— the *Persephone*—remains motionless in the middle of the fray. This is partly because its captain wants to avoid attracting attention. It's partly because he doesn't know what to do.

Abel stands alone on the bridge, attempting to order his thoughts. Normally he has no difficulty doing so; one of the advantages of being the galaxy's most advanced mech—an artificial, cybernetic intelligence—is the ability to think clearly and logically even at times of crisis.

But he's never known grief like this before. Never known this depth of fear. These emotions seem to have a paralyzing effect on the rational mind. He'll have to analyze later. For now he can only stare at the viewscreen, smell the blood drying on his coverall, and draw what conclusions are possible from the scene before him.

The Earth ships have all been destroyed or have retreated, Abel reasons. *The forces of planet Genesis, along with their new Vagabond allies from the Krall Consortium, have won a resounding victory. Earth's attempt at biological warfare has not only failed to defeat Genesis, but has also alienated people throughout the colony worlds of the Loop. The course of this war has been fundamentally changed. For the first time, Genesis has a real chance to win its independence.*

Noemi would be thrilled by her homeworld's triumph. Genesis has been fighting for more than thirty years, and all the people's efforts, all their prayers to the various deities they believe in, have done so little until now. Even the gods of mythology can't help a nation that's fallen so far behind on technology—especially not against an imperial planet that uses warrior mechs to do its fighting.

But even in the aftermath of this gargantuan battle, it's obvious to Abel that what turned the tide wasn't any epic clash of armed forces. The course of this war was changed by Noemi Vidal.

At only seventeen years old, Noemi was a veteran of dozens of space battles. She'd even volunteered for a suicide mission, willing to give her life for Genesis. However, before that mission could begin, she found the galaxy's most advanced mech—one loyal to his creator, the genius Earth cyberneticist Burton Mansfield—Abel himself.

When they met, he followed his programming, while she followed her military training. In other words, they tried to kill each other. But they forged a partnership, one that over time has become much more, a friendship that, at least for Abel, has ripened into love.

She even taught him to recognize Earth's tyranny over the colony worlds, which is why he can look at this battle scene—bloody and terrible though it is—with some satisfaction.

And how would it look to Noemi?

He can imagine her smile, bright enough to light up the entire bridge if not all of space surrounding them, shining more brilliantly than a supernova.

But Noemi Vidal is in sick bay, seriously injured, kept from death only by the chilly embrace of a cryosleep pod. He thinks he knows how to save her—though it will be risky for her, and even more dangerous for him. First he has to escape from this system, however, and so many variables are in play that he cannot yet sort them. Not with his mind blurred by the memory of Noemi lying wounded on the biobed in sick bay, almost dying, telling him good-bye—

A message crackles through the ship's comm signal: "Persephone, *this is Genesis Station Control.*" This is the antiquated space station Genesis has kept running near the farthest planet in their system, almost at the point of breakdown but still capable of scanning the area around the Gate. *"Respond or your ship will be apprehended and boarded."*

Abel snaps out of his fugue. The world makes sense again, and his first goal becomes clear: His ship *must not* be boarded.

He fundamentally distrusts the government of the planet Genesis, and as the station's suspicion proves, the feeling is entirely mutual. For a generation, they've fought a war against Earth's mechs and see them as nothing but killing machines. Briefly Abel believed Genesis's leaders capable of recognizing that he's different from other mechs, but he has since learned better.

To be fair, if they were to board his ship now, they *would* find a dead body on board. Specifically, the body of Darius Akide—a cyberneticist and the protégé of Abel's creator, Burton Mansfield, and later a member of Genesis's Elder Council. At least he was, until his death thirty-two minutes, four seconds ago. If Akide's body were found here, the

Genesis authorities would assume that Abel was the one who killed him. This assumption would be correct.

(Akide did try to kill Abel first, but he suspects the Genesis authorities won't accept that a machine has a right to self-defense.)

Even if he could talk his way out of that predicament, it would still take time he doesn't have to spare. Every second he's stuck in the Genesis system is one he can't spend working to save Noemi Vidal.

Again he envisions her as he last saw her a few moments ago, floating in the cryosleep chamber in front of him. Its opalescent fluid turned her blurry, pale, almost dreamlike. Her chin-length dark hair fanned out around her face like a halo; her exosuit drifted in shreds around her, torn edges singed dark by Akide's blaster. The terrible wound in her abdomen was mostly hidden by the cryosleep pod's silvery control panel, for which Abel was grateful.

No power in the six known worlds will keep him from saving Noemi's life. Genesis may have stopped Earth, but they won't stop Abel.

The *Persephone*'s proximity sentry begins to chirp. Multiple ships are moving through his general area, a mixture of Vagabond vessels and Genesis starfighters; the fleets are reassembling themselves post-battle, to take stock. At least one of those vessels must have been sent to pursue Abel by Genesis Station Control. Time to run or to fight.

If the planetary authorities already know Darius Akide boarded my ship, then they may have sent multiple starfighters to apprehend me, he reasons. The *Persephone* has no weapons as such, and what makeshift defenses it has couldn't stand up to starfighter attacks.

Abel looks up at the vast domed viewscreen dominating the darkened space of the bridge. Through the debris and ships surrounding him, he glimpses the Krall flagship, the *Katara*. It appears to be headed for one of Genesis's two moons, the one called Valhalla. This strikes him as a curious move, strategically speaking, unless Valhalla houses facilities he hasn't yet learned about. He'll have to inquire into that later.

For now, Abel has no time to jettison Akide's transport pod or his dead body, not without being observed. Therefore only one plan remains viable.

Run.

At cyborg speed, he moves to the helm and lays in a course that will take him to the Kismet Gate. His head throbs—a sensation he's never felt before, strange and unsettling, a reminder of his actions in the Battle of Genesis—but Abel remains focused. Engine ignition lights up the mag engines, creating the illusion of an enormous blazing torch in the dark of space. With one punch to the controls, the ship takes off at top speed.

Absolute top speed. *Overload.* Running the engines at

this level for more than a couple of hours would destroy them, and the ship, and everyone on board. But that's more than enough time to get away.

Or it should be. But one smaller craft is staying on him, pushing its engines even harder than Abel's pushing the *Persephone*. This doesn't seem like standard military procedure. But if his pursuer isn't sent by Genesis, who is it?

The speaker crackles, and a familiar voice says, *"Abel, slow down! What are you doing? Running away from being a war hero?"*

Virginia Redbird, scientist of Cray, is one of the precious few humans in the galaxy Abel considers a friend, and one of even fewer he would trust with Noemi's life. "Virginia, what are you doing here?" She doesn't lack courage, but she's no soldier.

"We got word that something mega weird was happening to the mechs in this fight, so I volunteered to come up here and take a good look—from a safe distance, of course, which wound up being a moot point because the fight was over before—"

"Please move away from the *Persephone* immediately," he replies. "It's important that you comply quickly." If Genesis comes after him, he doesn't want Virginia caught in the cross fire.

"Whoa. What's going on? Why aren't we headed back to Genesis for the victory parties?"

"I have to leave this system as soon as possible. You shouldn't come with me. It's safer for you here."

A pause follows. *"Okay, that sounds ominous and freaky as all get-out, but there's no way I'm letting you run off on your own. Because you're in trouble, aren't you?"*

He is. This would discourage most people from following him, but Virginia is drawn to trouble like iron filings to a magnet. Abel realizes it is possible to simultaneously feel admiration and chagrin.

"No reply means yes, huge trouble," Virginia says. *"There's no way I'm letting you go alone now!"*

Abel could attempt to evade her. However, Virginia Redbird is brilliant and resourceful. Coming up with a plan to elude her would take time and mental processing capacity he doesn't have to spare. "Then you need to board immediately."

"Are you going to tell me what the big rush is about?"

"I'll explain once you're aboard." She'll join him before he can rid his ship of Akide's body, so he'll have to confess to murdering a human. His programming should have prevented that in any circumstance other than saving another human's life—and Noemi had already been wounded. Virginia may well be unnerved by his ability to commit homicide. She might even turn against him.

The other voice breaks through comms again. *"Genesis Station Control to* Persephone, *you are moving away from the station instead of reporting—"*

"This is *Persephone*," Abel says. "We've taken post-battle damage. The danger of explosion is too great to risk station landing at present. I'm moving to a safer distance to complete repairs."

(A ship as small as his exploding in space is no risk to anyone, really, at any but the most immediate distances. However, human instinct makes them wary of explosions, regardless of actual danger. This instinct is one Abel doesn't share, and can therefore use.)

After a pause, the station says, "*You will complete repairs and approach the station within thirty minutes.*"

"I'm having trouble reading you," he lies smoothly. "Communications damaged. I'll contact you when I have a clear signal."

"*Confirmed.*" The station officer sounds suspicious. However, if they suspected that Akide's dead body was in a lab on Abel's ship, they'd be on their way to capture the *Persephone* already.

Which means Abel's actually going to make it out of here.

He attaches Virginia's transport craft via the tractor beam and pulls her in; it takes a long time to do so safely at these speeds, but he estimates she'll be aboard 6.21 minutes before they reach the Kismet Gate. Normally he'd go to the docking bay to welcome her, but instead he watches the sensors. He doesn't glance away even once. If anyone else pursues them—a command ship more aware of Akide's fate than the station is—

Nobody pursues. Genesis authorities must be disorganized in the aftermath of the fight, too much so to keep track of every one of the hundreds of unfamiliar ships soaring through their space. Abel has rarely been so grateful for human inefficiency.

After several minutes, as the space battle vanishes into the distant black, the proximity beacons inform him that Virginia's craft is being brought on board. He still doesn't look up, not until the doors slide open and Virginia Redbird strides onto the bridge.

She's an imposing figure—tall for a human female, with a lean and angular face. Her bright red exosuit is a match for the dyed streaks in her long brown hair. She's so visibly worried that Abel first thinks she has somehow learned about Noemi.

Instead, Virginia says, "Abel, what's with the transport pod in your docking bay? Who else is on board?"

She would've seen it as her craft was brought through the air lock. "No one else is aboard the *Persephone* at this time, besides yourself and Noemi."

"So where's Noemi?"

"In sick bay."

"I guess she's not too badly hurt, since she flew out there in my corsair, and the corsair doesn't look any worse than it did a day ago. Which is to say it looks terrible, because you two ran it ragged on Haven, but someday you will earn my forgiveness." Before Abel can correct her about Noemi's injuries, Virginia continues, "The one I'm worried about is you."

"Me?"

"Don't brush this off." She steps closer to him, studying his face intently. "What happened to those mechs during the battle—that had to be you. I don't see *how*, exactly, but absolutely no one else in the galaxy, and I am being literal about this—nobody else could even begin to shut them all down like that."

By *them* she means Earth's warrior mechs. Midway through the Battle of Genesis, they quit attacking the opposing forces and began attacking one another instead. Genesis hardly needed to fire a shot after that. As Virginia surmised, Abel was the one who reprogrammed the mechs. He feels as if he should be proud of this accomplishment— this unprecedented expansion of his abilities—but instead he hesitates. If he talks about what he did in the battle, he'll have to talk about the way it affected him.

But Virginia won't be put off for long. Abel admits, "I connected myself to the ship and used its comm waves to reprogram the mechs to attack one another." His head throbs again, echoing the pain he felt during the battle itself. Several minutes into his first ever headache, he's decided he doesn't like it. "It was...an overreach of my abilities, perhaps. But it was necessary."

Virginia's dark eyes widen. "You're bleeding."

Abel puts his hand to his face. The nosebleed he had during the battle has mostly stopped, but there's a slight damp warmth at the edge of his nostril. "It's nothing."

"Excuse me, but if your head *spurts blood*, it's definitely something! What exactly did you mean by 'overreach'?"

"You may have to help me determine that later, after we've gone through the Kismet Gate." It's approaching fast, already visible as a faint silvery speck far ahead.

"The Kismet Gate? The one with thousands of magnetic mines around it to make it absolutely impossible for anyone to fly through it and survive? *That* Kismet Gate?"

Abel simply replies, "Strap yourself in."

"Why are we leaving Genesis?" Virginia protests. "And when is Noemi going to get her butt down here? Does she need help in sick bay? None of this makes any sense!"

"Noemi is in cryosleep."

Nobody goes into cryosleep unless the alternative is death. Virginia knows this. Her face falls as she whispers, "Oh, God. What happened?"

"I'll explain everything," he promises, then wishes he hadn't. "After the minefield."

"Oh, crap." But she takes her seat and fastens the safety straps, preparing for the ride.

As the Kismet Gate opens before them, a wide silver ring shimmering brightly, Abel can't shake the thought that Noemi ought to be here. She should be by his side. He wants so badly to hear her voice, to see the way her eyes light up when they approach a Gate. To him, sometimes, Gates are no more than machines that generate artificial wormholes, allowing instantaneous travel to another part of the galaxy.

To Noemi, a Gate is always a miracle. The worlds are infinitely more beautiful through her eyes.

This time, he must go on without her.

2

PILOTING THROUGH A MAGNETIC MINEFIELD REQUIRES reflexes faster than any human possesses. Only a mech could do it—and most mechs fast enough for the work don't have the brainpower to handle the thousands upon thousands of split-second calculations necessary.

Which means Abel is probably the only individual in the galaxy capable of flying through the minefield on the other side of the Kismet Gate, a fact in which he usually takes pride.

At the moment, he has no time for vanity. His mind fills with velocities and trajectories, the track of each separate mine headed toward them. It seems to him that the blackness of space is crisscrossed with golden lines of light, most of them converging on the *Persephone*'s position. But he can change that position by the millisecond. Every swoop and spiral of their course dodges another mine and sends it colliding with another. Their destructions look like fireworks exploding. Abel has enough mental process free to take in the sight, and find it beautiful.

Virginia does not. For several seconds after they've cleared the minefield, she remains motionless at her station, eyes wide, face pale. Abel has begun to wonder if he should administer treatment for shock when she finally breathes a heavy sigh. "Okay. We're not dead. Congratulations, us."

He feels the congratulations should properly belong only to him, but it would be unseemly to point this out.

Still staring at the viewscreen, she says, "What sociopathic madman designed that? The head of the amusement park in hell?"

"The minefield was the work of a team of designers tasked with permanently sealing the Kismet Gate without destroying it, in order to deny Genesis the chance to interact with other colony worlds and perhaps foment wider rebellion—"

"I wasn't asking for History 101," Virginia says. "Or Basic Military Strategy. I meant, what kind of sadist would inflict that kind of terror on people?"

She's being facetious, which Abel has learned is one way Virginia handles stress. He replies, "Terror was surely not the intended result. Most humans would be killed within a fraction of a second after entering the minefield, leaving little time for fear."

Virginia gives him a dark look, but already her quick mind is moving on. "Okay. Enough of our near-death experience. What happened to Noemi?"

No answer but the truth will do.

• • •

Twelve point one three minutes later, he stands beside Virginia in sick bay. Noemi floats before them, lost in the all-encompassing oblivion of cryosleep. Virginia stares up at the pod, expressionless, hugging herself. Abel wonders whether she's upset about what happened to Noemi, or afraid of him.

He told Virginia the harder part first. She said nothing as she looked at Darius Akide's body in the lab. After that, Abel could only bring her here. If she must think of him as a murderer, he at least wants her to understand why.

Humans find silence awkward within a matter of seconds. Abel suffers no such insecurities, yet even he knows Virginia has gone too long without speaking. He ventures, "I haven't identified the error in my programming that allowed me to kill Akide. However, it may reassure you to know that I think only such a rare confluence of traumatic incidents could have affected me so radically. Under normal conditions, I don't believe myself to be dangerous."

"What the—Abel, *of course* you're not dangerous." Virginia hugs herself more tightly as she says it. "Somebody you love got killed—or nearly killed—right in front of your eyes. The person who shot her had just tried to kill *you*. I'm pretty sure a majority of humans would've done what you did, or at least tried to. And no jury would convict them for it."

"Because they are humans," he says. "A jury would judge me differently."

"Damn straight they would. They'd shut you down *fast*. Nobody can ever know about this. Not ever, ever, ever."

Virginia has taken his side. She's weighed his actions as she would a human's, allowing for fear, anger, and love—all the feelings mechs aren't supposed to possess. At any other time, Abel would've been both relieved and delighted. But as he gazes at Noemi, he can find only limited satisfaction. Knowing how slim a chance she has, and the price he may have to pay for that chance...he won't feel anything approaching relief or delight for a long time to come.

"Not to be negative," Virginia says, "but if I'm interpreting these readouts correctly—and maybe I'm not! Medicine isn't one of my things! But...it looks to me like the level of damage here is more than artificial organs can fix. Her nervous system seems to be—not functioning on its own. And nerves are the hardest thing to rebuild—"

"Your interpretation is correct." Abel puts one hand against the cool surface of the pod. It is an irrational impulse, but one he can't resist. "Noemi cannot be healed through conventional means. Yet the advent of organic mech technology suggests potential medical applications, which I believe can save her."

"Wait, what?" Virginia turns from the cryosleep pod to stare at Abel in bewilderment. She helped him uncover the research on organic mechs, so it's not the technology that has surprised her. It's the idea of using it on humans. "Can that even be done?"

"No one has done it yet," he admits, "but I've run two hundred and eighty-nine mental simulations in the past hour, and in two hundred and seventeen of them, Noemi could be restored to life."

"When did you run—oh, you ran the simulations in your huge mech brain while you were doing twelve other things at once," Virginia concludes. "Simulations are one thing, Abel. This is reality. Nobody's ever attempted human/cybernetic synthesis on this level. Not even on Cray, and we do experiments all day long! So there's literally nobody to help us—and this next-gen organic stuff isn't even commercially available yet—"

"Gillian Shearer, as the developer of organic tech, has a supply of the necessary materials. I believe she could help me use that technology to heal Noemi. Therefore I'm traveling back to Haven."

Virginia stares at him for so long that he wonders if

she failed to process his statement. Perhaps he should've treated her for shock after all. Before he can repeat his words, Virginia shakes her head in what appears to be disbelief. "Going *back* to Haven? To Gillian Shearer? The woman who's planning on *ripping out your consciousness* so she can give your body over to her sicko dad? Gillian thinks of you as nothing more than Burton Mansfield's ticket to immortality. If she ever gets her hands on you again, she'll steal your body and destroy your soul."

Abel replies, "That means I have something to bargain with."

"No, Abel. You can't. You can't trade yourself to Gillian for this. Noemi wouldn't want you to."

"Noemi has endangered herself for me in the past. She'd understand." Virginia won't, however, so he adds, "I'll only go through with the trade if absolutely necessary. It's possible I might be able to steal the technology from Gillian's lab instead." This seems unlikely in the extreme, but Abel sees no need to mention that.

He doesn't have to. Virginia already knows. "Is that supposed to sound reassuring? Because it doesn't."

Noemi's voice echoes in Abel's mind: *You're terrible at comforting people.* As she floats only centimeters in front of him, seemingly far away and lost even though he has a plan that should guarantee her survival and safety, he feels a wave of longing so powerful that it becomes a physical sensation—a warmth rushing through him, painful and yet somehow beautiful at the same time.

He'll have to ask Noemi how that can be possible. She'll know.

"Wait, wait." Virginia holds up her hands, as if she could physically hold him back from this decision. "Are you going to Haven to heal Noemi or...or to *repair* her?"

"Both," he says. "Noemi cannot survive without ceasing to be fully human. But this wouldn't be the same as taking her consciousness and putting it in a mech body. Instead, her own body would be altered. Transformed. She'd become a sort of hybrid, both mech and human."

Virginia's unease only deepens. "Are you sure she'd be okay with that? You know what Genesis teaches about mechs. You know that better than anyone."

Even after Abel helped save the people of Genesis from a deadly biological weapon, their Elder Council still judged him to be no more than a soulless automaton, unfit to remain on their world. "Noemi's different," he says. "She knows who and what I am. She was the first person to believe that I have a soul."

This is less persuasive than he expected it to be. "I don't know. Sometimes it's easier to accept differences in someone else than it is to accept them in yourself."

Abel finds this so illogical, even by human standards

of irrationality, that he sees no need to address it further. Noemi will awaken stronger. Faster. Better. More important is the simple fact that she *will* awaken. She'll live. Nothing else matters.

Virginia's eyes narrow with suspicion. "You're not usually hell-bent on doing something this batcrap loony. Are you sure you're thinking rationally? Or is this maybe Directive One at work?"

Directive One lies at the core of Abel's programming. It tells him to obey and protect his creator—Burton Mansfield, Gillian's father—above any other priority in the universe, including preserving his own life. That directive would command him to travel to Haven to hand himself over. Abel always believed Directive One held complete power over him, until the day Mansfield commanded him to kill Noemi.

Love is stronger than any programming.

"This isn't about Directive One," he says. "I only have one way to save Noemi. I won't fail her, even if the cost is my life."

Virginia looks stricken as she steps closer and puts one hand on his shoulder. "Listen. We'll think of something, okay? Something else. There has to be a way to—"

Proximity alarms wail yet again. Abel frowns. Nobody pursued them through the Genesis system to the Kismet Gate, or could've made it through the minefield if they had.

Nobody in the Kismet system would be looking for them. He changes his ship's ID codes regularly in order to avoid detection. Nor should they have run into a standard patrol. Kismet is a pleasure planet, a tropical getaway for the elite and a source of ill-paying, miserable jobs for everyone else. Neither group would have any reason to search the area near the Kismet Gate.

Virginia has come to the same conclusions. "We shouldn't have company out here in the boonies of space. That makes me nervous."

"Agreed." Abel crosses to the nearest console and brings up scanner readings. The screen fills with an image of nearby outer space that should be empty—

—and absolutely is not.

After 2.1 seconds, Virginia says, "Uh, Abel? Remember that broadcast we sent right before we traveled to the Genesis system?" She gestures at the screen, which shows numerous Vagabond vessels, Stronghold starfighters, and even the white hulks of Damocles ships. "I think we might've kinda…started a war."

3

THE PLANET KISMET IS OFTEN CALLED A PARADISE. HUMANS are given to extravagant exaggeration of the things they admire, but the first time Abel saw Kismet for himself, he knew that description was deserved. It hangs in space like a milky amethyst, promising lavender beaches and lilac skies. In a galaxy of increasing desperation, Kismet has long been the one oasis of beauty, peace, and ease.

No longer.

The pale violet planet itself is unchanged—but a large area of space, from within Kismet's orbit to the edge of this system, is patrolled by hundreds of Earth ships. There are so many ships that their electronic signals on the viewscreen look like luminous chains binding the planet tight. Abel switches to regular view and focuses his vision to greater and greater degrees of magnification until he can make out each individual craft.

Virginia does the human equivalent, squinting at the viewscreen. "Damocles ships. I see two."

"Three." Abel's scanned the far horizon already.

"How are there even Damocles ships there? How are they *anywhere*? I thought Earth threw every Damocles ship they had at the Battle of Genesis. Where, as you'll remember, we totally took them down. I mean, a couple of them escaped, but they limped away. There's no chance they were sent right back out to harass Kismet."

Abel swiftly adjusts the console screen magnification so Virginia can stop squinting. "We did considerable damage at the Battle of Genesis, but Earth must possess more Damocles vessels than we thought."

She huffs in exasperation. "I'm a mad scientist, so I get the appeal of unstoppable killer androids, but, you know, you can have too much of a good thing."

Abel ignores this, concentrating on the far more pressing matter of the Earth scout ship that has left its patrol formation and is now approaching their position. For 2.13 seconds, he considers evading it, but rejects the idea. Running away would only spark their suspicion. They can't afford to be suspicious.

They need to be *extremely boring*.

Virginia's distraction is so complete that she startles when a voice through the comms barks, "*No ships are authorized to travel through this area. Identify yourself.*" The tone is meant to rattle whoever hears it.

Abel is not easily rattled. "This is the free ship—*Charon*." The pause before giving his ship its latest pseudonym is fortunately not long enough for a human to notice. He reset the ship's internal codes, which will be sufficient to disguise them as a ship that's never visited Kismet before, thus avoiding any possible traps previously set by the late Burton Mansfield. "We're Vagabond traders. We came to the edge of this system some weeks ago, searching for asteroid metals and ores for mining."

"There are few asteroids in this area."

A brief vision of Humphrey Bogart in *Casablanca* flickers in Abel's mind as he answers, "I was misinformed."

"You're within proximity of the Kismet Gate."

Very quietly, Virginia murmurs, "Maybe Earth thinks Genesis might send someone through. Maybe that's why they're patrolling out here."

This seems unlikely. The minefield is impassable for humans, and Genesis refuses to use mechs. Kismet must be on security alert for other reasons. Either way, he must be careful.

To the comms he replies, "We thought a less traveled area might offer greater mining potential. Less likelihood that asteroids would already have been tapped for all valuable ores and minerals."

By now the suspicion in the scout pilot's voice is obvious. *"You want to explain that 'mining potential' for me?"*

Abel has one more weapon at his disposal, an ability he was programmed for but rarely speaks of: extreme attention to detail.

"It is true that the collective mass of the asteroids in this sector is between one-thirtieth and one-fortieth of Earth mass, much lower than the collective mass of the more commonly mined asteroid belts. However, these asteroids contain much higher than average levels of tungsten and magnetite. Let me pull up my charts." Abel doesn't need charts for this; he does, however, need the Kismet pilot to believe it's a human on the other end of this comm line. "Here it is—to be precise, this area shows signs of possessing seventy-one point four two three eight zero six percent more magnetite than would be found in the most commonly mined areas of the Kuiper Belt. Therefore, the potential haul from our current position is equal to or greater than it would be in any of the known belts. For instance, the Watchtower Belt in the Stronghold system has a collective mass of only one-third Earth mass, but has sixty-two point five one nine six six seven percent less tungsten than—"

"*Okay. Got it.*" The pilot's irritation is clear, even through the distortion of the speaker. "*Go about your business. Don't approach the Kismet Gate minefield, for your own safety; if you get damaged, nobody's coming to rescue you. Exploring through the system will be treated as hostile action.*"

"We're happy to comply. *Charon* out."

Abel snaps off the comms and looks over at Virginia, who shakes her head in disbelief. "You were practically holding up a huge glowing sign that says I AM A MECH. No human would ever pour out stats like that. Not even off a chart."

"As far as that pilot knows, no mech would either—at least not in a situation like this. There are no other mech captains of their own ships, none who live as free traders and would be in a position to have that conversation at all." Abel smiles—briefly, and not broadly, but it's the first he's managed since Noemi was injured. "Therefore, the pilot interpreted my response as that of a human. A pedantic, annoying human. The kind he would want to stop talking to as soon as possible."

Virginia laughs. "You're something else, Abel."

He's familiar with the colloquial phrase. It's complimentary in the vaguest possible way. But he can't help thinking of it literally. *I am "something else." Neither wholly mech nor wholly human. I am unique in the galaxy. I am alone.*

Soon, Noemi will be unique, too. But he intends to make sure she never feels alone.

Moving back to the ops station, Virginia studies the readings from Kismet in more depth; her eyes widen as she takes in the Damocles ships again. She rubs her arms, the kind of self-soothing gesture intelligent humans often use to filter out other stimuli while they concentrate. "This is mass military action. The Battle of Genesis set Earth off, didn't it? When we beat them, they realized they had a real fight on their hands."

"I think the stimulus came before the battle," Abel says. "I believe it began the moment Noemi spoke to the worlds."

• • •

Abel possesses eidetic memory. He perfectly recalls all the information and sensations he perceives, forever. As a student of cybernetics, among other sciences, Virginia knows this about him.

Yet she insists on replaying Noemi's message anyway, "to check." It's an emotional response, not a logical one, but he indulges it. He's found that attempts to make humans act rationally are often futile.

"*The truth about the Cobweb plague—both on Genesis and throughout the galaxy at large—has been kept from you.*" Noemi's voice echoes within the *Persephone* bridge. The audio recording is of the highest quality, and yet Abel could never be deceived by it. There is an emptiness there, a hollowness, that betrays Noemi's absence. This is an echo, no more.

"*Another Gate in Earth's solar system—a secret Gate, one that leads to the planet Haven, a habitable world that's been kept secret, too.... Find that Gate, and you'll know Earth's been lying to you. Find Haven, and you'll know why Earth created Cobweb in the first place."*

Virginia shuts off Noemi's recorded voice. "There's nothing about the other colony worlds of the Loop," she says. "Absolutely zero about Kismet. So why is Earth patrolling this place almost as hard as Genesis, i.e., the world Earth's actually at war with?"

"Think about what Noemi said. 'Find that Gate.' Almost no one else in the galaxy knows the location of the Haven Gate. Therefore Vagabonds and other travelers must be flooding every system."

Slowly Virginia nods. "While they're looking in the wrong places, they're getting frustrated. Which means they might combine forces. Make alliances. Figure out how to stand up against Earth. And maybe Kismet made trouble first."

"Exactly. There may be unrest on the other colony worlds of the Loop as well. That's why we broadcast the message to all the planets—in hopes some would rise up and join our alliance. It appears our plan was even more effective than we'd projected." For entire planets to rise against Earth—even planets as relatively pampered and privileged as Kismet—the levels of anger out there on the Loop must be incendiary. "Unfortunately, Earth had an effective counterstrategy of their own."

Shaking her head, Virginia mutters, "How are we supposed to counter *that*?"

"I cannot say."

Large-scale military strategy is beyond his purpose. With Noemi Vidal by his side, Abel can fight for Genesis and all the other colony planets. He can take up arms against Earth. With Noemi unconscious, endangered, suspended between life and death? He can only fight for her.

•　•　•

The military vessels aren't interested in one small ship flying to the Cray Gate, headed out of the Kismet system. So the *Persephone* makes good time and passes through without incident.

Virginia brings up the image of Cray on the viewscreen; its red-orange surface turns everything on the bridge faintly crimson. This world is not being patrolled like Kismet. Apparently Cray's privileged scientists have so far remained loyal to Earth.

(At the outskirts of the system, scans pick up a few Vagabond vessels searching for the Haven Gate, in vain. But they're far away from Cray itself, not a factor for either Earth or Abel to consider.)

"Nobody down there knows what I've done," Virginia murmurs. "I mean, Ludwig and Fon and the other Razers know about you and about Noemi and about the Cobweb plague—"

It was Virginia's Razer friends who realized the new, even deadlier form of the Cobweb virus had to have been engineered in the underground labs of Cray. That virus had been used as a bioweapon against Genesis, one that would've won the war for Earth—if Ludwig and Fon hadn't stolen the genetic information that allowed a cure to be developed. Abel wonders whether the elders of Genesis would express even a fraction of the gratitude the Razers deserve, or write them off as products of a corrupt system. Probably humans would have better luck.

"I helped put together Genesis's war fleet with the Vagabonds. I took part in battle," Virginia continues. "Well. I mean, mostly I watched the battle, but I played a big part in getting thousands of ships there! Nobody on Cray would ever believe it."

"Let's hope not," Abel says.

"Exactly. Someday I'm going back—someday soon— and I'd rather not do it as a war criminal, you know? Which I guess is technically what I am. But not after we overthrow Earth. Then I get to be a hero of the revolution." She grins with pride. "That has a nice ring to it, huh? 'Hero of the revolution.'"

"Certainly it's better than 'war criminal,'" Abel says as he inputs a course to the Stronghold Gate.

Virginia's smile dims when she looks down at her console.

"We're running the mag engines way beneath capacity. I get that we can't overload again yet, but we could move faster than this."

"That might attract more attention from the military, which I'd prefer to avoid. Besides, Noemi is stable in cryosleep. As long as this ship is safe, she is, too. Therefore my first responsibility is to protect the ship." Abel rises from his chair. "My second responsibility is to my friends, which is why I need you to return to Cray immediately."

She blinks at him, as though unable to process his words. "But you're headed to Haven! You've got to try to steal all this stuff from Gillian Shearer, or else you're going to get yourself killed—"

"There's a reasonably high probability of that. It's a risk I'm willing to take, for Noemi. But I'm not willing to put you at risk, too."

Virginia doesn't budge. "It's my choice to make."

"No. This is my ship. I decide who travels with it. And I won't be carrying you any farther than Cray."

She lifts her chin, using every centimeter of height she has over him. "How do you intend to make me leave? Throw me out an air lock?"

"Unnecessary—and, as exposure to deep space would be fatal to humans, counterproductive to my goal of protecting you. I would instead render you unconscious and put you aboard an orbital scanner I retrofitted as an emergency escape pod three months ago. By removing the sensory equipment and installing emergency air packs, I've made it capable of sustaining human life for approximately fifty-five hours. You could make it to Cray within"—Abel updates his calculations based on their current position— "nine point three hours. The nutrient bars and water supply inside will keep you nourished. I apologize for the primitive zero-G waste-processing unit, but I understand most humans get used to the vacuum effect, eventually."

"You'd *knock me out*? You would, wouldn't you?" Virginia's face flushes, and she balls her hands into fists. Is she going to try to knock him out first? Abel hopes she doesn't break her fingers in the process. Instead, she sputters, "You're about to shoot me into space, you—you— *overgrown toaster!*"

"Not if you'll take your corsair and leave freely. I'd greatly prefer that option. I suspect you would, too. The vacuum effect of a primitive waste-processing unit has been known to cause chafing on—"

"I get it, I get it." She slumps in defeat. "I know your specs as well as anybody, Abel. I'd have to be an idiot to try to fight you. If you keep acting like a big, heroic, self-sacrificing doofus, I'll leave the ship like you asked—but you won't think about it?"

"I've already run the calculation of your probable death on Haven six thousand four hundred and seventy-five times. No scenario offers you better than a thirty-two per-cent chance of survival."

A long pause follows. Virginia finally says, "No decimal points?"

"That one came out even."

"Come on. My chances have to be better than that."

"For most human passengers, they would be. However, you would insist on attempting to rescue me, Noemi, or both. These attempts would no doubt be intelligent but also doomed. Therefore your survival chances are very low. Regardless, I can't accept those odds, and you shouldn't either."

"You know me too well." She sighs. "Don't guess you're going to tell me the odds of your survival."

"No." They're much worse than Virginia's, but he has to do this. She doesn't. "Where we're going, you can't follow. Virginia, I hope we meet again, but if we don't, thank you for teaching me what friendship can be."

Her brown eyes well with tears. "Damn it, Abel, you're making me cry."

"Better here than in zero-G."

She makes a sound that is somehow both a sob and a laugh. He takes her arm and begins guiding her back down to the docking bay, and her corsair, and escape. No doubt she'll protest her expulsion at least one more time, but Abel now feels 88.21 percent certain he'll be able to make her leave, and is ready to administer unconsciousness via an injection if not. Either way, Virginia's headed to Cray.

Maybe he won't be able to restore Noemi's life. Maybe he'll lose his own. Virginia's the only one he knows he can save.

4

Twenty-one hours after Virginia's reluctant departure, the *Persephone* reaches the Haven Gate.

To Abel's relief, the gate remains relatively unguarded
so far. The few patrol vessels in the area are easily eluded,
and he slips through undetected.

Earth is still trying to hide the Gate, he muses. *Noemi's
message made the entire galaxy aware of Haven's existence.
Literal millions of people will be searching for the Gate Earth
tried so hard to keep secret. Putting a full military guard
around it would only draw attention to the area, making its
discovery more likely.*

Despite this attempt at concealment, Abel predicts the
Gate will be found, and soon. Haven provides one of the
few potential homes in the galaxy. It is nearly as large and
as potentially fertile as Genesis. Humans can survive there,
provided they've either survived the Cobweb plague—
a disease designed to bioengineer humans for this very

environment—or undergone a treatment protocol with a weakened form of the virus. Given the disastrous spread of Cobweb, millions if not billions of people are prepared for this new world.

More than that, they're desperate. Earth's climate has been unhealthy for generations and will soon no longer support human life. If the billions of people about to be displaced thought they might find a home on Genesis after winning the Liberty War, Earth's defeat in the last battle will have convinced them otherwise.

Other ships will follow, Abel thinks. *Haven won't stay hidden much longer.*

Flying into its frosty atmosphere, Abel again notes the pale cloudless sky, which is scalloped with the silvery crescents of some of the planet's fifteen moons. Forests of dark-blue conifers stand out against the endless blanket of snow. The only animal life he observes comes in the form of swirling clouds of marsupial bats. He's deduced that many other animals live here—these forms of plant life require insect fertilization, at minimum—but the ship's sensors don't pick them up in the immediate area.

What they do pick up is the Winter Castle.

It shines like a palace of crystal on the horizon. The structure is less a single building, more an enclosed town. Abel only observed it from a distance before, but now that the *Persephone* is drawing closer, he can fully appreciate both its beauty and its genius. Most human observers would think the tall, prismatic spires were merely lovely, but Abel recognizes the glitter of solar micro-panels. They must generate a tremendous amount of power, more than enough for the few hundred people who live there now. The passengers on the crashed *Osiris* hadn't made it as far as the Winter Castle when he was last here approximately two weeks earlier, but he detects flickers of light within windows, the distant hum of energy. The survivors have made that trek and are settling into their new home.

As he zooms in closer, he can detect greenery inside— arboretums and hydroponic gardens have been built. The plant life will both purify the atmosphere and provide fresh, healthy food. Only one set of doors is visible, but he spots many small hatches that could release mechs or ships to gather anything needed and bring it back to those inside.

It is a work of brilliance. Abel recognizes it as he would his own fingerprint. Both he and the Winter Castle can only have been designed by the same person: Burton Mansfield.

He glances toward the shadow on the horizon that marks the wreckage of the *Osiris*. That ship brought these settlers here, with Mansfield aboard—and with Noemi as Mansfield's prisoner. It, too, was a kind of artwork, beautiful and brilliant at once.

Now it is charred metal and broken tile. It is the grave for Mansfield's body.

Abel wonders if he, too, is about to be used up, burnt up. Whether he will become just the marker for a soul that used to exist.

• • •

He lands his ship in a small cavern approximately two kilometers from the Winter Castle. Purple crystals glint dully from the *Persephone's* landing lights as he settles it down. A scan of the surrounding geology suggests these crystals are amethysts, but this interests Abel less than the fact that sensors would have difficulty penetrating the cave walls and finding the *Persephone*. He's hidden his ship as well as he possibly can.

Of course he'll have to lead others here eventually. But by the time he returns, a bargain will have been struck. Noemi will be safe. The cavern must protect her until then.

He hesitates at the door, tempted to turn back and look at Noemi one more time. But he doesn't. It would be entirely irrational, and for the next few hours, he may do better listening to his machine programming rather than his human soul.

At his belt, he attaches a personal force field—the sort of thing normally worn with an exosuit for protection from exposure to deep space. His color vision tints gray— a natural side effect of the field. Such things are virtually never used without exosuits, because their energies would disrupt human brain waves. Abel's skull is made of stronger stuff. The field is nearly invisible, betrayed only by a faint golden glow along his skin.

Shielded only by this and his hyperwarm parka, Abel sets out toward the Winter Castle.

Gillian Shearer is almost certainly a person in authority among the humans currently living on Haven, he reasons as he trudges through the thick snow. *Most likely she is the principal authority—*

His thought stops. His movement stops.

Pain arcs through every millimeter of his body, so shocking that he almost can't process it. He topples sideways into the snow, utterly stiff. Most humans would be knocked unconscious, but Abel stays awake. Barely.

A stun weapon, he thinks, insofar as he can think. Force fields don't provide complete protection from those. Someone or, more likely, something is patrolling the area, and little time remains for him to escape.

He tries moving his hand. It twitches, nothing more. Still, it's a start. He's encouraged for the 18.11 seconds before he hears footsteps crunching in the snow.

When the Charlie mech leans over him, blaster in hand, Abel tries to speak but can't yet. All his hopes of bargaining with Gillian—of making his surrender mean something—are at risk. He can't do anything as the mech grasps Abel's arm in its hand.

Then the Charlie stumbles to the side. Just a step—no more—and immediately it appears to recover itself. The strangeness of seeing a clumsy mech would, at any other time, excite Abel's curiosity. Now he simply lies there as the Charlie lifts its wrist to its face and begins speaking into the small comm strapped to his glove: "The model sought by Dr. Shearer has been identified and apprehended."

Abel had hoped to negotiate as a free man. He must prepare to do so as a prisoner.

• • •

He is transported to Shearer's lab in an enormous white sack. This is unfortunate for two reasons. First, it gives him very little chance to work out the inner schematics of the Winter Castle.

Second, it's completely undignified. The second reason is far less important than the first, but he's keenly aware of it as he's dumped out on the floor of a room that's entirely, pristinely white.

"At last," says Gillian Shearer. "Model One A."

Abel manages to prop himself up and look at her. She's shorter than the average human female, but she radiates authority. Confidence. Power. Her brilliant red hair and blue eyes stand out sharply in this white-on-white laboratory, including the coverall she wears. Gillian is ready to get to work.

He knew her as a little girl. She had seemed to love him in those days. That time seems longer ago than it was.

Then she surprises him. "You came back to Haven of your own free will. You had no logical reason to do that, and multiple reasons not to. Did Directive One finally kick in?"

Gillian, just like her father, can't fully accept that Abel's core programming no longer controls him. He says, "No. I have a proposition to make."

The corner of her mouth twitches in a smile. "You're not in a position to declare terms."

"Don't be so sure." He points to the small box at his belt. This isn't much of a gambit, but it's all he's got.

Gillian's face falls as she recognizes the faint shimmer of the force field. "They didn't take that from you?"

"The mechs you sent after me can't think for themselves, as you must be aware. Even if they could, I've set the force field to deactivate only when a code is input. An incorrect code will result in a self-destruct—not tremendously powerful, as explosions go, but it would be sufficient to destroy me." Stiff from the electromagnetic "squeeze" of the field, Abel rises to his feet.

"You're having trouble moving?" Gillian regains some of her smugness. "Doesn't look like you can wear that field forever."

"I can." *With great effort,* he doesn't add. Abel needs to

keep the bargaining advantage. "Also, you should know that I've recently taken damage—possibly significant damage to key systems. It's the kind of damage unlikely to show up on a scan. The kind that might prevent you from achieving your goal."

"You could be bluffing about the damage," Gillian says. "But why come here if you legitimately thought you had nothing to bargain with?"

The rhetorical question is more for herself than for Abel. He continues, "I also want to give you a challenge. The chance to do something unique in the world of organic cybernetics. Something your father never even attempted."

She pauses for 1.5 seconds. Abel knows Gillian is loyal to her father, but he's studied her recent cybernetic work. She obviously wants to make breakthroughs of her own. "What would that be?"

"Noemi Vidal has been seriously injured. She needs more organ replacements than the human body will accept. No standard medical treatment can save her. However, if you were to use some of the organic technology you've developed—and you were to transplant it into Noemi's body while she's still alive—"

"You want to use cybernetic parts as med tech?" Gillian hasn't spent much of her life trying to heal human bodies; she'd rather make them obsolete. But the novelty of this idea obviously intrigues her. "How would that work?"

"I don't know any better than you do," Abel admits. "However, I would work alongside you to come up with the correct process."

"It's going to take days, weeks. It could even take months. My father shouldn't have to wait so long in limbo—"

"The alternative is waiting forever," he points out.

She folds her arms in front of her. "There's no guarantee of success. I want your word you'll surrender yourself to me at the end, regardless."

"You can't think much of your father's programming, if you think he would've made me foolish enough to take such a deal." Abel shakes his head. "You need incentive to succeed."

Gillian narrows her eyes. "You'll find it difficult to escape, you know. You're on my planet. In my castle."

"I appreciate a challenge. I hope you do as well."

After a long pause, she murmurs, "After modification on this scale, the patient would—well, would no longer be entirely human. It would be a hybrid. A true human-mech hybrid."

"You're interested," Abel says.

"Yes. And you understand the price."

He nods. This is something he's realized from the beginning.

She raises her head. "You'll shut off the force field. You'll surrender to me. And you will allow me to transfer my father's consciousness into your body—which is what you were made to do in the first place." The last words are spit at him, as though it were indecent of Abel to fight such a cruel fate.

He must lay out his conditions. "I'll do all this…upon Noemi Vidal's recovery to consciousness and her free departure from the planet Haven in my ship."

"She'll be an unprecedented leap forward in cybernetics," Gillian argues. "I should get the chance to study her. To analyze how a mech nervous system interacts with a mostly human body."

"I'm afraid you'll have to reserve that honor for your next test subject. Noemi leaves Haven, alive and well, or there's no deal."

White-faced, Gillian straightens. "My father deserves his chance to come back from the dead. He earned it the day he made you."

Yes, this is what he was made for. The reason he was born. Mansfield never saw Abel as anything but a potential vessel for his own mind, thoughts, and ambitions. The fact that Abel's own soul will be destroyed in the transfer… that never mattered much to Mansfield.

Now it doesn't matter to Abel either. Not if it saves Noemi.

● ● ●

The following fifteen days, twenty-one hours, and five minutes are filled with unique intellectual challenges, the sort of thing Abel would enjoy under other circumstances. But even science is no fun under this kind of pressure.

If he gets anything wrong, Noemi will die.

The cryosleep pod is brought inside like a glass coffin from a fairy tale, held high on mech shoulders, opalescent fluid swirling within. It is settled in the middle of the stark white lab, the center around which they all rotate. Noemi remains in the pod during the long days in which Abel and Gillian try to invent a new field of science on the spot.

"She won't be able to coordinate mech parts and human movement," Gillian says late one night, as they work outside the pod. "A human nervous system won't do it."

"You want to implant a cybernetic one?" Abel's unsure about this, though he sees the need as well as Gillian does. "Supplementing a human nervous system with a cybernetic one has never been done—not with clone parts, donors, ever."

"You want to leave her completely unable to function?" Gillian raises an eyebrow. "This is your option. If I didn't think it would work, I wouldn't offer it, would I?"

Remaining unspoken are the words *because I have to succeed to destroy you.*

It must be human, this desire to avoid the inevitable. But Abel cannot let Noemi continue to linger between life and death. "Let's design the nervous system."

In some ways, this process is deeply intimate: Abel

examines every nerve ending in Noemi's body, watches the slowly undulating patterns of her unconscious brain activity, traces the flow of her blood. But that intimacy makes what should be routine feel savage—like removing her pulpy, ruined liver from her open abdomen with his own hands, seeing his gloves become red and slippery from the gore. Or shearing her hair from her head, preparing to slice through her skull to unite her mech and human brains.

The odds of Noemi's survival improve as he and Gillian work, but they're never good enough for him. It seems impossible that Noemi will ever emerge whole again—that she could be the same again.

She won't be the same, he reminds himself. *But she'll still be Noemi.*

Why doesn't it feel like enough?

Maybe because he knows he won't be there with her.

Finally, there comes a point where every test has been run, every procedure performed. Abel and Gillian have managed to work side by side all these days without ever looking each other in the eye, but she does so at last as she says, "We have to take her off systems. See if she survives."

"I know," Abel says, but he doesn't move away from the modified pod they've built. Noemi lies still within it, lungs breathing only on cue. Will they continue once the machines are shut off?

Only one way to find out.

5

HEAT—INSIDE HER BODY, INSIDE HER SKIN, AS THOUGH
her skeleton had become a kind of gentle fire.

Light—not visible with her eyes shut, yet somehow sensed,
fully known.

Stillness—within her chest, where always before a heart
had beat.

Now, at the core of her, is . . . something else.

Noemi Vidal opens her eyes. The brilliance of the light
shining down on her blinds her to anything else, but she
knows she is not alone.

"Don't move," says a female voice. It's one Noemi's heard
before, though she can't place it.

Nor can she disobey the voice, because she's realizing she
couldn't move much if she wanted to. Her limbs and reflexes
don't seem to be paralyzed; it's more as if they were—
waiting. And somehow that feels right. It's as though this
motionlessness is as much a part of her as her skin.

Though some of her skin feels odd, too, sort of prickly…
her chest and belly, her breasts, her sides…a painless
throbbing in her head…

*Darius Akide. Abel laid flat, unconscious, endangered.
The blaster in Akide's hand. The terrible scorching pain—*

—I'm going to find Esther's star. Come to me there someday—

Noemi closes her eyes tightly, trying to ward off the nightmare. That has to be a nightmare, not memory, because if it
were a memory, Noemi couldn't be here. Couldn't be anywhere. In her bad dream, Akide betrayed both her and Abel.

Akide killed her.

Whatever strange situation she's in at the moment,
Noemi's absolutely sure this isn't heaven.

*I thought I read once that if you died in your dream, you
would wake up. But I'm not awake—not completely—why
can't I wake all the way up?*

Mist shivers through her. Sort of. *Mist* is the only
word Noemi has for the ethereal coldness that's unfurl-
ing beneath her skin, tendrils spreading out thinner and
finer within her as the sensation reaches her extremities.
It's contained within her skin, and yet somehow it feels
as though it contains her. Nausea clenches her belly, and
Noemi moans.

"She's hurting," says a male voice. Noemi knows that
one, too—knows it, loves it, understands he's trying to
protect her—

"It's within acceptable parameters." It's the same woman from before, even colder.

"Acceptable to you, perhaps. Not to me. We must—"

"Must what? Leave her as she is? That's impossible."

The voices bounce back and forth, back and forth, always falling silent one word before Noemi can recognize them.

The male voice says, "How much worse will this get?"

"How would I know? We're in uncharted territory, and there's no way out but through. Her vitals are strong; there's no reason not to finish bringing her online."

A new fire sparks into flame within Noemi. This one burns inside her head. It doesn't hurt. If anything, it feels good, like she's being warmed up where she hadn't even realized how cold she truly was. Her mind seems to sway toward that flame—

Strange thoughts, feelings, data pour into her brain, shattering all rational thought. There's no way to think, not when she has to *process.*

Elbow joint currently resting at one hundred twenty degrees, flesh 89 percent healed, blood flow optimized.

Liver functions successfully rerouted, healing around excised organ at 71 percent, kidneys shifting abdominal location as body adjusts to new parameters.

Artificial rib splice into living skeleton continuing.

"Processor functions normally," says the female voice.

"I wish I had better readings, for next time. A pity we had to rush this."

A memory takes shape in Noemi's buzzing brain: *A ship's hold filled with broken mech tanks and injured, sobbing people. A woman with damp red hair, crawling toward a child who is not a child. "I'm sorry we had to rush—it's going to be all right—"*

Gillian Shearer. The person speaking is Gillian Shearer, daughter of Burton Mansfield, as zealously loyal to him as any cult follower could be. How can Gillian be here, in the Genesis system?

Am I still in the Genesis system? What happened? Where am I? Noemi tries to remember, but her brain will show her nothing but that bad dream, over and over and over— Darius Akide firing his blaster—

The weird voice in Noemi's head reports, Memory accuracy verified.

No. No, it can't be—I'm dreaming the voice, too—

Gillian says, "Initial activations complete."

All the bright light around Noemi instantly switches to total darkness. Suddenly she can move—she knows this, on a level she can't define, even before she tries to act on it. The darkness splits along its seams, and Noemi figures out that she's in a pod, one that's opening around her like the petals of a flower in the sun. Instead of sunshine, though, what's revealed is a blindingly light room. A row of expressionless mechs stands at guard, near what must be a door. Machines beep and whirr, like scientific instruments.

Is this Shearer's lab? Noemi's terror deepens; the cold misty tendrils within her continue to spread. That lab ought to be half a galaxy away. *Am I on Haven? How is that possible?*

She doesn't know and doesn't care. The one thing she's sure of is that being under Gillian Shearer's control is very, very bad, and she has to get out of here, this second. Noemi sits up—

—or tries to. Her torso rises, but her balance is shot, or isn't even in existence, because she leans so far to the right that she nearly falls off the strange bed she's lying on. Jerking to the left makes it even worse, and this time she does fall. The floor is only about half a meter down, but pain flares through her rib cage and along the seams in her skin.

Seams?

As she lies there on the floor, useless and limp, she hears two sets of footsteps approach her, and Shearer speaks, her voice sharper and less muffled. "We just got done fixing her, and she's determined to break herself again already."

"She can't walk. She can't move. What have you done to her?"

It's the male voice again, and this time it, too, awakens a memory: *An upside-down theater on a crashed spacecraft.*

Red velvet and broken mosaics. Blue eyes looking at her as though she were a miracle. "Maybe I'm programming a new Directive One for myself."

Past and present finally connect. Hope bursts through the confusion and nausea like sunshine through clouds. Noemi manages to speak. *"Abel?"*

More gently he says, "I'm here."

He kneels next to her. Bright light shines behind him, obscuring his features, but she knows Abel's face by heart. He's conscious, free, totally functional—he's *alive*. In the dream, Akide had overpowered him and would surely have destroyed Abel. Thank God it was only a nightmare after all. The voice in her head was only part of the bad dream. Wasn't it? Noemi feels the impulse to sigh in relief, but her chest doesn't do it. Physically it feels...unnecessary.

What feels necessary is being with Abel. Remaining close to him. Making sure that anywhere she goes, he comes with her—

"All her nervous system functions are normal," Shearer continues. She steps close enough for Noemi to see her, that signal-flare-red hair pulled back in a tight bun. "If our projections prove accurate, motor control should adjust within the next day or so."

The hardness in Abel's expression when he looks up at Shearer is startling. Noemi's never seen him look like that. Never seen him *angry*. "You told me the cerebellum implant would coordinate motor reflexes with the new nervous system."

"It's calibrating as we speak. Give it time. This is unprecedented, on every level."

"What is she talking about? Is—is that Shearer?" Noemi manages to roll onto her back. Now that she looks directly up at Abel, she can see a faint shimmer along his skin. Is she hallucinating?

"You're disoriented," Abel says quietly. "We shouldn't get into all the details now."

She wants to protest that she's fine—that he should explain the confusing jumble of bad dreams and memories inside her head—but everything tilts sideways again, and she has to fight not to vomit.

"Do you remember being shot by Darius Akide?" Abel asks.

Noemi winces with both present and remembered pain. "Oh my God."

"I will take that as a yes," Abel says, with his usual precision. "Your injuries were too great to be healed by any medical means. My only chance to save you was through cybernetics."

"What?" Noemi tries again to sit up, and fails. "You're not making sense—I'm not awake yet—"

"The damage to your body went beyond what artificial organs alone could fix," he continues. His voice sounds so gentle, so kind, so *wrong* for the strange things he's saying. "Without central processing through a cybernetic nervous system, you couldn't have survived. So we gave you one."

Cybernetics inside her? "That's not possible."

"It is now," Abel replies.

"But—I'm *human*—"

"Not so much, anymore," says Shearer. Noemi's helpless bewilderment must be amusing for her, to judge by the cruel smile on her face. "You now contain a high percentage of mech components. To be exact, I've replaced your entire cardiopulmonary system and your liver, along with a few bones of your skeleton, and I've significantly enhanced your nervous system. You wouldn't have been able to coordinate all of that with only a human mind, so I added a processor to your brain. Don't worry about the hair, by the way. It should grow back even faster now, actually, between the regenerative fluid and more efficient processing of nutrients overall."

Why is she talking about nutrients? Who cares about my hair? Noemi wants to scream. All she can understand in her present confusion is that she's been altered—blood and bones and brain—and that the person responsible is Gillian Shearer, who would gladly see Noemi and Abel dead. Shearer would only have changed her into—

A monster, her brain supplies.

But as she looks at Abel's gentle, worried face, she finds

a tiny shred of hope. *He wouldn't let Shearer do anything terrible to me. He wouldn't let her transform me from human into... into something else.*

She has to stay with Abel. That's the only thing she knows.

"You're a hybrid now, Noemi," Shearer continues. "Half human, half mech. Well. Maybe three-quarters human, one-quarter mech?"

"Exact percentages are beside the point," Abel says.

He said percentages didn't matter? That can't be right. Maybe this is just the most vivid, awful nightmare of her life.

"Are you certain her functions will normalize?" he asks.

Shearer nods. "As certain as it's possible to be. She is, after all, the first of her kind. My innovation. My creation."

The thought of belonging to Shearer in any way is too grotesque to bear. Noemi looks up at Abel and says the only thing she knows for sure: "We have to get out of here." She tries to reach toward him and to her relief finds that she can—but he pulls back. That's when she recognizes the gold-tinged shimmer around Abel's body—a portable force field.

But that's meant to shield you from the cold vacuum of deep space. In-atmosphere, a field like that would deflect blasters and physical force, though it would also disorient anyone wearing it. Anyone human, anyway. Not Abel. *But why would he be wearing it in a laboratory?*

For protection.

Noemi looks over at Shearer again. They must be on

Haven. Abel came here—risked his life—to save her. Whatever the hell has been done to her, he was trying to save her.

Abel says, "I want to see Noemi fully functional before we complete the deal."

Shearer folds her arms, and her voice is like ice. "That's going to take days. This has gone on long enough."

"That wasn't our agreement," he says flatly. "Noemi must be safe and well."

Why would Gillian Shearer be willing to save me? It's not like she's our friend. She'd only help me if Abel had something she wanted, and there's nothing she wants more than...
Abel himself.

At last Noemi understands why they're on Haven. She knows the bargain Abel has made.

"No," she whispers. She shakes her head, or tries to, but it lolls to one side. Why does she have to be so weak and helpless? Why doesn't she have her own body? Why is any of this happening? "You can't do this, Abel. Come on— we'll get out of this, together—"

Neither he nor Shearer listens to her. Shearer says, "She *is* well. The rest is just healing and adjustment. As for safe—how do you suggest we arrange that?"

Abel never looks away from Shearer's face. "Permit me to load Noemi onto my ship and program a course for the Haven Gate. Then you allow me to monitor sensors until I can tell she's safely out of range."

Shearer purses her lips thoughtfully, then nods. "That's fair."

Noemi finds her full voice. "Abel, stop! Don't do this."

"It's already done." He looks back at her at last, his expression so tender, so sad, that tears prickle in her eyes. "I tried to die for you once before. You declined. This time, I must insist."

They're about to have the argument of all arguments. If he thought she was mad when she nearly jettisoned him out an air lock—

The cold silvery mist snakes through her body again, wreathing around her skull. It doesn't hurt, but it muddies her mind again, until she's only able to hold on to a few basic thoughts.

She can't stop them. This is going to happen. Has already happened.

Noemi is nothing God ever made, and Abel is dying.

6

SHE'S ALIVE.

Abel keeps coming back to this thought every few seconds. That reaction makes little sense; technically speaking, Noemi has been alive this entire time, and has only shifted to a new form of being. Still, he aimed for the impossible, and it has been achieved.

Granted, his probability of surviving this trip to Haven is currently at a discouragingly low 3.3 percent. That's irrelevant. Noemi's probabilities are shifting, but at minimum she has a 94 percent chance.

Gillian finally bows her head in assent. "You can take Vidal to your ship. But you're going under guard, and if you make one move, they won't aim for you. They'll aim for her." Her blue eyes turn toward Noemi.

"I won't attempt to escape," Abel says.

She snaps, "Your promises are meaningless."

"It isn't a promise. It's a necessity. I couldn't attempt to take off without risking the destruction of my ship, and Noemi along with it. I wouldn't have gone to so much trouble to save her if I were going to immediately endanger her again."

Noemi groans in discomfort, or maybe in protest. He can't tell, because her eyes have become unfocused, her body limp. The cybernetic nervous system must have just deepened its penetration into her brain. Adjustment will take time; he wishes he could help her through it.

But she's strong, resourceful, adaptable. She'll triumph in her new body. His assistance is not required.

Gillian's blue eyes narrow, like laser pinpoints in the stark white laboratory. "We could take her to the ship for you."

"And trust you to see her safely offworld?" Abel raises an eyebrow. "Our past encounters suggest that trusting you would be highly unwise."

"You've developed an attitude, haven't you?"

"You can call it an attitude if you wish," he says. "I call it self-respect."

Gillian Shearer has no answer for that. She allows Abel to load Noemi back onto the biobed; the warrior mechs that align around him are the only additional show of force Gillian needs. The mech who first captured Abel is still moving a little too slowly, but it is operating well within acceptable parameters. If Gillian notices the mech's flaws, she doesn't show it. She just watches as Abel eases Noemi's biobed out the door, mechs marching behind him.

The biobed's antigravity casters keep it hovering; even a human could push it with ease. As a precaution, Abel flips on energy bands that glow around Noemi's wrists and legs. The bands are normally meant to keep unconscious patients secure. They should prevent her from hurting herself before she gains some control.

Seventy-eight seconds later, Noemi stirs, awake again. She blinks up into the light as he pushes the biobed down a long white corridor with gleaming walls. "It's just a bad dream," she murmurs. "A bad dream. That's all. This isn't real."

Humans sometimes say such things rhetorically, as an expression of dismay. Abel believes Noemi is being literal. She doesn't yet trust the new information from her transformed body. Her still-growing cybernetic nervous system can't make sense of her unfamiliar surroundings. It will be a long time before she can marvel at her new capacities, abilities, strength. Instead, in this moment, she's…confused and afraid. He'd hoped to guide her through more of the transition, but he probably won't get the chance.

It's uncomfortable to see her that way, but it's for the best. If she can't fully process what's happening to either of them, maybe his fate will hurt her less.

"Stay calm," he says to Noemi. "Everything will be all right."

Behind him march the six warrior mechs—three Charlies and three Queens—who have been assigned to make sure that everything will definitely *not* be all right, at least not for Abel. They'll force Abel to leave the ship and take him back to Gillian Shearer and his imminent death.

Still, he hasn't given up. Shearer has a 96.7 percent chance of successfully completing the consciousness transfer. Yet she might realize the task to be impossible, or discover that Mansfield's soul has degraded in storage. Three point three percent isn't a promising chance, but it isn't nothing. Any value above zero equals hope.

Though it's hard to concentrate on such things when Noemi lies so close to him, breathing and blinking and almost entirely awake—her brown eyes open and searching for him—

Analyze, he tells himself, and gets back to it.

Gillian's laboratory seems to have been located near the heart of the Winter Castle. It would be logical for residences and important scientific facilities to be centralized, and therefore offer the most protection from intruders and the sharp Haven cold. However, his exit doesn't take him through the rest of the castle. Instead, the warrior mechs lead him through empty underground passageways. Abel would assume them to be service corridors, were it not for the elaborate iridescent patterns painted along every wall.

Perhaps the opulence of the Winter Castle extends even to its most basic areas.

Their group passes through a type of insulating lock into a kind of gear room stocked with hyperwarm coats, thick gloves, and insulating coveralls. Neither Abel nor the mechs behind him take any of the cold-weather gear; he can do without it for the limited time they'll be in the snow. Behind the gear racks in the distance, he sees another kind of man-shaped machine—not mechs but enormous Smashers, robots designed for deep-earth mining. They're two and a half meters high, more than half a meter wide, all in dark colors like navy, brown, and black. The rounded plates of their torsos and limbs make them look benign, but they can punch through sheer rock. Smashers created the tunnels of Cray and are carving out iron ore on Stronghold. There's little they can't overpower. But Abel can think of no way to turn the Smashers against the mechs guarding him.

Could I seal off the air lock? Trap them inside while I return to the Persephone? But he can't leave the *Persephone* here on Haven while he attempts to escape and return to it. He has to get Noemi safely away from this place as fast as he can.

Nor can he fight six warrior mechs hand to hand. He would risk the fight if it didn't mean risking Noemi's life, too. That is unacceptable.

Saving her means letting her go and accepting his fate.

•   •   •

Noemi remains too dazed to object until they board the *Persephone.* At first her eyes light up; familiar surroundings must comfort her. But Abel sees her watching the mechs behind him.

"Did I dream Gillian?" she whispers. Her memory has not yet achieved normal functionality. "This isn't real, is it? This voice in my head keeps saying it is, but the voice can't be real either." Despite her confusion, she sounds so alert that he's encouraged—until she tries to sit up. The snap of the energy bands shouldn't hurt, but it stuns her again. Her new brain functions and nerve endings don't know how to process the input yet.

Noemi's adaptation will be a fascinating process to witness. Abel wishes he were going to get the chance to witness it.

"I preprogrammed a course back to the verge of the Haven Gate," he tells her. Right now it won't make much sense to her, but her additional brain components should be able to replay it all. "You don't have to do a thing. Just rest."

"Don't do it," she pleads. "Kill me—deactivate me, whatever it would be now. Tell Gillian the deal's off."

"If you should see Harriet and Zayan again, please apologize for my abrupt departure. I would've liked to tell them good-bye." He thinks of his Vagabond crew members, remembers the ready way they both smiled. "If you decide to pilot the *Persephone* as your own ship from now on, you could offer them places on your crew, though I suspect they'll choose to settle on Genesis. Give my regards to Ephraim as well, and as for Virginia—" Abel pauses. "If you get in touch with her, even send her a prerecorded message, that will be enough. She'll know what's happened."

"I don't understand—" Noemi writhes in the grip of the energy bands. "Let me up!"

He snaps off the energy beams, freeing her. She rises immediately, only to wobble off balance and fall from the biobed. Abel had already lowered it, so she only rolls a few centimeters to the docking bay door. From the doorway, the mechs stand rigidly at attention. Probably they're counting down a set number of minutes before they will force him to leave the ship or simply kill Noemi.

"Why can't I move normally?" Noemi's fear is turning into panic. "What is this voice in my head telling me about the other mechs? Make this stop, please—"

"I can't do that." He smiles at her, hoping to be reassuring. "Noemi, you can do only one thing for me—lead a long and happy life."

She doesn't reply at first, just stares at him with eyes that are welling with tears. Finally she chokes out, "You're going to do this, aren't you? No matter what I say. Because I can't stop you."

Abel nods. "I'm sorry."

Noemi rakes her hands over her close-shorn scalp. The skin regenerators have almost finished sealing over the incisions from her surgery. Few human women shave their heads, for various sociological reasons, but Abel finds Noemi even more beautiful this way. Nothing distracts attention away from her large, dark eyes. Her voice is raspy as she says, "I wouldn't have wanted this."

"You had no chance to determine your own fate. I had to decide for us both. I chose you."

She shakes her head. "You keep giving yourself away for me—like your life doesn't even belong to you—"

"It does," he says. "Or it did. It's worth it."

Noemi wipes at her cheeks as she says, "We were just starting."

She means them, he realizes, as a romantic couple. They were going to travel through the stars together, on the adventure she'd dreamed of always. He wishes he could've had that time with her. Even a day of it. That would be more joyful than most human lifetimes.

Abel reaches toward her, then stops. The shimmer of the force field around him means he can't touch her. It would have meant so much to him to kiss her farewell, or even hold her hand. But Gillian's mechs remain behind him, ready to pounce, and apparently programmed to give him no more time.

The mechs step forward in unison. Two strong hands seize Abel by the shoulders and pull him to his feet. Noemi cries out in dismay, "No. Abel, don't!"

He pushes one control on the nearest panel, activating the time-delayed autotakeoff. Soon she'll leave this planet and take her place among the stars.

"Good-bye," he says as they pull him back off the ship, into the snow. Abel watches her face until the last moment when the door pinwheels shut, separating them forever.

7

Metal floor, alloy composed primarily of steel with a significant amount of aluminum, precise percentages undetermined. Metallurgical analysis advised.

So says the unwelcome intruder in Noemi's brain.

All she wants is to be able to get herself *off* the floor, to the bridge, and back to Abel. Instead, she's lying there, heavier than she ought to be, an outsider within her own skin.

At first she thinks of the heaviness as exhaustion, but when she tries to turn over, she becomes sharply aware that the new weight is literal. The devices Gillian Shearer put in her gut are heavier than her organs, heavier than her bones. Her own body seems impossible to lift. Noemi might as well be shackled to the floor.

The eerie mist reaching through her entire body blooms cold at the very base of her neck. The sensation makes her shudder in horror—but her focus improves. Her thoughts order themselves. She's rational again. Awake again.

I must be able to walk and move normally, she tells herself. *At least eventually. Abel traded himself for this…whatever this is. He wouldn't have done that for nothing. He wouldn't let Shearer destroy me. And if Shearer wanted me dead, she could just have shot me.*

Instead, she made me a…hybrid.

Noemi has no idea what that might mean, really. Every time her dazed mind tries to turn to it, her thoughts go blank. The knowledge is like a light too bright to be looked at directly.

However, she's still a soldier. Her military training taught her that when her life is on the line, there's only thing to do: attack. Fight to kill, and you might survive. Fighting with no other goal than not dying? That's how you wind up dead. Learning to walk and move again is her next fight.

Don't think about it, Noemi tells herself. *Just do it.*

There's no other way for her to get back to Abel, and she knows she must get back to Abel. She feels like she knows almost nothing else.

This time, when she rolls over, she makes it. Pushing herself up onto her hands and knees takes long seconds— maybe minutes—but it seems to Noemi that the more she moves, the easier it gets. Which isn't the same thing as being *easy,* but it's progress.

The weight inside isn't that heavy—it just feels different— you can do it.

Finally she rises to her feet, probably wobblier than she could've been since she was a toddler. Noemi holds her arms out wide to improve her balance as she half walks, half stumbles to the door.

When it slides open for her, admitting her to the *Persephone*, tears come to her eyes. She can't say whether that's out of physical pain, or the joy of being someplace sort of like home again, or the terror that she'll never again feel really at home anywhere.

What happens to her is irrelevant compared to what happens to Abel.

She forces her way up the long spiral corridor, left shoulder pressed against the walls. Every one of the arched struts forces her to stop and shuffle her way around it, but each goes slightly faster than the one before. She tries to make herself happy with the progress, but happiness is a long way away.

When Noemi reaches the bridge doors, she breathes a sigh of relief. She stumbles toward them—and collides with the solid metal. Normally the doors would've slid open for her automatically. Are they malfunctioning? Maybe this ship's as broken as she is. She puts her hand to the control panel nearby to open the doors manually, but they still don't budge.

"*Hello, Noemi,*" says Abel's voice. She startles, jolted by the sudden hope that somehow he's here, that he's saved himself. But it's only a recording. *"Given your well-documented history of refusing to follow instructions, as well as your general disregard for your safety, there was a ninety-three point zero seven percent chance that you'd try to return to Haven. I therefore hardwired the bridge and other navigational controls not to respond to you until at least thirty-five hours after leaving the planet. I appreciate your desire to rescue me, but I can't allow you to endanger yourself."*

"So I'm supposed to let you *die* for me?" Noemi's hoarse voice echoes in the empty corridor, reminding her that she's alone—more alone than she's ever been. She feels tiny. Useless. Even if she could return to Haven, what could she do, one girl against dozens of mechs and an entire winter fortress?

No. She can't afford to start thinking that way. The one absolute way to fail Abel would be to quit trying.

Okay. I can't get onto the bridge the normal way. I can't think of alternatives when I'm this panicky and upset. So if I want to get back to Abel quickly enough to help him, I first need to calm down. She laughs once, a brittle sound. Has she ever been this far from calm?

The only thing that would help her would be understanding more of what's been done to her. She might be able to figure that out in sick bay.

Painstakingly, Noemi works her way up the rest of the corridor, cursing Burton Mansfield or whoever it was who decided sick bay should be at the very top of the *Perse-phone*. Although she keeps herself braced against the wall throughout, her speed continues to improve.

Walking is occurring approximately 1.65 times faster than three minutes before, says the intruder in her brain.

At last she stumbles through the doors into sick bay. She sees one biobed—knows she was there not long ago—and memory jolts her, searing her soul:

Akide staring at her, horrified by the blaster in his hand, by what he'd done.

Abel picking her up from the floor.

Telling him to find her in Esther's star, and then the great onrushing dark—

That would've been her death. It wasn't a bad way to die: not alone, fairly quick, without getting anyone else hurt. After two years of combat duty in the Liberty War, Noemi has seen enough death to know the many ways it can come, and how horrible it can be. A good death is a rare gift, and she feels oddly cheated of it.

But Abel has given her more life, life she intends to use.

Noemi looks at the wall of cryosleep pods. One of the pods is missing, the floor beneath it gleaming with fluid. Soaking-wet scraps of dark green material float in the puddles there—the remnants of her exosuit. Noemi puts one hand to her belly to feel the loose garment of coarse white fabric she wears.

Who put this on me? God, I hope it was Abel. Not that she's 100 percent ready for him to see her naked yet, but better him than Gillian Shearer. Just the thought of being seen by those cold, clinical blue eyes makes her shudder. She's been violated enough for one day.

It's unlike Abel not to have cleaned up the cryosleep pod. He must've been rushed, and even upset. More upset than Noemi's ever seen him. But she can imagine it. The same fear rattles in her chest now.

She makes her way to one of the biobeds and sets it for a standard scan. It's not 0.7 seconds before the abnormalities begin to show up on the nearby screen. Noemi's eyes widen as she takes in the dark, too-angular shape within her abdomen instead of her internal organs. Worse is the dull silhouette of something embedded within the lobes of her brain. Scariest of all is the silvery tangle of thin lines that follow her every nerve and blood vessel—the cybernetic nervous system, the thing that makes her less human, more mech.

That's the part she'd like to ditch. But how is she supposed to get that out?

Noemi lets her head fall back on the biobed and stares blankly at the ceiling. Understanding what she's become hasn't calmed her down. It's plunged her into something as heavy as lead and dark as space.

She closes her eyes in despair, then opens them. *Wait. What happened to Darius Akide?*

The Elder was on this ship. He shot her from only a meter or two—

—1.689 meters, whispers the thing in her head—

—away from this very biobed. Abel was completely incapacitated at the time. Obviously he got the better of Akide, but how? When and how did Akide leave the *Persephone*?

Her skin prickles with fear when she wonders if he's still aboard. He could be waiting in any room, any side corridor, blaster in his hand—

Abel wouldn't have let that happen, she reminds herself. Still, the mystery of Akide's whereabouts is one Noemi would like to solve.

The nearest control panel crackles with sound. *"Hullo out there! What system is this?"*

It's not a voice she's ever heard before. Doesn't sound like Earth authorities. No Remedy warship would greet anyone so warmly. So who is it?

Noemi pushes herself upright. This time she's able to rise to her feet fairly smoothly. Another few steps and she's able to brace herself on the wall next to the computer panel. A few quick inputs will reroute communication to sick bay. "This is the free ship *Persephone*, and you're in the Haven system."

Her answer is a whoop of pure glee. *"This is it! This is it! By all the gods, we found Haven!"* The screen flickers, patching in visual as well, revealing a shabby ship's bridge peopled by eight Vagabonds, every single one of them laughing, crying, or both.

It's a few minutes before there's any break in the ruckus, which lets Noemi say, "I'm trying to get back to Haven—"

"This is the free ship Altamura, also bound for Haven. Those damned Earthers couldn't stand in our way for long, huh?"

"No. They couldn't." Despite everything, she begins to smile.

One of the Vagabonds points at Noemi. *"Listen to her voice. Isn't that the girl from the audio?"*

The stout captain holds out her arms as though she could embrace Noemi through the comm channel. *"It is you, isn't it? The very one who told us about Haven to begin with! Here to guide all of us to our new home."*

"That was me on the signal," she confirms. "Noemi Vidal of the planet Genesis. I could use some—"

"Told you it wasn't in the Kismet system," cries a Vagabond who's pouring something fizzy out of a bottle into cups for his fellow shipmates. *"That Remedy signal wouldn't steer us wrong!"*

The woman he's talking to is grinning with joy, but she still retorts, *"There's odd things afoot near Kismet. So it wasn't the Haven Gate. Doesn't mean it was nothing. And I still don't trust Remedy as far as I can throw 'em."*

"How many ships are there?" Noemi tries. Maybe if she

can calm them down enough to talk about themselves, they might then listen to her.

With a cackle, the captain cries, "*Dozens! Maybe even hundreds! We put together a group for this run, and we struck gold!*"

Hundreds? Noemi switches the screen to an external view. What she sees isn't the usual endless void of outer space, but a flotilla of Vagabond ships, each of them brilliant with multicolored patterns. A few plainer, newer ships must be Earth ships themselves—but civilian ships, piloted by humans who are as sick of Earth's leaders as any colony world.

Noemi's smile widens. "No. Earth couldn't stay in our way for long."

As she watches, another dozen ships appear. Then another. The flotilla is becoming a fleet. Literally thousands of humans are headed to Haven as fast as they can go.

"*Altamura*," she says, loudly enough to break through their party, "my autopilot's malfunctioning. It's trying to drag me back through the Haven Gate, which is the exact opposite of where I want to go. Any chance you guys could give me a tow?" The autopilot will shut down when a tow beam locks on, as a safety precaution to keep the ship from being torn apart.

"*You've got it,* Persephone! *Get ready for a bump.*"

Did Abel take this into account, too? Will another of his fail-safes shut down the tow?

No. The entire ship shudders from the impact of the beam, and Noemi tumbles to her knees. Falling down doesn't even bother her, not once she realizes she's finally headed back to Haven.

As dozens more ships continue to appear in the space around her, she thinks, *Please, God, let us make it there in time.*

Abel can't have long left.

8

ABEL STANDS IN A KIND OF CAGE MADE OF LIGHT—SENSOR
beams that periodically sweep different sections of his body,
checking and rechecking data. Gillian Shearer stands on the
far side of the lab, staring at his readouts rather than at her
prisoner himself. Some murderers might do this as a way
of dehumanizing their victim, but Gillian never thought of
him as the equal of a human.

This is merely caution. She took his report of damage
seriously, which was both wise of her and lucky for him. In
theory, more time in captivity should mean more chances
for him to escape.

In reality, no chances have yet become apparent. Rather
than becoming discouraged, Abel remains focused. He
doesn't need many chances, only one.

One that needs to arrive soon. To be precise, within the
next 9.87 minutes.

"Internal wireless capabilities are almost completely shot," Gillian says. "How did you do this?"

"Genesis forces were under heavy fire in the most recent battle."

"And you got hit?" She raises one eyebrow, as starkly red as a scar. "I'm surprised you came out as well as you did."

"My ability for self-repair is considerable," Abel points out. Both of his previous two statements were factual, but neither was relevant. He has no intention of telling Gillian what he was able to do at the Battle of Genesis—how he reached out with the machine side of himself and stopped Earth's mechs from attacking Genesis forces. Instead, they destroyed one another. That ability has proved dangerous, and Abel's unsure the circumstances will ever be dire enough for him to do that again. But if Gillian ever learned the full truth, she would no doubt launch into other tests and experiments equally painful and even more hazardous.

However, that might buy him more time....

"It doesn't surprise me that your non-wired communications overloaded. They're a generation out of date." Gillian's fingertips fly over her console as she speaks. Still she doesn't look up. "That's really the only way in which you're outdated, Model One A. You don't come close to Tether capability."

"Tether capability?" Abel frowns. "I've never heard of this, and I've been studying cybernetic advancements."

Gillian shrugs. "Nobody much talks about the Tether. It would be like—like designing the fastest spaceship known to humankind and talking about the color of the chairs. Tether tech is simple. It's functional. It's…invisible, the way the best technologies should be."

"Is it hardware or software?"

"Both, in a manner of speaking," Gillian says. "AI systems designed to communicate wirelessly usually have immense storage for complex signals, plus the bandwidth to handle Tether-coded signals. You know, ships, massive mainframes, remote-intercept data solids, that kind of thing. Mechs, however, don't have that bandwidth or that storage. So they require certain hardware, which you lack."

Abel feels almost offended. "I've never noticed any lack."

"Only machines programmed to analyze communication would ever notice the difference. Well, other machines and my father. So we should get that taken care of before we do anything else."

How perverse of her to keep saying "we," Abel thinks. *As though I were cooperating.*

Gillian steps closer, a small silver cylinder held within her fingers. "I can do the hardware update manually. Fortunately we don't have to open up your cranium; it's easiest to just go up the nose."

Easiest for her, she means.

The following few minutes are incredibly uncomfortable. Abel feels the cool metal being pushed up his nostril, then the burst of pain as it begins moving through the membranes that seal off his brain. Blood wells up anew, trickling from his nose and staining Gillian's glove. He can taste it in the back of his throat. A human undergoing this would either panic or pass out, probably both, before their inevitable death. Abel simply forces himself to think about something else. Something more pleasant. Which in this case could be nearly anything in the galaxy.

What he chooses to think about is Noemi's getaway. By now she should be at least halfway to the Haven Gate. She should also have regained some basic motor control, which means she'll also have tried to rescue him and found his fail-safe message. At this very moment, Abel calculates, there is an 86.39 percent chance that Noemi is *absolutely furious.*

He imagines her fury, and smiles.

"That felt good to you?" Gillian gives him a look as she strips off her bloody gloves. "It shouldn't have."

"It was bearable," Abel says. He swallows another gulp of blood as she squirts a medi-gel up his nose to seal off the worst of the bleeding.

"Good. Time to test it out." She taps in a command on the console, then pauses. "Anything?"

"No."

"I'll know if you're lying."

"Then you should know that I'm not." Abel "hears" nothing, receives no data.

With a scowl, Gillian turns back to her control panels, studying readouts for a clue as to what might've gone wrong. Surely, with her expertise, she's more than capable of simple hardware installation. Apparently she erred this time, but she'll get it right soon. So this delay seems unlikely to last long.

Stall, he thinks. It is his one productive option.

So he asks, "Are you certain Professor Mansfield's consciousness was fully preserved?" It would be especially galling for his soul to be destroyed to make room for another if that other is unable to function.

"Oh, yes." A flicker of dismay remains on Gillian's face, but she must not be that worried, because she's already getting back to work. "We've been working on consciousness storage for a long time, you know."

"At least since my creation," he says.

She laughs. "Long before that! There wouldn't have been any point to you otherwise."

That stings—and yet, he sees the logic of it.

She continues, "Father first became interested when Mummy became ill. He's always hoped to find a home for her. Someday, we will."

Gillian's gaze turns toward a wall of devices and components—a memory storage unit here, a metal knee joint there. One item on the shelves is different from the others: a box of ornately carved wood. He ought to have noticed it before. The box is large enough to contain a remote-intercept data solid, the kind of thing Mansfield uses to contain a soul.

"Your father managed to preserve the consciousness of the late Robin Mansfield," Abel says. "He could do it perfectly that long ago?"

The brief cheer on her face fades. "Not perfectly," she admits.

"How do you know that? How do you know she's stored at all?" Consciousness transfer is probably Mansfield's single most brilliant achievement, and it's the one Abel has deliberately refused to learn about. It is, after all, the way he'll die.

Gillian replies, "We tried developing a written interface, but she couldn't respond to that. So I suggested—I was a girl, understand—I suggested a Ouija board."

"A...Ouija board." Abel tries to imagine Burton Mansfield stooping to this, and can't. Yet it must've happened.

"We magnetized a planchette so Mum was able to move a cursor on the board. She spelled out words, and answered yes-or-no questions." Gillian isn't looking directly at Abel any longer; this part is harder for her to remember.

"Mummy got some of the questions wrong, and some of what she said made no sense. So, obviously, there's been consciousness damage, or incomplete storage. But it is her. She's in there."

"But you have no Inheritor mech for her, nor can you build one," Abel says. For an Inheritor to take on someone else's consciousness, it must be created using genetic material from that same person, taken during their youth. This is something Mansfield didn't discover until Robin Mansfield had been dead for decades.

Gillian shrugs, trying to come across as casual. "We'll have to come up with a different solution for her. But we will. Soon the whole family will be together again."

She thinks she'll get them all back: her mother, her father, and Simon, the young son she lost only a few months ago. The first attempt at loading Simon's consciousness into a mech body ended tragically; the body wasn't fully developed, and nobody had prepared the child for the shocking transformation. Simon couldn't understand what had happened to him—and his resulting terror and anger had contributed to fatal malfunctions. Surely Robin Mansfield would be even more confused, if her damaged consciousness is still capable of a state of mind that could be called confusion....

Abel realizes he's trying to solve Mansfield's problems instead of looking out for his own safety. Directive One still has its power.

"*Dr. Shearer, we have a proximity alert,*" intones the voice of a Queen mech, through one small speaker that must connect this lab to the Winter Castle's central security. "*We've detected multiple ships on planetary approach.*"

Gillian gapes with shock. She takes two steps from the console, staring up at the speaker as though it were the source of the problem and not the messenger. "That can't be right. How could anyone possibly—what are *you* grinning about?"

Abel continues to grin. "Did I not mention that Noemi informed the entire galaxy of Haven's existence more than a week ago?"

"*What?*"

"Millions of people from Earth, Stronghold, Kismet— even the Vagabonds—they're all looking for a new home," he says. "The kind of home they might have on Haven. Although we did not give them the specific coordinates of the Haven Gate, the search would've been intense, and has now been successful. I'd predict at least hundreds of ships are on their way here now. Within days, there'll be thousands. Even tens of thousands."

Cold fury in every syllable, she says, "This world is ours."

"You should tell that to the overwhelming majority of its population, as of a few minutes from now." Abel's never been so polite, so crisp, so formal. Puncturing at least one of Gillian Shearer's ambitions feels richly satisfying. He reminds himself to study human concepts of revenge. "By tomorrow, the Winter Castle may be no more than a small town. That would give you the approximate authority of—a mayor?"

Gillian mutters a word so obscene that Abel's been programmed never to repeat it, then dashes out the door. She leaves him alone, unguarded.

His one chance has come.

9

THE *PERSEPHONE* PLOPS INTO A GIANT SNOWDRIFT.
Displaced air and snow whirl out and around the silvery
ship, a nine-meter-high cyclone that would normally draw
unwelcome attention from the nearby Winter Castle.

At the moment, Noemi doubts the castle dwellers have
even noticed her one little ship in the middle of *this*.

Ships land all around her—cruisers, corsairs, freighters,
every kind of vessel imaginable. Briefly Noemi's surprised
so many of them have chosen to land on this particular area
of Haven, when they have an entire world to settle on. *Their
scans found signs of human life and habitation*, she realizes.
But that leads her to wonder, *So did they want to come after
the original settlers, steal their resources, get back at them for
trying to hide this world from the rest of humanity?*

She remembers the elated cheers of the Vagabond crew
when they recognized her voice. They would've sent messages
about her to other ships in their group, too. (*Vagabond fleets*

run on two things, Harriet Dixon explained once, months ago. *Fuel and gossip.*) Noemi's message before the Battle of Genesis made its way across the entire galaxy, which was what she'd hoped; humanity needed to know about Haven. She hadn't reckoned on the fact that they would also know *her.*

"Just my voice," she murmurs to herself as she clumsily seals her excursion boots. "And my name, I guess. But only a handful of people have seen my face." It's small comfort. Noemi was taught since childhood not to trust anyone from Earth or the other colony worlds of the Loop. She's learned better…but that doesn't mean she's comfortable being so exposed to all of them.

A topological map of Haven unfolds in her mind, precise to the centimeter. She knows the outline of each continent, the depth of every ocean. Mountain ridges, mineral deposits, seismic surveys, meteorological reports—

"Stop it!" Noemi shouts. Her voice echoes in the emptiness of the docking bay. The brain implant goes quiet, probably by chance. She doesn't think it responds to verbal commands. She knows only one fact about the thing in her head: It's beyond her control.

Maybe Abel can teach her how to shut this thing up.

Abel. She has to get back to Abel. Nothing else matters.

Awkwardly she finishes putting on a hyperwarm parka, then hurries from the *Persephone* into the snow. Her steps remain unsteady, but she's getting the hang of walking again. Before, it was like trying to walk after a bad concussion; now it's more like someone spun her around on the swings for too long.

Still awful. But better.

Dozens of ships nearby are releasing their passengers. More cyclones of snow, more silvery shapes in the sky. A small family vessel is near enough for the mother to wave cheerily at Noemi and cry out, in a heavy Russian accent, "Your ship—they told us which it was. They say you are Vidal of Genesis! Here to lead us against the thieves of this world!"

"I'm not here to lead anybody," Noemi protests.

"Once we're all prepared, we're going to attack," calls the father, a burly man with a bushy red beard. He points toward the gleaming opalescent spires of the Winter Castle. "They've got food in there, eh? Supplies? More than all of these ships managed to put together, I'll bet. They should share that along with their planet!"

"No, don't!" Noemi agrees with the sentiment, but she also knows the risks. "They'll have guards. You should wait until—" *Until what? Until the Winter Castle welcomes them with open arms? That's going to be a while.*

The father laughs. "Wait, wait, wait! Earth tells us to wait for permission. Remedy tells us to wait because we'll get sick. They just want to keep this world from us! No thanks."

With a jolt, she realizes the ramifications of what he's saying. *Remedy tells us we'll get sick.* In other words, Remedy spoke out about the dangers of Haven. This family heard the warnings that no human could survive here without having first survived the Cobweb virus. And they didn't believe it. They came anyway. Other people landing on this planet have probably done the same thing. How many? Dozens, hundreds, thousands? This, she thinks, is what happens when a population has been lied to for too long. They lose the ability to trust.

If people who haven't survived Cobweb don't leave Haven, they'll die within 5.16 days.

"No. Not decimals," she growls at the thing in her head. *"Please not decimals."*

Noemi wonders how to convince these people of the danger—but already, at least three dozen ships have landed in the near vicinity, and the sky is speckled with more to come. People are racing out of their vessels, laughing in delight, hugging both friends and strangers, starting snowball fights. They're in no mood to listen to anyone, even the person who told them about Haven in the first place.

Reluctantly, she decides to warn them later. They'll be easier to convince in a couple of days, once they've started feeling strange. Right now all that matters is getting to Abel.

He could already be dead.

He could. But she refuses to believe it. She has what the people of Earth don't—the power of faith.

Noemi pushes on through the snow, ignoring the ships landing around her. When she sees a few snowmobiles streak from the Winter Castle, she mentally prepares herself for attack. Surely these belong to warrior mechs on patrol. She also focuses on the small bays the snowmobiles exited from. Would those be as tightly guarded as regular doors? Could they be hacked? Might she have time to get in while one of the snowmobiles returns?

Her vision suddenly magnifies the doors, which is helpful but also makes her so dizzy she stumbles to one side. Can she not even trust her own eyes?

A flume of snow sprays up around Noemi, disorienting her again. Staggering to one side, she sees the swirling white disperse to reveal a Queen mech. Already the mech has leaped from her snowmobile to aim a blaster at Noemi.

Does she recognize me? Is she a mech who guarded Abel? One of the frustrations of going up against fighter mechs is never being able to tell the damned things apart.

"No humans not previously approved are authorized to be here," the Queen says flatly. "Depart immediately."

Okay. She doesn't know who I am, and she won't tell Shearer I'm here. It's not much of a relief, but Noemi will take what she can get. "I've already had Cobweb," she tries.

"Haven's safe for me." Maybe the Queen's deep programming will require her to prioritize humans in more danger.

No such luck. "You are not authorized," the Queen repeats. She levels her blaster. "This is your last warning before execut—"

Noemi reaches out to knock the blaster aside. At least, that's the plan. But she moves at unthinkable speed—like her arm has decided on its own what to do—and slams into the Queen's arm with so much force that it snaps at the elbow. It dangles strangely, blood oozing where Noemi's blow impacted with the metal skeleton to cut the flesh open.

"Oh my God," she whispers, staring at her hand. It hurts, but it's not broken. Shouldn't it be broken, after hitting metal like that?

The Queen, programmed to ignore input that humans would call *pain*, simply leans down to take the blaster in her other hand. Noemi moves faster, shoving the Queen with all her new strength. When the Queen goes flying several meters into the snow, Noemi stares. The scene ought to be ordinary—she's killed hundreds of mechs in battle. But it's *how* the mech died that's shocking. Noemi practically punched through metal without even trying. Her body is a stranger to her, capable of doing incredible harm, even accidentally.

I could kill someone without meaning to. I could kill a friend. Anyone. Would I even care?

What the hell am I?

By this time mechs are confronting Vagabond landing parties all around her. The guard forces seem to be stretched thin—no doubt Shearer wasn't anticipating an invasion like this—and the Vagabonds are fighting back. Blaster bolts sear the air, melt the snow.

Noemi has no idea what to do to help the Vagabonds. For now, they're on their own. She has to get to Abel.

Within 2.2 seconds, she's on the Queen's snowmobile, gunning the motor. She takes off at top speed through the snow, circling back toward the Winter Castle. Either the doors will be programmed to automatically open for one of their own vehicles, or she'll have to try swerving at the last minute. Given the state of her coordination, there's a decent chance she'll wind up as a red splat on the white walls.

When she's within four meters, the door opens. Noemi zooms through the dark tunnel and into the heart of the Winter Castle.

• • •

All the fighter mechs must be out in the snow or guarding more sensitive areas inside, because Noemi faces no resistance on her way through the vehicle bay other than a hapless George model, easily dispatched with one blaster bolt. When she reaches the bay door, however, it doesn't automatically slide open. No manual controls are visible. She considers firing her blaster at it, but that's more likely to set off an alert than open the door.

Instead, she tries accessing verbal controls. "Open door."

"State your name," it intones.

Pretty basic security, but effective enough in a structure designed to be inhabited by only the elite few on an otherwise deserted planet. Noemi knows better than to try Gillian Shearer's name; the Winter Castle's AI is probably programmed to track Shearer's location every second.

There was one passenger on the *Osiris* who had been kind to Noemi, though—someone without any particular rank. So she ventures, "Delphine Ondimba?"

The doors slide open.

Thank you, Delphine! Noemi limps into the heart of the Winter Castle. *Now I just have to find the lab, though there's no telling where that is—*

The thing in her brain starts up again, displaying a schematic superimposed over her entire field of vision. Her dizziness worsens, and again she thinks she might vomit. The nausea is worth it when she recognizes this as a full blueprint of the Winter Castle. It must be part of a basic data fill, something ready to be programmed into all mechs created on Haven. She doesn't even have to concentrate to highlight Shearer's lab near the very heart of the complex.

Or the lifts that go not only up and down but also sideways, to carry passengers around in the blink of an eye.

Noemi makes it to the nearest lift door and manages to stand upright until it opens and she sees she'll be riding alone. So she slumps against the wall as it whirs toward the lab, trying to gather herself. Maybe she'll have to fight more mechs. Maybe Shearer will pick up a blaster herself. *Power through it,* Noemi tells herself. *Get Abel free, and then he can help you.*

Though she's not sure what to make of the last help he gave her.

It doesn't matter. Nothing matters but getting to Abel while he's still alive.

The lab has no separate security. In fact, it seems to contain no one. Noemi stands just shy of the doors' sensors, readies her blaster, and calls on what little she knows of Gillian Shearer to formulate a plan of attack.

She's not a trained soldier. She's a civilian, an amateur. That's not as reassuring as it should be. Shearer's a zealot, someone who doesn't care about her own safety compared to serving her father's cause. That means she won't hold back the way an average civilian would. In desperate circumstances, the untrained can be even more dangerous, because there's no knowing what to expect.

Noemi braces herself, then rushes through the doors that slide open for her, ready for anything—

—except the sight of Abel, pinned to the ceiling by energy beams.

"Abel!" she cries out. "Oh, thank God."

He stares as if in disbelief. "But—my fail-safes—it should have been impossible for you to return to Haven."

A smile stretches across her face. "You're not actually perfect, Abel. You just think you are." Relief floods through her, a physical sensation that's almost dizzying. *I made it in time. I made it. We'll make it.* Noemi lowers her weapon as she realizes Abel's alone in the room. "Where's Shearer?"

"Supervising the counterattack against the Vagabonds currently landing on Haven," he says, with as much dignity as he can manage in his current predicament. "There are of course too many ships landing for her to control, but it seems Gillian never surrenders control without a fight."

Noemi stumbles into the lab. "Why did Shearer pin you to the ceiling?"

"She didn't." He looks sheepish. "I was held in a more ordinary energy cage on the floor below. When Gillian went to repel the next wave of settlers, I tried to escape by changing the polarity of the beams. This did not proceed as smoothly as I'd hoped."

"You pinned *yourself* to the ceiling," Noemi says, shaking her head. The motion makes her head whirl all over again, and she braces herself against the nearest wall. "Tell me how to shut this thing off."

"Noemi? Are you all right?" How like Abel, to worry about her while he's effectively stuck three meters above the ground.

"I don't feel very good." The understatement is so absurd she wants to laugh, or cry. "So help me get you down. That way you can get us both out of here."

"We should begin with you turning to the controls directly to your left."

She goes to the correct panel, inputs the coding as he dictates, and sends Abel plummeting down from the ceiling. He manages to twist around in time to land on his feet as silently as a cat.

When he embraces her, she hugs him back—gently, because of her foreign, dangerous strength. Besides, she couldn't hug him tightly enough. It's impossible. Nothing could express how she feels, holding him after she thought he was lost forever.

Though of course they're still on a hostile alien world, surrounded by mechs who would kill her on sight and capture him—but no. If Noemi thinks of all the complications now, she'll scare herself beyond the ability to think straight. They both have to think straight if they're going to survive this.

She closes her eyes and tells herself, *Abel can make everything right. He always does.* And she wills herself to believe it.

10

NOEMI'S COORDINATION HASN'T IMPROVED ENOUGH FOR her to move quickly. Abel lifts her onto his back and runs for the perimeter of the Winter Castle complex. Although they startle a handful of humans on the way—former *Osiris* passengers, no doubt shocked to be discovered here on their "secret" planet—nobody attempts to stop them.

Gillian Shearer doesn't know we've escaped yet. The Charlies and Queens are busy with their futile attempt to turn back the tide of ships headed for Haven. Only a handful of the Castle residents would recognize us. We have an 81.87 percent chance of making it to the vehicle bay without being stopped.

Once they're out in the snow, however, they'll be exposed and the dangers will increase...but perhaps it would be better to turn to that challenge when they face it.

The fighter mechs must be using nearly every snowmobile the Winter Castle possesses, but three remain. Abel settles Noemi on the fastest model and takes the piloting position. Her arms wrap around his waist as he powers up the machine, then zooms toward the bright rectangle of sunlight that marks their way out.

Abel had calculated that the landing force would be many hundreds of ships. At the moment, he seems to have slightly overestimated the number—and yet, he hadn't factored in the sheer chaos of their arrival.

He steers them across the snow, Noemi's arms still clasped around his waist. In a dozen directions around them, scenes of violence and fear play out. Nearby, a Vagabond family whose ship is painted with the old Russian flag is apparently beating a Charlie mech to circuits. Farther away, blaster bolts sizzle through snow, and human shapes fall. The carnage is useless; the wave of settlers will be beyond any control. And yet the mechs fight on.

Gillian Shearer never knows when to quit.

The grayish sky overhead reveals still more ships coming, casting dark specks over the light of Haven's many moons. If they're lucky, Gillian won't realize Abel's escaped the lab until he and Noemi are already halfway to the Gate.

She doesn't. Their luck holds. They make it to their ship unharmed.

Never before has the *Persephone*'s teardrop shape looked so welcome. Abel ditches the snowmobile, helps Noemi aboard, and takes off as fast as cybernetically possible. The course has already been laid in; he only needs to reactivate the autopilot he'd set up for Noemi's use alone, with a few modifications for different phases of lunar orbit. Within 4.71 minutes, they're rocketing up from the surface, headed for deep space.

He watches in satisfaction as Haven shrinks on the bridge viewscreen. When the doors slide open, he turns to see Noemi shakily making her way toward the ops station.

"We're free," he says. It is truer for them both than it has ever been before.

Noemi doesn't appear to feel the same way. Her eyes don't meet his as she flops into her seat. "Is this what freedom feels like?"

This statement is difficult to interpret. "What troubles you?"

She gives him a look as though he'd begun speaking in a language she doesn't know. "Abel...do you even realize what happened to me? What Shearer did to me?"

"You mean your hybridization? That's what we're calling the process, for now; it is an unprecedented medical procedure, one we invented, and admittedly all the ramifications are not yet known. But I supervised Gillian's work, so I'm as familiar with the procedure as anyone." Perhaps Noemi was too dazed to make much sense of the explanation they gave her earlier. "You were too seriously wounded for medical intervention. Your only chance at survival was through the implantation and integration of organic mech parts. Gillian Shearer—"

"No. I understand that." She pauses, then adds, "I *do* understand," as though she were convincing herself. Her gaze remains fixed on the floor. "But you don't realize how it *feels*. I don't know how to walk. How strong I am, or how fast I move, or how I feel, or—or anything. I'm not even at home in my own body."

"You're in a new state," he says. "A period of transition is inevitable."

"And how long will that take? Hours or years or what?"

Abel has to admit, "I don't know."

"Oh my God, how long will I live?" Noemi's eyes widen. "Do I still have a normal human life span or will I live for a couple of centuries, like a mech? I know I'm not totally a mech, but I—I'm not *fully human* anymore either."

Abel wishes she would look up at him. "You're the best of both, I think."

Noemi brushes her hand along her scalp. A faint fuzz of hair has already grown back. "That's what you see. The rest of the galaxy is going to think I'm a freak."

"Surely that is irrelevant compared with your own self-image—"

"First of all, I *don't know* what my self-image is right now, but since I can't even walk straight, it's not super high.

Second, it's not irrelevant! The way people treat you—it matters. I'm going to have to lie about what I am—"

"I lie by omission," Abel offers. "It's an easy habit to acquire."

Noemi shoots back, "I don't want to live a lie."

He has no response for that.

The silence that stretches out between them lasts a mere 7.3 seconds, but seems to last longer. Abel has always known that humans perceive time differently than mechs—faster when busy or happy, slower when bored or sad. However, this illusion is apparently one he can share under conditions of sufficient awkwardness.

Why is Noemi so unhappy? Surely she can't be displeased that he saved her life. If she were, that would mean she thinks of being part mech as being less than human. The transitive property would then indicate that she thought of *him* as less than human. Since very early in their relationship, Noemi has always accepted him as her equal.

Hasn't she?

Abel finds this question so disquieting that he immediately pushes it aside. "How do you feel?"

"Tired. I'm going to try to get some rest. It's weird how cryosleep makes you really tired. If you're asleep for days or weeks or months on end, you ought to at least be well-rested, right?" Noemi blinks. "My brain just told me the physiological explanation for that."

"It will be a new experience for me, not having to explain so many things to you."

She gives him the look that means *What you just said isn't what you should've said.* He'll analyze his error later. Maybe Noemi is merely exhausted into unusual levels of irritability. Humans are like that sometimes, and despite her fears, she is still mostly human.

"Well, call me for the Haven Gate." She rises to her feet and stumbles toward the door. The clumsiness is so unfamiliar, so unlike her, that he briefly glimpses how alien her body must have become. "Zayan and Harriet both said they refuse to sleep their way through a Gate ever again, because apparently dreams get beyond bizarre."

Abel has heard them complain about this before. Zayan once dreamed he had become a lasagna—to be specific, a lasagna with opinions about politics, frustrated about its inability to share these thoughts with a galaxy not yet ready to listen to pasta. "I'll summon you for the Gate," Abel agrees.

As the bridge doors slide open for her, Noemi pauses. "Abel, thanks for being willing to make that sacrifice for me. For taking that chance. Even if right now I feel like—" She sighs. "It means a lot."

Abel can only answer, "Always."

Their eyes meet, and the strangeness between them fades—until she turns and trudges toward the door.

He settles into his captain's chair, attempting to analyze her earlier reactions. Yes, the experience of suddenly gaining mech capabilities must be overwhelming to a limited human mind. Yet Noemi almost seems to be rejecting her new status entirely.

She accepts me as the equal of a human, Abel reasons. *Why can't she then accept herself?*

Perhaps he was wrong about Noemi's acceptance. Her total repudiation of her own mech half indicates a level of—underestimation, or even contempt. In her eyes, he might not truly be as alive and valid an individual as a human being. Maybe she never saw him as being "as good as." Only "good enough" to merit rights of his own.

The difference between those things is far larger than he would've anticipated.

Just before reaching the door, Noemi stops short and looks back at him in fear. "Oh my God. Darius Akide. Where is he? How did you get away from him?"

Abel remembers the crunch of Akide's spinal cord between his hands. His initial impulse had been to tell Noemi about this immediately—but now things are uneasy between them. Is this really the time to tell her he's capable of killing humans without orders, without needing to save anyone?

He says, "I overpowered Akide, and ejected him and his transfer pod while you were in cryosleep."

Every word of that is accurate. He simply omitted the fact that when he put Darius Akide in the pod, Akide was already dead.

Noemi pauses, then slowly, haltingly walks back toward Abel. "If you'd told me that earlier, I would've believed you. But now I can't help but listen to the voice in my head that's analyzing every single thing you left out of that story."

Indirectness will not serve me as well in the future, he thinks.

"Tell me the whole truth," she insists.

It's been a long time since Abel wasn't sure he could trust Noemi with the whole truth about anything. His trepidation doesn't change the fact that he owes her that truth. "I killed him."

She sways on her feet. For 3.1 seconds, dreadful suspense stretches between them. Then she shakes her head, as though to clear it, and says, "It was self-defense. Of course. Akide was trying to kidnap you—I saw it myself. He was going to use you to destroy the Genesis Gate, which means he was trying to kill you—"

"This is all true," Abel says. He stands up, as rigidly correct as he was on the day they met. "However, I didn't kill him in self-defense. I killed Akide because I thought Akide had killed you. It was an act of fury. An act of revenge. It was murder."

Noemi puts her hand to her mouth. Is she trying to

remain silent? Afraid she'll throw up? Abel's programming doesn't allow him to guess.

He continues, "My programming ought to prevent me from killing a human for any reason besides defending another human. It didn't. Instead, the killing felt—natural, instinctive. It took me a while to understand why, but finally I realized that was because what I did had nothing to do with being a mech. That was my human side. Killing Akide was the most human thing I've ever done. If that's humanity, I must again question why so many humans consider themselves superior to mechs."

She winces as though his words had caused her physical pain. He waits for her answer, expecting it to be terrible. Maybe she doesn't trust him any longer.

When she speaks, however, she surprises him: "Does Genesis know?"

"Do you mean, have the authorities learned that I killed Darius Akide?" Noemi nods, so Abel continues, "I'm not sure. As he was operating with the authority of the Council, they must at least know that he set out to apprehend me in the immediate aftermath of the Battle of Genesis. By this point, they'll be aware that Akide failed to execute his plan. But I don't have sufficient data to determine whether they know that Akide reached my ship, or that he's dead."

Grimacing, she asks, "What did you do with... with the body?"

"I put it back in his transport pod and ejected that pod just before leaving the Cray system, on a trajectory that should've sent it crashing into the other planet in that system. As that world is even hotter than Cray, with an almost wholly volcanic surface, Akide and his pod would've been vaporized. I calculate only a five point two two percent chance that the pod would be detected by Cray sensors, and only a zero point eight one percent chance that Cray would've had any chance to intervene between detecting the pod and its destruction."

Another long silence stretches between them; Abel refuses to measure this one. Finally, Noemi begins to nod. "Good."

"Good?"

"He tried to kill you. He basically *did* kill me. Genesis would've let him get away with that. If you'd left Akide alive, he would've stopped you from saving me. So as far as I'm concerned, he got what he deserved."

It's Abel's turn to stare. "I would've thought revenge was a value inconsistent with Christianity."

"It should be," Noemi agrees. "But pretty much all of human history proves that wrong. Besides, I've never been a perfect Christian. I've tried, and I've tried, and I've studied my Second Catholic catechism until I almost have it memorized, and none of it changes the fact that I'm almost glad Akide's dead."

She's disquieted; Abel can tell. This discord between her beliefs and her feelings is one they should get into sometime.

But not now.

"You're tired," he says gently. "Try to rest. We'll talk about it more later."

"I don't care if we never talk about it again," Noemi insists, but she turns to go. Maybe she's only sleepy, or maybe she needs some time alone to think about this.

Abel knows he does.

11

As requested, Abel awakens Noemi via comms before going through the Haven Gate. She makes her way to the bridge a few minutes later, wearing her sleep-rumpled gear from before. Walking is…easier. Not normal, still uneven, but better.

Abel and Shearer said I have a cybernetic nervous system now, Noemi thinks. She can feel the cool, misty traces of it through every centimeter in her body—from thin tickles just beneath her skin to deep, chilly streaks that reach into her brain. It's supposed to meld with the rest of her body soon, until it feels natural. Like it belongs there. Which it doesn't yet.

Not even Shearer or Abel could tell her how long her adjustment is going to take. Noemi wonders whether she's ever going to feel whole again.

At least she and Abel are together.

She moves slowly enough that she's still in the corridor,

a few meters shy of the bridge, when the *Persephone* hits the Haven Gate. Traveling through a Gate has always been disorienting for Noemi, along with pretty much every other human being in the galaxy. Light bends in ways it shouldn't. Sound warps. Any sense of up versus down, right versus left, gets lost for a few seconds that seem to last way too long.

Abel has always been completely unfazed by the process. Noemi decides that if there's any upside to being — whatever she is now—then at least it won't be as bad going through the Haven Gate.

It isn't as bad.

It's *worse*.

Half of Noemi's body can handle it; half can't. Her mind seems to think the best way to handle this is to tear itself in two. Static drowns out her thoughts, and pain ripples through her limbs, her abdomen, and her throbbing head. Noemi clutches one of the wall struts as if it were a life preserver in a stormy ocean and prays for it to be over.

Does God listen to the prayers of mechs? She never had to ask herself that before. Abel doesn't pray; he doesn't believe.

The static stops so suddenly that Noemi startles. Reality takes shape around her again, like the crystals of a kaleidoscope settling into a pattern. Swallowing the last of her queasiness, she straightens up and tells herself, *This is how things are now. Deal with it.*

What other choice do you have?

Still troubled, she walks onto the bridge and halts in her tracks at the sight on the viewscreen. "Holy cats," she murmurs.

"Is that a reference to the Egyptian goddess Bast?" Abel says. He's a little too precise, too eager. This is how he acted in the early days, before they knew what to make of each other. "A preliminary search of my records suggests this as the only major feline deity, but I could scan deeper for lesser-known mythologies."

"It's just a saying. It means—*that*."

She gapes at the enormity of the melee in the distance: thousands of ships, facing off against Earth scouts and one another, all of them attempting to pass through the Haven Gate.

As enormous as Gates are, they can only allow so many ships through at a time. That might be dozens of personal craft, even hundreds—but only two or three Damocles ships or larger freighters could transit together. The unwelcome thing in Noemi's head tells her that at least 3,956 ships have massed around the Haven Gate, and plain logic tells her that number will probably double within a day.

"You saw how many ships were landing on Haven," Abel points out. "Remedy seems to have sent out some information about the Gate's location, though the galactic search would no doubt have turned it up before too long."

"It's not the number of people that surprises me—at least, not only that." Harriet and Zayan told her word spread fast among the Vagabonds, but this seems incredible. "What I really can't believe is that Earth's trying to control this," she says. "The people know about Haven now. The home humanity's needed for centuries? This Gate is a sign pointing the way. They won't be denied."

"Or even delayed," Abel adds. "Unfortunately."

"Unfortunately? What's 'unfortunate' about humans finally having a real future?" Noemi thinks it's high time Earth got stuck with a situation beyond its ability to dominate. But then her memory offers up the Russian family, so sure that Earth was lying about the toxicity of Haven's atmosphere, and she remembers how careless they're all being. "You mean Cobweb. They're ignoring the warnings about Cobweb."

"You were entirely clear that the planet is only safe for those who've already suffered the Cobweb plague, or undergone the specialized treatment given to the passengers of the *Osiris*," Abel reassures her. "But it appears many of them refused to prepare."

Exhaustion sinks into Noemi's bones, into her soul. When she transmitted that message galaxy-wide, she lit a fuse without knowing whether it led to a firecracker or a bomb. At the time it seemed brave, even necessary; now she feels like the same immature, impulsive idiot she's always been.

"Noemi," Abel says, coming closer to her. "Your message was entirely clear. Their misunderstandings are their own. You aren't to blame."

She nods, even though her bruised heart can't believe it. "We should get out of here. But where do we go?" It seems important to set a destination, to have one solid goal in the middle of all this confusion.

"That is a difficult question to answer."

They fled Haven because they had to, for Abel's safety, but Noemi is newly, sharply aware that there aren't many other places for them to go. Genesis is impossible, because Abel could easily be arrested for murder. Earth is impossible, because they'd both be in constant risk of getting arrested for treason. Cray doesn't accept outsiders at random; only the most elite scientists and students are allowed to live there. "Kismet's too expensive for the likes of us, and Stronghold—" Her memories of the place are largely blurred by fever, because Abel took her there to save her from her own bout of the Cobweb virus. But she remembers it as a gray, chilly, forbidding place, as craggy and hard as the ores mined there. Is that their only option?

"Our first destination should be Cray," Abel says, surprising her. "I want to make sure Virginia Redbird arrived home safely, and she may be able to help us with whatever counterfeit permits and identities we'll need going forward."

Noemi nods. It's only an interim plan, not a final

answer, but it helps to have one decision made. "We'll go via Stronghold, right?" Her hands lay in a course—more swiftly than she could've done it before. This counts as an "improvement," but it still feels weird.

No other vessels react to their departure. Earth's ships are too busy trying to block travelers heading toward the Haven Gate to care about their one little ship heading away from it. This is what safe looks like, for now.

She becomes aware that the silence has stretched out too long. When she glances back at Abel, he squares his shoulders, as though for courage. He says, "I sense that there are tensions between us. Perhaps it would be better to discuss them now, while we have time and safety...relatively speaking."

Taken aback, Noemi says, "Um, okay. What tensions?"

"You seem displeased at your new nature as a mech-human hybrid."

"It's bizarre," she says shortly.

"Was I wrong, then? My only alternative would've been to let you go, and I was not—*am* not willing to do that."

"Abel, no. I'm not angry with you. I'm just...*angry*." With a heavy sigh, Noemi turns to face him. "My whole life has to change. Who I am, what I am, what I can do with my life...it all vanished in an instant, and I have no idea what comes next. That's scary. A lot of times, when humans get scared, we also get angry."

Hopefully, Abel says, "You mean you don't blame me for your transformation?"

"I remember what it was like when Esther was wounded. Even though Esther said she didn't want artificial organs, I tried to make you implant them anyway. When it came right down to it, I was ready to do anything if it would save her. That's how love works." He lifts his chin, a silent acknowledgment of his love for her. She feels too shy to meet his gaze as she adds, "I guess there's no way to love without being a little bit selfish. You want to give everything to the other person, but there's also something you want for yourself, more than you've ever wanted anything before."

"I wanted you to live," Abel says. "That's all." He's never put expectations on how he feels for her, never acted like that required her to feel the exact same way. Maybe that gives her time to figure out how she does feel, because right now she doesn't have a damned clue. The only thing she knows is that they should be together.

When he smiles, reassured, she manages to smile back. But she thinks, *What kind of life is this going to be?*

• • •

It takes hours more to reach the next Gate, hours Noemi largely spends conked out in her bunk. Cryosleep's even more exhausting than the data in her head suggests; maybe the official information doesn't take into account how the experience actually feels. Or maybe none of those scientists ever went through it themselves.

Abel sleeps, too. At first she's surprised—Abel doesn't need sleep the same way humans do—but then she does the math. He hasn't had other crew members to help run the ship in days or weeks, and he spent even more time working in the lab to bring her back to life. He's had to be on constant lookout for attack by Earth ships or Gillian Shearer's mechs. He was captured and treated like an experiment in a lab, very nearly getting killed in the process.

Even mechs get tired sometimes, Noemi figures. *Maybe that's another reason I'm not bouncing back yet.*

It would've been better if they could've slept in the same room—maybe even the same bed. Noemi isn't completely sure if she's ready to take the huge leap forward of sharing a bed, given what might happen between them. She only knows it would be good to see him. Better to touch him.

As she's lying under the covers, awake but only barely aware of it, the comms chime with an incoming live transmission. Noemi sits upright and jabs at the nearest panel with her finger. "Patch me through," she says to the computer.

Abel's voice through the speaker answers her, "*I awakened just in time to hear the chime and have already patched the message through, though not yet begun conversation—*"

She manages not to groan in frustration. "Will you just patch us both through?"

Another chime, and then a deep, unfamiliar voice says, *"Krall Consortium vessel* Maputo *to the free ship* Persephone. *Do you read us?"*

"We read you," Noemi says. Maybe she should let Abel handle this, as the captain, but she was in charge of the negotiations with the Consortium. "Have you been looking for us? If so, why?"

"All Consortium vessels have been on the lookout for you since shortly after the Battle of Genesis," replies the *Maputo.* *"The alliance between our Consortium and Genesis holds. Your assistance is required for the next and final stage of the Liberty War."*

Hope blossoms in Noemi's heart. Abel told her once that she had her own version of Directive One: her powerful instinct to protect her homeworld. She hadn't known she'd ever be able to help Genesis again.

"You have our attention, Maputo," says Abel. *"Please elaborate."*

"The information is coded in-person only," says the deep voice. Vagabonds distrust digital communications, which can so easily be altered; the most important conversations only take place when both parties are face-to-face. *"Can you rendezvous with the* Katara *on Stronghold?"*

Noemi raises her eyebrows, and suspects Abel's just as surprised as she is. The *Katara* is the flagship of the Krall Consortium, the personal vessel of Dagmar Krall herself.

"We can," Noemi says. "When?"

"*Twenty-one hours from now,*" says the *Maputo*. "*Do not land on Stronghold without first confirming the rendezvous with the* Katara *in orbit. The situation on the planet is volatile.*"

"Understood," Abel says. "*Is there any other critical information?*"

"*Negative.* Maputo *out.*"

A crackle of static indicates the comm channel to the *Maputo* has been closed, but the connection between Noemi and Abel is still live. She says, "Do you trust them?"

"*On the balance, yes. They've taken a side in the Liberty War; their concerns are Genesis's concerns, for now, and vice versa. The Vagabonds have no reason to turn against Genesis, and every reason to remain allied against Earth.*"

"Agreed," Noemi says. "Just the same, I'm keeping my eye on them."

"*Very wise.*"

• • •

Everything goes well during their voyage to Stronghold—until they're both on the bridge, ready to settle the *Persephone* into orbit. That's when a red warning light begins to flash on its console. From her position at ops, Noemi brings up the data and frowns. "We've got issues with the mag engines."

Almost instantly, Abel's at her side, studying the same data. "I've put them into overload too often," he says. "I always allowed for several hours or days of rest before those uses, but still—too many overloads is too much wear."

"Can we fix this?" Noemi doesn't want to have to find a new ship. That would be complicated and dangerous, and besides, *Persephone* is almost like home.

"Yes, it's fixable," he says. "However, we'll need to obtain the necessary parts."

Sensors indicate that the *Katara* hasn't reached Stronghold yet. "I guess we won't be able to borrow them from the Consortium," Noemi says.

"Not unless we wait, and I would prefer to begin repairs sooner rather than later."

"Then 'sooner' means we've got to land on the planet."

They share looks of dismay. Whether or not they trust Dagmar Krall, they'd rather wait for her. Breaking the rules of this rendezvous might be enough to scare off the *Katara*, and ruin any chance Noemi has of helping Genesis again.

But they have no choice. It's run the risk of being stranded in deep space—or head to Stronghold.

12

THE *PERSEPHONE* HAS ONLY LANDED ON STRONGHOLD once before. At the time, Noemi had been delirious, suffering in the high fever of the Cobweb virus. Abel, overcome with fear for her, had paid relatively little attention to their surroundings. But one of the advantages of a cybernetic brain is the ability to recall even those things that went unnoticed before. He calls up the memories, scans the images and sounds, and compares them to what they see now.

Noemi's recall cannot be as detailed. Not only did she have only fallible human memory at the time, but she spent most of their time on the planet too sick to be coherent. Yet he must be underestimating human memory, because she recognizes this as the spaceport they landed at before, and sees all the ways in which it has changed. The contrasts are even sharper to her than they are to him.

"*Look* at this," she whispers as they walk through the crowded port. (Her steps are still too slow, slightly halting, as though she'd sprained an ankle recently—an ordinary occurrence, not one anyone will remark on.) The spaceport resembles most architecture on Stronghold: thick, made of stone, Brutalist in its starkness. However, she's pointing out the graffiti painted and scratched on every pillar, every floor: *Our Worlds Belong to Us. Haven for All Humanity.* "It's finally happening! They're all rising up against Earth."

"Not all. Your visual sensors should be more acute— can you make that out?" Abel gestures to a distant arch that leads to the outside. The words scrawled there say *Genesis Lies.*

She brushes one hand over her nearly bare scalp, an uncertain gesture, but she doesn't flinch. "Sure, not everyone believes in us. But there must be some threat of an uprising. That scene near the Haven Gate? That doesn't suggest a galaxy at peace."

He nods, conceding the point. "Several Damocles ships were patrolling a large area of the Kismet system when I came through, and a few scouts were monitoring the area near the minefield. It's already clear from the Damocles we've seen that Earth has greater military reserves than was ever publicly reported. If they haven't already run into substantive resistance, they expect to, and soon."

Encouraged, Noemi begins to smile. "There must be graffiti like this on all the colony worlds. The planets are figuring out that they could stand up to Earth together in a way they never could alone. As far as I'm concerned, that's good news."

"There's an ancient Russian proverb," Abel says. "It goes, 'Never celebrate the death of the czar.'"

Noemi frowns. "You mean—don't get excited about one power falling before you know what might replace it."

"Exactly. No one should take heart when war begins."

Her grin fades as she takes this in, and for a moment he wishes he hadn't said it. Maybe he should've let her take her happiness where she could. Yet that would be patronizing her—treating her as less than the intelligent, courageous person he knows her to be. As she grapples with this transition, he must not take it easy on her; she'd hate that, and tune him out immediately. He must trust in her as he always has.

Noemi shrugs, and her voice is hard as she replies, "Maybe the rest of the galaxy can be scared about 'the start of the war.' *My* war began before I was born. I've never known anything else."

"I stand corrected," Abel says, and leaves it at that.

Stronghold is not a beautiful world. Someday, if terraforming efforts fully take root, it might become warm, green, and welcoming. At present, it is nothing but a flat gray sky stretched over endless black sand. The broad banners that fly from most arches and buildings provide only flickers of color in the vast, stony monotony. Its horizon is dotted with mines, smelting factories, and the like. The industrial smoke this planet produces is deliberately sent into the atmosphere to warm the climate; its sluggish gray swirls drift slowly toward the clouds. Stronghold is Earth's quarry, its mother lode of every vital metal and mineral. It is the colony world Earth can least afford to lose.

Genesis and Stronghold would make uneasy allies, he thinks. *Terraforming through pollutants, deep-earth mining— these are the practices Genesis has forbidden. After Earth's defeat, wouldn't they inevitably turn on each other?*

The galaxy may find out.

A quick scan at a public kiosk reveals the location of the closest repair depot, which requires only a short trip via public tram. The depot is located at the edge of a mine, which must be why it's surrounded by and filled with gray-plated Smashers. This is the work their enormous, powerful bodies were built to do. The hulking, humanoid shapes of them form an eerie maze leading to the heart of the depot.

To Abel's mild surprise, the head of repairs is human: squat and pale-skinned, with a thick shock of gray hair and a name tag that reads HELGA. She appears to supervise a number of Item models, all of whom are tinkering with various machines. She sucks on a mint stick as she scans the dataread they brought, with its diagrams of the *Persephone's* damage. "Not pretty," Helga says. "Why were you two running around like flighted mammals out of the depths of purgatory and burning out your engines like that?"

He tries to think of a valid excuse, but as usual, Noemi is quicker with this sort of thing. "Don't know if you noticed, but there's a war brewing. We get away from trouble as fast as we can, and these days? There's trouble everywhere."

Helga nods. "Fair enough. Well, we've got the parts and can send 'em over to fix you up in a jiffy. Just as soon as you transfer the credits—" She lifts up her own dataread, which displays a figure Abel finds staggering.

"That's more than four times the usual price," he says. If Helga thinks he's too naïve to understand when he's being swindled, she'll soon know better.

But her grin is knowing. "Like the lady said—don't know if you noticed, but there's a war on. Plus every Vagabond and his great-aunt Mildred is headed to Haven, so they're all fixing up their ships for the big voyage. Supply shortages plus shipping delays mean higher prices." Helga sighs heavily. "Listen, kids, I'm making less profit on this work than I did before. Hardly any, to tell you the truth. But we've got to stay in business, and I can't stay in business if nobody can afford repairs, so here I am practically working for free."

No doubt Helga is exaggerating—but Abel suspects she isn't exaggerating much. The problems she describes are logical; he ought to have projected this possibility from the start. Worrying about Noemi has left him very little mental energy to consider anything else.

Noemi leans closer to him and murmurs, "Can you pay for this?"

He's put aside almost all his profits from Vagabonding; with no taste for luxury, he's kept his money available for emergencies. Yet some emergencies go beyond planning. "Almost, but not quite."

"So what are we supposed to do?" She puts one hand to her shorn temple.

A loud metallic clatter startles them both. Abel looks over to see that an Item has dropped one of its tools onto the concrete floor. Such a slip is rare for the dexterous Item models. Not unheard of, by any means—but Abel notes it.

"Not again. These damned things have been giving me trouble all week," Helga mutters.

As the head of repairs bustles over to investigate her malfunctioning mech, Noemi resumes speaking. "The last time we had to earn money was back in the Kismet system, and I doubt Stronghold has a tourism industry to support."

"The obvious option is of course—"

"*Not* prostitution," she insists. Humor glints in her dark eyes. No doubt she remembers Abel's offer to take up the "oldest profession" in order to earn funds on their very first journey. "Stop kidding around."

Abel wasn't joking, but there seems no point to admitting it now. "Our choices are therefore limited. Perhaps we should ask Helga—"

"Vidal of Genesis."

Startled, Abel turns toward the voice whispering at his shoulder; Noemi moves even faster—equally startling—and seizes the cloaked speaker's arm. "Who's looking for her?" she demands.

The tall man in the green cloak pulls back his hood, revealing East Asian heritage and a metallic scrollwork tattoo along one side of his face. "Call me Yeoh."

"What is your business, Yeoh?" Abel remains careful not to admit that Noemi is "Vidal of Genesis."

Yeoh says, "You were instructed to wait for a rendezvous with the *Katara*."

Noemi visibly relaxes at the mention of Dagmar Krall's flagship. Abel remains wary, but contact with the Consortium is more likely to help them than hurt them. "Our ship is having engine trouble," he says. "We'd hoped to obtain repair parts and return to deep space, but we are, as the saying goes, 'flat broke.'"

Although Yeoh doesn't reply, the explanation seems to satisfy him. "Lucky for you, the commodore has her own reasons for being planetside. Follow me."

Noemi smiles brilliantly at Abel as she falls into step behind Yeoh, who's heading into the bustling crowd near the repair station. He remains at her elbow, ready for any sort of ambush.

Expecting betrayal where there is no motive for betrayal

could be considered paranoia, Abel tells himself. Perhaps he's becoming neurotic. What might Burton Mansfield have made of that?

• • •

The cheapest form of insulation on Stronghold must be the soil of the planet itself. That's Abel's best theory for why all the planet's entertainment venues are located underground. Not deep within subterranean caverns, like the entire civilization on Cray—but half-buried, with only long, narrow windows near the ceilings to let in the weak sunlight. The café Yeoh leads them into uses actual wax candles for additional illumination; they burn within lanterns hanging from the ceiling beams or tiny votives atop each table.

At a table in the far corner sits Dagmar Krall. Abel automatically runs a physiognomy scan that confirms it's really her, but even a human would already know. Krall's appearance is striking: blond hair that hangs freely, and large, unusually wide-set eyes. Her clothing is more subdued than that of the average colorful Vagabond's, perhaps as a nod to her authority over the largest private fleet in the galaxy—or to dispel the many rumors that she's less of a businesswoman, more of a pirate queen.

They last saw Dagmar Krall in the Battle of Genesis, leading the *Katara* and her entire Consortium against

Earth's fleet. She seems to have moved from defending Genesis to helping that planet take the offensive.

Noemi and Abel take the chairs opposite Krall. Yeoh remains standing two meters away, tacitly guarding them from detection.

Or, Abel thinks, *guarding Krall from us.* The faint distrust he feels is no doubt mutual.

"A lot of people are wondering where you guys are," says Krall, by way of hello.

Noemi's expression darkens. "The Genesis authorities? Are they looking for Abel?"

Krall raises an eyebrow. "Should they be?"

Abel judges it most prudent not to answer this.

But Dagmar Krall doesn't seem to expect an answer. She continues, "You left some Vagabond crew back on Genesis wondering where their captain went."

"We had an emergency," Abel says, leaving it at that. "Besides, I believed Harriet Dixon and Zayan Thakur intended to settle on Genesis permanently."

"Doesn't mean they don't wonder where you are." Krall's eyes study Noemi intently. "Nice haircut."

"Oh. Um, thanks." Noemi ducks her head. She's in no hurry to explain what she's become, at least not to Dagmar Krall, which Abel considers wise. "But we didn't come here to discuss hairstyles. The message from the *Maputo* talked about helping Genesis."

Krall leans forward, lowering her voice. "I assume you both know what I mean by *Bellum Sanctum*?"

"Of course." Abel is programmed with a full knowledge of Latin, as well as thirty-one other languages, both living and dead. "The phrase translates as 'holy war.'"

"It's more than that," Noemi interjects. Her excitement is palpable.

"What do you mean?" he asks her.

Eagerly she explains, "We learned about this in tactics training. Genesis always had a kind of masterstroke weapon—one they'd kept in reserve in the early days of the war. But they waited too long to use it. It was an offensive weapon, not defensive. We couldn't use it until Genesis was in a position of strength, which it hasn't been for thirty years."

"What precisely does it do?"

"I never had that kind of security clearance," Noemi says. "They weren't giving us details. If we'd known what it was, we might have hesitated in battle. They taught us not to hesitate in war. Hesitation ruins everything."

"Not everything," Krall says. "In this case, the Battle of Genesis means your homeworld is back in a position of strength. Some Consortium ships and others from the Vagabond fleet are now acting as Genesis's operatives in the greater galaxy. And right now, we're working to get everything ready for Bellum Sanctum to be used at last."

It strikes Abel that Krall is talking around the particulars of the Bellum Sanctum plan. Possibly this is only discretion in a public location. But he notes this for future consideration.

Noemi's too elated to notice any evasion, at least for the moment. "That means the end of the war. It means victory at last."

Abel finds himself remembering Darius Akide's desperation during their final, fatal encounter. Akide didn't act like a man who knew Genesis had a weapon that would give them victory. Yet as a member of the Elder Council, wouldn't he have known that?

Krall interrupts his train of thought. "If we're going to help with Bellum Sanctum, we have work to do in the Kismet system. They've stepped up security there—"

"Exponentially," Abel says. "Does Earth suspect a major Genesis strategy is about to be deployed?"

"Doubt it." Krall's expression becomes faraway, uncertain. "I have my own suspicions about the Kismet system, but that's for another day. The point is, we need your help there, as soon as possible."

"Why?" Noemi's already beginning to think through the question in more depth. Her delight at the thought of Genesis's victory hasn't completely overridden her rational mind. "You're the leader of the biggest fleet in the galaxy, outside of Earth's military. We're two people in a decades-old science vessel that doesn't even have weapons."

Krall nods, acknowledging this. "But one of those people

is the single most advanced mech ever created. Human talent alone can't get the job done. We need you, Abel."

He glances at Noemi, who is in all probability thinking the same thing he is: that as a hybrid between mech and human, she might be as useful to Krall, and to Genesis, as he could be. Still, there's nothing to gain from telling Dagmar Krall about Noemi's hybridization, which means it's not yet worth even the very minor risk.

"Although Genesis has little use for me," Abel says, "I am willing to undertake this work on that world's behalf, once the full Bellum Sanctum strategy has been explained to us and I've heard exactly what you need me to—"

"Commodore!" Yeoh leans over the table, his face stricken. He gestures toward a comm link at his belt. "We're picking up signals from Stronghold security—they've received reports of Krall Consortium activity."

"Well," Dagmar Krall says, "we knew taking sides in the war would win us new enemies. Looks like Stronghold is one of them."

Yeoh nods. "They're already sending out patrols."

Immediately Krall stands, wrapping her scarf around her neck. With a wolfish grin, she says, "Looks like we'll be discussing this further in the Kismet system. For now, we have more important things to do. Like *run*."

13

Run.

It feels like more than a statement. It feels like a command. The diagram of the way they came toward this café drops into Noemi's head, unsummoned. It's terrifying how quickly the mech within her responds to this command, how strongly she feels the need to get out of here as fast as possible—

But in this case, the human within her agrees completely. She leaps away from their table, grabs Abel's hand, and runs as quickly as she can.

Abel's swift reflexes mean he's with her, stride for stride. Usually, when they're running for their lives, she can sense him holding himself back so as not to leave her behind. He's still doing it—though not as much. Her legs are fully human, but her brain's sending messages at double or triple the rate it did before. She doesn't have full mech speed, but she's running faster than virtually any human could.

Good. That means they can stay together.

People spin out of their way as they dash by—flattening themselves against walls, yelping in surprise. She pays them no mind. Right now, the crowd is just one more obstacle between them and the *Persephone.*

"If it helps," Abel calls over the din of the crowd, "Stronghold security is only looking for Consortium members. Not for us."

"So far as we know! I'm not hanging around to find out whether they've tied us to Krall."

"Agreed," Abel states, his attention still on the path ahead.

As the spaceport appears in the distance, a Queen model steps in front of them, halting Noemi and Abel in place. She curses herself for not bringing her blaster along.

The programming inside her urges her forward, and Noemi grabs the Queen by the shoulders to push her aside. This ought to start hand-to-hand combat—but instead, the Queen shuffles sideways, then drops to the ground.

What the hell? Noemi thinks.

A human security guard comes hurrying to the fallen Queen, shouting into the comm unit strapped to his wrist, "We've got another mech breakdown! Sector nine, section one—"

Another?

Abel pulls Noemi forward. "We can't slow down."

"Right, of course." Panting, she accelerates again, keeping her eyes on the spaceport looming larger as they go. The Queen's appearance means they have to hurry. Either Stronghold is looking for the *Persephone* after all, or their frantic dash has betrayed them as allies of the Consortium.

They're within fifty meters of the spaceport, when Noemi catches sight of that wall of Smashers, the giant mining robots still standing there, waiting to be deployed.

Except that they *have* been deployed. They're stepping out of their metal frameworks, their heavy feet plodding upon the ground. One of the Smashers begins scanning, then stops when it reaches her and Abel. Another Smasher turns toward them. Then another.

"Abel?" Noemi calls. "What's happening?"

"I can only conjecture, but I believe that due to regular fighter mech malfunction, Stronghold is now using mining robots for security."

"You mean, those monsters are coming after us?"

"Unfortunately, yes."

The Smasher closest to them leaps forward and swings a long arm, nearly striking Abel in the head—a blow that would surely have decapitated him. Noemi's entire mind floods with the need to protect Abel—to put herself between him and harm.

She tries to stay calm, reminding herself, *Smashers don't have cybernetic brains like Queens and Charlies, so they can't launch a strategized attack.*

But they *do* have enormous metal frames and the ability to punch through solid rock.

The trajectories in Noemi's head appear again, pointing out the swiftest way for them to reach the ship. She doesn't like the answer, but it's their best chance, so she takes it.

Noemi takes a deep breath and runs straight for the center of the line of Smashers beginning to approach them. At the last moment, she ducks down to roll between a Smasher's enormous feet. Abel's mind must've shown him the same route, because he's right behind her.

A metal fist slams down mere centimeters from her head, so hard dust flies in the air and the impact jolts her nearly as much as a real blow. Noemi skitters out of the way, pulling Abel with her.

"Are Smashers fast?" she yells as they start running again.

"So it would seem," Abel answers. The pounding of heavy Smasher feet is getting louder by the step.

"There!" she shouts, pointing to a nearby transport, hardly more than a hovering sled. "Let's go!" They leap on board, activate the controls, and take off. It's not a tremendously fast vehicle, but it moves more quickly than Smashers can run. As the mining robots lumber in pursuit, Noemi shouts over the roar of wind, "They're not that far behind!"

"I calculate we can make it to the *Persephone*. Whether we'll have time to take off again is another question."

They came to this planet for repairs the ship hasn't had. "The mag engines—"

"If I deactivate certain safety limits, the engines should at least get us to the Cray system, perhaps one trip more." He doesn't have to add, *And no farther.*

The two of them zoom along mere centimeters above the desolate, crater-pocked terrain. She looks back at the enormous, mindless robots chasing them—demolishing everything in their path in their thoughtless pursuit. There's no question that the Smashers are capable of living up to their name; any single one of them could kill both her and Abel with a single punch.

The sled zips to the spaceport doors. They leap off and run through the nearest entry. Noemi breathes out in relief. "Thank God. The doors are too small for the Smashers to get through."

"That should help us," Abel agrees.

Which is exactly when the first Smasher crashes through the wall. Chunks of stone fly around the room, chips like shrapnel, and Noemi barely has time to cover her face from the debris.

No time to think. All her strength and will are directed at running as fast as she can. She and Abel tear through the spaceport, trying to ignore the metallic din behind them.

Glancing back once, she sees the Smashers coming toward them like a metal tsunami.

Finally the *Persephone* comes into sight. Abel shouts, "I'm going to get the ship ready for takeoff. Just close it up for launch."

Normally he would never leave her behind. He trusts her abilities in a way he didn't before. It would be more gratifying if she didn't feel like he was trusting her for *not* being human. She yells no more than "Go!"

Abel takes off ahead of her, disappearing into the silver teardrop of their ship. Noemi keeps running, and by now she can dare to hope. While Smashers can go through walls—are more or less built to do precisely that—they might have safeguards to keep them from damaging human machinery. If so, they won't punch through the *Persephone*'s hull.

If not, she and Abel will have to steal another ship or die trying. Probably the latter.

Running through the *Persephone*'s door feels like crossing the finish line of a marathon in first place. Noemi begins cycling through launch procedures, her sweat a cool sheen on her skin, and when she hears the Smashers clank outside the door, terror seizes her as if in a fist. She freezes in place, unable to move, unsure whether it would do any good if she could.

The Smashers don't burst through.

Noemi slumps against the wall of the docking bay in

relief. The things are programmed to preserve spacecraft. That means she and Abel are going to make it.

An enormous metal sphere rolls through the entry into the docking bay, then unfolds itself. As the Smasher takes its true shape again, she yells, "Oh, come on!"

The thing in her head pulls out a memory—one Noemi has been too frantic to recall on her own. She studied robots and cybernetics in military training, to a limited degree; she only learned how to destroy them.

Shape-modification technology usually routes all functions through a certain kind of core connector, says the military instructor from long ago in her head. Noemi can envision the diagram her squadron was shown. That connector looks a lot like the arc-shaped protrusion from the side of the Smasher's head.

Noemi jumps onto the Smasher, leaping as high as she can—high enough to clutch the thing's shoulder and pull herself up. It isn't programmed to deal with humans coming at it instead of running away. So it stands there dumbly, trying to process a solution, for the half second it takes her to grab that core connector and rip it out.

The Smasher staggers backward. Noemi jumps down, clutching the bundle of wires in her left hand, breathing hard. As she hits the panel to close the *Persephone*'s bay door, she sees the lights in its cranium dome go dim.

Abel must've completed takeoff prep, because the door

belatedly pinwheels shut. At least no more Smashers can get inside. She sags against the wall in relief.

Through the speaker, she hears Abel: *"I show us ready for takeoff. Can you confirm?"*

"Confirmed. Get us the hell out of here."

The ship lifts off that instant, and she feels the shivery moment when artificial gravity kicks in.

Abel says, *"Are you all right?"*

"Exhausted. But yeah, I'm all right. No security ships came after us?"

"A few ships seem to have engaged with the Vagabond fleet, but the Katara *and most of the others appear to have gotten away safely."*

The plan to win the war for Genesis remains safe. Grinning, Noemi says, "Oh, by the way, we now have a Smasher of our very own."

"We have a what?"

She's finally astonished Abel. As exhausted as Noemi is, she can't help being a little proud.

• • •

Noemi takes some time to rest while Abel checks the engines and examines their new Smasher for himself. She makes it back to the bridge before him, which gives her a little time to look over the engine readouts. They are... not good.

It's a miracle we've made it this far, she thinks. *We're good for one more trip through a Gate, the end. Even that is at a higher risk level than I'd like to run.* Captain Baz would've grounded any starfighter with engines twice as sturdy as these.

Yet her new understanding of probabilities makes her feel better about these numbers than she would've before. Is that more sensible? Or would good old human fear serve them better right now?

I guess we'll find out when the ship doesn't blow up, Noemi tells herself. *Or when it does.*

Abel reappears on the bridge smudged with grease and looking satisfied with himself. "It's a very interesting inner matrix," he says. "The Smashers are capable of significant intelligence upgrades, if desired."

"What would we do with an intelligent Smasher?" She laughs. "I think I should be the only 'significant upgrade' for a while."

His pleased expression fades. "Do you still resent your hybridization?"

That takes a moment to process. "Wait. What?"

"Have you not forgiven me for making you part mech?" As it often does when he's feeling vulnerable, Abel's mech precision kicks in. "Or, rather, for requesting that Gillian Shearer make you part mech—"

"Hold it right there," Noemi says. "Forgive you? Abel,

you *saved my life*. That's not the way I'd have wanted it saved, but I know you didn't have any other options."

He blinks as he considers her words. When he speaks again, his tone isn't as cool—but still wary. "You dislike being a mech-human hybrid. You've said so. To be part mech is to be lesser. Which means I, too, am lesser than a human."

Her face flushes hot, as though she'd been struck. "No, Abel. How can you say that? I've always—ever since I realized what you were, who you were, that you had a soul, I've always defended you! I've always said you were the equal of any human, and better than most of them. So where are you getting this 'lesser' stuff?"

"You repeatedly expressed dismay about your new physical and mental functions—though admittedly less, as you've adjusted more—"

"Exactly. I've been trying to adjust." Noemi calms herself, trying to think less about his accusation, more about how threatened he must feel. "Abel, nobody wants their body changed around without permission. Even if it's necessary! Nobody wants to wake up and find out they have to relearn how to walk, or even how to think. That doesn't mean it can't be done. That doesn't mean you're 'less' than before, or—or that you hate the parts of you that have changed. But it's scary as hell."

When his eyes meet hers, he looks like himself again, so they're getting somewhere.

She sighs as some of her own words replay in her head. "I guess maybe I sounded . . . a little harsh, in the beginning. But did you expect me to be fine with everything right away? Did you think being a mech's so much greater than being human that I wouldn't need any time to adjust?"

"Of course not." Abel pauses. Maybe he's rethinking some of the stuff he said, too. "It's possible I focused on the physical issues inherent in the transition, while underestimating the emotional difficulty you would face."

Noemi folds her arms. "You think?"

This time, thank goodness, he recognizes the humor. His smile has rarely been as welcome.

"Humans need to get used to anything new. Like body parts. *Definitely* including body parts."

"I understand," he says. "I'll be more understanding of your transition in future."

"Hopefully I'm past the worst of it," Noemi says.

Abel hesitates before asking, "Should I assume that all . . . adjustments to personal interrelationships made before your hybridization are now to be considered 'on hold,' as part of this transition?"

It takes her 2.1 seconds to parse that. "You mean—you and me."

Abel's blue eyes meet hers. "Yes."

They'd made some decisions, right before the Battle of Genesis. Noemi remembers the lightness, the *rightness* of her choice to travel through the stars with Abel. The way it felt to run into his arms. The intensity of their kiss.

Can she be as sure of that any longer? Can she be that sure about anything?

Noemi can't entirely trust the mind and body she has now. Maybe she has to put her faith in the person she was before.

"I guess I still want us to be together." She takes a deep breath. "I don't know how that works any more than you do, but I'd like to find out."

"You would?" He looks at her with such hope. Such simple, unguarded love. The beauty of it feels like it could crack her heart open. This must be the right choice after all.

"Yeah." Noemi slides her arms around his neck, pulling him closer. "I think I would."

Abel leans close for a kiss, whispering against her lips, "Then let's begin."

14

ABEL UNDERSTANDS THE MECHANICS OF HOW HUMANS express physical affection. His databanks include all relevant biological information, a wealth of fiction portraying love and passion, and sociological input into the nuances of mating from sources as diverse as the twentieth-century manual *The Joy of Sex* to the second-century Sanskrit text the *Kama Sutra*.

(Several *Kama Sutra* postures would be difficult or impossible for humans to achieve, much less maintain. They are well within Abel's parameters.)

However, his actual experience falls far short of his knowledge. Without emotion, Abel does not possess desire—he'd never fallen in love before Noemi, and so had never felt it for himself.

She has taught him this, and is now teaching him many things more.

"You really never wanted to kiss anyone else?" Noemi murmurs as they cuddle together on one of the lower crew bunks. (Not his bed, nor hers—that would suggest a progression to greater intimacy than Abel is willing to presume.) "Not even the tiniest flicker of curiosity?"

"I felt curiosity," he admits. "But that's not the same thing as desire—at least, not for me."

She lies next to him, touching from their feet to their thighs to their bellies to their heads. Abel rests his cheek against her forehead; from this angle he can just see her kiss-swollen lips. He's not yet sure whether they're done kissing for the time being, or whether this is merely a pause. A pause seems infinitely preferable to stopping.

Noemi idly rubs one of the arms he's wrapped around her. "So it was impossible for you to feel physical, um, needs before you fell in love with a woman?"

"Strictly speaking, it could as easily have been a man I first fell in love with. I possess no inherent sexual orientation or preferences."

She looks up at him in dismay. "Are you—programmed not to feel emotions without, uh, stimulus?"

"I'm programmed with a deep feeling of devotion," Abel admits. "That was meant to be directed only at Burton Mansfield, in order to make me obey his orders, even the ones that lead to self-destruction. But with you, I believe that devotion grew into something far more powerful."

She frowns. "Devotion is a part of your programming? Is it a part of mine now?"

Abel considers this. "Unlikely. Mine was a special program, not a standard function of mech hardware."

Noemi smiles, apparently reassured, but still curious. "So you could've fallen in love with—well, anybody? Just whoever showed up at the right time?"

"Not just anybody." He rolls her over onto her back, the better to look down into her eyes. "It seems I would only have felt romantic love for someone brave, and forthright, and intelligent. Someone who had high ideals and challenged herself to meet them. Someone who wasn't afraid to hope. Someone who could look at me and see not a machine, but a person. I think such people are very rare."

To Abel this seems like no more than a recitation of the facts, but Noemi's dark eyes well with tears. "I think you're the only person who could've seen anything that good in me."

"Not the only one," he says. "Just the first of many."

Her only reply to this is to pull him down for another kiss, and it's the only answer Abel needs.

●　●　●

They had first planned to go to Cray only to check on Virginia. Abel now hopes that they can also talk her or some of her Razer friends into helping them repair the *Persephone*'s engines. The trick will be managing this without attracting undue attention.

"So, do we pretend to be games merchants again?" she says once they've returned to the bridge. "Or do you have a better plan?"

"Actually, I do. Weeks ago, while investigating Gillian Shearer and Mansfield Cybernetics, Virginia and I set up false records that establish me as her 'cousin.' Family members are allowed to visit Cray, as long as they don't come too often or stay too long." Abel considers this. "Our stay will be short, so I doubt we'll run into any problems."

She raises an eyebrow. "Our stay on Stronghold was short."

"Your point is well taken."

Noemi makes her way to the ops station as she says, "Cousins, huh? You two look so much alike."

Virginia is several centimeters taller than Abel, and dark where he's fair. He can see the humor. "If asked, I'll say I was adopted."

That makes Noemi laugh out loud.

Her mood remains buoyant as they approach Cray for landing. Abel, too, is encouraged by the lack of any extra military presence. No Damocles ships surround the dull reddish planet. Its citizens are almost all scientists, brought to this planet as children, separated from their families and taught that their first loyalty is to Earth. They're pampered and privileged, allowed to spend their entire lives in a kind of intellectual playground. If the revelations about

Haven have shaken Cray's ties to Earth, there are no visible signs so far.

As for the biological warfare—Earth's attempt to destroy Genesis with a deadlier form of Cobweb—that weapon was created here. Every other world and all the Vagabonds may be outraged at the thought of biological weapons, but at least some of the people on Cray agreed with their use. They helped it happen, after all.

In other words, Abel and Noemi have enemies here. They just don't know who they are.

When he says as much, she replies, "So, we just don't cause any trouble."

"You believe that this is possible, all past experience to the contrary?"

"Let me try to be optimistic, okay?"

Landing permission is swiftly granted. Although his last visit was less than four weeks earlier, apparently "Cousin Abel" hasn't visited often enough to raise suspicion—yet. As he and Noemi disembark, there's no sign of surveillance, only a couple of George models placidly recording data.

Noemi's expression darkens. "Do you know what I mean when I say it's too quiet?"

"I'm familiar with the euphemism, but I see no grounds for concern. Don't indulge in paranoia." Abel refuses to surrender to neuroticism just yet.

"It's not paranoid to be on our guard. For anyone, but especially for us."

"I only meant to reassure you," he says. "Though I must point out that your commitment to optimism has already faltered."

"You're still terrible at comforting people."

It's an old joke between them. This reference is further evidence that their interactions are becoming normal again. Abel smiles to himself.

He goes to a communications kiosk at the edge of the hangar and punches in the codes for Redbird, V. Almost instantly the screen lights up with Virginia's face. She grins, as she always does, but her expression is edged with anxiety. *"Cousin Abel! Thank goodness. I didn't know when you'd come back again."*

"I wanted to surprise you," Abel says. "Noemi's here, too."

Next to him, Noemi leans close enough to wave at the camera. Virginia brightens. *"Well, sounds like it's time to celebrate! Would you like to meet up for dinner? And maybe we can get a look at your ship."*

"A look at our ship?" Noemi frowns, then goes very still. Abel knows she's realized what he determined almost from the beginning: Virginia is afraid her communications are being monitored.

Cray authorities suspect dissent, he reasons. *Even sabotage. Genesis, a world with lower levels of technology, found the cure for the weaponized Cobweb virus within weeks. It would be logical to conclude Genesis had help, and the authorities would know that help could only have come from Cray itself.*

As he thinks through this, he keeps his tone casual. "Yes, you should come by before dinner. Who'll be with you?"

"Just Ludwig, Fon, and me." Virginia points to a spot off camera. *"We'll come to the docking bay as soon as we can!"*

Instead, red warning lights begin to flash—not in the space dock, but within the Razers' hideout. Instantly Abel realizes that Cray authorities must already have suspected who the guilty parties were; they were monitoring communications, waiting for something incriminating—such as a strong hint that someone badly wanted to escape the planet. He and Virginia just provided that hint.

"Oh crap. Oh no." Virginia whirls toward the still-unseen Ludwig and Fon. *"Override the locks, now!"*

"We're going to have company," Noemi mutters as space dock doors begin to clank open nearby. "Lots of it."

Within 0.52 seconds, Abel has pulled up the area schematics he studied on his first visit to Cray. A human's memory would retain only a few details, if any. He sees them in his mind in complete detail. "Virginia, you must get to the Caldera Four observatory platform. All of you, as fast as possible."

"Caldera Four?" Virginia yelps. *"Talk about going from the frying pan to the—"* But she shuts off communications, and he knows they'll meet him and Noemi there if they can.

A blaster bolt hits the wall near them, and Abel mentally adds, *If we make it there ourselves.*

"Get down!" Noemi shoves him toward the nearest cover, a pile of crates. Abel's shocked at the force of her push, the confidence of her defense. She aims her blaster and starts firing, every single bolt precision aimed.

The Charlies and Queens fire back in a standard pattern. Yet their accuracy is below regular parameters—perhaps most humans wouldn't notice it, but Abel does. Noemi seems to as well, probably due to her military training. She is therefore relatively safe. This frees him to concentrate for the 2.7 seconds it takes to map the quickest route to Caldera Four. As soon as he's sure, he shouts, "Head for the ship!"

Noemi keeps returning fire the whole way, but her greater speed means she reaches the *Persephone* only moments after him. As she dashes into the bridge, sweaty but not winded, she says, "Did you notice the mechs?"

"Yes. They're not performing up to usual standards."

"We've seen some other breakdowns," she says as she takes her position at the navigation console. "What's up with that?"

"I don't know," Abel admits. He knows only two things: The mech malfunctions have happened too often to be dismissed as mere coincidence, and he and Noemi don't have time to investigate while Virginia and her friends are in danger. "Are you familiar with the definition of a caldera?"

Noemi's eyes widen. "Wait—that's not just a name? We're really headed to a caldera?"

"You did notice that this is a planet with significant volcanic activity?"

Any further protests are cut off by the vibration of the mag engines coming online—which isn't exactly what it ought to be. Only microns off, but still, wrong. No full human could tell the difference, but Noemi's additional senses must make her as aware of the danger as he is. They didn't even get a chance to make repairs on Cray.

"If the engines break down," she says, "will we go dead in space and freeze to death? Or will we explode?"

"Unknown."

"Again, not comforting!"

"With us, the truth rarely is." The *Persephone* lifts off from the pad, still maneuvering well. It's about to be put to the test.

Noemi points to her ops screen. "They're locking down the spaceport exits."

"We're not exiting the conventional way," he explains. Holding the mag engines at minimal power, he takes the ship not upward, but forward, all the way to the edge of their platform—

—then down, into the depths of Cray's caves.

These underground tunnels are the reason this planet is habitable. They form laboratories, house humans, and conduct air. The schematics Abel saw months ago laid out very clearly the nearby location of some large, undeveloped aeration tunnels—which means he and Noemi are now making their way through solid rock. Uneven rock. Rock caves that twist and turn, or rise and fall, very sharply. And that are sometimes less than two meters wider than his ship. Even knowing the layout, it's all Abel can do to keep from crashing.

To her credit, Noemi doesn't scream. She says only, "The thing in my brain is telling me how much trouble we're in, down to the decimal point."

"As is mine."

"I bet you're going to say there's no way to shut that voice off."

"I've never tried." If he were ever going to start, this would not be a bad time. But Abel's programming directs him to deal with problems rather than deny them.

Noemi sucks in a breath as they take a particularly narrow turn. For a moment the viewscreen seems to show nothing but rock in any direction. But external sensors indicate the temperature is rising—sharply—which means their goal is close.

When the *Persephone* reaches a semi-transparent barrier, Abel recalculates its strength before crashing through. In that second, the heat sensors blaze red, a warning against temperatures too intense for humans to survive. Visuals shimmer and warp; the light turns crimson.

Beneath them gapes the open maw of a volcano.

Properly, a *caldera* should only refer to a supervolcano. On Cray, where volcanoes are more plentiful than clouds, the crater hardly counts. But it would be a caldera on Earth, which must have led to this name, which feels true enough as they look down into the vast sea of bubbling magma far beneath them.

Noemi stares into it for a moment, and he prepares himself for the inevitable questions. They don't come. She must finally be listening to the data within. "The scientists studying this must have a heat-shielded area to protect them during observations, right? Is that where the others are going to meet us?"

"Exactly." Abel steers the ship toward a far platform. As they get closer, they can see the faint shimmer of a minor energy shield—something the *Persephone* can easily fly through—and, beyond it, the shapes of three people running at top speed.

"There's no place for us to land," Noemi says, getting to her feet. "I'll get some tow ropes ready."

He doesn't bother agreeing. She knows as well as he does what must be done, and he must concentrate on flying. The intense heat of the volcano warps the air, creating unpredictable crosscurrents and downdrafts; it's all he can do to keep the ship steady.

Breaking through the energy barrier shakes them only

slightly. Once it's done, Abel uses the tractor beam to anchor the *Persephone* to the rock just below the platform, then runs down to the docking bay to help Noemi.

This should be the easy part, he reminds himself. The fact that towing people up from a volcano counts as *easy* in this scenario is somewhat discouraging.

When he reaches the bay, Noemi already has the towlines ready. They're magnetic cables, normally used for tethering a ship in low to zero gravity. However, they're also capable of latching on to whatever metal a person has on them. Even a buckle or a bracelet will do.

The door pinwheels open, and a wave of hot air hits them as intensely as opening an oven—the shield keeps out all but a fraction of the volcano's heat, but that fraction is enough to stagger a human. On the platform 27.11 meters beneath them stand Virginia, Ludwig, and Fon, all in orange coveralls, each one looking more terrified than the last.

"I'll aim for Virginia." Abel readies himself. "You aim for Ludwig. Fon is small enough that either of the others should be able to bring her with them." Noemi stares down at the towline in her hands, which he takes for assent.

Instantly he calculates the weight, distance, vector— and he throws.

The towline flings toward Virginia, snapping around her like the tentacles of a kraken from myth, its magnetic charge drawn to the metal of her coverall. He can hear

Virginia's protesting screech even over the roar of the engines, but what this rescue method lacks in dignity it makes up for in efficiency. Abel hits the control to bring the towline in, and Virginia zooms toward them at top speed.

Noemi hasn't yet thrown her line. She clutches it to her, staring down at Ludwig and Fon in mute horror.

"We have to go," Abel says. Should he do this for her? No—he must continue to steady Virginia's towline. "You're strong enough to throw it."

That's not what was worrying her. "Different voices in my head are telling me different things about how to throw it—about whether I even can—"

"Trust the machine."

Noemi throws it. It lands only one meter behind Ludwig, only two behind Fon. They both turn and run for it. The instant they grab hold of the line, Noemi yanks it back with all her strength—

—her strength that, thanks to her cybernetic nervous system, is now measurably greater than before—

—and the towline slams into the edge of the open doors with so much force that it breaks. The length of it tumbles down uselessly onto the platform, sending Ludwig and Fon sprawling. Even from this distance, Abel can calculate that the girl has at minimum broken an arm. Ludwig sees Fon lying there and crawls toward her. When he scoops Fon up into his burly arms, her black hair swirls around them like ink in water. They look up in hope, and Abel accelerates Virginia's ascent, in hopes of having time to throw again—

It's already too late. The platform doors open, and Charlies and Queens run out, blasters ready. Impossible to say whether these mechs are malfunctioning, like some others they've seen, but it doesn't matter. They have Ludwig and Fon at point-blank range.

Virginia's towline snaps her into the bay, sending her rolling across the floor until she thuds into the inert Smasher. Instantly she's pushing its coils away, scrambling to her feet. "They've got Ludwig and Fon! We have to go back!"

"We can't," Abel says. He cannot allow himself to empathize. Someone has to be cold and rigid, or else none of them will escape. "They're already in custody, and if we don't leave immediately, we will be, too."

"No." Virginia turns back to the door, through which the guards can be seen cuffing Fon and Ludwig. "No."

Abel hits the controls. The door spirals shut, closing off the sight of her friends' capture. As he runs back up to the bridge, he calculates a 67.87 percent chance that either Noemi or Virginia will hurry after in an attempt to stop him.

Neither of them does. It seems humans are in fact able to recognize futility.

15

FOR SEVERAL LONG SECONDS, NOEMI CAN'T MOVE. SHE keeps staring at the closed door, as if she could will it to pinwheel open again. This time she would see the scene from minutes ago, back when there was still a chance to save Ludwig and Fon. She wouldn't break the towline. She would get it right. She'd save everyone.

Instead, she's standing in near darkness, motionless, listening to Virginia sob.

Noemi can say nothing other than "I'm sorry."

"Sorry? You're *sorry?*" Virginia slaps her open hand against the wall; the thud reverberates through the entire bay. "You let Ludwig and Fon get captured, which means they're going to go to prison for years if not for the rest of their lives, and *you're sorry?*"

Eyes blurring with tears, Noemi drops her head in shame.

Virginia paces the length of the bay, hands fisted in her long, red-streaked hair, so tense it seems she could shatter with any step. "Back when we first met seven months ago, you guys showed up on Cray and needed our help. We gave it to you. You needed me to help break Robot Boy out of prison, which could've put me in prison, too, or even gotten me killed. I did it anyway. Helped Abel hack into Mansfield Cybernetics corporate secrets, even though I had bad dreams about freakin' warrior mechs crashing into my bedroom at night for solid months after that. Went all the way through an unknown Gate to a mystery world. Went to Genesis to help you guys win a war—a war against the planet I was born on! I did *all* of this, rescued you two over and over and *over*, and I never asked for anything until now, and instead *you ruined my friends' lives*."

There's no way to counter this, because every word is true. Without Virginia Redbird, Noemi knows she and Abel wouldn't have gotten very far. "I screwed it up. All of it. Not just the towline—from the very beginning—"

Virginia snaps, "Stop with the self-pity. It's not going to make me less angry with you."

That stings. Noemi didn't say any of that to somehow get herself off the hook; she knows how badly she's messed up. But that's not what Virginia needs to hear. "I just meant—if I could do it differently, I would. And I know you would, too."

Virginia stops pacing, sighs deeply, and slumps against the nearby Smasher as though it were a wall. "No, I wouldn't. Wish I could say that was because I'd never leave people in trouble behind. The truth is…all this running around, breaking the law, it made me feel important. *Special.* On a planet where everyone's a genius, 'special' is kind of hard to come by. But working with the famous Model One A? Going on secret missions with a soldier from Genesis? That proved I was smarter than anyone. I wanted to be forever captain." She closes her eyes, like she doesn't even want to see anymore. "And I'm jerk enough to do all that over again, just like before. Except this time I wouldn't bring my friends into it. I'd keep them safe. Nobody's neck would be on the line but mine."

What would I do over? Noemi wonders. She couldn't not volunteer for the Masada Run. Couldn't let Esther die without trying to rescue her, couldn't leave Abel trapped and alone in his ship. All along, she's done her absolute best. Fought as hard as she knew how. So many terrible things have happened that it seems like there ought to be some action she'd change, something she'd do or wouldn't do—but she can't think of it. The past seven months of her life, she thought she was choosing her own course. Instead, she was locked into an autopilot that has steered her to this.

The ship shudders, and she remembers that they still have to escape from Cray. More correctly, Abel is trying to escape, taking them with him, and she draws comfort from that. Her military instincts tell her to go to the bridge, but what could she do? Either Abel and the engines can handle it or they'll all die.

Virginia sniffles, and her voice is hoarse as she says, "Oh. By the way—"

Noemi steels herself for the next accusation. Probably she deserves this one, too. "Yeah?"

"Congrats on not being dead." This time, when their eyes meet, Virginia manages a watery smile. "So they did it, huh? Figured out how to put mech systems in a human body? You're going to be in every cybernetics course from now on, you know."

"Great," Noemi says wearily. "Just great."

"I need to congratulate Abel, too. When last I looked in on our heroes, you were in cryosleep and Abel was headed to Haven to strike a really terrible bargain, if he couldn't find any other way out of it." Virginia shudders at the thought of another friend in danger. "But it looks like he managed to get away again."

"Actually, I'm the one who got us out of there. I wasn't going to leave him behind." Noemi gestures toward her close-shorn hair; the pale white edges of some incisions are still slightly visible at her hairline. "But yeah. They figured out how to make me...well, half mech."

Apparently the only thing that can distract Virginia from grief is brand-new technology, like the stuff woven through Noemi's blood and bone. She sounds slightly less miserable as she asks, "You're a hybrid now, right? Part mech, part human? Because that is mega, super, colossal badass."

"It doesn't feel that way," Noemi admits. "Not always. Sometimes it feels like my own body doesn't belong to me anymore. Like my brain is split in two and I don't know which half to listen to. I know I'll get the hang of it—I can even see how it's going to be great—but I can't take back what just happened. I'm stronger than I was, not mech strong but, still, more, and I didn't realize how hard I'd yanked the towline until it broke, and—" *And Ludwig and Fon were lost.*

Silence stretches between them again, long enough for Noemi to figure that Abel must've gotten the ship out of trouble. Otherwise they'd be dead by now.

"Listen," Virginia says. "I get that being part mech has to be the weirdest weird in Weirdtown. It's weirdness I hope to study in depth as soon as we're not running for our lives. But you're here and you're alive, and I'm not in the mood to be sorry that at least some of my friends are still here with me. Okay?" Despite what is clearly her best effort, her eyes well with tears, and Virginia begins to cry.

"Okay." Noemi gathers Virginia into a tight hug. That's all she can do.

• • •

Virginia turns out to have stayed up most of the previous forty hours, worrying about whether she and her friends would get caught.

"First they tried to dig into our Razer data," she says

as Noemi leads her through the *Persephone*'s spiral corridor. "We'd set up a fake layer of info for them to tap into, so we dodged that bullet, but we knew the authorities weren't going to stop there. Everyone on Cray was totally paranoid—like, they thought Earth was invincible, that *we made* Earth invincible, and then the Battle of Genesis proved otherwise. Some people thought Earth would punish us, and other people were sure it could only be sabotage, and overnight we went from this whole planet of happy nerds to a place where nobody trusted anybody anymore."

Fascinating as this is, Noemi can hardly take it in. She's too worried about Virginia. "You need to sleep."

"How am I supposed to sleep?"

"With a sedative."

Virginia sighs. "Yeah, that oughta do it."

The sedatives in the ship's stores are applied via patch. Noemi peels one and sticks it on the inside of Virginia's wrist, where blood vessels are close to the skin, so it will take effect faster. Even as they leave sick bay, Virginia is already swaying on her feet, and Noemi has to steady her. This task can't distract her from the slightly odd vibration she feels through the floor. Maybe a human would miss it, but her mech senses won't let her tune it out.

The *Persephone* can't put off repairs much longer, or they'll wind up dead in space.

Maybe Abel thinks that's a viable option, Noemi muses

as she watches Virginia groggily stumble into her bunk. He spent thirty years waiting to get picked up last time. He was bored and lonely, but not in danger. Not even uncomfortable. Does he think she ought to be able to handle that, now that she's half mech?

It's impossible, she thinks, walking back down the corridor. *Even if my body can take it, my mind can't. There would be nothing to see, nothing to do. Abel would be my whole world.*

Noemi pauses, putting her hand to her mouth as she remembers their first kiss. They had been in the pod where he'd been marooned, floating in zero-G just like he had for those thirty years. Then she thinks of the hours they recently spent curled up in a bunk together, kissing so many times she lost count, until she felt giddy and happy and spent.

Having Abel as her whole world might not be all bad. . . .

Still, she'd rather choose on her own terms when she and Abel tune out the rest of the galaxy. If the *Persephone* breaks down, there's no telling when they'd be found, or by whom.

Will they ever get a chance to learn what they could be to each other? Or will they always be hunted, in constant danger, on the run?

Sometimes Noemi feels like she's been running forever.

• • •

When they reach the Cray Gate several hours later, Noemi's at navigation and Abel's at ops when the doors slide open.

Virginia wanders in, wearing a pair of pajamas—bright blue, with tiny pineapples patterned across the fabric.

In reply to their questioning looks, Virginia says, "I found them in one of the abandoned crew lockers. Don't give me that look, okay? I need all the comfort I can get right now."

The joke is too raw; Virginia's pain is too new. Noemi tries to play along, though, holding up her hands in surrender. "No argument here."

"Personally, I think they're pretty sexy stuff." Virginia turns, modeling the oversize, gaudy things as though they were high fashion. "Maybe I'll set a trend."

"Pineapple pajamas will sweep the whole galaxy," Noemi agrees. Abel seems at a loss as to how to play along, so she gives him a more pragmatic topic of conversation. "How many hours until we reach Kismet?"

Before Abel can answer, sensors begin beeping. Virginia peers down at the ops console and says, "Oh, yay, another war fleet! Today is turning out so well."

"Damocles ships?" Noemi looks down at her controls in alarm—but the Earth patrols are centered around one particular area of the system, fairly far away.

"No Damocles. This war fleet is ours," Abel says.

The viewscreen zeroes in on the distant signals to reveal Vagabond vessels—and among them is the *Katara*. Noemi breathes out in relief. "They made it."

"Who made it?" Virginia squints. "Wait, that's the Krall Consortium flagship, right? What is this, some kind of space party?"

"We'll explain shortly." Abel opens communications. "This is the free ship *Persephone*, to the Vagabond fleet, calling any officer authorized to make contact."

In only seconds, the viewscreen changes from a starfield to the face of Dagmar Krall, one eyebrow raised. *"I do recognize you and your ship, you know. It's only been a few hours! Besides, I don't meet with fully sentient mechs every day."*

"Now you get two for the price of one," Virginia mutters, too low for anyone but Noemi to overhear.

"I would imagine you meet with sentient mechs about as often as I meet with the leader of the largest Vagabond trading group in the galaxy. Which is to say, exactly as much, as we are the only two individuals who fully meet those descriptions," Abel replies.

Noemi smiles. Abel's not great at banter yet, but apparently he's trying.

He continues, "We're very glad to see you. Although we intend to help you as discussed, our engines have reached a critical state of disrepair. We need parts we don't have—"

"But we probably do." Krall is already nodding. *"Send the specs over, and we'll set up a transfer immediately."*

"Thank you," Abel says. He's visibly relieved—a rarity

for him. He must've been even more worried than Noemi had realized.

Krall replies, *"No thanks necessary. Genesis is the Consortium's single most important ally. You're working to help Genesis win the war. That means we need to repair your ship as much as we'd need to repair our own."*

As soon as comms go silent, Virginia says, "Anybody else wondering if this makes us pirates, too?"

"Like she said, it's for Genesis," Noemi says. Already she feels encouraged again. Dagmar Krall is a ruthless woman, and her Consortium is as likely to be involved in piracy as it is in free trading. But Krall takes her allegiance to Genesis seriously, and has already fought a fierce battle for their freedom. She's playing a key role in the Bellum Sanctum strategy, and the best help and protection they could've found.

The *Persephone* is once again a ship on a mission, and Noemi is once again a soldier with purpose.

16

TRUE TO HER WORD, DAGMAR KRALL PROVIDES THE necessary repair parts within minutes. Instead of merely sending over an equipment pod, a simple corsair comes over, piloted by Krall's most trusted lieutenant, who also happens to be her wife. Anjuli Patil hasn't come here only as a favor, however; she's also tasked with briefing them on the mission.

"Not even I'm privy to all the details," Anjuli says as she hands Abel his next repair tool. She's perched on a corner console in the engine room, wearing a gold sari, dark red tattoos along her arms, and an easy smile. "But as I understand it, the Bellum Sanctum device has been kept undercover in a base on one of the moons of Genesis. Which—you know, I wouldn't have thought you guys even had a lunar base, what with being so anti-technology and all—"

"We *do* have a space fleet," Noemi says dryly.

"Yeah, you're no Luddites," Virginia says from her place

on the floor; she's lying on her back beneath one of the mag field generators, only her feet visible as she assists with repairs. "You've got a space fleet—one made up of decades-old ships, run from government buildings that don't even use artificial light during the day—"

"We're not against technology in and of itself," Noemi insists. "Just its overuse."

Abel points out, "To be fair, 'overuse' is a term that can be interpreted many different ways." The look Noemi gives him suggests that he should let her handle the rest of this conversation.

For her part, Anjuli is undaunted. "Well, it's a massive electromagnetic device that ought to have the power to scramble pretty much all communications, planetwide, for as long as it's functioning. If we can protect that device, it could function for *years*. If Earth can't talk to the colony worlds—if they can't talk to their ships, or give orders to the Damocles—that will bring them to their knees, almost instantly."

"Very likely," Abel agrees. It strikes him as odd that a "masterstroke weapon" would be so benign, something that might take no lives whatsoever. But if any planet were to create such a weapon, it would be Genesis. Mostly he's reassured that the full plan has finally been revealed to them. His earlier suspicion of Dagmar Krall appears to have no merit.

"As you can imagine," Anjuli adds, "the Bellum Sanctum device requires a massive engine—one in better repair than Genesis has."

Noemi stands in the doorway, leaning against the jamb. "When you say big…how big?"

Anjuli takes a deep breath. "We're here to steal one of the minefield generator engines."

Up until this point, Virginia has been on her back so deep beneath the engine workings that Abel can only see her legs from the knee down. Now she rolls out on her hover platform with wide eyes. "Excuse me? Tell me you didn't just say what I think you said."

Abel understands her astonishment. Already his mind is unfolding the various scenarios for this engine's location and retrieval; all of them are, at best, extremely challenging.

"I don't understand," Noemi says. "The mines are magnetic. They work together to power the entire minefield grid. They don't need an overall generator engine."

Anjuli answers even before Abel can. "They don't any longer, no—but they once did. Magnetic minefields are easy to maintain, but difficult to set up. There's a period of weeks or months when the mines are being deployed, but the master grid isn't yet activated, which means—"

"That the mines would just blow each other up," Noemi concludes. Abel is pleased at this evidence that she's listening more readily to her data implant. "It's like...like you need a framework for them to hold on to, before the minefield is complete."

Nodding, he says, "Generating such a framework would require extremely large amounts of energy."

"Huge. Enormous. Gigantic." Virginia's eyes are round. "That thing's not just floating around in space, is it?"

Anjuli beams, as though they were discussing a far more cheerful subject. "Of course not! It's located on the outermost planetoid of the Kismet system—a ball of frozen rock, devoid of any useful minerals, totally deserted. The engine was buried deep, with extremely strong automatic security that's still up and running."

"How do you know?" Virginia says. "That was a generation ago. Security could've broken down by now."

Until this, Anjuli Patil has seemed like one of those humans whose good mood is constant and self-perpetuating; the laugh lines on her face seem to confirm this. Now, however, her smile falters. "Genesis leadership sent us to investigate almost immediately after the Battle of Genesis. Three people made separate attempts to enter. None of them survived."

Noemi crosses herself, but is too much of a soldier to remain stricken. "Let me guess—this security is something only an advanced mech could get through?"

Anjuli shrugs. "Maybe some incredibly talented human somewhere could pull it off. But how many more people have to get killed trying? Besides, the real challenge is what happens when the engine gets turned on."

"Vibrational effects," Abel says. His memory banks have little detailed information about such engines, but enough for him to have extrapolated the likely problems. "Such engines have a stabilizer field, but it doesn't take hold until three seconds after ignition. Until then, the full vibration of the engines is in effect."

Virginia makes a face. "Big whoop. Three seconds of shaking? Doesn't seem like a big deal."

"The vibration levels would disorient a human to the point of losing consciousness and would cause severe concussion. The likelihood of brain injury would be over ninety-six percent." Abel doesn't add the decimal points, as they vary by age and size of the theoretical human involved. "This is why such engines are always activated by mechs—and even some mechs are destroyed in the process."

There are no exact data on how many mechs are destroyed this way. It's not considered important enough to take note of.

"Exactly," Anjuli says. "You should take a look at the specs before you decide whether you're willing to do this, Abel."

Abel makes one more adjustment to the engine and watches the indicators curve back toward normal. His ship will endure.

Now he just has to find out if *he* will.

• • •

The task ahead is theoretically survivable, Abel reminds himself several hours later, as he begins his descent into the access tube.

Tube is not the most accurate description of this: a three-hundred-meter tunnel carved into the core of this desolate frozen rock. It's a small planetoid, so it has no atmosphere to protect him and so little gravity that it cannot steady him. The main difference between being here and being in deep space is that, here, Abel's in a lot more danger.

The tunnel leads straight down, deep underground, and is only just wide enough to admit one individual in an exosuit. Dozens of sensor rings line the tunnel, glowing faintly orange in the darkness. There is no other illumination, save for the safety lights on his exosuit.

If he touches a sensor ring, it will explode. If he damages his exosuit, he'll be exposed to the cold vacuum of space, which will kill him faster than he'll be able to return to the surface for rescue. And he has to successfully deactivate every sensor ring as he goes, or else removing the massive engine will set off a chain of explosions that will destroy him and the engine both.

No one part of this is overwhelmingly likely to be fatal, although taken all together it is extremely hazardous. But the real danger will begin only after he's entered the disruptor engine.

This fact is not reassuring.

The comm unit in his helmet crackles with Noemi's voice: *"Ready?"*

There's no point in discussing his qualms; she knows the hazards already. He says only "Yes."

Abel sinks deeper into the tunnel, reaches the first sensor ring, and sets to work deactivating it. The small control lever above each ring has to be pushed into the open position. Doing so without damaging his exosuit is difficult—it requires real physical effort—but he manages. The second one goes like that, and the third, and all the way through to the eighth.

Yet as he begins work on the eighth, he notices a small panel embedded deep in the stone—one not noted on the earlier plans. "Abel to *Persephone*," he says. "I believe I've found a secret security fail-safe that—"

Red lights activate on the panel. Abel shoves himself beneath it 0.113 seconds before a laser grid snaps into place above him, the beams sizzling at an intensity capable of slicing his body in half.

"Abel?" The fear in Noemi's voice is unmistakable. *"Abel, do you read?"*

"I'm all right," he says, looking down to see that an identical grid is glowing above the next sensor ring. "Unfortunately I appear to have activated a secondary line of security."

"Can you deactivate it?"

"Yes." The secondary security is, in and of itself, not very worrying. However, his review of the engine specs suggests this level of security may have activated other defense systems within the engine.

"I wish I were there with you—"

"Better that you aren't," he says. Abel can face these dangers, but it would be far more distracting if Noemi had to face them, too. His concern for her would undoubtedly occupy a large portion of his conscious thoughts, all of which need to be focused on his own survival.

Abel deactivates one of the fields, then another, then another. By now he is half a kilometer within the moon. Nonetheless, it is not a relief when he sees the rough bronze-colored surface of the engine beneath him. He reaches down, readies himself, and hits the activation panel embedded within its surface.

A hatch slides open—revealing dozens of rows of spikes

thrashing within, extending and retracting in patterns incomprehensible to humans, too fast for their eyes to focus on. Abel, however, is not a human and can therefore focus on each spike. Logically this is an advantage, but he can take little satisfaction in it.

"I'm here," he says.

Through comms Noemi answers, *"Can you patch in a visual for us?"*

"I think you'd prefer it if I didn't."

"It's that bad?"

"I'm going in." Abel leaves it at that.

Noemi hesitates before saying, very quietly, *"Be careful."*

She means for him to take care of himself, rather than be careful on the mission. His value to her as an individual is greater than the sum of all the things he can accomplish. Abel wonders if Burton Mansfield could ever have understood that.

He lowers himself through the first layer of spikes, just before they punch through their holes with a CRUNCH. Holding his body in a tight crouch, Abel counts off the seconds until the pattern offers his next opening—

Go!

The spikes CRUNCH just above his head, so close that he feels a vague thump on his helmet. If the helmet is critically damaged, he'll be as dead as though the spikes had pierced his skull.

No human could ever pass through here, he silently reasons as he continues making his way to the center of the disruptor engine. *Even if they possessed the pattern recognition skills and reflexes necessary, stress reactions would swiftly become extreme and incapacitate them.*

It subjectively feels much longer, but it's only 12.1 minutes before he reaches the internal engine controls. Once he's at the controls, floating in zero-G, he speaks through comms again. "I'm in."

"Thank God," Noemi breathes. *"But how are you going to get out again?"*

"That part is easier."

He levels his feet toward the floor, then turns on his mag boots. They thud down heavily, metal on metal, magnetism doing the work of gravity. This allows Abel to more closely study the small control area.

The engine is designed to operate almost as an independent vessel; most deep-space machines of such enormous size are, for ease of transport. Secondary mag engines are attached and will power on when he activates the primary engine. When those secondary engines come online, they'll activate other ship systems—such as vibration dampeners.

The trick is surviving the three seconds before the dampeners take effect.

A human might hesitate, take a deep breath, or say a prayer. Abel simply reaches for the control panel. None of his actions now make any difference in the ultimate outcome; he has to take the risk, regardless. He'll survive or he won't. He sees no point in dreading either alternative.

There's no air to transmit sound, but the vibration through the floor is enough. A dull roar fills Abel's helmet as his entire body shudders. The shaking grows violent; Abel goes limp, trying not to resist—resisting will only get him hurt—but the thrashing is so bad it may make no difference.

Within his skin, he is vividly aware of what is metal and what is flesh. They damage at different rates. Both are at risk if this doesn't—

An energy field closes around him, pillowy as cotton. Abel can still feel the vibration in his feet, but he's able to stand steady. Although his head throbs, his nose doesn't start bleeding again. (A relief, as this would be especially unpleasant in zero-G.) An internal sweep reveals that he has survived with only minor damage.

Abel allows himself a smile as the vibrations grow more violent and spread outward from the engine into the surrounding rock.

Cracks appear in the stone surrounding the engine. Dust floats like fog, unhampered by gravity, but it doesn't obscure the destruction breaking out all around. Abel braces himself as quakes ripple out in greater and greater strength—then cuts the power down to baseline.

It looks like he's adrift in opaque mist. When he switches out of human vision, however, and scans more closely, he's able to see the larger cavern that's been carved in the center of this planetoid.

"Abel to *Persephone*—"

"*Oh my God*," Noemi says in a rush, "*the sensor readings we're getting—it's exploding!*"

"Not so much exploding as liquefying," he answers cheerfully. "Regardless, it's finished. I'm safe within the engine, and a large space has been carved out from the center of the planetoid. Mining ship lasers should be able to cut a passageway for me to maneuver out within one point one four hours."

"*Then...then you've done it. You've saved Genesis.*" Noemi's joy is evident in every syllable she speaks. "*On behalf of my ungrateful planet, thank you.*"

"I didn't do it for them," he says. "At least, not primarily. I did it for you."

Within another hour and a half, the engine is free in space, surrounded by trails of space dust, ready to fight for Genesis. In the distance, the Krall Consortium ships are flashing their lights in applause.

● ● ●

Multiple Consortium ships focus tractor beams on the engine in order to tow it from the system. As a convoy, they may attract attention—but from a distance, the engine will look like just another ship on sensor scans. This should allow them to tow it to the Earth system, where the plan appears to be to hide it in the asteroid belt between Mars and Jupiter, where it will be hooked up to the communications jammer. After that, it will be ready for battle.

The Genesis forces will be in position to attack as soon as the Bellum Sanctum order is given. Earth will hardly have time to mount a defense.

So Abel expects something of a hero's welcome upon his return to the *Persephone*. Instead, as he uses the propulsion pack on his belt to return to the ship, he hears Noemi say via comms, *"We've got trouble."*

"More?" Abel says. He looks around, but from this vantage point he can see little but his ship ahead of him and blackness all around. "This is a prodigious amount of trouble, even for us."

Virginia's laughter doesn't conceal her nervousness. *"Never rains but it pours. We've got an incoming Damocles."*

A human might panic. Abel simply adjusts the propulsion pack to maximum speed.

Once he's on board, he hurries onto the bridge in his exosuit. On the viewscreen is an image of an enormous Damocles ship that has lumbered to the edge of the vast minefield, approaching closer to their position.

"They weren't anywhere near this sector," Noemi

mutters as she runs scans. "You think they're programmed to protect the minefield if they see other ships in the area?"

"A logical possibility." Abel has passed through the minefield before, but always in a small, single ship that might go undetected by a Damocles. Dagmar Krall's flagship and the other Vagabond vessels must have attracted more attention.

From a distance, the Kismet minefield is invisible to the human eye, but Abel's sharper vision picks up the tiny, dully bronze pinpoints against the blackness. Every one of those promises death to a ship that gets any closer to the Kismet Gate. The Gate hangs in space, a shimmering silver ring promising as much power and bloodshed as anything out of the ancient novelist Tolkien. With the Damocles approaching from the heart of the system, the dangers surrounding them are considerable.

"This isn't a normal Damocles ship," Noemi says. "This one's huge. At least double the size of the old ones. How many mechs does that thing carry?"

"Too many," Virginia says. "Nothing else matters."

"If we run for it, we're going to draw more of the fleet near Kismet toward us," Krall says via comms. *"But I sure as hell don't know how we're supposed to take down a Damocles."*

Abel does some quick calculations. "It would be inadvisable for us to allow the Damocles to get close enough for me to pit the mechs against each other again."

"*Is that what happened at the Battle of Genesis?*" Krall says. "*You turned the mechs on each other? Interesting trick.*"

"Yes." Abel thinks of the immense pain he felt, the way his nose bled afterward, and the damage he took. Gillian repaired that damage, but that avenue isn't open to him again. "This time, we'll require a different strategy."

Noemi squares her shoulders. "We have to attack them. Head-on, immediately."

"Attack?" Krall and Virginia say, almost in unison. Abel's almost as surprised, though he swiftly follows her line of thought.

"We go in as a unit," Noemi continues as though the others hadn't spoken. "All our ships, together. That's what it will take to go up against a Damocles. If we wait, or go in at anything less than full force, we're just giving them time to signal for reinforcements."

"That fleet would attack us after we fought a Damocles!" Virginia protests.

Noemi answers, "They would—but we might have time to get away first."

"*They'll chase us all the way to the Cray Gate,*" Krall says.

"Even if they do, they won't be able to keep up. We'll have hours in the Cray system to scatter. Some ships can hide through the Blind Gate; others can head straight for the Stronghold Gate; and a few of you might even be able to get landing clearance on Cray." Noemi's dark eyes are unfocused, an expression Abel has learned to associate with intense thought. "With the incredibly high levels of space traffic all over the place, and the general disorder? We'll have time to get good and lost."

Krall's tone shifts from alarmed to merely wary. *"That's assuming their fleet isn't trailing behind them even now."*

Noemi shakes her head. "Take it from someone who's fought against a lot of Damocles: Every single one of them is assumed to be able to take care of a whole lot of enemy ships. So the others will hold back from an initial fight; as far as they know, it's taken care of. But if we scatter, they'll pursue immediately."

"This way we only have to fight one Damocles," Krall says. *"The bad news is even one Damocles is hard to kill."*

Finishing his inner calculations of risk and probability, Abel says, "As previously indicated, I won't be able to send a single command to all the mechs at once this time." He thinks back to Gillian's failed effort to install Tether technology in his brain. Would that tech help him control other mechs, or perform other useful feats? Silently he reminds himself to explore his Tether capabilities in the near future. "But I should be able to interfere with their operating systems, which will make each individual Queen and Charlie far less effective. That gives the Kismet vessels a chance to escape."

"Life would be a lot easier if we could get through that

Kismet Gate," Krall grouses. "*Which is why the damned minefield is there in the first place.*"

Abel and Noemi exchange glances as Virginia shudders. As the only individual capable of piloting safely through the Kismet minefield, he could volunteer to take the *Katara* through. But that would only maroon the rest of the fleet in the Kismet system.

He may be the most advanced mech in the galaxy, Abel thinks, but he has *some* limits.

"*Okay, back to reality, which is a big fight in the near future. We'll provide cover for the* Persephone *while Abel takes care of those mechs.*" Krall now sounds more confident. Abel wishes he felt the same. "*Heading in on your mark.*"

By now Virginia's long face has gone slack with dismay. "Tell me that we don't have to do what I think we have to do."

"We have to let the Damocles get closer before we attack," Noemi says.

"That's what I thought we had to do." Virginia slumps back in her seat. "Oh, rapture."

In precisely sixteen seconds, the Damocles is in range. Its white bulk fills most of the viewscreen as its panels open to release flocks of warrior mechs. Queens and Charlies zoom out in their exoskeletal suits, more like flexible ship hulls than regular exosuits; these turn each mech into something that can move as fast as a starfighter and is equally hard to damage. Most of the mechs head toward the *Katara*, the largest ship—but that still leaves dozens free to head straight for the *Persephone*.

"Incoming," mutters Noemi. The mechs are approaching fast.

At the Battle of Genesis, Abel had to tie his entire consciousness to the ship in order to reprogram the attacking mechs. For what he needs to do now, he requires only a partial connection. Once he's accomplished that, he chooses one of the closer mechs, a Charlie, and fires a beam that should scramble its navigation. The Charlie vibrates—in a human, the reaction would be called a seizure—then throws itself against another mech nearby. Exploding light and debris fill the viewscreen in the instant before Abel moves the screen to target again.

And again.

And again.

Most of the mechs spiral off into the oblivion of space, but a few others are destroyed.

Consortium ships do their part, firing on individual mechs or mimicking the scrambler signals from the *Persephone*. Mechs blow one another up, or zoom around crazily without direction, or even collide with some of the outermost mines in the minefield. In effect it creates a gap in the minefield—which could be dangerous for Genesis—but that hole is only on the outskirts, nowhere near the Gate itself.

Finally, the last few mechs fly back to the Damocles ship, which hangs still and ominous in the sky.

"Good work, Persephone," Krall says through the speakers. *"It looks like the Damocles has shut down completely."*

"More likely it's only in stasis," Abel replies. "Attempting to regenerate damaged mechs while all but shutting down core systems."

"Remember how we figured other Earth ships wouldn't show up while they thought a Damocles could take us out?" Virginia asks. "Well, now the Damocles is shut down. How are they going to react to that?"

"They'll come," Noemi says. "Not right away. But soon."

The enemy is asleep—but not for long.

17

NOEMI'S PULSE POUNDS LIKE A DRUMBEAT IN HER VEINS—
a military tattoo, a call to action. Her whole life, she's been
afraid of Damocles ships. Every history holo they watched
in school showed the enormous hulk of a Damocles at the
heart of every battle. As soon as she began preliminary
military training at age twelve, she learned how dangerous they were. Like the proverbial sword they're named
for, Damocles ships hang above worlds as a constant, silent
threat of the damage Earth can do—and will do—to any
planet that steps out of line.

What she sees now should be impossible: a Damocles
ship stalled, silent and helpless. Abel's shut them down...
at least for the time being. Other Earth ships will soon
respond to this shutdown, but at the moment they remain
in place, still operating under the protocol that one Damocles is enough to win any battle.

That gives us a brief opening, she thinks. *We shouldn't waste it.*

"Nobody's ever stopped a Damocles before," she says to Abel. Virginia's stepped out, so they're alone on the bridge. He listens to her quietly, patiently. Has anyone else ever listened to her the way he does? "Not like this. They're supposed to be invulnerable, but that's impossible. Any machine can break."

She half expects Abel to protest that *he* couldn't, but he remains focused. "Your reasoning is sound. In point of fact, I believe Damocles ships may be designed to be broken—when it is desirable for them to break."

That makes Noemi wrinkle her nose. *"Desirable* for them to break?" Then it hits her. "In case of capture—or boarding—there would have to be a self-destruct."

He nods. "My memory banks include no plans or specifications for Damocles ships, but it is rational to assume that some kind of self-destruct or singular override exists. Earth's military strategists have always been keenly aware that an exceptionally talented opponent might develop a way to 'hack' the Queens and Charlies, essentially switching the side the mechs were fighting for in the middle of a battle."

"That's close to what you did at the Battle of Genesis, right?" Noemi says.

"Close, but not exactly. There I turned the mechs against *each other.*"

"Has anyone ever pulled that off?"

"No," Abel replies, dashing that particular hope before Noemi had even fully imagined it. But he continues, "It is even possible one Damocles's self-destruction might trigger others, to prevent the hacking of multiple ships."

The possibilities seem to light up Noemi's mind. "You mean, they're interconnected? We could maybe take out more than one Damocles at the same time?"

Abel nods. "If they were close enough to be in communication with each other...possibly."

Dagmar Krall's voice comes through the speakers again. *"We've come up with a plan. One of our transports is critically damaged. The crew's already evacuating. Once that's done, we could program its autopilot to fly straight into the Damocles. The resulting explosion ought to take the Damocles out."*

"That plan has an excellent chance of success," Abel says.

Noemi stifles a laugh. *Whenever a human has a good idea*, she thinks, *he acts so* surprised.

But this time, another human has an even better idea. "Commodore Krall," Noemi says, "I'd like to hold off on your plan for a while."

Krall sounds annoyed. *"I thought you guys said that thing would wake up again soon."*

"It will," Noemi says, "but while it's in dormant mode, we have an incredible opportunity. Nobody outside of Earth's most elite security forces has ever boarded a Damocles vessel.

Nobody human, I mean. Earth keeps it that way so nobody can know what the ships' vulnerabilities are. If these mechs stay asleep long enough for us to get on board and run a few scans, we could do so much more than destroy this one Damocles. We might learn how to destroy them *all.*"

Any senior officer in the Genesis military would've wanted to debate this for days. Apparently pirate queens are more adaptable. *"That would be an intelligence coup,"* Krall says. *"Could change the whole shape of the war—but only if we have time to get in and out before the fighter mechs in this thing wake up. Do we, Abel?"*

"I cannot be sure," he says. "With no definite data on the Damocles ship's construction, there's no way for me to come up with an estimate."

Noemi's mech mind agrees with this, but her humanity decides to keep pushing. "There's no reason to think we don't have time to get over there," she says as Virginia walks back onto the bridge. "It takes time for them to run reboot and repair cycles on fighter mechs. So the Damocles ought to stay in stasis for at least a few minutes—long enough for us to board. Right?"

Although Abel looks like he wishes he could answer otherwise, he says, "That is correct."

Virginia has stopped in her tracks. In a low whisper, as if to herself, she says, "I leave the bridge for *five minutes* and they're planning a field trip to a Damocles."

"It's important," Noemi says to her.

"It had better be!" retorts Virginia.

"Well, if we don't know how much time we have," Krall says, *"we shouldn't waste any more of it. I'll send a couple of* Katara *crew members out in a shuttle immediately to join you."*

"We'll meet them there," Noemi promises.

Abel snaps off communications, which means he's on board with the plan. Still, he looks uneasy. "I don't know if I can monitor the mechs as well from an exosuit. That means I wouldn't have any advance warning of when the Damocles will become active again."

"That's why you shouldn't go." Noemi has always felt safer with Abel by her side. Now, however, he can protect her best from the bridge. "We need you here on the *Persephone*, using its sensors to monitor the situation. There's no way I'm not getting a look inside. And, Virginia—if you're willing to chance it, you could open up the onboard AI better than anyone."

"I love a mystery," Virginia quips, but without her usual enthusiasm. Her expression is shadowed; her eyes lowered.

Noemi thinks, *She won't take risks so casually, not after Ludwig and Fon.*

Still, that's not the same as never taking risks again. "Sure," Virginia says. She's already regaining some of her bravado. "Never let it be said I missed a chance to spy on super-secret tech."

Abel remains disquieted—Noemi can tell—but he nods. "I can devise no logical objection to your plan."

"See, when you made me part mech, you lost the upper hand."

He's evolved enough to know when she's teasing. He smiles. "We shall see."

"Then that's settled." With a nod, Noemi says, "Let's go."

• • •

Her courage remains strong until they get within a hundred meters of the Damocles. Noemi takes in the enormity of it—the vastness of the long, angular metal structure, the way it seems heavy even in vacuum. She's never been this close to a Damocles before. If she had, she would've been killed.

Through the speaker of her exosuit's helmet, Noemi hears Virginia say, "*Ugly mother, isn't it?*"

"It'll look prettier blowing up," Noemi responds.

She and Virginia left the *Persephone* in exosuits powered by thrusters, until the shuttle from the *Katara* snagged them via towline. They're currently being dragged in—a routine process, and an easy one, since there's no resistance in space. But it makes Noemi feel out of control. She hates that feeling.

It fades as the shuttle gradually nears the Damocles. Shuttles are slowpokes, as spacecraft go: They can barely match one-fifth the speed of the *Persephone*. But their small size and precise handling makes them good for approaches like this.

The Damocles side panels open upward, like wings, revealing shimmering distortion fields within. Those won't keep them out, but they've always prevented any unauthorized human from looking inside.

Until now.

The shuttle slips through the distortion field as easily as if it were the iridescent surface of a soap bubble. Noemi blinks as the prismatic haze vanishes—*pop*—and reveals the interior of the Damocles.

Her first thought is of Gothic cathedrals from Earth, the ones they studied in Galactic Civilization: a vast, dark, vaulted chamber, gray as stone. While she had expected some sort of launching bay, she hadn't anticipated that almost the entire ship would be hollow. There's no sign of living spaces within the ship, or anything like a bridge. Instead, she sees…racks. Long metal racks, thick and arched across the width of the ship.

Like a rib cage, Noemi thinks with disgust. But that's not the worst part.

The worst part is that the mechs hang from these racks, wearing their star-shaped exosuits folded partly around them like the wings of bats. And they're awake. Their eyes stare out from the suits, glinting oddly in the light from the shuttle. Cat's eyes do that. Those are the eyes of predators.

Virginia's seen it, too. *"They're watching us! We're about to get—wait. Why aren't we getting killed?"*

Noemi shakes her head. "I guess the mechs don't fall asleep in dormant mode. They're just...resting." Come to think of it, as far as she knows, Abel's the only mech in existence who truly sleeps.

"They're resting until the ship wakes up, which it will at any time, at which point these mechs will turn back into unstoppable killing machines," Virginia says. *"In case it wasn't completely obvious, we need to get the hell out of here."*

As creeped out as Noemi is, she won't head for the door just yet. "Let's learn what we can."

Turns out there's no locking station for a shuttle or any other small craft to securely dock within a Damocles, so they have to leave their ship free-floating within. The crew members from the *Katara* emerge in their own exosuits, which are older even than Noemi's, and shabby with wear. All of them are maneuvering as best they can in zero-G, which always feels a little like bobbing in unpredictable waters. But they manage to work fast, aiming scanners at every corner and cranny of the Damocles interior. Virginia spots a control panel three meters above them, one meant for humans to use while programming missions within the ship. She braces her feet against the shuttle's hull and pushes herself upward, as if flying, to see the panel for herself.

Noemi's first inclination is to use her own scanner, but

then she remembers that the hardware attached to her belt isn't nearly as badass as the hardware inside her head.

Trust it, she tells herself. *Give it a try.*

So she takes a deep breath and tries to silence her thoughts like she would in meditation. Normally that doesn't go very well. This time, however, when she quiets her mind, another voice is waiting.

Diameter of ship, twenty-eight meters. Length, forty-seven meters. Width, twenty-two meters. Probable alloy of hull—

The information pours into her, like water into a glass. Noemi originally found this eerie—and she still does—but she also sees the wonder of it. The beauty. Numbers aren't just numbers any longer; they're knowledge. The information glitters inside her mind like the facets of a jewel, dazzling her until she feels her throat tighten.

Is this what it's like inside Abel's head? If so, his universe is so much more beautiful than she ever imagined.

Don't cry in zero-G, she reminds herself. Tears and mucus floating around inside a helmet equals yuck. To collect herself, she pushes off the shuttle and soars up to where Virginia is working.

It looks like Virginia is scowling. "How's it going?" Noemi asks.

"I'm not at my most dexterous wearing exosuit gloves." Virginia holds out her hands and wiggles her fingers, which are encased in the slight puffiness of the suit. *"Yeah,*

I'm getting some information, but I could get so much more if I could just touch the damned thing."

"We'll be able to learn more from scans." The richness of the data inside Noemi's head still staggers her. From this she could fashion a nearly complete blueprint of an entire Damocles. In fact, the rush of information is making her dizzy, almost nauseated—but she figures she'll be able to overcome that, given time.

Virginia remains preoccupied by more immediate problems. *"Are the mechs looking at us? I think they're looking at us."*

Noemi allows her brain to compensate for the low light within; the mechs seem to sharpen. Row after row of Queens and Charlies stare at the intruders, watching them intently, waiting for activation that could come at any moment. She says only, "How much more time do you think you'll need to go through the available data?"

"I'm working! This looks promising—" Virginia wraps her legs around the pole of the control panel, allowing her to work with both hands at once.

"Promising?"

"Remember how you were talking about a fail-safe? Some kind of self-destruct?"

Fresh hope sparks within Noemi. "You found one?"

"Let me take a look. The trick is to make sure that's what it is without, you know, getting it started."

Virginia stabs at the control panel one more time, and the screen flashes red with warning. Noemi lights up. "You found it?"

"*Yeah.*" Virginia looks over at Noemi, wide-eyed. "*Unfortunately, I activated it.*"

It's as if the chill of absolute zero had penetrated Noemi's jumpsuit to freeze her to the marrow. "The Damocles is going to blow?"

"*In about five minutes,*" Virginia says weakly. "*Can we get ourselves out of explosion range that fast?*"

The intelligence inside Noemi's head knows exactly how fast a shuttle can fly, which means she can't deny the hard, instant truth: No. They can't.

18

ON THE *PERSEPHONE* BRIDGE, SENSORS GLARE ORANGE. Abel swiftly checks energy readouts, locates the rapidly increasing radiation levels, and realizes what's happening to the Damocles, even before Noemi's voice comes over the speakers: *"We're in trouble."*

He does the calculations in 0.041 seconds. "I'm on my way."

"Abel, no! You'll only get yourself—"

Static swallows the sounds of her voice, a by-product of the radiation emanating from the Damocles. He'll pretend he never heard it, if she tries to protest after he's rescued her and her party.

Because he *is* rescuing them.

Although he can't determine the precise time of detonation, an estimate can be posited based on the rate of radiation increase and a likely overload point for a vessel of this size. He doubts they have more than four minutes before the

Damocles destroys itself, and a shuttle isn't capable of flying out of range in that amount of time. There's no chance for any more elaborate retrieval mission; the most dangerous option is the only one with any chance of working.

He fires the engines, aims for the heart of the Damocles, and accelerates.

Exactly how he'll rescue Noemi and the others remains a mystery to him. Mansfield programmed Abel with a wealth of material on topics both critical and arcane, but not with the specs for a Damocles. That information was too closely guarded a secret. He can extrapolate—volume divided by estimated number of mechs transported—but he won't know anything certain until he can see for himself, which by then will be within two minutes of detonation.

But Noemi has been programmed, too, in a way. In the past they've agreed that if his Directive One is to protect and obey Burton Mansfield, hers is to protect and obey her homeworld as a soldier of Genesis. She's been trained in military procedure since she was no more than a child; that knowledge is a part of her.

Every rule of military procedure for a space emergency declares: *Stay with your ship or get back to it as fast as you can.*

He doesn't know what the Damocles may do, but he knows what *she'll* do as surely as though he'd programmed her himself.

Abel focuses on the controls as the *Persephone* zooms

toward the open hatches of the Damocles, piloting into the center of one of these darkly iridescent disruptor fields. It shimmers as he passes through, no more than glints of light at the edges of his vision. He fully dilates his pupils to get the best look at the inside—

—the glassy stares of warrior mechs meet him, feline and unnerving—

—but he disregards that input as soon as he sights the shuttle. The Krall Consortium crew members may not be as rigorously trained as Noemi, but they know enough to scramble back inside their spacecraft. But it takes even well-trained spacefarers a while to maneuver in zero-G. Only a couple of meters above the shuttle are Noemi and Virginia, using exosuit thrusters to return to the ship as well. It won't take them very long, but any delay wastes time they don't have.

At least there appears to be no docking mechanism at work, he thinks. *Detaching from such a mechanism would take seconds if not minutes. Instead, the shuttle is free to move.* This is one of his only sources of encouragement, so he concentrates strongly on it.

Abel's personal security/preservation programming urgently signals for him to depart; this information is worthy only of immediate deletion.

Instead, he brings the *Persephone* around in one large loop, one that gives Noemi the 4.1 seconds she needs to drop through the shuttle's hatch, Virginia at her side. He doesn't wait for the shuttle to be sealed, just accelerates toward it and activates the tractor beam.

The small bump he feels when his ship attaches the shuttle generates relief—more than it should, given that he's still in the heart of a Damocles that's going to explode in roughly 29.15 seconds. (His estimate is improving as he monitors radiation gain.) It's not much of a chance for them, but he'll take it.

Abel grabs the shuttle with the *Persephone*'s tractor beams, reeling it in closer than safety protocols suggest as he accelerates away. They hurtle into deep space again, coincidentally straight toward the *Katara*, but he doesn't slow down. He has 41.48 seconds to avoid a crash with the *Katara*, and only 3.5 to avoid imminent destruction.

At the last tenth of a second, he reroutes extra power to the shields, then spins his ship so that it's between the Damocles and the shuttle. He snaps off the viewscreen— more effective than closing his eyes, and he'll still be able to monitor sensors.

The only thing those sensors can tell him is whether he's going to live or die, information he's destined to find out one way or another . . . and yet he must watch.

He imagines Burton Mansfield saying, *So human.*

The domed viewscreen blinks off, draping the bridge in darkness. Abel sees the sensors flare from orange to red and braces himself in his captain's chair. The *Persephone* starts to shake violently, and he feels dozens of thuds of debris against the hull. If they punch through the surface, air pressure will be lost, and he'll be sucked into space to freeze.

(There were times he contemplated that, during his three decades trapped in the equipment pod bay. His programming doesn't allow for suicide except in response to certain directives, but it also ensures he's not afraid of death. So he had always been calm and curious as he wondered whether it would be better to die swiftly in the paralyzing cold, or be alone in the dark for another two or three centuries. As he never came to a final conclusion, he remained in the docking bay, reasoning that he could choose to exit the *Persephone* and end his life at any time, but once he'd done so, there would've been no turning back.)

He won't find out today. Although damage indicators light up the command consoles, none of that damage is critical. The shuttle is therefore all but guaranteed to be unharmed— but he doesn't trust his understanding of probabilities, sometimes, when it comes to Noemi. Instead, he brings the viewscreen back up and switches to rear cameras to see the shuttle for himself. Its hull remains completely intact.

As he watches, Noemi pushes herself up through the top hatch, zooming upward in space for only as long as it takes her to activate her exosuit's thrusters, which send her soaring back to the *Persephone*. Back to Abel.

Back home, he thinks.

Abel initiates the repair operations the ship can perform itself, then hurries down to the docking bay to welcome Noemi home—and Virginia, who appears to be only slightly behind her. (Krall's team takes their craft back to the *Katara*, which is somewhat disappointing for Abel; he's never had true guests before. But this is unimportant.) By the time he arrives, the air lock is already cycling. The moment the door releases, he opens it to see both Noemi and Virginia taking off their exosuit helmets. "Welcome back," he says.

Noemi steps through the door first, apparently unruffled. When she sees Abel, she grins. "Nice catch."

"I knew where you'd be."

Abel means it only as a statement of fact, but she gives him the kind of smile often described as melting. Only now does he realize the idiom refers not to the smile, but to the emotion inside the one who sees it. "You always do," Noemi says. "And I knew you'd be there. I knew I'd be with you again." She embraces him—only briefly, but it makes him long to kiss her again. Not once, but over and over, the way they did when they were cuddled together in the bunk.

Soon, maybe.

Virginia looks more shaken, but she's already thinking of next steps. "So, Damocles destroyed means we're okay—"

"For now," Noemi interjects. "But we need to get this

engine to Genesis forces right away. Every minute we wait is another minute Earth might send forces against us, or worse, recognize the Bellum Sanctum strategy."

"Hey, just had a potentially disturbing thought, as is my wont." Virginia sits down heavily and begins removing her boots. "Are we sure Dagmar's telling us the truth about Bellum Sanctum? Or did she just send us to pick up a big engine for her?"

"It would be tactically unwise and unlikely for the Krall Consortium to lie about the Bellum Sanctum only to obtain this engine," he says. "A machine of such size and power has few uses, none of which would be valuable in ordinary Vagabond work."

"Besides, they wouldn't even have known about the 'Bellum Sanctum' plan if they weren't working pretty closely with Genesis leaders," Noemi says. "So now we send this engine on its way to Genesis, and we find out how this war ends."

• • •

Three hours later, while the ship's systems run through another set of diagnostics to confirm their repairs, Abel sits alone in the docking bay.

Almost alone, he should say. He is kept company by the Smasher, which sits on the floor, patiently allowing him to tinker with its AI. Its awareness is, of course, only a fragment of what a normal mech's would be, much less a human's or Abel's own, but there's enough there for the work to feel…companionable.

Gillian Shearer had imperfectly installed Tether technology within Abel. Therefore, he'd decided to try installing that tech within the Smasher, to see if he could figure out where she'd gone wrong—the better to activate Tether abilities for himself. (Having escaped Gillian's clutches for good, he sees no reason not to update.) The flaw in her installation turned out to be minor—more an activation problem than anything else—which means he's already fully outfitted both the Smasher and himself.

So now he's indulging his curiosity, tinkering to see how much he might be able to develop the intelligence of lower-level robots. Currently he's installing significant enhancements to the Smasher's memory. To the best of Abel's knowledge, no one has ever done this before.

That's because there is no need for an intelligent Smasher. But Abel considers curiosity to be adequate motivation.

Besides, he's waiting for a visitor to the ship—one who announced herself twenty-nine minutes, point oh three seconds ago. Abel finds himself intrigued by the novelty. At last, a guest.

When the docking signal finally comes, he swiftly wraps his tools and leaves the bay just in time for the air lock to cycle and allow a transit pod to come inside. As it cycles back, pumping in atmosphere and restoring gravity, he counts the seconds until the door slides open again.

Standing in the center of the docking bay is Dagmar Krall. Her blond hair is now braided back from her face, and her clothes have returned to Vagabond gaudiness— a rich red tunic and gold pants that seem to be made of silk. The confidence radiating from her and the unwavering focus of those large eyes give her the ineffable quality humans call *presence*. No one would be surprised to learn she's the most powerful Consortium leader in the galaxy.

"Welcome to the *Persephone*, Commodore Krall," Abel says.

"Thanks." Her smile is warmer when she's not in her command chair. She seems almost relaxed. "I've been curious about this little ship."

"I would be pleased to offer you a tour." He used to give tours back in the early days, when this was Mansfield's ship. It will be more enjoyable to lead the tour as its captain.

"Sounds great. But first, I was hoping to speak with you privately, Abel." Her smile seems unexpectedly friendly. "About…an opportunity."

Intriguing. "What do you mean?"

"We're working with Genesis now," she says. "That alliance will hold until the war is won and my people who want homes on that planet have them. While some Genesis operatives have begun moving throughout the larger galaxy—"

"They have?" Abel wonders what kind of an intelligence service Genesis could possibly have, after three decades of isolation. They'll have to learn fast.

Krall nods. "I hear they've even sent a couple agents to Haven. But most of what Genesis needs done in the galaxy at large, the Consortium is sworn to do. Still—that won't last forever. We're going to win this war. With Bellum Sanctum about to deploy, it looks like we're going to win soon. The question is, what happens afterward?"

"I believe," Abel says, "that you're finally approaching the point."

"You're one of a kind," Krall replies, beginning to pace around him. "Not that I have to tell you that, but it bears repeating. You're the only mech of your kind, and your capabilities—the things you've done in this fight, in the Battle of Genesis—well, it's impressive."

Abel nods in acknowledgment. There is no need to thank her, since she is merely stating fact.

She continues circling him. "I've seen you turn the tide of battle twice now. You seem like a good man to have around. You're *useful*, Abel. That's more than you can say for most people. And it means you could do better than small-scale trading."

"Small-scale trading has proved reasonably successful for me so far." Abel doesn't intend to brag, but Harriet and Zayan have assured him that their profit margins are considerably larger than those of the average Vagabond vessel.

Krall bows her head, conceding the point. "I'd imagine you're doing as well as any single trader can out here. But you could do even better if you had more resources. More intel, from more corners of the galaxy. If you had allies sworn to help and defend you no matter what."

The conclusion finally presents itself to Abel. "You're recruiting the *Persephone* for the Krall Consortium."

"Think about it." Krall spreads her hands as though laying a banquet before him. "You'd get bigger jobs. Have backup and security. Partners get a cut of every deal. Your ship's smaller than I'd usually require for a captain to be a full partner, but in this case, the *Persephone*'s not the main asset I'm trying to bring into our fleet. It's you yourself. We'd have your crew in for specialized training—"

"I appreciate the offer." It is, in fact, the most flattering thing Abel's heard in a while. "However, I doubt we would work well together long-term."

"Why would you say that?"

"Forgive me, Commodore Krall—"

"Call me Dagmar."

"Forgive me, Dagmar," Abel continues without missing a beat. "But you are—in a manner of speaking—a pirate."

She laughs long and loud. "Yes, I break the laws. So do you. When Earth's the one defining what's right and what's wrong, sometimes it's better to be 'wrong.' We've both made that call plenty of times, haven't we?"

That is... a rational stance for her to take.

Maybe sensing his curiosity, Krall adds, "You have to consider the opportunities, too. Genesis may win its independence soon. That means trade, and the new trade routes won't solely be under Earth's control. On top of that, the galaxy's expanding! Haven won't be isolated for long, and—" She pauses, as if wondering whether to trust him with this. More quietly, she says, "Like we were discussing back on Stronghold, the military presence in Kismet is higher than that for any of the other colony worlds."

"Yes, though it's curiously far from Kismet itself."

"Very curious," Krall agrees. "So some of my scouts looked around. It turns out that at the edge of this system, tucked away in the orbit of a planetoid in the very center of this military presence, is an object under construction." Her eyes sparkle with excitement. "That object has only just become recognizable as another Gate."

Abel is as capable of being amazed as any human, it appears, because it takes him a full 0.72 seconds to speak. "A Gate to another secret world?" How many planets did Earth's elite intend to hide from the populace at large?

"Actually, I think this is on the up-and-up," Krall says. "There are signs Earth's rushing the construction, trying to get it ready double-quick. If they could announce another planet, one as good as Haven or better, it would go a long way toward defusing the public anger."

"But they won't know whether the planet is viable for human settlement until after the Gate's complete and the system's been explored in depth." Gates are built when long-range scanners find a world that shows promise—but thanks to the amount of time it takes light to traverse the galaxy, scans can only tell how a planet looked thousands if not millions of years ago. That's more than enough time for a sun to go supernova, for an enormous asteroid to crash onto the planet and wreck its ecosystem for geologic ages to come, and for any other number of catastrophes that would turn a potential home for humanity into just one more lifeless, useless rock.

"Exactly," Krall says. "So they're building that Gate in one hell of a hurry. At this rate, it looks like it won't be more than another year or so before it's fully operational. That's when the rest of the galaxy finds out about this. But my Consortium knows about it now, and that gives us a significant advantage. Whoever controls Kismet in the years to come is going to wield considerable power. With all these worlds coming together, and Earth probably losing absolute power—you see the possibilities, right?"

Abel does. He also understands the parts she didn't say, only implied.

"The only planet that should control Kismet," he says slowly, "is Kismet itself."

Impatiently, Krall waves her hand. "Well, of course. But we'd be working with Kismet, and Genesis as well, once the war is won. Colony worlds and Vagabonds would be leading the way at last. Isn't it about time?"

Perhaps she means well. Probably. The kind of person who enjoys the free life of a Vagabond usually isn't the kind who wants to impose a military dictatorship. But Krall is clearly unwilling to think about the full implications of this power. Her plan is all about knocking Earth down and making money in the chaos that is sure to follow.

Abel wants to plan beyond that. What shape will the galaxy take? How will the worlds work together, instead of merely following Earth's commands? Krall is interested in the wreck of a civilization; he's interested in the rebuilding of one.

"You'll undoubtedly do well with this plan," he says. "But Consortium life's not for me."

"You want your independence," Krall says with a nod, and it's surprising how disappointed she looks. Abel's flattered to think she was so interested.

His path, however, must be one of his own choosing... and he means for it to follow Noemi's path, wherever she may lead.

19

ALTHOUGH NOEMI WAS AT FIRST TOO EXCITED TO ASK many questions, the more she thinks about the Bellum Sanctum plan, the more she wishes she knew.

Holy war can be righteous, she thinks, *but it's been used to excuse a lot of terrible things, all the way back to the beginning of human history. It's important to ask whether a war is just before declaring it holy.*

Noemi's never had to question the morality of the Liberty War before. Protecting her world from Earth's ruinous rule—it was self-evident that this was a sacred duty. But the Liberty War has always been a defensive war. The few aggressive moves Genesis troops made in other star systems were only in the earliest days of the fight. By collapsing all of Earth's communications, Bellum Sanctum represents a shift from defending Genesis to attacking Earth.

Noemi's okay with that, in principle. Her family died after their vehicle happened to drive over unexploded ordnance—her earliest memories include the heat of the explosion; the coldness of the snow where she lay, too injured to move; and the tiny crumpled form of the baby brother she never got to watch growing up. If Bellum Sanctum causes deaths on Earth, it's only fair. Earth should know what it feels like—the grief, the fear, all of it.

But there's a thin line between *justice* and *vengeance*. Noemi wants to make sure she's on the right side.

She heads to bed while Abel's still talking with Dagmar Krall. Although she can't wait to hear everything about that conversation—and is even tempted to listen in via comms—two death-defying escapes in a row have left her wrung out and exhausted. Virginia put her pineapple pajamas back on and turned in almost immediately; it's high time Noemi followed suit.

But it's hard to get to sleep. She lies in her bunk, alternately drowsy and fitful, for what feels like hours before she finally dozes off.

Sometimes, when Noemi's sleeping, it seems like her brain keeps working on problems without her. While she's either completely out or dreaming surreal, unrelated things, her rational mind must remain awake, fitting together the various jagged edges of a problem until it appears whole.

This is one of those nights, because almost as soon as she awakens, she murmurs, "Darius Akide."

Akide knew what Bellum Sanctum was. He had to know,

as a member of the Elder Council. He also had to know that Genesis was finally in a position of strength and could go on the offensive. But he was still desperate to use Abel to close the Genesis Gate and end the war that way instead. Why would Akide feel like that if the Bellum Sanctum strategy was able to give Genesis the final victory?

Noemi believes there are only two possibilities: First, Akide might've believed Bellum Sanctum wouldn't work. The device is thirty years old; it could be broken down, maybe beyond repair. But it's the second option that makes her heart beat fast, makes her question every bit of rage she's felt for Darius Akide since he attacked her and Abel.

The second option is that Bellum Sanctum would work, but it isn't just about scrambling communications. It involves something else—something too terrible for Akide to contemplate. So terrible that he never wanted to see it used, not even against Earth. Once the Battle of Genesis had been won, though, he knew Genesis was finally in a position to use that ultimate weapon. Attacking us was an act of desperation. He was willing to destroy Abel—even to murder me—to keep our planet from using that weapon.

For that to be true, though, Bellum Sanctum would have to cause death, and on a massive scale.

Noemi can't be certain of any of this. Maybe she's making an ocean out of a trickle, as Mrs. Gatson used to say. She wants to think that her planet wouldn't ever devise a strategy so corrupt, so far removed from the teachings of any of the religious traditions on Genesis. Surely the people would rise up to protest anything truly cataclysmic.

Is the leadership of Genesis lying to the people? The same way they might be lying to me?

As she sits on her bed, breathing hard, the comms crackle with Virginia's voice. *"Ahoy there, mechs and half mechs! Looks like our happy little ragtag fleet is about to get another member."*

Noemi wipes her eyes and hits the toggle to open a two-way channel. "Do you mean another ship is approaching?"

"Isn't that what I just said?"

Abel's voice breaks in. *"Can you identify the approaching ship?"*

"No specific ID, but they're headed toward the Katara *for docking, so it looks like they're old friends. It's a weird model of ship—white, almost cylindrical—reminds me a lot of the* Dove *back on Genesis."*

Sucking in a sharp breath, Noemi realizes what this might mean. "Is there any chance it *is* the *Dove*?"

"You know, I think it is?" Virginia laughs. *"I guess the big battle showdown made it possible for a few Genesis ships to start wandering around the rest of the galaxy."*

At any other time, this would've been cause for Noemi to celebrate. Now, however, one question fills her mind: *Should we let the Consortium turn the engine over to a*

Genesis ship before we know the whole truth about Bellum Sanctum?

She hurries down the long spiral corridor of the *Persephone* to the bridge. Not only is she shaken by her fears about the Bellum Sanctum device, but she's also become unsteady again. Noemi had thought she was getting the hang of her new capabilities, but her hand and arm have started feeling twitchy. The invasive voice in her mind tells her things that aren't as relevant to what she's doing. Probably she's just still tired, but is this what it's going to be like every time she has to push herself to the limit? Her life involves a lot of that. A *lot*.

Abel must've gotten to the bridge right before her, because she walks in to see that he hasn't yet taken his seat in the captain's chair. On the viewscreen is an image of the ship that's unquestionably the *Dove*.

"We need to talk," Noemi says to Abel.

"Agreed."

She stares at the *Dove*, which seems to be getting too close. That must be her paranoia at work, though. Surely. "I've had some thoughts about the Bellum Sanctum strategy—realized some things we have to find out—"

"That's what you're worried about?" Abel looks completely confused.

Only then does she recall there's another reason to avoid the Genesis authorities—

Communications snap on, signaling an incoming message from the *Dove*. The voice that comes over says, *"Preliminary identification suggests this spacecraft is the independent ship* Persephone. *Do you deny this?"*

Noemi glances at Abel, who looks even more uncertain than she feels. Replying is up to her. Slowly she says, "This is the *Persephone.*"

Abel straightens in his seat. Virginia turns toward them, realization washing over her, too.

"Remain in position," snaps the voice from Genesis. *"You are hereby ordered to stand down and surrender the mech designated Model One A, also known as Abel, to us."*

Noemi's gut twists. "What for?"

From the speakers she hears, *"Model One A is wanted for the murder of Elder Darius Akide."*

They know.

Noemi turns to look back at Abel, whose expression has turned grim. Quickly she silences the comms. "You can't turn yourself in."

"I have no intention of doing so," Abel says, surprising her. His ability for self-sacrifice has a limit after all, and she's glad of it.

But how do they get out of this one?

Dagmar Krall's voice crackles over comms: *"Whoa, whoa, Dove, we never discussed any of this during our negotiations—"*

Whoever it is on the *Dove* snaps back, *"None of the*

agreements between us and the Vagabond fleet allows you to shelter a known murderer and refuse to deliver that murderer to justice."

"We gotta stall," Virginia mutters, before turning comm audio back on. "Um, we have innocent civilians on this ship who are totally innocent and shouldn't get blown up in deep space due to innocence. We're in agreement on that, right?"

"*Surrender Model One A,*" says the implacable voice on the other line. At the edge of Noemi's console, a flickering dot appears—the signal of whatever scout ship or starfighter the *Dove* has sent out to confront them. They aren't waiting for the *Persephone* to approach and be processed in an orderly fashion. This is an arrest. If a vessel resists arrest of a crew member, the penalties can be severe.

Noemi's pretty sure that the murder of a member of the Elder Council gets the worst penalty possible.

Virginia interjects, "Any chance of reasoning with these guys?"

"About the murder of an Elder?" Abel says crisply. "Highly unlikely."

"We have to try." Noemi grips her console, thinking hard. "It was self-defense. Genesis recognizes the right to self—"

"But it wasn't self-defense." Abel's blue eyes meet hers evenly. "It might've been, in other circumstances—but I shot Akide purely because he had shot you."

Sometimes Noemi wants to whack some sense into his thick metal skull. "Nobody has to know that, Abel!"

"Are you suggesting lying to a court of law?"

Is he going to try getting self-righteous on her? Noemi retorts, "We lie *a lot*, when we have to. I don't see any reason to stop now."

Virginia looks from one to the other, then back again, but keeps her mouth shut.

Nothing Noemi's saying seems to be sinking in. Abel acts like she hasn't even spoken, reopening the channel to the Genesis ship. "This is Model One A. I hereby confess to being the sole perpetrator of the murder of Elder Darius Akide. As one of my passengers previously indicated, there are innocent parties on board. Will you allow the others to leave this ship safely before you take any further action?"

A pause follows, but only briefly. "*Confirmed. Innocent parties aboard the* Persephone *have five minutes to abandon ship. After that, they will be considered as aiding and abetting the crime of murder.*"

"Oh, *come on*," Virginia mutters, but she's already rising to her feet.

Wait. That's it? It's over and done with? It's like the floor dematerialized under Noemi's feet. She doesn't have anywhere to stand. All she can do is fall.

Without once glancing back, Abel heads for the door. "We have to get you both into Noemi's starfighter," he says.

"It will be a crowded and uncomfortable trip, but the ship can safely transport the two of you."

"This can't be the only way," Noemi protests—but Abel's already walking off the bridge, and Virginia shrugs helplessly as she follows.

There's nothing for Noemi to do but catch up.

She hurries to the docking bay and shoulders her way past the bulky Smasher. There sits her old starfighter, and Virginia is already easing her way into the cockpit. Though it will be a tight fit, the little ship will hold two.

When Abel turns to her, his face remains a porcelain mask. "You must board. We have only two minutes and fifty-one seconds to go."

"Fifty point seven eight," Noemi answers.

The corner of his mouth lifts in something that's not quite a smile.

"It wasn't a *joke*." She has to ball her hands into fists to keep from shaking his shoulders. "It's just what I know, because of my mech half—"

"Which I would advise against mentioning on Genesis," he interjects.

Noemi ignores this. "—and it's enough time to come up with another plan! Enough time for us to get away!"

Abel shakes his head. "That would only put you in danger. You've been endangered because of me too often. Last time, you almost didn't survive."

Fury sparks into flame inside her, a firestorm that robs her of reason or kindness. "So you're going to make all the decisions for me. Like you did last time, when you turned me into something that isn't even human! How come you're the only one who gets to make decisions, Abel? You say you respect me, but somehow you're the one making all the rules."

He stares at her, obviously astonished. She expects him to be equally angry, or abashed, or possibly even ashamed. Instead, what she sees in his eyes is naked, vulnerable pain.

Quietly he says, "Not even human."

Great. Now he thinks I don't consider him the equal of a human anymore, and there's no time to convince him otherwise. Genesis is coming, and they will *fire to kill.* Noemi might take her chances, but she can't ask Virginia to take that chance with her.

She and Abel wasted the last minute they had to change their fates—even to say good-bye—on arguing.

"Okay," Noemi says. Her voice is hoarse. "Time to go."

Abel nods. His blue eyes are unfocused. The only time Noemi ever saw Abel so wounded was when he first realized Mansfield's true plan for him. She's hurt him as badly as Mansfield ever did.

They turn back to the cockpit of the starfighter. Virginia sits there, stiff and uncomfortable, clearly wishing she hadn't overheard what she just overheard. Noemi allows herself to be loaded into the starfighter, where she has to tuck in awkwardly along Virginia's side.

"Get away from the *Dove*," Noemi says to Abel. "It doesn't matter what else you do, okay? You only have to do one thing, and that's stay alive and free."

"I'd argue those are two things," Abel answers. His voice is dull and flat. "But your point is well taken. Find another ship as soon as you can."

There's no time for her to share her worries about Bellum Sanctum. She'll have to investigate that on her own.

Just before they seal the cockpit, Noemi says, "Abel?"

He'd been turning away, but he pauses. "Yes?"

She can only think of one thing, the one that matters more than anything else: "Please—please understand how I feel about you."

Abel turns his face toward her then, and their eyes meet with an intensity she's never felt before. They're communicating soul to soul. None of the obstacles the galaxy has thrown between them have the power to change that.

He whispers, "I'm afraid I finally do."

The cockpit cover slides over her and Virginia. Abel backs out just before the air lock tightens with a snap. Noemi closes her eyes as her starfighter bobs in zero-G, then zooms out into the emptiness of space. The *Persephone* becomes no more than a silver teardrop against the starry sky.

20

THE *DOVE* GAVE ABEL FIVE MINUTES TO GET NOEMI AND
Virginia to safety. Their starfighter launches within three.
But he doesn't fool himself into believing he's safe for the
remaining two minutes.

As far as the Genesis ship is concerned, the only innocent people have abandoned the *Persephone*. No: the only
people, period. Its crew has no reason not to fire on what
Genesis considers an unmanned ship, one that contains
a very deadly device—namely, Abel himself. He understands both that Dagmar Krall would like to help him, and
that she's not about to endanger her Consortium's alliance
with Genesis on the behalf of a single individual, no matter
how rare or valuable she might consider him to be.

Abel runs up the spiral corridor to the bridge. He has to
think of a way to evade the *Dove* long enough to—

—to what?

Abel is alone again, as alone as he was in that docking

bay for thirty years. But this time, it's worse. This time, he understands the meaning of camaraderie, friendship, even love. He thought he knew what it meant to be loved, but Noemi's deepest feelings for him seem to have been no more than programming. All his hopes for the future have been demolished. Existence seems to have no meaning, if it must be endured without love.

But he refuses to give up. While Abel can't fear death, he can and does want *more life*.

He wants to know how the Liberty War will end. Wants to find out what will happen with the masses emigrating to Haven, and whether the world behind the unfinished Gate will turn out to be as good or better. Eventually he'll want to know how Harriet and Zayan are doing; they plan to have a child together in the future, a child he would be eager to see. Virginia will undoubtedly travel a path both chaotic and brilliant, one well worth witnessing. Circumstances might allow them to resume their friendship someday.

And Noemi—

No, he'll never see her again. Never get the chance to love her, or be loved by her. But he might have the opportunity to hear of her—what adventures she'll undertake, what future she might have.

It would be enough just to glimpse that future. To know she was happy. No matter what she thinks of him, Abel will always want that for her.

It's reason enough to stay alive.

He dashes along the spiral corridor of the *Persephone* until he bursts onto the bridge. The viewscreen shows the starfighter slowly flying toward the *Dove*, on a course that is unnecessarily, but conveniently, between that fighter and the *Persephone*. As her farewell, Noemi's doing her best to give Abel a chance to escape. That opportunity is all he needs.

He takes the helm, bringing the ship around and firing his newly repaired mag engines. They roar into full power, their flare shining through the energy-field walls to look like impossible fire in space. Then he heads out at full speed, aiming straight at the far-distant Cray Gate, all the way across the Kismet system.

Of course the Genesis ship pursues. The *Persephone* began its life as a research vessel, one designed for precision more than for speed. Whatever purpose the *Dove* was originally intended for, apparently it was one that required higher velocities. One glance at the console tells Abel that his pursuer will catch up with him in no more than eight minutes, seven seconds.

But his readings tell him that the *Dove* engines lack one capability the *Persephone* has just regained: Its engines can't be switched into overload.

Abel does it. His well-repaired ship responds swiftly, smoothly, as though overload were no problem at all. As he rockets toward the Gate, he sees with satisfaction that the *Dove* is being left far behind.

But Noemi is being left behind, too, and so many of his own shattered hopes.

• • •

Abel decides to fly through the so-called Blind Gate—the surest way he knows to get away from it all.

Literally.

This Gate represents the worst-case scenario in humanity's search for livable planets: A likely world was found, a Gate was built, and an excursion party came through in hopes that nothing major had changed and settlements could be established. Instead, they discovered that two of the planet's moons had shattered, sending enormous, climate-destroying meteors crashing into its surface. Numerous new satellites, of irregular shape and orbit, render travel through this system dangerous. So humanity abandoned any hope of settling here.

Of course, some people *do* travel through the Blind Gate. It's a terrible place to live but a very, very good place to hide. Occasionally smugglers come through, or other individuals who are strongly motivated to keep their location unknown. Abel came here himself once before—with Noemi, when they needed to hide from the rest of the galaxy and repair his ship, then called the *Daedalus*.

This is where he showed her his favorite movie,

Casablanca. This is where he suggested making love—merely as a means of satisfying curiosity, or so he thought at the time. (Abel's greater understanding of his developing subconscious suggests that his request may have had then-unseen dimensions.)

It may have been unwise to come to a location where so many memories would make me miss Noemi, he thinks.

Yet where else could he go? He and Noemi are the only two living individuals who've made landfall in every single system connected to the Loop. Memories of her linger on Earth (in the ancient cobblestoned streets of London), on Genesis (near the open-air market by the river), on Cray (talking about the importance of faith while sitting under strings of fairy lights), on Stronghold (pretending to be husband and wife so he could stay with her in the hospital), on Haven (finding each other within the glittering wreckage of the *Osiris*), and even on Kismet—if its lunar station counts.

There's no escaping the memories. The entire galaxy is gilded with traces of Noemi Vidal, brighter in all the places she's ever been. Abel decides he wouldn't have it any other way.

• • •

After a full day of moody contemplation on a large asteroid, and one large collision coming closer than he would've liked, Abel makes plans to leave.

This raises the question of where, exactly, he should go. Now that Genesis ships are capable of traveling through the galaxy—even in limited numbers—he could be found and apprehended at any point. Unrest has spread throughout all the star systems of the Loop. It's a dangerous time to be the lone crew member of a small free ship.

He finally determines that safety is not to be found in a location. His best chance of it will be found in a group.

Dagmar Krall is betting heavily on the Kismet system representing a new seat of power after the Liberty War ends, and the new Gate has been built, Abel reasons. He hasn't been gone for that long. Therefore at least part of the Vagabond fleet will still be stationed there.

She is allied with Genesis now—but being allied to a world does not always mean *obeying* that world. Krall strikes Abel as someone who does not obey easily.

He returns to the Kismet system without incident and, as predicted, finds the Vagabond fleet still in place at the far edges of the minefield. Ship sensors quickly pick up the signal for the *Katara*, which he immediately hails.

Anjuli Patil's voice comes through comms: *"Free ship* Persephone, *we didn't expect to see you again so soon— maybe ever, after the way you took off. Good job with that, by the way!"*

"The surprise at my return is mutual," Abel says. "Please let Commodore Krall know that Abel, captain of the *Persephone*, has reconsidered her offer to join the Consortium. If it's still open—I accept."

• • •

He boards the *Katara* for what he expects to be a brief exchange of formalities with Dagmar Krall. But Krall's lieutenants—including, especially, her wife—don't want to leave it at that.

"We *must* have the tattoo!" Anjuli insists, holding Krall's arm affectionately as they all stroll through one of the tall central corridors of the *Katara*. Consortium members of various ages and races bustle through, conducting minor trade with one another, greeting old friends. "Every new pilot in the Consortium gets one. It's tradition."

Krall gives her a look that's equal parts warmth and exasperation. "It's one thing to ask humans to carry marks on our skins for the rest of our lives. That's another fifty or sixty years, tops. Abel can expect to be around, what—"

"Another two to three hundred years," Abel says. "But if the tattoo is traditional, I have no objection."

Anjuli's dark eyes light up. "You see?"

With a heavy sigh, Krall gives in. "Fine. Set up the ceremony."

Within half an hour, Abel sits shirtless in the center of a large meeting room at the heart of the *Katara*. He's on one chair; a grizzled, dark-skinned man is perched on the other, a tattoo gun in his hand as he starts work. Another forty-seven Consortium pilots have gathered together to watch, cheer, and drink.

Well, from the look of things, mostly to drink.

The first pinprick of pain stings Abel's upper arm. Fortunately, under controlled circumstances like this, he has the option of turning his pain receptors down to near numbness. He does so and watches with calm interest as his tattoo takes shape.

"It always starts with the silhouette of your ship," says the tattoo artist, who has told Abel to call him Barry. "So there's as many kinds of Consortium tattoos as there are kinds of ships. Lucky for us both, yours is easy."

Abel nods as a teardrop-shaped outline appears on his skin. As his skin isn't entirely human, the reaction to the ink is different; already he can see that the colors will be far more vibrant on his body than on most humans. "The tattoo starts with a silhouette. What next?"

"Above it, everyone gets a katara," Barry says. By this he means not the Consortium flagship but its namesake, a square-handled dagger traditional to India. As the blade is filled in, he continues, "Within the silhouette, you get whatever color you want—and as time goes by, we layer on that with symbols for your biggest deals and victories. Ought to work up something for the Battle of Genesis, huh?"

"I wasn't a Consortium member at that time," Abel points out. "Is that all?"

Barry chuckles. "Not quite all. Underneath your ship, you put one word. One thing you fight for more than anything else. That's what you're in the Consortium to win. So what's it going to be for you?"

The first word that comes to Abel is a name: *Noemi*.

But that's wrong. He's not in the Consortium to win her. Noemi will always be in his heart, no matter how many centuries he lives; a tattoo can't make his devotion to her greater. That would be impossible. And he doesn't want to be reminded of his short-lived hopes for the two of them every single time he sees his bare arm.

For now, he must define another primary goal.

"Well?" Barry prods.

"Freedom," Abel says. "The word you should write there is 'freedom.'"

The others around him hear that, even through their raucous carousing, and they cheer in approval. Abel smiles back at them, ignoring the tattoo needle and the tiny pinpricks of blood it leaves behind.

21

IT'S INCREDIBLY STRANGE TO NOEMI, TO BE ON A GENESIS ship flying freely through the other systems of the Loop.

Even weirder: The *Dove* is able to bring her back to her homeworld without facing more than token resistance from a handful of Queens and Charlies along the way.

("Bizarre, right?" Virginia mutters to her. "Is Earth, like, out of mechs or something?"

"No idea," Noemi says. She knows only that they should be meeting a lot more resistance than they are.)

Even a quick, uneventful journey back to Genesis takes days, and those days give her too much time to think. Too much time to remember the way Abel's eyes looked when she told him about the programmed feelings within her—to endure those feelings yearning for him every second of every hour—

Try not to think about it, Noemi says to herself. *If you keep thinking about it, you won't be able to bear it.*

The best way to use this time, she thinks, would be to investigate the Bellum Sanctum strategy further. Is it what they were told—a massive communications disruption—or something more sinister?

But her questions get her nowhere. Either the *Dove* crew members don't have clearance to know any more than she does, or they don't believe *she* has the clearance. She'll have to do more digging once she gets home.

Noemi has left the Genesis system two times and returned twice. (She isn't counting the time Abel took her away unconscious.) Both times she left, she had fought with all her body and soul to save Genesis—first in the Liberty War, then from the Cobweb plague. Both times, her welcome had been strained at best, and suspicious at worst.

This time, she didn't do a damned thing except get dragged back, so *this* is when her planet finally decides she's a hero.

"We've all seen the holos, Vidal," says Deirdre O'Farrell as she walks Noemi and Virginia through the spaceport. (O'Farrell! Who wouldn't even talk to her just a few short months ago!) Her face looks so unfamiliar with this huge smile. "Everyone knows that you went into the battle in a civilian ship, even though you were no longer with our fleet. No orders. Just pure loyalty to Genesis."

Another voice interjects, "Which I pointed out several times." Noemi turns to see Captain Baz coming toward her, a broad smile on her face.

The terrible numbness within Noemi cracks enough for her to smile back. "Captain. It's so good to see you—"

"None of that 'captain' stuff. You're a civilian now, remember?" Baz grins as she folds her dataread and digital scanner against her chest. "That means you get to call me Yasmeen."

Noemi pauses. She understands the compliment, but calling the captain by her first name feels...blasphemous. Maybe she'll get used to the idea, but for now, she intends to talk around it. "I guess that means you're not taking me back into the fleet?"

Baz shakes her head fondly. "You still want back in the fight." In the hangar, a couple dozen pilots remain at work on their starfighters. As Noemi walks through the space, smelling grease and ozone, she glimpses their furtive, admiring looks at her.

Where were all these guys when I was being treated like a pariah six months ago? But of course they were right here. It's the exact same people.

I didn't deserve to be an outcast then any more than I deserve to be a hero now.

"Listen," Noemi says, "I appreciate the warm welcome, but let's face it—I'm not the one who turned the tide at the Battle of Genesis. That was Abel."

O'Farrell freezes at the mention of Abel's name. The clatter and clang of repairs in the hangar goes silent.

Virginia gives the others a meaningful nod, backing Noemi up. Captain Baz smiles, but sadly. "How do you figure that, Vidal—I mean, Noemi? The mech's ship never flew into battle."

"No, because his ship had no weapons and couldn't have fought in the battle that way. Instead, he used his ship to send signals to the Queens and Charlies. He told them to stop firing on us and start blasting each other." Noemi stops, forcing both O'Farrell and Baz to face her. "That's what turned the tide."

O'Farrell scoffs, a sound that makes Noemi want to punch her freckled nose. "There's no way you can prove that."

Until this point, Virginia's been silent, but this comment pushes her to respond. "Um, excuse me, but there is. Provide me with holographic images and sensor scans from the battle, and I'm happy to go through them and show you second by second where the signals were sent, and how you can trace them." She folds her arms and uses all her considerable height to stare haughtily down at O'Farrell. "Assuming that your planet actually bothers taking scientific scans instead of leaving it all up to divination or alchemy or whatever—"

"Give her the scans," Noemi interjects, before Virginia can go past defending Abel and start ticking everyone off. "She'll show you."

Baz looks uncertain, which might be as good as they

can do right now. But O'Farrell's face has gone utterly cold. "The mech captured you. Sometimes hostages begin to sympathize with their captors—"

"That's not what's going on!" It would feel so good to put a fist through O'Farrell's face—but that won't help Abel. Besides, prickly pain tickles along the length of her left arm, and Noemi's not entirely sure her body would obey her. She might hit O'Farrell too hard, or even worse, not hard enough. "How can you not look at the evidence? How can you not realize what he's done for all of you?"

Quietly Baz says, "We realize the one most important thing, which is that Abel killed Elder Darius Akide. Unless you can prove that's not true either?"

"It's true," Noemi admits, "but you haven't asked why Abel did it."

"Mechs kill." O'Farrell's voice is flat. "That's what they're made to do."

"Not all mechs, and definitely not him!" *Deep breaths*, she tells herself. *Hang on.* Noemi can't fly off the handle now, not without wasting her chance to vindicate Abel. "He only shot Akide because Akide shot me. With a blaster. At close range."

Baz and O'Farrell share a look of mutual disbelief. It must sound insane, accusing an Elder of murder. Noemi would've thought so herself at any point in her life before the moment Darius Akide aimed his blaster at her and fired.

"Why would he do that?" O'Farrell demands.

"That's what I—what I've been wondering—" Noemi has to catch her breath. As she pauses, she sees flat incomprehension on Deirdre O'Farrell's face...but Captain Baz has gone pale. Does she know something?

Or maybe she's just worried because Noemi's on the verge of hyperventilating.

"Trust me," Virginia says, pushing into the conversation again. "I saw Noemi in the cryosleep pod afterward. That blaster bolt nearly ripped her in two."

"Why should I trust *you*?" O'Farrell says. "You're an outworlder." Virginia gives O'Farrell a look that could melt steel.

Noemi tries, "You can run scans. You can see what happened to me—" The breath catches in her throat again, and it takes her a moment to steady herself.

Virginia leans closer to her. "Hey, are you sure you're okay?"

"I don't feel good," she admits.

O'Farrell seems determined to stick to her captive theory, because she asks, "Did that mech do something to you?"

"He saved my life after Akide shot me in the gut at almost point-blank range," Noemi says.

"That wouldn't even be possible," Baz says quietly. "A blaster at that range—you'd be dead."

"I should be dead," Noemi agrees. Anger and exhaustion

are catching up with her; she's breathing too quickly and has started feeling woozy. She pushes on. "But Abel saved me. He saved me by—by changing me."

Baz frowns. "What do you mean, changing you?"

Noemi shouldn't even have said that much. She should try talking around it. But the fast, heavy pulse of her temples is too quick, and the world is dark around the edges, and somehow it's spinning, or falling, and she's falling, too.

• • •

A few hours later, she lies on a biobed in the Goshen hospital. Unlike the ones on the *Persephone*, this biobed is soft, with a cushy pillow, and a light cotton blanket has been wrapped around her. Soft afternoon light filters through the window, through which she can see the grassy meadows that skirt the city, the same meadows she and Esther ran through as children. She ought to feel swaddled, comforted, made whole.

Instead, she hears the murmurs of the physicians who don't know what to make of her. Noemi catches only a word here and there:

"Unprecedented."

"Irreversible."

"Appalling."

"Abomination."

Thank God at least one of the doctors can handle what she's become.

"This is amazing," says Ephraim Dunaway, who hurried from the capital to her bedside in order to help. He's one of the only physicians on Genesis who understands mech components at all. "This stuff goes beyond any bioengineering I've ever seen. Some of this is standard tech, but some of it—most of it, especially this cybernetic nervous system—this is a huge leap forward. It looks as organic as any other cells in the body. You couldn't tell those parts were artificial if it weren't for the accelerated functions."

"In other words, we couldn't tell the difference between a mech and a human?" The head doctor on Noemi's team recoils. "This is Earth's next conspiracy against us. While settlers keep showing up pretending to be desperate Vagabonds, playing on our sympathies—Earth could be putting newly engineered mechs in their ranks. Every off-worlder must be considered suspect."

Noemi feels sick, now more in her spirit than her body. "That's not true," she insists. "I'm the first person this has ever been done to. There aren't any others. You can't force out the Vagabonds—they need homes, they fought for you—"

"No political decisions will be made in this room," the doctor replies, his eyes narrowed. "I'll point out only that you have no way of knowing that you're the only one."

"Actually, I do, since the one and only person who can do this is Gillian Shearer, aka daughter of Burton Mansfield, also known as the would-be cult leader who's currently running things on Haven." For one moment Noemi wishes Abel had given her the *Persephone* and taken the starfighter for himself, only because then she could've showed these idiots more of the proof of where she's been, and what was done.

Her heart aches at the thought of Abel, but she pushes it aside.

Showing the doctors proof wouldn't have made a difference, because they aren't even listening to her. "You'll have to remain under observation," says the suspicious doctor. His tone makes it sound less like they're taking care of her, and more like she's under arrest.

She never really felt like she belonged on Genesis—but now she's more of an outcast than ever before.

As the other physicians file out, muttering among themselves, Ephraim stays beside her bed and takes her hand. He's a large man—tall and muscular, someone she'd expect to have become a soldier rather than a healer. Yet his gentleness is as much a part of him as his warm brown eyes or dark skin. His presence comforts her, gives her a sense of safety. "How do you feel, Noemi?"

"Awful," she admits. "But I don't know how much of that is the new components being weird, and how much of it is just not being able to stand any more stupidity." With a sigh, she lets her head fall back onto her pillow. "At least you're here. It helps to have someone who cares and actually knows what he's doing."

Ephraim sighs. "Let's get real. I don't know what I'm doing. No doctor in the worlds would. You're something that's never existed before. Evaluating your health is— well, for the time being, let's call it a challenge."

At least he didn't say it was impossible, Noemi thinks. But to judge by his expression, he might be thinking it.

Ephraim squeezes her arm, obviously trying to be reassuring. "Speaking of people who care, you've got some visitors."

That's when Virginia walks in, with Harriet Dixon and Zayan Thakur right behind her. While Virginia's wearing her usual stuff, Harriet and Zayan have abandoned their colorful patchwork Vagabond gear for simple Genesis tunics and leggings. But Harriet's brilliant smile is the same. "After the battle we thought—well, rumor had it you'd been blown up at the very end, when nobody saw. Good to see you alive and well again!"

"Sort of well, anyway," Zayan adds. "And Abel—it's not true what they're saying about him, is it?"

Noemi pauses before saying, "He did shoot Darius Akide, but only because Akide tried to kidnap him and then shot me." She doesn't repeat what Abel said to her about his lack of hesitation or remorse. Only someone who'd been in that same situation, who had been afraid for their own life and for that of the person they loved, could truly understand Abel's actions. "My body is all the proof the authorities need. Instead, they're only looking at me as some kind of freak."

Harriet and Zayan exchange a glance. "Virginia filled us in," Zayan says. "Part mech, huh? That sounds pretty badass."

Noemi sighs. "It was starting to be badass once I got used to it, but now—I don't know. Hopefully this is just more of the transition, but I feel strange. Kind of…wobbly, I guess."

With a shrug, Ephraim gestures toward her readouts. "Unfortunately, 'wobbly' is about as precise as your diagnosis gets. We have no idea how your vitals should look, post—uh, post-modification. So it's important to pay attention to how you feel. It's *vitally* important."

"It's hard to concentrate." Noemi sinks down onto her pillow. It's like someone tied an anchor to her heart, and it's dragging her to the depths. "I'll never see Abel again. He's all alone out there. Vulnerable. If Genesis doesn't hunt him down, Gillian Shearer might. And there's some huge military thing going on—" She catches herself. Probably Ephraim, Zayan, and Harriet know absolutely nothing about Bellum Sanctum, and it should stay that way. "I'm scared for him. That's all. I'd feel better if I could at least do something constructive, but I can't even get out of this bed."

As Noemi lies there, miserable and weak, an awkward silence stretches out. Nobody can reassure her about Abel, which means nobody knows what to say. Harriet and Zayan can't make up their minds where to look, and Ephraim's busying himself with the medical readouts again. Luckily,

Virginia never shuts up for along. "Okay, so, I'm going to be a little selfish here. Right now I'm stranded on a Luddite planet, totally out of the Loop in the literal and metaphorical senses, and not able to do a damn thing to help my friends under arrest on Cray. In other words, I need to get the hell off of Genesis. Work up a fake ID, figure out a new place to be and another life to live. But first, I've got to get out of here. Would flying that starfighter away from this rock do the trick, or would they shoot me down as some kind of conspirator?"

"I think you could leave," Noemi says, "but I'm not sure." Nausea wells up inside her, and she imagines that every false component in her arm and chest and head has begun to ache.

No. Not imagines. They do ache. Terribly.

Her stomach churns, and her head spins, and—

The next several seconds are no more than a blur. Noemi's body thrashes, and though she can barely think, she believes it must be trying to tear itself apart. The ache in her head sharpens until she feels like she's being cut in two. Her mind blurs with endless raw data that spills into her like a tsunami of meaningless numbers. Distantly she hears Ephraim say the word *seizure*, and it seems like that should explain what's happening, if she could think about it long enough.

She knows only one thing for sure: Her mech parts aren't making her better any longer.

Instead, they're making her sick.

22

ABEL HAD JOINED THE KRALL CONSORTIUM PRIMARILY to gain allies amid a galaxy in turmoil. The Liberty War—for so long confined to the Genesis system—now threatened to break out and encompass all the worlds of the Loop. It would be difficult for any ship with no home planet to make its way through such a war; it would be even more difficult for one with a fugitive for a captain. He'd anticipated that having allies in the trade would give him protection, and that his own considerable talents would make this an equitable exchange.

He hadn't anticipated that the Consortium would immediately pull him into military action.

"*Only* sort of *military*," says Anjuli Patil via comms, in the preliminary briefing. "*We probably won't see any combat.*"

"By a slim margin," Abel replies. "Specifically, there is a forty-seven point forty-eight percent chance of battle breaking out."

Anjuli's eyes widen. *"That high, huh?"* But she smiles bravely. *"The point is, there's a half-completed Gate in the Kismet system. If Earth retains control of that Gate, they retain control of the world on the other side. We can't allow that to happen."*

The long-term military strategy is sound. In the shorter term, Abel would consider it wiser to wait for this kind of action until Earth's dealing with conflict elsewhere—in other words, after some of the patrol ships in this area of the Kismet system had moved away.

But he may be overcautious. If they were to wait for another clash as major as the Battle of Genesis, they might be waiting a long time. The closer the Gate gets to completion, the more intense Earth's hold on the Kismet system will become.

"Very well," Abel says. "Send the necessary information, and the *Persephone* will be ready."

"Of course," Anjuli replies. Her pleasant tone is sincere, and yet within it Abel can hear a slight hesitation.

He knows why. It's because he just acted as though he had the right to refuse Krall's instructions.

Now that he's a member of the Consortium, he doesn't.

• • •

At Krall's signal, the Consortium moves in.

The Vagabond vessels crowd the perimeter of this

irregular, seemingly empty corner of space, their running lights shining like the stars of new constellations. More than one hundred ships are coasting in, from freighters to little skimmers, each vibrantly painted with patterns he recognizes from the art of various cultures: Maori, Navajo, Celtic. Abel's photographic memory informs him that dozens of these ships weren't present at the Battle of Genesis. Their crews must be later converts to the fight.

The uprising is getting larger, he thinks. *More and more people are joining the fight.*

Noemi would be so happy to know that—

Briefly, Abel closes his eyes, pushing aside the pain. He reminds himself that she will know, someday. It doesn't matter that he won't be the one to tell her.

When he opens his eyes again, he glimpses a flicker of movement at the most distant edge of his ship's sensors. Opening a channel throughout the Consortium fleet, he says, "We have smaller vessels deploying. Probable warrior mech presence."

"*Steady on, people.*" Krall's voice comes through the comms firm and strong. "*Shielded vessels, take point.*"

The *Persephone* is only here to add to the intimidating size of the Consortium fleet. His ship doesn't have battle shielding; it doesn't even have real weapons. Abel's always made it through combat via a combination of speed, strategy, and occasional use of lasers and comm signals—which aren't capable of damaging an enemy as much as of confusing it to the point of damaging itself.

In this conflict, the strategy isn't his to determine. Speed is something he can use only at Krall's request. He's been given a relatively safe position in the rear center of the fleet, but if the battle turns bad for the Consortium, even this good position won't protect him.

Besides, hiding from the fight seems…indecent.

(This can only be Noemi's influence.)

Abel continues scans as skirmishes begin on the edge of the fleet. Blaster bolts and weapons fire illuminate the black borders of open space. The entire bulk of the Consortium ships continue moving toward the center of this contested area of space—at which lies the half-completed Gate to a world unknown. They must secure that Gate, but that means they have to concentrate their forces into a single mass. But the Queens and Charlies that he can now see firing at the outermost ships—speeding in dangerous, irregular arcs like stinging wasps—they're free to protect themselves. Or to attack the vulnerable. To do anything their deadly programming suggests.

He reasons, *We must use their strategy against them.*

Abel accesses the thousands of forms of military strategy stored in his memory banks and chooses one of the simplest, and one of the most effective: the feint.

He opens a private channel to the *Katara*. "I think I can

draw many of them away from our fleet," he says as he steps to the ops panel and starts working. "Earth's military has become much too dependent on warrior mechs in recent decades. Deprive them of their Queens and Charlies, and they'll retreat."

"*We're trying to deprive them!*" replies Anjuli via comms. "*By* shooting *the damned things!*"

Abel wants to say the warrior mechs are too numerous and too quick for that, but the battle is proving that point for him. "I'm about to release a probe," he says instead. "Inform our ships to ignore that probe and any signals it sends. The rest should take care of itself. *Persephone* out."

With that, he turns his full attention to the probe.

This is no longer an accurate name for it. Once it was an ejectable sensor probe for Mansfield's research; Abel has since retrofitted it as an escape pod—the same one he offered Virginia Redbird, if she hadn't agreed to leave the ship for Cray.

Retrofitting the pod meant removing almost all its sensors, but some remain. Signals can be sent from within it, programmed remotely. So he programs it to send out the same type of scrambling signals he used to confuse the mechs at the minefield. This time, however, the scrambling isn't random. Abel gives it a focal point—a direction.

A direction the warrior mechs must follow.

In his determination to create the most advanced mech

of all time, Mansfield gave Abel at least part of the programming of each of the other twenty-five models of mech
in existence, from the culinary knowledge of a Baker to the
childcare technique of a Nan. Some models' programming
were installed in their entirety—including those for warrior mechs.

He knows their abilities. Knows their strategies. And
knows exactly which kind of signal they'll interpret as a
top-priority pursuit. Abel can imagine what Virginia Redbird would say about this: *You're basically putting up a huge
neon sign that reads "Chase me, losers!"*

"Exactly," he murmurs to himself, then launches the pod.

The silver streak of the pod vanishes into the blackness
of space on his viewscreen, just one flash among hundreds
in the battle that's begun. Normally Abel would switch to
more schematic sensor readings, but not this time. If this
plan works, the proof will be visible shortly.

Soon he picks up a small wave of mechs flying toward
one area at the very edge of the fight. Then another wave.
He allows himself to smile as more and more mechs change
their normal attack patterns to fly in pursuit of the pod.
Their gleaming exosuits form burnished arrows against the
darkness of space.

Over comms, Dagmar Krall says, *"Abel, you're even hand-
ier than I thought you'd be."*

"It's my nature." He feels justifiably proud, but apparently humans enjoy the pretense of humility. Abel's learning how to oblige them. It feels so unnatural, though. "The minute the Queens and Charlies are fully centralized around the pod, we should concentrate all fire."

"Already on it."

Within another 2 minutes, 49.1 seconds, every single warrior mech in the Earth fleet has congregated around the pod. The Earth ships are frantically sending signals, trying to get the mechs back into formation, but they can't counteract what Abel's just sent out.

At least, they can't do it in time.

Space lights up with weapons fire, and the explosions of mech after mech. Even before the Queens and Charlies are completely destroyed, the Earth fleet has begun to scatter; within minutes, they've vacated this area of space entirely. They're going to the only place reinforcements could come from—in other words, they're fleeing for the Cray Gate.

Which means this new Gate—the one that may someday lead to yet another home for humanity—belongs to the Consortium. To the people.

Noemi would be proud.

• • •

Once their presence around the Unknown Gate has been established, Dagmar Krall begins granting shore leaves. Kismet is apparently delighted at its liberation from Earth control; its planetary leaders have invited any and all Consortium members to make planetfall, to enjoy the famous beauty and luxury of this world. While many ships will, of course, have to remain in place to guard the Gate, Krall apparently sees no need to deny the others the spoils of victory.

Her announcement is met with yet more flashing-light "applause." For all their embrace of the spacefaring life, most Vagabonds love to put their feet on solid ground for a change. To smell fresh air. To have a true sky overhead instead of outer space.

The *Persephone* is included in the very first group of those cleared to visit Kismet. Probably it's meant as a reward for Abel's clever thinking during the battle. He needs no reward for that, and briefly considers giving up his leave to some other Vagabond ship, which might appreciate it more.

But he and Noemi never made planetfall on Kismet. It's the one world in the galaxy that isn't haunted by the ghosts of happier times, when they were together, facing every challenge, discovering each other.

Maybe, on Kismet, he'll miss her less. So he joins the first wave of travelers down to the surface.

Kismet is always described as dazzling: a waterworld with lilac oceans and lavender skies. Only 10 percent of its surface is land, made up entirely of tropical islands with white sand and soft winds. This makes the planet perfect for human habitation...in the short term.

But there's not enough landmass to house a huge population, much less grow the food to feed them. Kismet farms its seas, but anywhere beyond the narrow band of the tropics, those seas are inhabited by large, highly dangerous shark- and squid-like creatures. These alien creatures have proven themselves willing to devour human crops of the native kelp—or, on occasion, to eat the humans themselves. So there's a limit to how many people can live on the planet before overcrowding and food shortages set in.

Instead of responsibly peopling Kismet with a small, hardy group of settlers, Earth turned the planet into a kind of resort. Those rich and powerful enough could escape Earth's stagnant air for days, weeks, or months on the beach. Only a few thousand people have ever lived there full-time, and they were there to provide cocktails, massages, and hotel services for the wealthy guests.

Until now.

Abel steps out from the central spaceport of Isla de Fortuna, blinks, then minimizes his light intake by 30 percent. Pearlescent white sand shifts softly beneath his boots as he takes in the scene: Stretching along the beach is a long, palatial resort—or what was one, and is now a kind of central bartering market. The permanent inhabitants of Kismet once wore sarongs and shifts with various corporate logos on them, but now they dress more like Vagabonds, and trade like them, too. Booths exchange fruit for fish, fish for cloth, cloth for solar chargers, and so on. It's noisy and chaotic, but almost every person is grinning.

One's own mayhem is always better than anyone else's order, he thinks.

Most of the Vagabonds head straight for one of the fruit kiosks—in deep space, citrus is a rare luxury. Abel's more interested in a gathering closer to the seashore, where people are animatedly discussing a word he thinks he'd pick up on even without superhuman hearing: *Haven.*

"Come on," argues a woman wearing long black robes. "It can't be true. Who ever heard of a planet you can't live on unless you've had a disease first?"

"That's the whole reason the Cobweb virus exists," insists a man with a heavy French accent. "They were trying to make us ready to live on Haven. Making us sick the way it does—that's just the side effect."

A deep voice from the back says, "Four years ago my husband died of that 'side effect.' Mind how you talk about it."

The Frenchman holds out his hand. "Forgive me, my friend. I don't mean to make light of the subject. I only meant that we can't set foot on Haven without knowing that it's safe first. Rumors have it that the Vagabond settlers there are already dying by the thousands."

Abel thinks of the havoc he saw on Haven. It saved his

life, but by now humans are dying for no worse crime than wanting a home. Noemi warned them, but desperate people are never good at hearing what they don't want to hear.

"You're afraid of shadows and lies," insists the woman in black. "The so-called epidemic is just a cover-up, the story Earth tells to keep us from Haven."

"It isn't," Abel says. The entire group turns to stare at him. Although he's a stranger, they must recognize the absolute certainty in his voice. "I've been to Haven already—it was safe for me. But I took readings of the atmosphere while I was there. Toxicity levels will kill the average human within days. Only the genetic change worked by Cobweb makes survival possible."

The woman in black folds her arms. "How can this be true? If you were safe on Haven, you'd have stayed there!"

No point in getting into why he should never again set foot on Haven. Instead, he slightly reshapes the truth: "My companion badly needed medical treatment." A few nods follow; they approve of his prioritizing Noemi's health over his own comfort. Harriet and Zayan told him that, to Vagabonds, the most important virtue is loyalty.

The Frenchman asks, "Then what are we to do? Wait to get Cobweb, and hope we don't die?"

"Haven's original settlers were exposed to a weakened version of the virus—one that changed their bodies without making them as seriously ill." Abel considers the ramifications. "While there may not be a large store of that material on the planet at this time, both Haven and Earth must have the basic knowledge of the medical protocol. What you should do is negotiate for the raw information and materials to be distributed throughout the galaxy."

After a brief pause, the deep-voiced man says, "That's what the fight would be for, then. Not Haven, but the ability to live there."

It strikes Abel how different the future will be from anything that has ever been before. The newness and strangeness of it all is dizzying—and, in its own way, glorious.

Then he notices that one of the men in the surrounding crowd, one with a long mustache and a green cloak, is staring at him. His stare is intense and, if Abel's assessing human emotion correctly, hostile.

Abel's first thought is that he's been identified as a mech. But that makes no sense. He is mostly unknown to the galaxy at large.

But one planet's entire population has heard of him— and blames him for murder.

Genesis has been sending operatives out into the various systems of the Loop, Abel recalls. *That would include Kismet. And any information packets such operatives have received from Genesis could well include an image of one of their world's most wanted criminals.*

Me.

Perhaps this man isn't from Genesis, but the possibility cannot be ignored. Amid the various chatter of the group, he steps casually to the edge of it, then strolls away in the direction of the spaceport.

Abel doesn't glance back until he's stepping inside the *Persephone*. When he does, he sees he's been followed. The man with the long mustache stands in the far passageway, speaking into a comm unit.

The casual protocol serves no more purpose. Abel runs inside, sets the ship to prepare for takeoff, and begins strategizing. *Get back to the Consortium blockade around the Unknown Gate. They'll provide cover and protection.*

This is why Abel joined the Consortium in the first place. Space presents too many dangers to be faced alone. Allies are necessary. Flying out of Kismet atmosphere, back to the depths of space, feels like going home.

When he rejoins the Vagabond fleet, Abel considers the crisis passed—until the moment a tractor beam locks on to his ship, holding it fast.

A beam from the *Katara*.

"*Persephone* to *Katara*," Abel says into comms. "Is there a particular reason you've locked me into position?"

He hopes against hope that there's some other reason— repairs, maybe. Anything other than what he fears.

But then Krall's voice comes over the speaker, slow and sad. "*I'm genuinely sorry about this, Abel. You'd have been a fine member of the Consortium. Even in the past few days, you've proved your worth.*"

"But I'm worth more as a bounty for Genesis," he says dryly.

"*This isn't about money,*" Krall insists. "*This is about our alliance. We didn't join forces with Genesis because it was right or just. We did it so my people could have a world to live on. So they'd have homes. That means preserving the alliance is my top priority. When Genesis says they need a wanted criminal turned over to them—then that's what we have to do.*"

Abel says, "I understand." And he does. Dagmar Krall has made the only moral choice she could.

But that doesn't make it any easier when the power over his ship is transferred over to the smaller craft from Genesis. Abel can take no comfort from returning to Noemi's world—not even when it offers the chance of seeing her one last time. Not when he's being dragged back for his trial for murder.

And his execution.

23

NOEMI'S MEDICAL RECORDS TELL HER THAT THE SEIZURE only lasted for seventeen seconds. The eerily accurate time-keeper in her brain tells her it was actually 16.89 seconds from onset to end.

It's been a whole two days since then, and she's still stuck in her biobed. Her mech chronometer can't keep her from feeling like she's been in this hospital forever.

The feeling that she'll never get out—that might be a little too accurate.

"Feeling better?" Ephraim Dunaway asks as Noemi props herself up on her pillows early on the third morning of her stay. "How did that ion surge work?"

Noemi shrugs. A muscle in her arm twitches. "I don't feel any different. No better, no worse."

Ephraim brightens. "No worse?"

"I mean—no worse because of the ion thing. I think. But I'm still getting…slower, more tired." She scratches the pixie cap of regrown hair on her scalp. At least she still has full control of her fingers. So far. "Have you turned up anything?"

He sighs as he leans back against the wall and softly thumps his head against it once. "Not a damn thing. Genesis isn't exactly the place to be if you want to research cutting-edge organic mech components."

"Maybe it's not a mech thing," Noemi says. She's been brooding about this in her conscious hours. "Maybe it's a Gillian Shearer thing. My treatment was experimental. Do you think she might not have realized all the side effects of what she did to me?"

Ephraim nods. "Maybe she hasn't. Still, nothing about the materials or energy output within your body ought to be affecting you like this." He folds his arms, thoughtful. "You know, we use Tare mechs on Remedy ships. We haven't brought any of them planetside, because nobody's in a big hurry to put themselves in a mech's hands here on Genesis—but we've been using them to run labs, crunch data, synthesize treatments, all those kinds of things. But they've been making mistakes. Breaking down. Reports we've been getting from around the Loop suggest that's happening to a lot of mechs all over the galaxy."

"It is," Noemi says. Suddenly she feels cold, not from anything happening in her body, but from fear. "Abel and I saw malfunctioning mechs on Stronghold and Haven. We knew it was too many malfunctions to be only a coincidence, but we didn't get the chance to investigate. You think it might have something to do with what's happening to me?"

"It might not," Ephraim admits. "We just don't know. You're something that's never been seen before. We have to investigate every human cause of sickness and every reason a mech might break down. And if there are mass breakdowns going on out there, well, I don't think we can afford to ignore that."

Mechs are failing all over the galaxy. Will that catch up with Abel, too? Is he all right, wherever he is? "You guys must be studying the mechs. Trying to figure out what's going wrong."

"Up to this point, the mechs hadn't been a major priority," he replies. "Not with a whole planet still recovering from biological warfare. But now I'm going to take a more in-depth look at our malfunctioning Tares."

Ephraim stares at the window for a moment, and Noemi just watches him. After more than two days stuck in a biobed, even watching someone stare counts as entertainment.

She remembers meeting him at the hospital on Stronghold, the first time she was his patient. His imposing size and deep voice might've been intimidating if he hadn't been so kind to her during her illness—so warm and caring, unlike virtually anyone else on Stronghold. It turned out that his mother had been a soldier, one marooned on Genesis in the early days of the war, while she was pregnant. The people of Genesis had taken mercy on her and sent her home unharmed. So when he'd realized Noemi was a soldier of Genesis, he hadn't reported her to the authorities. Instead, Ephraim had risked his freedom to get her to safety.

"Do you regret it?" she asks.

He frowns in bemusement. "The ion surge?"

"No—I meant, back when we met, when you saved me and Abel from being arrested in the hospital on Stronghold." The memory of Abel in that hospital, holding her hand, pretending to be her husband... She'd give so much to hold his hand again.

"Saving us cost you your whole life there," Noemi continues. "Do you ever regret it?"

Ephraim shakes his head no. "That was a debt of honor. Genesis saved my mother's life; I saved a soldier of Genesis. As for the rest of it—well, I joined up with Remedy before I'd ever laid eyes on you. You don't join a resistance group without accepting that sooner or later, your life's going to be turned upside down. In my case, it happened to be sooner." A small smile appears on his full lips. "It's been one hell of a ride."

"Yeah. It has." Swooping through the mouth of a caldera to rescue Virginia. Running through snowdrifts to escape from Haven. Riding out the crash of the *Osiris*. Mansfield kidnapping Abel. Curling up with Abel in long-abandoned crew quarters to watch his favorite movie from the twentieth century, something called *Casablanca.*

Burying Esther in Kismet's star so she could warm and illuminate an entire world.

Quaking in the corridor of an unfamiliar ship, holding a blaster on the verge of dying, when the mech who'd been trying to kill her strolled up, introduced himself, and asked for his orders.

"Maybe it's a hardware problem," Ephraim says, bringing Noemi back to the here and now. "Maybe Shearer's technology wasn't quite ready yet. Maybe she hadn't tested it enough before she implanted it into you."

"Of course she'd tested it. Abel told me Shearer was trying to win investors from all over the world with her fantastic new organic-mech creations. Do you think she'd do that if she couldn't actually build the mechs?"

Ephraim stares at her for a long second, then does the last thing she would've expected: He starts to laugh.

She must look stricken, because he pulls himself together quickly. "Sorry, sorry. It's just—even now that I've spent a while on Genesis, I forget that this isn't really a capitalist society. If it were, you'd know that *hell, yeah,* Gillian Shearer would try to sell a product she hadn't perfected yet. That's how she'd get the money to perfect it. Assuming she could. If she couldn't—well, she'd still have the investors' money."

Capitalism sounds like a huge, confusing mess, and Noemi's glad she hasn't had much to do with it. "Shearer seemed to believe in herself pretty strongly. She believed even more in her father, to a degree that couldn't be rational." She struggles for the right words. "We're a society of faith, here on Genesis. But we're also a society of tolerance. That means accepting that not everyone will believe in precisely the same way we do. We're taught to guard against—I guess you'd call it zealotry. Believing that your way is the only way."

"I don't get it," Ephraim admits. "If you believe, don't you *have* to think your way is the only way?"

"Not at all. The opposite of faith isn't doubt. The opposite of faith is certainty." She told Abel that once; she feels the truth of it even more strongly now. Her catechism teacher would be proud of her, Noemi thinks, which would be the first time that stiff-necked guy had ever been proud of her for anything. "Human certainty is an illusion. Ultimate knowledge belongs to the divine. Being humble before God means accepting that you may not possess the only path to Him."

Ephraim doesn't quite know what to do with this, and she doesn't blame him. This is the closest she's ever come to preaching at her friends from other planets, something she absolutely doesn't want to do. But he needed to understand this to get what she has to say next. "Shearer doesn't have any doubts. Not about herself, her dad, their self-proclaimed mission, any of it."

"So what you're saying is, we won't get any help from a repentant Gillian Shearer," Ephraim says.

"We wouldn't have anyway." Which is true. But admitting how far she is from any answers, any help, just makes Noemi feel even more afraid.

The only person who might be able to deduce the real problem is Abel, the one person she'll never see again.

●　●　●

That evening, the hospital informs Noemi she has two visitors. Her condition has been stable long enough for her doctors to clear her for the public visiting area. Noemi slips into a cream-colored robe and pads down the hallway, holding on to Ephraim's arm for support. She's pleased that Harriet and Zayan must've come back to see her, although she would've thought Virginia would bring them directly to her room.

She walks into the visiting area looking for them. Instead, at one of the long white tables, she sees Mr. and Mrs. Gatson.

They were Esther's parents, and her own foster parents. It seems like she ought to be closer to the people who took her in after her mom, dad, and baby brother died. But Noemi thinks it would be easier for her to talk to complete strangers.

Once she takes her seat across from them, she gives Mrs. Gatson an uneven smile. "I'm glad you're okay," Noemi says. "When I was here last—we weren't sure."

"I'd been put in a medical coma," Mrs. Gatson says

briskly. "Records weren't kept in an orderly fashion during the worst of the epidemic, so I had to wake up before anyone knew who and where I was."

Mr. Gatson leans forward. "If you hadn't brought our world the cure, we might never have found her." Mrs. Gatson presses her lips together into a thin line; it's like she's embarrassed they have to get into the subject at all. Her husband might be here to express gratitude, but she certainly isn't.

"I guess you've heard what happened to me?" Noemi ventures. She can't imagine why else they'd be here.

Both of them nod. Mr. Gatson looks worried; Mrs. Gatson seems oddly... satisfied.

It's Mr. Gatson who speaks. "They can get this mechanical stuff out of you, can't they? I can't imagine how sickening it must be."

"*Half mech.*" Mrs. Gatson spits the words out like they were snake venom she'd sucked from a wound.

"We're trying to figure out how to handle it," Noemi says, which is the simplest version of the truth.

Mr. Gatson shakes his head. "When they told you what had happened, you must have felt so violated."

"I did, at first," she admits. It feels surprisingly good, being wholly open with him. That rarely happened before. "I'm getting used to it now, though. Whatever malfunction I'm dealing with—hopefully we can get past that, and then I can continue adapting."

Very carefully, Mr. Gatson asks, "You mean...you don't mind being turned into a mech?"

"Half mech," Noemi says. "I'd never have chosen this of my own free will. But it was an emergency. Abel did this to save my life. Without my mech half, I'd be dead."

Mrs. Gatson's pale, steely eyes meet hers. "There are fates worse than death."

Which means: *I'd rather you'd have been killed.*

Mr. Gatson must've heard it the exact same way Noemi did, because his face goes pale. His fingers close around his wife's forearm like he's holding her back. "I guess a lot of decisions are still being made. We don't get any say in them. But we wanted you to know, Noemi—" He pauses, then drops the act. "I wanted you to know that I hope you'll be well and happy soon, no matter what that might look like."

Tears well in her eyes. "Thank you." When their eyes meet, she and her foster dad finally experience one moment of true grace.

Mrs. Gatson turns her head toward the nearest chronometer, checking to see if it's time to leave yet.

• • •

Her foster dad's warmth is more surprising than her foster mom's coldness. As Noemi curls up to go to sleep, she thinks about Esther. She'd always wanted Noemi to be more truly a member of the family. Wherever Esther's soul is now, she's happy that Noemi and Mr. Gatson finally came together for a moment.

The next morning proves bleaker. Muscle spasms rack her limbs, and her headache throbs with every beat of her heart. Worse is the loneliness. The longing.

Where are you, Abel? I bet you'd know what's wrong with me. You could figure it out faster than all the human doctors put together. Noemi closes her eyes, thinking of the malfunctioning mechs they ran into on Stronghold and Haven. *Is it some kind of software virus, something spreading among mechs the way Cobweb spreads among people?*

If it's an epidemic among the mechs, then this could affect Abel, too. There's literally nowhere in the galaxy he could go to be safe.

Her comm unit chimes, and she taps the screen to answer. Maybe it's Virginia or Ephraim, updating her about their research—

But it isn't. Instead, she sees the gaunt face of Elder Cho. Behind him are the green banners of the Council chamber; this is official business.

"Elder Cho." Noemi inclines her head in respect. "To what do I owe the honor?"

Cho's face might as well be a mask. *"It has been previously determined by this Council that no mech shall ever be allowed residency on Genesis."*

Why are they calling to tell her *again* that Abel can't live here, especially since Abel's nowhere around?

Then realization strikes. Her frustration vanishes, leaving behind nothing but cold, numb shock. Noemi can only stare at Elder Cho as he continues, *"Due to your recent modifications, we have determined that you've essentially become another form of mech. Therefore your presence on Genesis cannot be tolerated. You must leave the planet immediately."*

"But—" Noemi swallows hard. "I was born here—my parents, my brother, they died in the Liberty War—I *fought* for Genesis! I fought in battle after battle, I volunteered for a *suicide mission*, I brought you the cure for Cobweb and a fleet of ships to fight with, and—"

"Noemi Vidal did these things," Cho says impassively. *"She was a great hero, in her way. But she was a human, one who no longer exists."*

They don't understand, because they won't. Zealotry never recognizes itself. She can't get through to them; she can only plead for mercy. "I'm sick. Dr. Dunaway's working on a treatment. If we don't find one in time—" She swallows hard. "If we don't, I could die."

Elder Cho doesn't flinch. "Noemi Vidal is already dead."

24

ABEL COULD FREE THE *PERSEPHONE* FROM THE TRACTOR beam of many different types of ships—virtually all non-military vessels, and approximately 66.86 percent of military ships as well. His ship was outfitted with top-level technology when it was built more than thirty years ago; he's updated it considerably in the past few months.

Unfortunately, the Genesis ship dragging him along is using tractor-beam tech that's fully half a century old. The mechanism is old-fashioned and not nearly as efficient—but it operates on a completely different system than Abel's ship does, which makes him powerless against it.

It is, he thinks, like being capable of breaking through any electronic lock in existence, only to be bound in iron chains.

So Abel's forced to simply wait as the *Persephone* is dragged through space—past Cray, past Stronghold—all the way back to Genesis.

He's not completely without hope. If he could escape from Gillian Shearer's lab on Haven, he can escape from Genesis. If Noemi has been taken to Genesis, as seems likely, she would no doubt try to help him.

Even if she thinks he's less than human in some way, Noemi would never ever abandon him to such a bleak fate.

However, for all Gillian's delusions of grandeur, she was in the end only one person, controlling one small town and a finite number of mechs. The Winter Castle's security has limits. Genesis, on the other hand, is an entire planet, its people hardened by decades of war. Even in the aftermath of the Cobweb plague, Genesis can field a strong military presence in space and on the ground. They will be harder to elude.

But perhaps not impossible.

Wait, he tells himself as they make their way through the outskirts of the Earth system. He's in his quarters, between repeat viewings of *Casablanca.* (He considers this the best way to kill time in captivity: watching your favorite movie while planning to escape.) *Wait for your chance. It could appear at any time, and you must be ready to seize it—*

At that moment the *Persephone* shudders.

Abel sits upright, evaluates the potential causes of strain, and then pauses the movie's playback at the first frame of Rick walking into the Blue Parrot. At full cyborg speed, he dashes back to the bridge.

On the viewscreen he sees the Genesis ship that took him captive in the middle of a firefight with another—a new one, but familiar in its design—

Out loud, Abel murmurs, "Remedy."

Remedy and Genesis are supposedly allies—but that alliance is between Genesis and the more moderate wing of Remedy. Ephraim's group. They don't speak for the entire movement.

It's instantly apparent that the Genesis vessel is outgunned. They hang on, though, fighting against the odds; he'd expect no less of soldiers who've endured the Liberty War.

He also expects them to lose, which means he's about to be free.

Remedy is a large resistance organization, leaderless, comprised of different wings with different philosophies; the various cells agree only that Earth's dominion over the planets must end. It began as a group of doctors who had realized the truth behind the Cobweb design—that it was designed by Earth and released deliberately into the galactic population long before the full risks were understood. Since that beginning, however, Remedy has expanded greatly. Some cells are more radical, more violent. Many have bombed public facilities on the various worlds, stooping to terrorism to accomplish their goals.

Given the armaments on this particular ship, Abel

suspects he's more likely to encounter Remedy terrorists than Remedy physicians. Either way, he's much more likely to be set free, or at least get the opportunity to escape. He disapproves of Remedy's terrorist actions, but he's in no position to quibble with the ideology of his liberators.

Finally the Genesis ship takes one hit too many. A faint wobble shakes the *Persephone*, which Abel instantly recognizes as the tractor beam's release. As the Genesis ship retreats, he takes his position at navigator, ready to set a new course to—well, he's not sure yet, but absolutely anywhere else.

Before he can do more than put his hands on the controls, another tractor beam seizes the *Persephone*.

Remedy has freed Abel from Genesis only to capture him in turn.

This is troubling, but also confusing. Remedy cannot be taking Abel captive for the same reasons the *Katara* did; they, too, have an alliance with Genesis, but if that was the Remedy ship's motivation, they would simply have left the *Persephone* under Genesis control.

Abel activates comms. "*Persephone* to Remedy vessel," he says, keeping his voice neutral. "Please state your business."

A visual signal appears on the viewscreen, revealing a face Abel knows. "*I suspected we might meet again. I never suspected it would be like this.*"

Abel greets this man in turn. "Captain Fouda."

Fouda led the terrorist cell of Remedy that attacked the *Osiris* and forced a crash landing on the surface of Haven. Remedy didn't yet know that Cobweb treatments were necessary to survive on that planet, which meant that most of Fouda's people died within days—including Riko Watanabe, the member of that cell who came closest to being their friend.

(Abel never condoned Riko's actions, but he understood the deprivation she'd come from. Her sense of justice had become warped, but she sincerely believed she was doing the right thing.)

But Fouda ought to feel *some* loyalty toward Abel. "Noemi and I negotiated with Gillian Shearer on your behalf," he says evenly. "We made sure the Remedy survivors would be welcomed into the Winter Castle. If Gillian failed to honor her end of the bargain—it would be unjust to blame us."

"*Shearer followed through,*" Fouda says heavily. He doesn't seem surprised to see Abel, which under the circumstances is rather strange. "*I blame you for nothing. But there are other members of Remedy who need homes on Haven—those our doctor friends look down upon, and are reluctant to welcome to Genesis.*"

By this Fouda means other terrorists.

"*She released me,*" Fouda continues, "*and promised to give Cobweb treatments to all the Remedy members who need it. Her only condition was that I . . . run an errand for her.*"

There's no need to ask what that "errand" is. Abel has already run through forty-one potential scenarios, and needs to run no more, because the most probable answer is clear. "Gillian bargained with you for treatments for the others," he says. "And I'm the price."

Fouda nods. "It's one I have to pay."

Both Fouda and Krall have thought of their people and not themselves. This should seem admirable, utterly benign.

Instead, in the name of what these people consider to be the common good, Abel has to die.

● ● ●

They make it through the frenzy at the Haven Gate swiftly; Earth seems almost to have given up trying to police the area. Fouda's ship tows the *Persephone* back through the Gate, through the system, into the atmosphere of Haven itself.

Abel could attempt to free his ship from the tractor beam, but Fouda's vessel has a far stronger tractor than most. The stress levels could well shatter the *Persephone*. Better to wait, and see if another opportunity arises.

So he simply watches their journey via the viewscreen as they arrive on Haven. On the horizon he sees the outline of the Winter Castle. Its pristine walls and many defenses have only slightly protected it from the enormous wave of change sweeping over Haven.

All around the Castle is an enormous bustling settlement that he can only think of as the "suburbs." These newcomers must originally have hoped to be taken inside, counting on a level of generosity Gillian Shearer doesn't have. That, or they hoped to conquer the Winter Castle for themselves, which means they weren't counting on a level of defense Gillian Shearer *does* have.

Since both those efforts failed, they've done the next best thing, and the smartest: They've completely surrounded the Winter Castle, so that anyone from the inside who wants to travel over ground will have to go through them. Going through them will mean getting permission. Getting permission means negotiating for some of the assets inside.

No matter how well provisioned or insulated they are, the residents of the Winter Castle can't stay within its walls forever. Someday they'll have to deal with these people; they'll have to rejoin the greater human society they tried so hard to reject. The few survivors of Remedy within the Castle must already be pushing for it.

Maybe there's no poetic justice for Abel, but there will be for the passengers of the *Osiris*.

Fouda drags Abel's ship well into the zone around the Winter Castle, very nearly to its border, where a checkpoint has been set up. As the *Persephone* settles into the snow, Abel heads down to the launching bay, preparing himself to fight if given the chance.

But he isn't.

When the bay door pinwheels open, a flurry of snow-flakes swirl in on the chilly breeze. Through that scattering of snow, Abel can see six Remedy members, each armed with blasters pointed directly at him. Behind them stands Captain Fouda, who looks unhappy but even more determined.

"She'd prefer to have you undamaged," Fouda says.

"I'm sure she would." Gillian needs to bring her father back into a body that's in perfect working order. For 1.13 seconds, Abel considers rushing the soldiers, forcing them to fire on him. Maybe he'd take so much damage the transfer would be impossible.

But Gillian would only repair him. There are disadvantages to being so hard to kill.

So Abel steps forward, allows his hands to be put in energy cuffs, and is led onto the surface, into the checkpoint zone.

Stretching out around this area, in every direction, is a vast camp composed of small ships, makeshift tents, temporary shelters being adapted for more permanent use, and dirt paths tramped down from the snow, in some places lined with stones on either side.

Fouda's team leads him toward the largest structure nearby, one situated near what looks like the primary entrance to the Winter Castle. This is more than a mere way station, however; the tented structure is bustling with activity. They step through the heavy, transparent tent flaps that serve as a door, and at one glance Abel recognizes this as a field hospital.

"We need more plasma in quadrant C," calls someone in the distance, which sends a woman hustling in that direction with a heavy crate in her arms. Makeshift bunks, seemingly created from former benches pulled out of their ships, lie in long lines under a thin roof supported only by poles. It looks flimsy at first. But the snow walls around the perimeter effectively cut the wind, and small solar energy pods have been distributed to ensure the entire building is reasonably warm.

"We need to bargain for a Tare," huffs the man who appears to be in charge, to his assistant. "We've been able to estimate the pediatric doses so far, but the tinier babies— we *have* to be precise, which means we need a Tare."

"More than one, if we can get it," pipes up a girl—no, a woman, albeit one so small, with such a high-pitched voice, that she could easily be taken for a child. Unlike the Vagabonds, who are wrapped in bulky patchwork coats sewn from various blankets, this woman is wrapped in a padded cloak of silvery velvet. "Shearer's got plenty of those, and she can spare a few. The only reason she hasn't traded them already is because she wants to break us down." Then she sighs. "I guess she probably still wants to break us down.

But she needs supplies, and access, and sooner or later, something's got to give."

The man in charge—a doctor, it seems—stares at this young woman with her halo of dark curls, then nods. "I hope we can trust you, Ms. Ondimba."

"You can," she says. "You'll see."

The name Ondimba is familiar to Abel. He pulls up the reference within 1.102 seconds: Noemi mentioned a Delphine Ondimba among the passengers on the *Osiris*. Most of those passengers were pampered and coddled, and thus useless when Remedy's terrorist wing attacked. According to Noemi, Delphine Ondimba had been the exception. She'd kept her wits about her, even devising a clever way to track their ship's journey from within a cargo hold.

"What is a passenger from the *Osiris* doing outside the Winter Castle?" Abel asks her. Fouda's men stare at him, but they don't try to stop the conversation.

"How did you know—oh." Delphine answers her own question by holding out her velvet cloak sleeves. "Only a couple dozen of us have left so far, but trust me, there's going to be more. Life in there is—it's unbearable."

"A life of unending elegance and privilege has become unbearable?" Abel stifles a smirk. It sounds as though Gillian Shearer's best-laid plans have gone awry.

"*Awful*," Delphine says with emphasis. She sits on the edge of an empty cot, looking slightly shell-shocked by the enormity of misery and want that surrounds them in this hospital. "Some people became disillusioned as soon as the *Osiris* crashed. I mean, after that, nobody was under any illusion that Mansfield or Shearer were as infallible as they claimed to be. We thought we'd be ushered in here by mechs ready to pamper us after the trip, you know? Instead, we had to hike here through the snow, *four whole kilometers*. We had enough mechs to carry the injured, but that meant we had to tow our possessions along with us— at least, the ones that survived the crash landing."

Only someone who had led an extraordinarily easy life would consider "walking with luggage" to be a great travail. Abel says only, "And after you reached the Winter Castle?"

"That's when the real problems started," Delphine says. "We were supposed to sit back and relax! Amuse ourselves all day long! Eat gourmet delicacies at every meal!"

"This is not what most people would describe as 'a problem,'" Abel replies.

"It isn't, for the first couple of days." Delphine sighs. "After that? It's just boring. I wanted to do something interesting—something *useful*. So did most other people. I thought I'd like simple food to eat, at least for a meal or two. I wanted to feel like I could touch something without leaving fingerprints all over it. The existence Mansfield dreamed up for us...it wasn't a life. Honestly, it felt like we were his pets in some enormous terrarium."

Abel's not surprised. "His psychology sometimes suggested that Professor Mansfield thought he was the only real person in the world, and the rest of us are only…puppets. Mechs and humans both." His own place in Mansfield's psyche is unique, Abel thinks, but perhaps not so different from the man's general attitude toward others.

Delphine gives him an odd look, perhaps wondering how he knows Mansfield that well, but she continues her story. "Then the Vagabond ships started landing, and people began getting sick. We wanted to help them, but Gillian absolutely wouldn't allow it. I mean, how cold can you be?"

"You *were* going to keep Haven a secret from the rest of the galaxy," Abel points out. "How different is that from what Gillian has done?"

This earns him a scowl. "Maybe Mansfield and Shearer thought they could keep a planet secret forever. Me? I figured there was no way we wouldn't be found eventually. Most of the others did, too. We just wanted a head start, you know?"

Abel doubts most of the other passengers' intentions were so benign. However, Delphine Ondimba seems sincere.

She continues, "Well, anyway, a bunch of us decided we'd had it. When we saw the Vagabond towns forming, we figured, if you can't beat 'em, join 'em." Delphine gestures around the field hospital, her smile tremulous. "Not that I have any idea what I'm supposed to be doing. Or where our food is going to be coming from. But—but we can make Shearer negotiate, and we're damn sure going to!"

Fouda finally speaks. "Now we have something to bargain with."

All the other Vagabonds in the field hospital seem to notice Abel's energy cuffs in the same instant. Some of them look alarmed; others look angry. "You said you were joining us!" Delphine cries. "That you'd come out to join forces with us—"

"Which in a sense I have." Fouda remains undaunted. "Gillian Shearer is no friend of mine. If she were, I'd have walked Abel straight in there. She's already offered me Cobweb treatments in exchange for him—but I see no reason not to up the price."

The man in charge of the hospital huffs, "If you think we're about to start trading human beings to Shearer—handing over our own—"

"This is no human," Fouda says. "It's a mech, and Shearer wants it."

Delphine Ondimba gasps in recognition. "I thought you looked familiar! You look like Professor Mansfield. *So much* like him! You have to be the mech Mansfield and Shearer were so desperate to get their hands on right after the *Osiris* crashed. What did they call you? Model One A?"

"I prefer Abel. And I suggest you negotiate with Gillian for whatever it is you need most. Ask for a working Tare model, and doses of the Cobweb protocol, and anything else you can think of." Abel squares his shoulders. "Trust me. She'll make the trade."

He accepts where he is, what's going to happen. What other option does he have? To run away, setting up a pursuit that would probably get many Vagabonds killed? To escape this planet and system, only to have the Krall Consortium drag him back here again? It appears that the fate Burton Mansfield designed for Abel is finally at hand.

This way, he'll be able to save lives. There will be those who'll remember him as a hero. At least his death will have some meaning.

If Noemi ever comes back here, Delphine will tell her we met. She'll say that I went to Shearer bravely, that I prioritized the welfare of others above my own. Of course Noemi knows Abel would do this. But he likes to think of her hearing it, of his courage being revealed to the one person who matters most.

Even that doesn't take away the sting of knowing that Burton Mansfield has finally won.

25

THE AUTHORITIES DO THIS MUCH FOR A SOLDIER OF Genesis who's seriously, maybe fatally, ill: They send her a transport to the nearest spaceport and give her a few hours to leave her homeland forever.

Noemi slowly walks across the tarmac. Balance requires concentration. Her bones ache as though someone had injected liquid oxygen into her marrow to freeze it solid, and the buzzing in her head is somewhere between "sinus infection" and "swarm of bees."

Look on the bright side, she tells herself. *You own absolutely nothing but the clothes on your back. So at least you don't have to carry any luggage?*

She sighs. Looking on the bright side isn't one of her core skills.

The landing pad designation on her dataread takes her to a small, unfamiliar vessel, one she's never seen before. It's about half the size of the *Persephone*, a sloping gray oval of a ship with a tiny cockpit. To judge by that and the modest engines, Noemi would guess that this ship is mostly meant to ferry cargo from deep-space ships to planets and back again—not to travel through multiple Gates to various worlds.

But the *Apollo Acestor* is the only ship Remedy could spare, and she knows she's lucky even to get that.

As she approaches the *Apollo Acestor*, Ephraim steps out. He's still wearing the pale blue robes of a Genesis physician, but he's got a rucksack over one shoulder that she'd bet contains spacefaring gear. When he sees Noemi, he hurries to her side. "What are you thinking? I told you I'd come by the hospital and get you."

Noemi sighs. "I decided to go ahead and take the transport the Elders offered me, before they thought better of it and banned me from public transit. Then you might've had to carry me piggyback all the way here."

"I could handle a piggyback ride!" he insists. "You *have* to be careful not to push yourself too hard."

"I'm just walking." She doesn't say that "just walking" takes all her effort. Ephraim already knows. "Did you get all the permissions you needed from the Council? You're sure you can return to Genesis whenever you want?"

He grins. "The Council said they'd 'leave it up to Remedy leadership' to decide whether I should be allowed back after helping an 'enemy mech.' The way they said it made me think they wanted Remedy to be the bad guys who'd tell me never to come back. Apparently they forgot that I kind of *am* Remedy leadership—as far as we have any."

The loose web of rebel cells that comprises Remedy includes people from several different planets and with many different philosophies, from humanitarian physicians to violent terrorists. Nobody's in charge. When their spacecraft came together to defend her planet from biological warfare, their spokesperson was chosen almost at random—but Ephraim Dunaway's the guy they chose.

More gently, he adds, "Don't worry, okay? I can return if I want to." His tone of voice tells her that he does want to— soon, and maybe for good. After growing up on cold, hostile Stronghold, then breathing Earth's smoggy air while living undercover, he must see Genesis as a paradise.

The thing is, Noemi does, too. Even now, when she's being cast out forever, Genesis seems to her to be the closest thing to heaven.

She gazes toward the distance, where the grasslands begin. When they were little, she and Esther would chase each other through the tall grasses outside Goshen, the soft rushing sounds of it broken only by their laughter. Noemi had sometimes imagined taking Abel there; she had a daydream of them flirting, laughing, playing chase. He'd probably ask what the point of playing chase even was, but maybe he'd figure it out after he caught her....

Ephraim's forehead furrows with concern. "Hey. You okay?"

Noemi hopes he's only worried about her physical health. The thought of him seeing how sad she is and pitying her—it makes her cringe. "Sure. Well, I'm the same. That's going to have to count as 'okay' for now."

"I'm setting up regenerative equipment in the *Apollo Acestor* lab." He pats her shoulder as the two of them begin walking up the gangway into the ship. "It's not like we have tons to work with in here, but I think we can at least keep your condition from getting any worse for a while. That buys us some time to figure out what's really going on."

They step into the ship, which feels cramped and dark inside. As Noemi's eyes adjust, she realizes the tiny bay is already almost filled by her freshly repaired starfighter. Two legs stick out from under it, surrounded by tools.

"No offense," Virginia says, her voice slightly muffled, "but your planet is kind of boring. Gorgeous! But boring. You think I'm going to stay anyplace that doesn't stock the latest Han Zhi holos? Not likely. So I'm grabbing the first ride off this rock."

Noemi has to swallow hard before she can answer. "It's dangerous for you to leave Genesis. On Cray you could be arrested—"

"We're not headed to Cray." Virginia skims out from beneath the corsair, lying on her back. The slim hoverboard beneath her causes enough static for a few strands of her hair to float around. "Wait. *Are* we headed to Cray? Because if so, tell me now. I like to avoid active arrest warrants."

"You know we're not headed to Cray," Noemi says.

"Yeah, I know." Virginia's wide grin changes to a scowl. "You're not going to get mushy about this, are you? Because this isn't one hundred percent selfless. Genesis really isn't the best place for me. I might not know where that best place is, exactly, but it's going to involve way more tech. So I'm only being, like, eighty-nine percent selfless. You should still be in awe of my saintly nature, but—"

Noemi drops to her knees and hugs Virginia. She has to be careful with the hug—it's difficult for her to judge her strength—but she does her best.

Virginia murmurs, "I tried to save two of my friends and failed. I'm not going to fail anyone else."

"You've *never* failed me." Noemi's throat is tight. "You never would."

"All right, all right," Virginia says gruffly as she pushes Noemi back. "But I've hit my mush limit for the day."

A knock on the entry ramp makes them all look around to see someone walking on board. "Captain Baz?" Noemi asks in wonder. "What are you doing here? Just—saying good-bye?" She always liked the captain, but she'd never imagined Baz took such a personal interest in her.

"Actually, I was hoping to have a word with you." Baz's

dark eyes flicker over to Ephraim, then to Virginia. To her, they're offworlders—not people she's ready to trust.

"Uh, sure. Come with me." Noemi leads Baz into the *Apollo Acestor*, which lets her take her own look around. There's not much besides a basic bridge/engine room combo, a tiny mess hall, and crew quarters so tiny they make military bunks look luxurious. The mess seems as good a place as any for a conference.

As they sit at the one table, Baz says intently, "Word has it you're one of the people who helped obtain the engine for—for Bellum Sanctum."

"Yep, that's me," Noemi says. "Obtainer of the engine for the plan that's supposed to end the Liberty War for good. And still, the Council's throwing me off my own planet."

But Yasmeen Baz doesn't look like she's here to share her anger at the injustice. Her expression is unfamiliar, because Noemi's never seen it on her captain's face before. It's fear.

Quietly Noemi says, "Darius Akide attacked Abel because he wanted to use him to close the Gate. I've been thinking about it, and if Akide realized Bellum Sanctum was a possibility after the Battle of Genesis, he was still willing to commit murder and close the Gate forever. That suggests Akide didn't want to use the Bellum Sanctum strategy. So that makes me believe that the strategy is something besides a communications scramble." She pauses, then adds the fear she's hardly even dared think inside her own head, much less speak aloud. "That it's something terrible."

"You've always been sharp, Vidal—I mean, Noemi." By now Baz's voice is hardly more than a whisper. "Are you familiar with core disruptor technology?"

Noemi blinks. "I think so. But that's not weaponry, is it? It's a machine that digs deeply into a space object and then explodes it completely. That's how miners blow up larger asteroids, to get at the ores inside."

"Most of the time, yes." Baz fiddles with the loose edge of her headscarf, betraying her nervousness. "Once, however, Earth tried to use a core disruptor as a weapon. Despite heavy resistance from our troops, they were able to place an unprecedentedly large disruptor deep within a cave on our moon Bodhi. The goal was to destroy it."

"Wait. Earth was going to blow up *a moon*?" The repercussions are as obvious as they are horrifying. "How much of that debris would've rained down on us from outer space? People would've been killed! The climate would've been—"

"Substantially altered for a generation or two," Baz says, nodding. "Which Earth preferred to avoid—they've always wanted to start moving people onto Genesis immediately. But this was their last-ditch weapon. If they'd used it, the population on Genesis would have been reduced to a fraction of its former self, unable to fight back. Our environment would've healed within fifty to seventy-five years—in time for Earth's population to finally claim it as their own. When the tide of battle turned, and we were able to push Earth mostly out of our system—that's when they tried to use the core disruptor."

After Earth's use of biological warfare, Noemi had thought nothing that world could do would ever again shock her with its evil. She was wrong. "But Earth's plan failed. The core disruptor didn't destroy Bodhi."

"No," Baz says. "A Genesis team was able to deactivate it in time. The disruptor remained deep within the cave on Bodhi, still intact. It only lacked power. This engine, the one brought to us from the Kismet system—it's more than strong enough to power the disruptor again."

No. It can't be. Noemi rises to her feet and backs away from Baz, as though the distance would somehow get her farther away from this terrible truth. "You mean—" Her mouth is dry, and she has to swallow before she can finish speaking. "Genesis intends to use the core disruptor against Earth's moon?" *But that's one of the largest moons in any solar system—it plays a huge role in Earth's weather— its destruction would be even more terrible for Earth than Bodhi's would've been for Genesis—*

"They don't plan to use it against Earth's moon," Baz

says. "The Bellum Sanctum strategy would use the disruptor against Earth itself."

The leadership of Genesis means to destroy Earth.

Noemi slumps against the wall. Tears well in Baz's eyes. This is a horror too great for any words. It is a sin beyond redemption—Second Catholic catechism would say such a thing is impossible, but Noemi now believes that part of the catechism is wrong. No god in any theology would forgive this depth of evil.

And I gave them the engine to do it, she thinks, sickened to the point of dizziness. *Abel and I risked our lives for this. For the murder of billions of people. For the destruction of everything beautiful that humanity has ever built. For the extinction of every animal and plant that's managed to hold on through their environments' devastation. For the greatest crime human beings have ever known.*

No wonder Darius Akide was willing to commit murder to stop this from happening. He was exchanging two lives— Abel's and mine—for the lives of billions.

Finally, Noemi manages to say, "As much as Earth is hated, I can't believe anyone would agree to go through with this."

"No, you're right. That's why the plan is top secret. My squadron's been chosen to escort the core disruptor into the Earth system and aim it at the ocean floor; that's the only reason I know." Baz turns her teary eyes toward the ceiling. "We were congratulated for earning this 'incredible honor.' I could protest—pull us off the assignment—but then, if there's any chance of stopping this thing, I want to be there. I want to play a role."

"We can stop it?" Noemi gasps as she seizes on this brief hope.

"I don't know," Baz admits. "There are other escort squadrons, too. But if anyone else can create a diversion—or find allies for us—"

"I'll do it," Noemi promises, without hesitation. She has no idea how to do this. She's not even sure she'll be alive in another few days, if this mech virus or whatever it is keeps wreaking havoc with her innards. But she'll fight for this to her last breath. "When do they plan to bring the core disruptor to the Earth system?"

"They're still installing the new engine, which buys us time—but the current timeline suggests we'll go through the Genesis Gate with it in eight days." Baz shakes her head in dismay. "Did you ever think we'd be defending Earth against Genesis?"

"We're not defending Earth. We're defending *Genesis*," Noemi insists. Her Directive One remains intact; at this moment, it feels stronger than ever. "Not Earth. If we won the Liberty War like this—Genesis wouldn't just be destroying Earth. We'd be destroying ourselves. Our culture, everything we hold sacred...after Bellum Sanctum, all of that would only be empty words."

"You're right," Baz says. Then she repeats it, as if to convince herself, "You're absolutely right."

It's unbelievable, but true. Noemi murmurs, "The only way we can save our way of life...is to save Earth."

26

ABEL COULD TEAR THROUGH ANY PHYSICAL RESTRAINT, but the small energy bands on the biobed gurney hold him firmly in place. So he can only lie still and stare up at the ceiling as he's hauled back into Gillian Shearer's laboratory.

Gillian sits at the far edge of the lab at her desk. It remains as brightly, fiercely white as he remembered: ceiling, walls, floor, even the desk. The harsh light from overhead reveals how thin her red hair is and makes her look haggard. Then again, Abel muses, anyone who'd endured what she had in the past year would look haggard: She'd left her home planet for good, crashed on a completely different planet, and is now trying to hold on to absolute power from a cramped laboratory, despite dwindling support. Hundreds of thousands, if not millions, of people are landing on this planet, and it won't be long before they notice how many vital resources the Winter Castle is trying to hoard.

Most important of all, she lost her father. She lost her

son. Grief doesn't excuse her behavior, in Abel's opinion, but perhaps it helps explain it.

Gillian holds out her hand, and the Tare accompanying Abel's mobile biobed puts a dataread into it. The Tare is operating smoothly and effectively, with no signs of the malfunctions he's seen galaxy-wide.

Scientists say the last human sense to fade upon death is hearing. For mechs, it must be curiosity. Despite the fact that he'll never be able to use this information, Abel has to ask. "Are you aware that mechs throughout the galaxy are breaking down, while yours remain in normal working order?"

To his surprise, Gillian chuckles. She sounds eerily like her father. "Just like Dad, not to release the update before we left. Of course, he'd hoped he'd be able to deploy it himself. Now he'll have the chance."

"Update? Mechs are breaking down because they lack—an update?" Abel focuses all his concentration on this new information, rather than on what's happening to him. The word reckons back to an earlier stage of technology, centuries before, in its lawless days—"This is planned obsolescence. You've begun designing mechs *intended* to break down within a certain amount of time."

"An archaic concept, I know," Gillian says, tapping on her screen. "But it's one my father and I thought it wise to revive, before the journey of the *Osiris*. Our community on

Haven would need a way to make profit. Mansfield Cybernetics had to remain the sole source of the mechs the galaxy relies on. What better way than by making sure they'd need to come to us to keep the mechs they already have?"

The concept is both ingenious and diabolical; Abel has no trouble believing Burton Mansfield would come up with it. "I appear to be immune."

"You're unique, Abel. You've always had a singular destiny. What point would there be in my father designing his own future body to break down?" Gillian's smile has taken on the glassy, impersonal quality he's learned to fear. It's the expression of a worshipper, not a daughter. "But the planned obsolescence looks even further into the future. When we've created our Inheritors—when we alone have created and perfected the next generation of mechs—we can phase out the old ones. We'll be able to provide the galaxy with something so much better."

More mechs with souls, still bound in servitude to humanity. Abel has always been afraid for the Inheritors and the bleak future they might face, but he's suddenly seized by an even greater horror, one that even eclipses his own fate.

Noemi.

She's part mech now. Some of the software runs on the implant within her brain. Will she break down, too? She hadn't when she left the *Persephone*, but that could be due to no more than later installation of—

Gillian breaks his train of thought by adding, "My father will be able to release the updates himself, soon—assuming you're back in working order."

She taps in some command at her console. The slight tingles in Abel's head, as well as the faint silvery whispers at the very edges of his hearing, inform him of what she'll learn from the scan that's being run: His Tether is now fully functional.

"Good." Gillian sits upright, and the spark returns to her intensely blue eyes. "We can finally begin." She gets to her feet and repeats, in a reverent whisper, "Finally."

From the white pod of her desk, she draws two containers. One is a dodecahedron, faintly glowing. Abel recognizes this as the special data solid developed to hold the entirety of a human consciousness. The other is a humbler wooden box, one old enough to show some signs of wear, which must contain another data solid.

The first holds the mind of Gillian's father and Abel's creator, Burton Mansfield. The second holds her mother—at least, in theory. Mansfield's tech wasn't nearly as good at the time of Robin Mansfield's death as it is now. She died more than thirty years ago. Whatever's kept in there might not bear much resemblance to the living woman before. The few words it was able to conjure on a Ouija board appear to have proved that much.

But Gillian isn't thinking about that right now. She's

focused purely on making Abel fulfill the purpose he was made for: housing Mansfield's soul, at the cost of his own.

"Time to finish hooking you up." Gillian holds up another chilly cluster of diodes. "Just a few more applied to your skin, and we'll have full coverage."

Abel has been stripped to his underwear, which he finds somewhat undignified—not that it matters much at this point. He doesn't feel fear as much as he feels…defeated.

"It's curious," Abel says as the diodes are applied to his legs, "how enthusiastic you and your father are about immortality."

Gillian doesn't even look up at him. She's too busy with Mansfield's data solid. "My father removed your fear of mortality via your programming. It's highly unnatural, not to fear death. You can't imagine how humans feel."

"I don't have to imagine. Mansfield programmed me with data about the human psyche in all its forms." Real-life interpretation has sometimes proved trickier than the textbook examples in his head—but Abel understands the basics. "However, immortality has its own drawbacks, which you don't seem to have considered. For instance, what if you're marooned in a spaceship? Unable to escape, unable even to deactivate yourself. I made it through thirty years of that, but it was difficult. And my consciousness is wholly artificial. A more human mind…I think someone could very easily go insane."

Gillian still doesn't look up. "Getting marooned like that seems unlikely."

"Once I would've thought so, too." Abel glances at Gillian, whose head is bent over her work. While he isn't afraid, he finds that he would like someone to look him in the eye. To *see* him, during these last moments of his existence. She never glances away from the diodes.

"If that's the scariest possibility you can come up with— well, I think that conversation's over, don't you?" Her tone could now be described as "smug," which Abel considers extremely rude.

He replies, "That's not the scariest possibility. The scariest possibility is outliving anyone who may care about you. Everyone, perhaps. Without love, I think immortality could only be very bitter."

She blinks, apparently still surprised that Abel might talk about emotions. "My father will have love. He'll have me."

Abel says the hardest truth he knows: "Your father hasn't loved anyone but himself for a long time."

Gillian finally looks at him then. The porcelain mask of indifference is broken; her hand trembles, but she keeps her firm grip on the data solid. "You don't understand," she says.

But he does. Abel realizes that Gillian believes this act will at long last win her father's love. There was a time he wanted that love, too. He couldn't help but want it. On some level he still does, even though he's learned Burton Mansfield's love is a prize not worth having. That's the nature of children, when it comes to their fathers.

His father never did love him. Now Abel's existence will end, for the pleasure of an egomaniac who felt entitled to more than one life.

What was the point of gaining consciousness, living independently, striking out on his own if it only led to this?

Then Abel thinks of Noemi. She was the point. She still is. She was worth it.

Gillian places the data solid in a reader, which begins to glow. Abel feels a faint tingle along the diodes. This is it.

What should his last words be?

"I was lucky," he says, surprising himself. Yet instantly he knows those were the right words. He's been so lucky just to exist. Just to have experienced the universe.

Gillian pays no attention. "Initializing," she says, and—

The room goes gray. Then it vanishes, not into blackness but into memory. Light seems to blaze in front of Abel, meaningless until he realizes where he is: back in the basement laboratory in London, the place where he was born. He can feel the pink goo dripping from him, remember the faint itch of his skin as his neurons came online.

Another flash of light—

"There you go," Mansfield says, watching Abel tentatively *begin pedaling a bicycle. "Let's see those reflexes at work."*

Balancing is a more complex skill than his programming suggested it would be, but Abel can do it. He pedals faster, then faster, until he's zooming down a hill. This is... this must be what humans call fun. Maybe his creator could come up with a way to allow mechs to fly—bioengineered wings, perhaps—

Light swirls around him again, dizzying in its intensity.

Amid a raid by the German authorities, Captain Renault says, "I am shocked, shocked to find that gambling is going on in here!"

At that moment a waiter appears at his side. "Your winnings, sir."

Renault easily replies, "Oh, thank you very much." Abel laughs out loud.

"You're learning how to respond to narratives," Mansfield murmurs. *"Good, good."* His hand flicks toward the screen, turning off Casablanca *as though there could be no reason to continue. Abel is disappointed, but makes plans to sneak up here at night to watch the rest of the movie.*

Light. Movement.

"Captain Gee?" Abel floats in zero gravity, pushing the comm panel within the equipment pod bay for the fourth time. "Dr. Mansfield? The air locks have closed. Power is offline to the pod bay."

The small windows in the bay reveal the greenish flash of weapons from the furious space battle being waged just outside. The Daedalus *has been hit—Abel can deduce that if*

*nothing else—but how badly? Is Mansfield dead? Directive
One blazes bright inside him, demanding that he go save his
creator, but he can't.*

One more shudder, and the ship goes dark.

Light again, and the contrast nearly overwhelms him.

*"What are my orders?" Abel says, looking down at the girl
huddled on the floor, a nearly spent blaster clutched in her
hands. She has tan skin and chin-length black hair. Her wide,
dark eyes stare up at him as if she doesn't dare believe him. He
doesn't mind. Humans sometimes require long periods of time
to understand transitions his brain comprehends at once.*

*Besides, it's pleasant to see a human again after so long,
even if she is a soldier of Genesis. Pleasant to talk again. And
soon, perhaps, he will even be spoken to—*

There's another flash of light, but this one is different.
Abel feels as though his memories have become less real,
more remote, mere fragments of color in a constantly turning kaleidoscope. He can catch glimpses—kissing Noemi
in zero-G, leaping with her across a snowy crevasse in the
wreck of the *Osiris*—but he can't inhabit them any longer.

His memories are being removed from his body.

The body that is no longer really his.

Someone's there with him, in his own head. Abel can't
see or hear anything, yet he senses another presence. Maybe
this is what it's like for humans, when they "just know"
somebody has walked into a room behind their back.

Father, Abel thinks.

Hello, my boy.

Light flashes again:

Standing in the basement laboratory and seeing Model One A sit up for the first time. As the gestational fluid drips away, he's able to make out the mech's features—features so very like his own, when he was young, though perhaps a bit more handsome. Satisfaction flows through him as he sees his masterwork, his future—

Light.

"Don't do this," Robin pleads. *She's become so frail these past few months, almost skeletal; it hurts to see her like this. Although she tries to push the diodes away, her hands are too weak to manage it.*

He doesn't want to think about how she's hurting. He doesn't have to. He has another plan.

"You'll wake up in a whole new body," he promises. *"Even if it takes me my entire life, I promise you, I'll find a way to bring you back."*

"Please, just let me go," she groans, *but he ignores her. He has work to do.*

The kaleidoscope spins again, but this time the fragments are unknown to Abel. They must be memories belonging to Burton Mansfield, but he's losing his ability to even see them, much less make sense of them. The only physical sensation he has left feels vaguely like floating.

"I can hear Gilly," Mansfield says. It's hard to tell whether he's talking to Abel or to himself. There's not much difference anymore. "Can't see her yet, but I can hear."

Abel can't hear or see. He's floating away from anything he's ever seen, or felt, or known.

If a mech has a soul, can that soul go to heaven? Abel's never had any personal interest in an afterlife, but he wouldn't mind heaven. If heaven exists, Noemi will be there someday. He's sure of that. He would so like to see her again.

She was the best part of his life.

"At last," Mansfield says. This time, he's unmistakably speaking to Abel. "You've found our fate at last. Why did you fight it for so long? Wouldn't it have been better to just give in?"

"No."

That's the last Abel can say. He isn't floating anymore. He isn't anywhere anymore. A great blackness envelops him within and without, neither frightening nor comforting, because it is all there is.

He has been evicted from his own body. That ought to be death…

…but somehow it is not.

27

BELLUM SANCTUM IS EATING NOEMI'S BRAIN. OR BURNING it. *Consuming* it, anyway, until she can hardly think about anything else.

There's nothing worse than knowing a disaster is coming while having *absolutely no idea* how to stop it.

"Tell the media!" Virginia suggests as she prepares a small vial of nanotech fluid that—in theory—might help keep Noemi's breakdowns at bay. She wants to be as functional as possible before the *Apollo Acestor* takes off. "Say, hey, Genesis, your Council's leading you straight to hell! Or does the Council control the media?"

"They don't. We have a free press. But who's going to believe me?" Noemi settles herself onto the *Apollo Acestor*'s small biobed. "As far as most people on Genesis are considered, I'm not even human anymore. They wouldn't trust me if I pointed out the sun is in the sky—much less if I tried to tell them about something like this."

Ephraim takes the vial from Virginia, pops it into a syringe, and injects it into Noemi's arm. It doesn't hurt, save for a faint cold sting. "Why can't your Captain Baz report it? They'd believe her, right?"

"Not now that she's violated military security. If anyone found out what she'd done, she'd be considered an oath breaker. On Genesis, we don't look kindly on those."

Noemi senses the fluid course through her; internal sensors track its passage, which seems like unnecessary information, almost creepy to know. More welcome is the return of her balance. Although Ephraim and Virginia warned her that the nanotech fluid is only a temporary fix at best, she's grateful for any break in the misery.

"So, you have a free press, but nobody's going to talk to that free press, because nobody's going to listen to anybody they don't want to believe anyway," Virginia says. "Am I getting the picture here?"

"Unfortunately." Noemi's heart sinks. Is Genesis nothing like the world she grew up believing in?

Then Ephraim says, "It's not so different on Stronghold— or on Earth, or Cray, or anywhere else. Humans in general tend to hear only what they want to hear, and nobody wants to hear about a damned doomsday weapon."

Okay, so, Genesis isn't awful. Humans are awful. Noemi sighs. Maybe she should be glad not to be entirely human anymore. Maybe Abel's arrogance is more like common sense.

Maybe Abel can help.

Abel was the one individual in the galaxy capable of turning that engine back on. Turning it off again might not be as dangerous—but it is hard to be sure. He's certainly the only one who's had substantial experience with the engine in the past couple of decades.

From the moment Noemi learned she was an exile from Genesis, she's known she wanted to find Abel again. In some ways they parted badly—she shouldn't have said that, about him making decisions for her, and she suspects he took it as something far uglier than she intended.

But she believes in Abel. She trusts his love for her. Above all, she can count on him to do the right thing.

So once the *Apollo Acestor* has left Genesis, they need to find Abel. However, she also needs a plan of her own. It's a big galaxy, Abel won't know she's looking for him, and locating him might take more time than Earth has left. What can she do?

"We have to figure out some way to warn Earth," Noemi says. This is treason, and every word of it stings. But Bellum Sanctum is treason, too, and infinitely worse—because it betrays every principle her world was founded upon. "The Vagabonds call me 'Vidal of Genesis.' So people out in the galaxy already know my voice. So maybe Earth's leaders would listen to me before they threw me in jail. And maybe they can figure out a way to stop this thing."

Virginia and Ephraim exchange looks across the dim, cramped sick bay. Finally, Virginia says, "I'd call that our best plan, if it weren't our *only* plan."

Noemi hops off the biobed, grateful to feel semi-functional again. "Then let's get moving."

The next few minutes pass in a blur of systems checks. All three of them are double-checking the docking bay, when the thumping of footsteps on the gangway makes them all look up. Harriet Dixon and Zayan Thakur rush in, and even in the shadowy bay, she can see that they appear worried.

From the air lock door, Ephraim calls, "You guys coming along? Thought you were settling here for good."

"That's the plan," Harriet says in a rush. "We still hope we can settle on Genesis someday, but that's not why we're here."

Looking grave, Zayan says, "Abel's in trouble."

"I was getting to that!" Harriet protests.

"Wait, wait." Noemi steadies herself with a hand against the wall. The urge to find him again spikes within her, almost painful in its intensity. "What do you mean, Abel's in trouble? Did he try to come back to Genesis?"

It feels good to think he might've risked everything to be with her again. It shouldn't.

"He didn't *try* to come back. He's being *forced* to," Harriet says. "See, Vagabonds know other Vagabonds. We help each other out with deep space repairs, information about routes, that kind of thing."

Zayan cuts in. "We know a guy who knows a guy who knows someone on the *Katara*. And the word is that Dagmar Krall gave Abel a place in the Consortium, but Genesis realized he was hiding with them, and the Elder Council demanded that Krall hand Abel over at once, to face trial on Genesis for Akide's murder. Otherwise their alliance was over."

Noemi's voice shakes as she concludes, "And Krall chose the alliance."

They're going to bring Abel back here to kill him.

I will never *let that happen.*

But Harriet surprises her. "No. I mean, yes, Krall chose the alliance, but another friend of ours who mines on the outer reaches of the Earth system said that the Genesis ship transporting him ran into trouble and is broadcasting throughout the whole system that another ship stole their prisoner."

"You mean Abel escaped?" Noemi's relief at the thought outweighs the flash of disappointment that she now has no excuse to find him again.

Zayan shakes his head sadly. "Nope. He didn't escape. Remedy took him prisoner instead."

"Abel's not having a great week," Virginia says.

The joke falls flat. Noemi doesn't care. What is going on?

"I don't understand," Ephraim protests. "Remedy is allied with Genesis! We're not their enemies, at any rate. So why would anyone who belongs to Remedy attack a Genesis ship to get Abel? Nobody in Remedy has any motive to do it."

"Someone clearly does." Noemi straightens as the pieces fall into place in her mind. "There are Remedy members trying to survive on Haven. A lot of them need medical treatment."

"How is that a motive for Remedy to go after Abel?" Virginia says.

"Think it through." For days, Noemi has felt off balance, confused, unsure. But now she's absolutely certain, and as horrible as the situation is, at least she finally knows what's happening, and what she has to do. "There's only one person in the galaxy who wants Abel in custody more than Genesis does. Only one other person who'd put a price on his head."

Virginia's eyes widen. *"Gillian frickin' Shearer."*

Harriet covers her face with her hands; both Zayan and Ephraim groan. It's all too clear what's happened to Abel—and the terrible fate he's about to face.

"We have to get to Abel, as fast as we possibly can," Noemi says. Her own fate doesn't matter now. The danger doesn't matter either, because Abel can be in no greater danger than he already is. But that doesn't mean she can forget everything else. "The fastest way back to Haven is through the Earth system, and we were headed there anyway. We can warn them about Bellum Sanctum on the way."

"Bellum Sanctum?" Zayan asks. "What in the worlds is that?"

"Oh, we are in an entire vortex of trouble, my friend," Virginia replies. "Explanations later. For now, just go with it."

Noemi hardly hears any of this. Her mind's racing too fast, fueled by desperation. "We'll send a message in the Earth system. Multiple messages, to every government center on Earth, and the offworld bases. We'll even warn the mining stations near the asteroid belt. We can do all of that on our way to the Haven Gate. And we'll make sure they believed our message when we check in on our way back, after rescuing Abel."

She knows it might not be that easy. If there's already been time for the news of Abel's capture to have reached Genesis, then there's surely been time for Gillian Shearer to have wiped Abel's soul.

Still, she has to try. Even if there's only one chance in a million to save Abel, Noemi has to give him that chance.

When she lifts her head, she sees that same conviction reflected in every person around her. Abel means more to her than to anyone else here—but he means a lot, to everyone. They all want to rescue him. They're all in this together.

Harriet and Zayan exchange glances before Zayan says, "If you think you could use a couple of extra hands—"

"We're leaving immediately," Ephraim says. "It's going to be crowded, but if you're ready, let's go."

"We're ready," Harriet says, clasping Zayan's hand.

Virginia hurries into the ship; no doubt she's headed to choose her ideal spot on the bridge. Harriet and Zayan follow. Noemi hears Zayan mutter under his breath, "I *told* you we should've packed some clothes."

•   •   •

They fly through the Earth system at top speed, launching beacons and sending signals every chance they get. The *Apollo Acestor* isn't as fast as the *Persephone*, and it doesn't have as many signaling options, but this is the only ship they have. That makes it the only chance Earth has.

The only chance Abel has.

I'm coming, Noemi thinks over and over, between message packets, between dizzy spells. *Please hang on. I'm coming as fast as I can.*

The waiting might be easier if she felt like her warnings were getting anywhere. She'd like to think that they're doing some good. But if anyone from Earth attempts to answer their messages, the *Apollo Acestor* gets no sign of it.

"I don't like this," Ephraim mutters as they soar toward Neptune and the Haven Gate. "Noemi—I know how important saving Abel is to you. It's important to me, too. That doesn't change the fact that saving Earth has to be our priority."

"I agree." Noemi keeps staring at the viewscreen, as though the power of her concentration could move this ship faster. She feels as if she could push it past the speed of light. "But if Earth won't listen to the messages, how much more luck do you think we'd have in person?"

"You've got a point." Ephraim sighs heavily. "I hope to hell they're listening."

The cold horror of suspense doesn't dissipate until they reach Neptune, where, amid the frenzy around the Haven Gate, the *Apollo Acestor* slips through easily. They're not bothered on their way through the system or landing on the planet either. *At least we caught a break there*, Noemi thinks. *We deserve at least one.*

She'd known that settlers were descending on Haven, but she hadn't realized how quickly they'd organize into, well, *cities*. The *Apollo Acestor* lands at a makeshift pad, with several individuals apparently hard at work already. A young man with an Afro hurries up with a dataread in his hands and a grin on his face. "Welcome to Haven! We're helping people get settled—trying to spread everyone around—"

"That's a great idea," Virginia says as they all hurry off the ship, hyperwarm jackets sealed against the cold. "But we're just visiting."

He blinks. "We already have *tourists*? Wow."

"Not that kind of visit." Noemi adjusts her holster, feels the reassuring heft of her blaster. "We've got to get into the Winter Castle. More to the point, we've got to get someone out of it. And this time, I'd rather not have to fight Queens and Charlies the entire way in."

Although the young man still looks flummoxed, he directs them to the "hospital," a hastily put-together place, not unlike the triage stations sometimes set up on base after especially devastating battles. Apparently the head of the hospital handles negotiations with the Winter Castle.

That's mildly surprising—she still doesn't understand how these "negotiations" work—but Noemi gets the shock of her life when she sees who one of the volunteer nurses is.

"Noemi!" Delphine cries, hurrying toward her with open arms. Noemi hugs her back, almost on autopilot. It's not like they became close on the *Osiris*, exactly, but it is sort of good to see her again.

"What are you doing out here?" Noemi asks.

Delphine makes a face. "Getting out from under Gillian Shearer's thumb. Trying to learn how to do something useful." Then, to Noemi's astonishment, she adds, "You've come for Abel, haven't you?"

"You've met Abel? You've seen him?" Noemi's heart sinks. "How long has he been in there?"

"I saw him early yesterday, when the Remedy ship returned. Captain Fouda and the head of the hospital did a lot of negotiating before allowing Abel through to the Winter Castle."

"Fouda?" Noemi says in amazement. "That son of a bitch! We saved him!"

"I know," Delphine says miserably. "And I don't agree with exchanging people—even robot people—for some sort of bargain, like they're just goods to be traded. I think it's wrong. But I'm not the one in charge, and we need so much medicine here, and a couple of Tares aren't working properly—excuse me, what are you doing with that medkit?"

"Using it." Ephraim's gaze takes in the dozens of patients lying on cots and stretchers. "I'm a doctor, and one who knows a lot about the Cobweb protocol."

"A doctor?" Delphine says, almost reverently. "We need real doctors. I think we only have three of them here, and hundreds of patients."

The tall man who must be in charge has overheard and steps into the conversation. "Thank God we have another physician here. Anything you could do—"

"I'm all yours the minute we get Abel out, which hopefully won't be long." Ephraim's loyalty surprises and moves Noemi, and she smiles for the first time in what feels like forever. As he finishes making notes on a patient's chart, he turns to her and asks, "So you say you know how to get into the Winter Castle?"

Noemi looks toward the transport doors she saw last time. "Last time I got into the Winter Castle the same way the mechs got out. So if we're going to try that, we need Shearer to send out her mechs." She turns to the head of the hospital. "Do you think a few Vagabonds might be willing to help us rescue our friend by causing a distraction?"

Although she expects an argument, the tall man simply inclines his head in respect. "I recognize your voice now, Vidal of Genesis. You gave us this world. Giving you a distraction in return is the least we can do."

Not only do they get the promise of a distraction but they also get the loan of a few snowmobiles. Once they've got these in position, Ephraim starts counting things off. "Okay, Harriet and Zayan, you'll be a team. Noemi, you stick with me and Virginia—oh, holy hell, Virginia!"

Virginia, who's refastening her boots, looks up at him in confusion. "What?"

"You—Harriet and Zayan, too, I think—" Ephraim's eyes are wide. "Have you already had Cobweb? If not, Haven's going to kill you. The entire place is toxic! Me, I had Cobweb as a kid, but if you haven't, this is *bad*."

Harriet gasps, and Virginia puts her fingers to her throat as though to check her pulse. Noemi makes a gesture meant to communicate, *Calm down, guys.* "It takes two or three days for the toxicity to sink in. The Remedy fighters were fine at first. And as far as I know, the effects wear off after leaving the planet."

Ephraim still doesn't look happy. "How do you guys feel?"

"Fine, I guess?" Harriet squares her shoulders, visibly summoning courage. "It's got to be a short stay, but that's true regardless, right?"

Ephraim nods reluctantly. "Okay. We break into two teams."

"Three," Noemi says. She may be sick and not quite herself, but she's still the military strategist here. "You guys should go in teams of two, because you need backup. But I've been here before. I can go alone. And the more teams we have, the faster we'll be able to find Abel."

More teams *are* better. Also, the others don't need to drag around someone whose inner circuitry might go haywire at any time, possibly betraying their position and getting them killed.

She watches the other four glance at one another; they're not totally buying her reasoning. But no one protests. Instead, Zayan says, "You're the soldier, so your plan goes."

Virginia checks her weapon. "Three teams. Let's do it."

Noemi speaks into the comm unit linked to the Vagabonds who've agreed to help: "Flight team, *go.*"

Ship engines hiss and hum in the distance, sending up sprays of snow on the horizon. As they stand by their snowmobiles, they watch five volunteer Vagabond ships rocket toward the Winter Castle, flying high enough to avoid hitting it, but low enough to set off every proximity alert in the place. Even at this distance, they can hear the faint wail of the faraway klaxons.

As the ships spin back around to buzz the castle one more time, some of the ground-level hatches open. Queens and Charlies zoom out on snowmobiles, their eyes raised to the sky, their weapons aimed upward. The scanner counts off the meters as Noemi's teammates get on their three snowmobiles and fire them up. Virginia rides behind Ephraim; Zayan holds on to Harriet's waist; and Noemi takes her own.

Noemi raises her hand and chops down through the air: *Go.*

• • •

Ten minutes later, creeping down a corridor with her back sliding along one wall, Noemi thinks, *Why does the Winter Castle have to be so damned big?*

The place is beautiful in the same ornate, overdone manner as the *Osiris*. Instead of the golds, turquoises, and siennas of that ship, the Winter Castle is decorated purely in white, silver, and pale blue. The designers must have taken their inspiration from snowflakes, because every window is hexagonal, as are the floor plans of many rooms. Intricate filigree decorates even the service corridors, adding traces of sparkle. Noemi can only imagine the ornate splendor of the bedrooms and amusement areas where the rich and powerful were meant to play.

Her attention to these details doesn't make her forget the small security cameras every fifty meters or so. She just has to hope Gillian and her mechs are so caught up in fending off the Vagabonds outside that they aren't paying any attention to what's going on inside.

Footsteps around the next corner make Noemi freeze. She readies her blaster, thankful that at the moment she's stable and steady. *Take me to Gillian Shearer's laboratory,* she rehearses in her head. *Do it, and nobody has to get killed.* Nobody's going to get killed regardless, but whoever's in the next room doesn't have to know that.

Better to choose the moment of confrontation rather than wait to be surprised. She takes a deep breath and spins around the corner. "Take me to—*Abel!*"

"I realized someone had managed to get in." Abel smiles. His face is alight with relief, and something else—it looks somewhat like satisfaction. "I hoped it would be you."

It's him. It's really him. He must've found another way to escape when Gillian was called away to deal with the Vagabonds. And he didn't pin himself to the ceiling this time. Abel's all right!

Noemi flings her arms around him in relief so profound it feels almost like rapture. "How did you manage to hold Shearer off? Are you okay?"

"I'm better than I've been in a long time." He embraces her, too, gingerly at first, then more firmly. "Are you alone?"

"No. Let me signal the others and we can get out of here." Swiftly, Noemi hits the code on her comm unit that will signal the other teams to hurry back to their snowmobiles. The signal doesn't go through—they're too deep within—but they should only have to travel another few meters to have better luck. This was all so much easier than she thought it would be; it feels like a miracle.

Except that it's somehow oddly... off.

"I was delighted when I saw you on security cams," Abel says, tilting his head. "But I wasn't sure you'd ever come back to Haven."

"Don't you get it?" Noemi asks. "We found out you were in trouble! I'd *never* leave you in danger. In fact, I don't think I want to leave you at all, ever. Besides, there's something about—about Bellum..."

Her voice falters as she trails off. Abel's reaction feels wrong to her. He's focused on different things than she'd expect. Why?

For reassurance, she looks into Abel's blue eyes.

No. She's looking into blue eyes.

But this isn't Abel.

28

ABEL APPEARS TO HAVE NO PHYSICAL FORM. THIS IS peculiar, but he thinks he can adjust.

It surprises him how difficult it is to order his thoughts without anchoring them in physical space. Learning to do so would no doubt be an excellent long-term goal, but he's eager to figure out precisely how it is he still exists. Therefore a mental shortcut is in order.

He visualizes his surroundings, trying to come up with images that would match the vague sensations at the edge of his consciousness. After an immeasurable while, the oblivion acquires a sort of grayness. The grayness coalesces into fog, and finally, as he concentrates, the fog dissipates into a fine mist. Abel finds himself standing in a kind of grotto, where both water and stone are in soft shades of greenish gray. Light of some sort allows him to see, but he can find no obvious source for it.

Then he realizes that, in this place, his body seems to glow. It is, perhaps, the illumination of thought.

"How can I possibly continue to exist?" Abel says. The grotto is solid enough for his voice to echo slightly. "My memories were removed from my body. That should have destroyed my consciousness."

His first thought is that maybe Burton Mansfield didn't manage to get Abel entirely out of his head. Maybe he's still in there, being forced to operate as Mansfield's subconscious. If so, he intends to fill his creator's dreams with enough horrors to keep a Freudian analyst busy for years.

But Abel senses that he's left his former body completely.

Perhaps Noemi's right about the existence of an afterlife, he thinks. Does the soul live on after death? Is there some kind of heaven, even for mechs? If so, it seems mechs must construct their own. Abel looks around the grotto, which isn't the most compelling location he's ever seen. He might want to try creating something more festive.

In the mist, he glimpses a kind of shape, more solid than the others. It moves, and Abel realizes he isn't alone.

Is this God? If so, how interesting.

The figure speaks with a female voice. "It's not so dark anymore."

"No," Abel answers. "I appear to be glowing. Is that by design?"

"Design," she repeats. Although her tone is uncertain, the word could be interpreted as a reply to his question. It seems possible that this indeed is some manner of deity.

He straightens. "May I ask if you are an entity, or a representative of entities, that could be understood as godlike or divine? If so, can you tell me whether you were ever accurately understood and worshipped by a human religion, and if so, which one?" Identification is important. If he's dealing with a deity that resembles the Christian Holy Spirit, Abel will conduct himself differently than he would with, say, Hel, the Norse goddess of death.

After a long moment, the voice laughs. "No. No. I'm no god. No god at all, no god anywhere. I just got stuck here by someone who pretends to be a god."

Disappointing, but not uninteresting. Abel resets to agnosticism and carries on. "Can you explain exactly where we are?"

"Are you real?" She sounds somewhat more focused. "Your accent is rather similar to mine. I've imagined so many things, so many, many things. Wonderful and horrible, over and over, all these years. But I never imagined another voice before. So maybe you *are* real."

"I believe myself to still be real," Abel says, "though the nature of my existence is currently in some doubt. It's entirely possible that I exist only within another person's mind, but you are not that person. Do you also believe yourself to be real?" Abel has never had another conversation where so little could be taken for granted.

She replies, "I was once. I was, wasn't I? I was real, and then Burt made me something else entirely."

Burt. Abel remembers what he'd seen in Gillian's laboratory, remembers her story of a broken, half-stored consciousness forced to communicate via Ouija board. "Are you the late Robin Mansfield?"

"My name. You said—oh, I had no idea how good it would be to hear my name again!"

The shape in the fog moves as though to stand, and as it does so, it clarifies into human form, glowing as brightly as his own. Although Robin Mansfield died before he was constructed, Abel has seen many images of her, so he recognizes her long face, high cheekbones, and soft auburn hair. Is she asserting her own appearance, or is Abel constructing her image from those long-ago photographs and videos? Either way, she stands before him, an uncertain smile on her face, wreathed in some sort of garment that might be made of nothing more than fog. Whatever he and Robin Mansfield are now, they are no longer alone.

The moment of recognition seems to have focused Robin considerably. "Who are you?" she asks.

"I'm called Abel. Model One A of the Mansfield Cybernetics line."

Her face falls. "Oh no. Burt said—he said Model One A

would be for him, a mech that wouldn't be a person until he lived in it, but would also somehow be a person even before that—somehow—"

"I am a mech with a soul," Abel confirms. He could argue that the existence of a soul has now been scientifically proven. Noemi would be proud. "I attempted to escape Professor Mansfield to lead my own life, but your daughter, Gillian, recaptured me. She's grown into a cyberneticist as well, by the way. She downloaded Mansfield's consciousness into my body, and now I'm...here."

"Wherever here is," Robin says. Her tone has become distant again.

"The likeliest hypothesis is that we're both trapped in a complex data solid."

"It falls pretty short of paradise." With a sigh, she steps closer to Abel, examining him. "You look so much like him when he was young. Before he got hardened, while he could still relate to his fellow human beings. Burt made you in his image. I guess he's still playing god."

"It's one of Professor Mansfield's favorite pursuits," Abel says.

"So he captured your soul, too, put you here—"

"Actually, I believe both Mansfield and Gillian intended to erase my soul. But I traveled out of my body under my own power somehow."

It's the Tether, Abel realizes. Tether technology is both

hardware and software. But Abel's software is more than just programming; it is part of his essence, his *self*. When Gillian upgraded him for her father's convenience, she didn't think about what it would mean for Abel. Hardly surprising, since she never considered Abel's well-being at all.

However, it appears Gillian has altered Abel's consciousness on the most basic level. He isn't just able to transfer messages with the Tether; he can subconsciously transfer his very soul, to anywhere in the galaxy.

Abel corrects himself. He can transfer his soul to any receptor with sufficient bandwidth and memory storage that happens to be within range. Not quite anywhere.

But it was enough to save him from death.

Robin Mansfield is staring at him dazedly. Already she's losing focus again. Abel quickly resumes the conversation. "My survival was accidental, an instinctive reliance on my Tether technology." This is the likeliest hypothesis by far, so Abel speaks as though it were certain. "Whereas you were transferred into a data solid, I appear to have transmitted *myself* into one."

"It's horrible, isn't it?" she says, sorrow in every syllable. "Not yet, for you. Not at first. But wait a month. Or a year. Or a decade. Or—or—forever, I think I've been in here forever—"

"You died approximately thirty-four years ago. Have you been conscious all this time?"

She nods. "You can't imagine how it's been."

"I can, actually." He says this as kindly as he can, because he knows how much this hurts. "Mansfield abandoned ship during a battle in the Liberty War. He stranded me inside it for thirty years, entirely alone. My surroundings were at least concrete and physical, but that wasn't much consolation."

Robin shakes her head mournfully, and her glow dims. The shadows within the grotto deepen. "Burt could look at me like I was the most precious thing in the worlds," she murmurs. Thinking of her husband seems to focus her—probably through the pain it causes her. "That look would keep you with him long after you knew better. But finally you'd realize that he wasn't smiling at you, wasn't loving you. He was only loving his own brilliance in using you."

"Unfortunately," Abel says, "I didn't know better until he told me himself." How cheerfully Mansfield had announced his plan for Abel. How happy he expected Abel to be at the chance to die in his creator's service. "I understand what you mean about him. The way he could smile through you."

"I went mad so many times." Robin gazes around the grotto. "Sometimes that was easier. The time didn't quite seem real then. Or every once in a while, I'd pull myself together enough to have fun in here. I could picture the French Alps, or the Scottish Highlands, or even imagine myself looking up at the stars. But it never held. The constellations would shift, or the mountains would melt, and always, always, I was left alone with my own mind. No one should ever be so alone."

Abel couldn't manipulate his reality within the *Daedalus* equipment pod bay. Which alternative is better? He peers intently into the mist, willing it to change shape.

The grotto floor flattens; the cave overhead soars up into infinite darkness. What had been mist turns into clouds overhead and low, rolling fog on the ground. Greenish gray fades into shades of silver. Abel stands on an airplane runway, wearing a trench coat and fedora, and Robin wears the uniform of a French officer during World War II.

She looks down at herself in bemusement. "What is this?"

"It's the end of my favorite movie. *Casablanca*. You appear to be in the role of Captain Renault."

"*Casablanca*. I know that one. I *remember*!" Robin's laugh turns out to be beautiful. "Shouldn't I be dressed like—like—the one in white, who was so pretty—"

"Ilsa," Abel says. "But Noemi would always be my Ilsa."

"Noemi," Robin repeats, wonder in her voice. "You love this person?"

He nods as he stares into the fog surrounding the airstrip. Maybe, if he thinks hard enough, Noemi will come walking toward him in one of Ingrid Bergman's costumes—

But no. It would not really be Noemi, just an illusion of

her. Spending time with an illusion who couldn't truly love him back would only drive him mad.

Robin adjusts her cap, then nods toward the propeller plane that's waiting farther down the runway. "This time, I think Rick should get on board."

"Are we going to continue the story?" In no religion listed in any of his databanks has Abel ever seen a theory of the afterlife that involved spending all eternity making up movie sequels with near strangers. It could, he supposes, be worse.

"Don't you understand?" Robin asks, her eyes alight. "If you brought yourself here, then you also have the power to leave."

"True." Abel ought to have understood this before. Then again, dying and entering the afterlife is something of a shock. It hampers comprehensive analysis. Abel decides not to make a habit of it.

Robin's soul is currently nestled in an ornate wooden box sitting on Gillian Shearer's desk. It seems possible, maybe probable, that he's in there with her. But can he remove himself from the box as easily as he arrived? Is there another potential holder for his soul—one from which he might be able to take action?

"They haven't always left me alone in here," Robin murmurs. "I could tell they were trying to talk to me. But their voices were only echoes, without any real words, and they made me move around this—this triangular thing that pointed to letters—"

"It was a Ouija board."

Robin huffs and rolls her eyes, and it's such an ordinary human gesture that she seems, for an instant, truly alive. "Well, they know I'm in here, at least. Which means they could potentially figure out you're in here, too. I don't think you want them to do that."

"No." Surely Robin's data solid is periodically scanned for deterioration. If he were detected within it, Abel anticipates he would be immediately deleted. "We ought to travel to another, more recent data solid. We could find one that's already installed for direct interface with the Winter Castle computer systems, which would give us both access to much more information—"

"No," Robin says softly. "Not we. Just you. I can't make that journey anymore, if I ever could."

"Why not?" Abel realizes that he understands, in some instinctive way, how to exist as data. Perhaps that's natural for anyone whose soul is fundamentally software. Robin Mansfield cannot share those instincts. After this long, however, she ought to have some idea how to do it, and he could teach her the rest. "There are possibilities for our future existence outside of this data solid—which admittedly are all more theoretical than immediate. Still, we have reason to hope."

"I'm not really myself any longer." Robin paces around him on the tarmac, her boots shiny in the glare of the airport lights. "I remember Burt—remember loving him, then almost hating him—but I don't recall where we met. Did he ever tell you? I think he proposed to me at his PhD ceremony, but I don't have any idea how long we were together before that. Did we have a wedding? It's just...a blur. I think I knew all of that when I first woke up in here, but I don't anymore. It's all gone."

Data degradation, he realizes. The changes Gillian feared are real, and perhaps worse than she knew. Mansfield stored his dead wife's consciousness in a far more primitive form, generations of tech back from what he used for himself. While enough of Robin remains for them to have this conversation, this is still only a fragment. She's incomplete, becoming more and more so as time goes by.

"When you say the name Gillian"—Robin's voice quivers with pain—"I know that's my daughter. I remember being pregnant with her, I put my hands on my belly and loved her even before she was born, but I don't remember her face. I must've seen her face sometime, but I can't think of it at all. If I were myself, I'd know my own little girl. Wouldn't I?"

Gently, Abel says, "Yes. I think you would."

They can build no mech body for Robin's soul to dwell in. Mansfield has no genetic samples fresh enough to successfully create an Inheritor for his late wife. Barring a major leap forward in technology—which might be decades or even centuries away, if it ever came at all—Robin is eternally trapped, with no end in sight.

It's very like Mansfield to assume he'll conquer all obstacles sooner or later. Abel cannot share this delusion. Apparently, Robin can't either.

Robin straightens, tugs on her French uniform jacket, and turns to face him. "I'm so tired of it now. So tired of feeling my mind break down, bit by bit. I thought in the beginning that maybe I'd been freed from death itself. Now I understand that it wasn't perfect freedom I'd been given. It's only perfect isolation."

"Isolation is worse than any death." Abel thinks back to those thirty years in the pod bay. The only thing that makes the memory bearable is the knowledge that it ended.

He reaches out with his consciousness, instinctively, and senses a way out. Maybe not his final destination—but it would work for now. And from there, he can continue the search.

When his eyes next meet Robin's, she obviously knows their time together is at an end.

"Please," she says. "When you talk with Burt and Gillian,

tell them to please, finally, let me go. Let me find peace. Tell them it's what I want."

"They're unlikely to agree," he says.

"Then please, find a way to kill me. Or delete me. Whatever you'd call it." Robin's hand rests against his chest for a moment. It's the only touch they share, startlingly real. "Just promise me you'll end this, however you can."

Abel nods. She steps away from him, turns toward the phone booth, and walks away, perhaps to round up the usual suspects.

He turns up the collar of his trench coat and walks toward the plane. There's no pilot, and yet somehow he knows he has to generate the feeling of movement. The sense that a transition is not only necessary but also allowed.

So he reaches into his pocket and pulls out his papers. To the ether he says, "Signed by General Weygand himself."

The papers worked in *Casablanca*. They work here. The propellers spin, and the airplane begins to rumble forward on the runway. Abel sits back, and at the moment he feels the plane's wheels leave the ground, he closes his eyes.

He can't imagine where he's going. He can only reach out—out past this data solid, past this room, past the Winter Castle itself—searching for something he'll only know when he finds it.

And then he does.

29

NOEMI STAGGERS BACKWARD. "PROFESSOR MANSFIELD," she whispers.

Mansfield grins at her with Abel's face. "Miss Vidal. What a pleasure it is to see you again."

Whatever control she'd regained over her body is gone; she feels like she might crumple to the floor, lose consciousness, explode. Usually she'd strike back at anyone or anything that hurt the ones she loves, but she can't attack Abel's body. It's still precious to her even when his soul is gone.

Gone.

The hand that closes around her forearm doesn't touch her the way Abel would've. Mansfield's grip is as hard and merciless as a steel cuff as he says, "You've become far more interesting than when we last met. More interesting, and less human."

Noemi's eyes well with tears, but she won't allow herself to cry. Only inside her head does she wail: *Abel's gone,*

Abel's gone, we're too late, he's gone. Out loud, she says only, "Whatever your daughter did to me didn't work. I'm already breaking down."

He isn't dismayed. "Bluffing me, Miss Vidal?"

"No." How much she'd like to slap him, but it's Abel's face, even without Abel behind it. "If you keep me here, you'll see the truth soon enough."

"Oh, don't worry," he says. "You won't be going anywhere."

His speaking patterns, the tones of his voice—he doesn't sound like Abel at all. How could she have been fooled by this golem, even for a moment? Maybe she only saw what she wanted to see.

Mansfield cocks his head, studying her. "There's no way we'd ever let you go. The first hybrid between human and mech? The prototype? We have a great deal of research to do."

"What are you going to do, dissect me?"

"Only as a last resort." The simplicity of Mansfield's answer chills Noemi to the marrow. "This is a whole new technology that could help humanity. It would be selfish not to share the knowledge."

"You're the most selfish person I've ever met," Noemi says. "All you want is profit."

"You don't think this technology can save lives?"

Gauging by the way Noemi feels right now, hybridization seems more likely to end lives than save them. "Let's just say you're not ready to make mech-human hybrids yet. Seems like a lot of your big projects aren't 'quite ready.' They don't usually wind up being what you promised at all. The *Osiris* was supposed to be this big secret, but Remedy found out about it in time to crash it on Haven. The Inheritors were supposed to be ready to provide eternal life right away, but what happened with Simon proved they're not even close. And you've still learned *nothing*." Her voice shakes, but she wills herself to keep speaking, to spear him with every word. "The galaxy calls you a genius, and I guess you must have been. Once. A really long time ago."

The spear draws blood. Noemi sees Mansfield pull back; his expression darkens with anger and contempt that have no right to be on Abel's gentle face. "You're speaking rather hastily for someone who's soon going to be a subject in my lab."

Mansfield wants that threat to scare her, but Noemi is past all that. She laughs at him. "I don't think I'll be around much longer. I know Abel's gone. The rest is noise."

Could Ephraim's team, or Harriet's, still find her in time? Noemi can't even bring herself to hope for that. They're in other parts of the Winter Castle, maybe headed back to the snowmobiles by now. Besides, even if they did find her, Mansfield would attack them. She knows how much damage Abel's body can do.

From a comm unit at Mansfield's belt comes Shearer's voice. "Do you need assistance, Dad? I can have some mechs on the way to you in seconds."

"Don't be ridiculous," Mansfield snaps. "Since when have I needed anyone's help?"

Mansfield literally thinks he's better than every other human and mech in creation. Including Noemi. Including his own daughter. Dazedly Noemi wonders whether Shearer knows this, and if so, why she'd destroy someone as beautiful as Abel just to bring this bastard back from the dead.

Really, though, Noemi knows why. It's the same reason why she was willing to fight and die for Genesis even after her planet wrote her off as a lying traitor. The reason why it hurt Abel to prioritize his own life over Mansfield's. There's always one core purpose in our hearts that we'll sacrifice anything for.

Noemi thinks, *Love is Directive One.*

Mansfield isn't dwelling on his daughter's concern for him; he's too busy studying Noemi. He lets go of her arm to pace around her. "Maybe someday hybrids could outpace even mechs as fine as myself—but not yet. Not for a long while. For now I am more efficient, stronger, smarter than any other being in creation. *I am indestructible.*" Mansfield's voice behind her back makes Noemi shudder. She can feel her hair standing on end. "I have capabilities beyond any human. I can begin my work anew, and I can go beyond it. Create wonders the galaxy has never seen. Make the worlds everything they should be."

Noemi grits her teeth. "You mean, you're going to play God."

"Someone should, don't you think? Oh, that's right. You're from Genesis. You think angels are playing harps up in the clouds, and you can leave everything up to them. Didn't you ever hear it said that God helps those who help themselves?"

The contempt within her bubbles hot, like liquid iron being poured into her veins to go hard and strong. "You think believers are like children. You don't think anyone's really seen the universe for what it is, except for you."

"I don't think it," Mansfield says. "I *know*."

He continues pacing around her, his gaze intent and alien. Glimpsing his profile, Noemi wishes it were Abel next to her—wishes it with all her will, her blood, her bone. If wishing could change reality, Mansfield would vanish in that instant, and Abel's soul would light up behind those blue eyes again.

But any soldier who's been to war knows what wishing is worth.

Instead, she gazes past Mansfield to the far corridor. According to the blueprint of the Winter Castle inside her head, this corridor should lead away from the hub, closer to the perimeter of the building.

You aren't faster than he is, she tells herself. *You aren't stronger. But he's even less used to his mech body than you are to yours. You're also mad as hell, and if you catch a lucky break, maybe that adrenaline can get you out of here.*

Escape feels so useless. What else can she do to prevent Earth's destruction? Nothing comes to mind. She's lost Abel, just like she lost Esther. The two people in her life who trusted her the most, gave her the most—who *loved* her—she failed to protect either of them. They're both dead partly because she was too damn slow to save them. There's no way to repent for that. No way to redeem it.

And Abel was so gentle. For all the raw information in his databanks, he always remained so innocent. So open to exploration, discovery, joy. If anyone deserved more than his fair share of life, it was him. Instead, Noemi's left with the hollow hurt of knowing he spent about 90 percent of his life trapped in an equipment pod bay, without gravity or light or companionship—but never, never without hope.

All his hope turned out to be in vain.

But he didn't only have hopes for himself, Noemi remembers. Abel had hopes for her, too. He gave up so much to give her a chance to live. She won't waste it.

Far corridor, she tells herself. *You just need one shot at the far corridor.*

Mansfield continues circling her. "Personally, I suspect you only need a software update. I can't know for sure until I get you to my lab. For now, though, let's assume that you are breaking down, as you claim. Physically, probably, I could fix you. Mentally? You're a hazard. It's really not worth repairing you." His voice goes even colder. "Well then, I guess I'll have to remake you into something much more useful."

He steps behind her. She has a clear shot to the corridor. *Go.*

Noemi bolts forward, using every bit of power she has—human, mech, all of it. Her balance is uneven, but she's upright, and her newly fast reflexes still work. If the corridor wavers and splits into two corridors as her vision doubles, it doesn't matter as long as she aims for the middle. When she reaches the corridor, her footsteps echoing against the curved, iridescent walls, she tries to calculate how long it would take her to reach the snowmobile—of all the times for that voice in her head to fall silent instead of giving her information—

Mansfield's weight slams into her back; his arms seize her as she thuds into the wall and onto the floor. She'd forgotten how heavy that body is. Winded, Noemi struggles for breath, wriggles in an effort to escape his grip, but it's no use. She fights him even as he pins her to the ground and peers down at her like a hawk sighting its prey.

"You're trembling," he says. "Are you so scared of a face you claimed to love?"

Noemi never claimed to love Abel. She wishes she had, because she knows now that she did. Abel never even got to hear her say those words. Regret consumes her, threatens to swallow her whole.

But Noemi spits back, "You don't look like him." A sob catches in her throat. "I could always see Abel's soul. And I can see that you have none."

"Enough." Mansfield shakes his head at her as though she were a naughty little girl who refused to follow the playground rules. "Let's get you to the lab."

Noemi tries to be brave. She has to face that this is the end of her life, at least in any form she'd ever want to live it.

The floor shudders. Then it shudders again. A distant thudding comes closer. Mansfield sits up, clearly as confused by this as she is, though not alarmed.

At least, he's not alarmed until the nearby wall collapses, breaking outward in a spray of dust and shimmer. They both stare as the miasma settles to reveal an enormous dark shape, something with arms and legs—

"A Smasher?" Mansfield gapes at it as it lumbers forward, all two and a half meters of gray hulking metal, its immense weight shaking the foundation of the Winter Castle itself. "Who the bloody hell programmed a mining droid to come through here?"

"No one," the Smasher says in a tinny, monotone voice from the small speaker at the center of its chest. "It was my idea."

Noemi stares. Smashers don't have ideas. Smashers also don't attack humans. But this one grabs Mansfield in one of its enormous, multipronged hands, and tugs him away from Noemi easily. She skitters backward, crab-walking away from the bizarre scene.

Am I hallucinating? Am I breaking down completely? Is this mech brain failure or something?

"Abort previous protocol," Mansfield barks, trying to sound authoritative while clutched in the Smasher's hand like a toddler's dolly. "Delete instructions. Initiate dormant mode."

"I'd rather not," the Smasher replies. It lumbers to a nearby chute with the genteel label REFUSE, instead of GARBAGE. It opens the broad door and drops Mansfield unceremoniously through it. Noemi hears him shouting as he thuds against the walls all the way down to wherever the castle garbage ends up. It would've been incredibly satisfying to watch, if Noemi wasn't pretty sure she's headed there next.

Look for an emergency alarm. See if you can hit it. Whatever security Shearer's got would probably target the Smasher and maybe you'd get your chance to escape. This plan dies as soon as Noemi thinks of it, because already the Smasher is plodding toward her. It stops a few steps short of her and says, in its flat voice, "The garbage chute won't kill Professor Mansfield. I chose to leave his body intact, since I hope to have use of it again."

Hope had died inside Noemi's heart. Now it's born once more, along with the single soul she loves most in the whole galaxy. "Oh my God," she whispers. *"Abel?"*

30

SMASHERS DON'T HAVE EYES, EXACTLY; MINING ROBOTS don't need to distinguish fine shades of color or the subtleties of light. They have scanners, which provide a rough sensory map that can be used for digging out ore, properly loading carriers, or carrying out occasional demolitions work, as well as metallurgical analysis.

The scanners give Abel only a grainy, colorless image of Noemi, but it's enough.

"A curious experience, being a Smasher," he says as he lifts Noemi and carries her away from the rubble of the smashed wall. "This physical form is much more cumbersome, but much more powerful."

If he's correctly interpreting her blurry expression, Noemi is still dazed with astonishment. "How—how is this possible?"

"As you know, I—at least, my old body—was recently

outfitted with Tether hardware and software. My consciousness and the software appear to have fused in some sense, until using the Tether has become almost automatic. A kind of instinct. Fortunately, as part of an experiment, I installed the Tether inside the Smasher we picked up on Stronghold. While I was at the task, I also put in considerable extra memory storage, purely out of curiosity." Proximity alerts at Abel's shoulders warn him that the corridor is narrowing. He sidesteps carefully through the next door. "As it turns out, this gave me a way out of data containment after Mansfield had extracted my soul. The *Persephone* had been abandoned not far from the perimeter of the Winter Castle, which meant that the Smasher was within range. Granted, his form is rather graceless, and I hope not to keep it for very much longer. In our current situation, however, it's the most useful receptacle for my soul. And it has certain advantages. For example—"

With his free "hand," he punches through the nearest wall, creating a passageway that will allow them to quickly reach the perimeter of the Winter Castle. The boom echoes through the corridors. Security is likely to arrive soon; Abel's surprised it hasn't already.

Noemi touches the broad hull he has for a chest, the sensory dome he has for a head. Her hands seem so small against his new, massive bulk. "A home for your soul," she repeats, her voice trembling. "Your soul left your body, and now you're—you're free."

He thinks she may be close to tears. Perhaps she's merely overwhelmed, but Abel can imagine that this transformation might have certain theological aspects. "Do you consider my survival proof of the soul's survival after death?"

"I don't need proof for that," she says. The grainy gray image is clear enough for him to see her crooked smile— or perhaps he's filling the incomplete visual data with his own memories of her. Abel could never forget any of her expressions, any centimeter of her face. "Besides, this isn't like anything else that's ever happened in the history of the worlds. You're something humanity has never seen before."

In Abel's opinion, this has been true since his manufacture, but he elects not to point this out. His resurrection on Haven is not only unprecedented, but unanticipated.

If humanity doesn't know how to treat mechs with souls while they're alive, then they certainly cannot be trusted to preserve and protect those souls after the deaths of their physical bodies. Should Inheritors have to accept the mortality of the soul even if, for them, it would be avoidable? Ethicists will debate this without coming up with any definite answers for decades, if not centuries.

That would be fine, if Inheritors wouldn't be invented until centuries in the future. But Inheritors will exist very soon. They're already on the verge of being made. Gillian and Mansfield have a lab ready and waiting here inside the Winter Castle.

Within his cradled arm, Noemi tenses. "Someone's coming. *Lots* of someones." Abel's audio input is extremely weak, but he's begun to pick up slight vibrations in the floor. Noemi scrambles against him, making him think she's trying to escape, until he sees her level her blaster over his arm. "Just turn me to face them. I've got the rest."

Even with his limited vision, Abel can tell her aim is unsteady. Is she truly so upset?

Either way, her assistance is unnecessary. "Save your weapon's charge. We may need it later."

"But how do we—"

Three Queens and a Charlie burst from the next door, all of them fully functional, armed, and ready for combat. These are warrior models, designed to kill humans…

…but they're not much good against Smashers.

Abel spreads the broad mining claw he has for a hand and swats them aside. The mechs tumble across the room, slam into the far wall, and sprawl on the floor. Two of them have already deactivated, and the other two struggle to get up and return to the fight. Abel folds the claw into a fist and brings it down once on each mech, hard. After that, nothing remains but blood and wire.

Noemi shivers hard enough for his dull sensors to feel it. He says, "If it helps, don't look at them."

"Abel—" She sounds winded. "I've been killing mechs since I turned fifteen. This isn't anything new."

"Then why are you shaking?"

"I'm sick," she says. "Or breaking down. Whatever you'd call it. We don't know what's going wrong with me, or whether it has anything to do with the other mech breakdowns going on throughout the galaxy—I don't guess anyone *can* know—"

"You're lacking a software update," Abel says. "At least, that's the cause of the other breakdowns, and I suspect the tech implanted within you had the same expiration date."

"Wait, really?" Noemi seems confused. "How can every mech in the galaxy need updating?"

"Because Mansfield and Shearer stood to make a profit on it," Abel replies. "They've updated their own models, of course. If we can retrieve a destroyed mech from this area, I can probably determine and replicate the update."

She laughs weakly. "Is there anything you can't do?"

"At the moment, many things." Nor is Abel absolutely certain that he can fix what's wrong with Noemi. However, he suspects that mentioning this would count as being "terrible at comforting people."

"There's more that you don't know," she says, her voice

breaking. "Genesis is about to strike, using the Bellum Sanctum—"

"And the Liberty War will be won. Congratulations."

"You don't understand, Abel." Noemi looks up at him, and her voice is pleading. "We have to *stop Genesis*."

As he continues their journey back to Noemi's party's snowmobiles, she explains to him what Bellum Sanctum is. Abel had considered himself incapable of being further surprised by human savagery, but it seems he was wrong.

"If Earth hasn't listened to the warnings we sent and doesn't act until it's too late—or if Earth can't defend itself against a core disruptor at all—then we have to figure out some other way to stop this," she finally concludes. "I was wondering—you were the only one who could turn that engine on. How hard will it be to turn it off?"

"Vibrational stresses will still be extreme. As I understand it, mechs or more basic machines generally undertake this task. So I would be a natural candidate to deactivate the engine. I will, however, need my original body to do so, or at least one smaller and more dexterous than this." What is he to do, if he can't reclaim his body? Maybe he could upgrade the memory of a higher-capacity mech like a Queen or Item—but with these enormous, clumsy hands, he's not sure he'd be able to do that. "Burton Mansfield's occupation of my body is proving inconvenient not only to me but also to the billions of other people whose lives are at risk."

"It was so grotesque, seeing him in you—in your body." Noemi shudders.

"When did he tell you who he really was?" Abel hopes she hadn't kissed him yet. He would be very, very angry if he learned Mansfield had taken advantage of Noemi in that way.

"He didn't tell me. I knew it wasn't you in there. I'd realized that after just a few seconds." Noemi's voice has begun to tremble again, and this time he doesn't think it has anything to do with her health. "I know you, Abel. I know your soul, and it's sweeter and purer and better than any human soul I've ever encountered. I know you, I trust you, and I believe in you."

It's more than he ever dreamed he would hear from her. Beyond his wildest hopes. But Abel knows he must ask: "You aren't angry that I helped turn you into a hybrid mech? You don't think being a mech is 'less' than being a human?"

"No, I don't," Noemi says. "I got upset when Genesis came after you and you didn't listen to me. You have to get better at solving problems *with* me, not *for* me. But that never made me think less of you. I *couldn't* think less of you, and I don't ever want to leave you. Not ever again."

Abel isn't as certain. Yet the way she looks up at him, the expression in her eyes... surely that's reason to hope.

But the trembling isn't just emotion. Noemi is badly in

need of repair, and they're in hostile territory. They must hurry.

Rather than remind her of her illness, Abel says, "I look forward to kissing you when I'm once again in a body with nerve endings."

Noemi's laugh encourages him. "Yeah, a human-shaped body might come in handy for that."

This phrase is evocative of many possibilities, but Abel sorts them as lower priority.

Noemi, too, seems to be refocusing on the essentials of survival. "Harriet and Zayan came with me," she says. "Virginia and Ephraim, too. We're supposed to rendezvous back at the snowmobiles—if they haven't been captured, or gotten lost."

"I'll locate the others."

Lumbering to the nearest control panel, Abel interfaces with it and pulls up security video, sector by sector, flipping through it as quickly as his duller sensors will allow.

Area: Central laboratory. Gillian Shearer is furiously typing into a control panel as she shouts, *"I'm trying to open the hatches!"*

"Well, they're not opening!" says Mansfield's voice, via his comm link. *"I'm stuck in here with the junk, and I can't believe my own daughter doesn't have enough wherewithal to do something about it!"*

Apparently Mansfield's escape from the garbage is taking a while. Good.

"Alert security," Mansfield's voice continues. *"They should be on the lookout for that Vidal girl and a Smasher."*

Gillian frowns. *"A Smasher?"*

As entertaining as it would be to continue eavesdropping, Abel knows it's time to move on.

Area: Internal defense. Various Queens and Charlies stand in formation. There are two dozen—an intimidating number to fight, but not a large enough number for the total defense of the Winter Castle in the long term. He makes note of this for later.

Area: Repair and regeneration. In this room he sees empty mech tanks, which are waiting to incubate Inheritors. The next step in mech development, mechs who will be able to procreate and feel emotion. Who will have souls. Each of them will have a Directive One buried deep within their programming, and they'll have to obey it—and Mansfield, no doubt. No human law will prevent it, and no human will care. They will have to surrender their bodies, their lives, on command.

Organic mechs aren't the future of cybernetics, Abel thinks. *They are the future of slavery.*

But he must move on.

Area: Refuse processing. Burton Mansfield wades through the sludge and muck accumulated at the bottom of the

Winter Castle, sopping wet and filthy, and clearly furious. This view is a waste of 0.021 seconds, as Abel knows none of the members of Noemi's party are there—but he doesn't regret looking.

Area: Climatological research. Harriet and Zayan dart through one of the doors, keeping their backs to the wall.

Area: Kitchen 4. Virginia and Ephraim sneak between two tables. As they hurry by, Virginia grabs a frosted pastry from a platter and starts munching.

"Located," he tells Noemi.

"Then signal them," she says. "Let them know it's time to get the hell out of here."

• • •

Abel reaches the snowmobile bay first, Noemi in his arms, which proves fortunate. When Zayan and Harriet run in, they reach for their weapons. Only Noemi's presence keeps them from firing. (A Smasher hull would withstand significant blaster damage, but they might've accidentally struck Noemi in the process.) Even with her there to help him explain, they find his transition...difficult to comprehend.

"*This* is Abel," Zayan repeats. "This big mining thing right here?" He knocks against the metal "chest" for emphasis, which Abel finds somewhat impolite but not worth mentioning.

"It is me," Abel promises. "For instance, I know that you

found the floating food at Montgolfier extremely repellent, and that if you and Harriet fulfill your plans of having a child someday, you particularly like the names Swathi and Martin."

Harriet's face lights up, and she squeezes Zayan's hand. "I like Martin, too." Her biggest grin is reserved for Abel. "Welcome back from the dead, if that's the right term."

"It will do for now." He recalls Robin Mansfield, still trapped in an afterlife that is no life at all. He intends to keep his oath to set her free, but he must get Noemi to safety first.

Noemi sags against him, her limbs limp. The shock of Mansfield's attack and his rescue must've sent adrenaline coursing through her body, keeping her alert. Now it's worn off, and her weakened condition is clear. She murmurs, "We have to wait for—"

Blaster fire down the corridor startles the humans. Abel redirects his audio input in time for Ephraim's voice to echo through the corridor: "Come on! Move!"

"I'm moving!" Virginia shrieks, the last word almost obscured by more blasters and the pounding of footsteps.

As ever, Noemi rallies for combat. "Harriet, Zayan, get on a snowmobile and go! We'll be right behind you."

"No." Abel deposits her on a snowmobile and motions to Harriet to take the controls. "You can't help Ephraim and Virginia in your condition. I should be more than capable of defending them on the way out."

"But—" Noemi starts to protest, then goes pale. She sways sideways and catches herself just as Harriet hops aboard the snowmobile. Zayan's already on another one, understanding how short time is. Still, Noemi can't quite give up her need to fight. "I don't want to leave them behind."

Abel says, "You aren't. I'm still here."

Harriet guns the engine, and the snowmobile zips forward. Noemi grabs Harriet's waist, allowing herself to be taken away. She must feel even worse than she's letting on. Zayan's right behind them, and within 3.72 seconds, both snowmobiles have zoomed through the open bay doors, into the brilliant light reflected from the snow.

Immediately afterward Ephraim runs in, sweating and breathing hard. Abel decides explanations will take too long. Instead, he sweeps Ephraim up in one claw, giving him a shake that sends his blaster tumbling to the floor.

"What the hell?" Ephraim yells. He struggles to free himself, which proves to be impossible. Abel spreads the other arm wide, ready to catch Virginia when she comes through.

She doesn't.

Instead, he hears a security door sliding shut.

Virginia's voice comes through Ephraim's commlink. *"The door is blocked, so I'm going to go deeper in. See if I can't mess this place up from the inside out."*

"No!" Ephraim fights even harder to escape Abel's grasp. "Virginia! Don't do this!"

"*Too late, buddy.*" She cackles with what sounds like genuine glee. "*I can't get out, so I'm going to do some serious espionage before they catch me.*"

How like Virginia, Abel thinks, to turn a no-win scenario into a chance to cause mayhem. The plan is too risky, and he would physically remove her by force if he could—but without knowing her location, he can't.

He *can* tell that another two mechs are bursting through a side door—and the portal to the outside is grinding shut. If he's going to get Ephraim to safety, he has to go now.

He has to leave Virginia behind.

Abel turns and runs to the door. Blaster fire scores his back, but he keeps going. There's nothing to do but save those he can.

31

THE WIND BUFFETS NOEMI'S FACE, HOWLS IN HER EARS.
She can see nothing but a pale sky above and white snow
below. Harriet is only a dark warm shadow she's holding
on to to keep herself from floating away from this body,
this planet, until she's nothing but a soul.

Like Abel, she thinks through a haze. *Just like Abel.*

Through the rush of air around her she hears distant
blaster fire. The soldier inside her reawakens, pulling her
back into the here and now. They're escaping from the
Winter Castle, and she can't fall apart yet.

Harriet curves sharply as she brings the snowmobile to
a stop near the makeshift Vagabond hospital. The curving
motion sends a flume of snow spraying out around them.
The sudden stop dizzies Noemi all over again. She closes
her eyes, takes a deep breath, and only then climbs off.

A few seconds behind them is Zayan. His snowmobile

halts close enough to send snow flying; the cool speckles against Noemi's hot cheek feel good. She must be feverish. Through the spangling of snowflakes on her eyelashes, she sees him run to Harriet. The two of them embrace tightly, and it hits Noemi how much they must care about Abel. Risking their own lives would be one thing, but they're willing to risk each other. That's so much harder.

Noemi takes one step back and wobbles on uncertain ground. It's not much of a tilt, but she loses her balance completely and topples back into the thick snow. Directly above her, one of Haven's largest moons is full, occupying almost a quarter of the afternoon sky. She stares up at it, breathing deeply, trying to regather her strength. *You're almost done. Abel's going to get out of there—the part of him that matters, anyway—and once you're all safe, you can rest. You can be healed. Abel's body can be regained later. Just keep going.*

"Noemi?" Delphine kneels by her side. "Are you okay?"

"Just dizzy," Noemi says as she lets Delphine help her sit up, then stand. Her knees feel watery, and pain shoots through her spine as though someone has sliced her nerves, but she keeps her soldier's reserve on her face. The others have worried about her enough.

"There!" Zayan yells, pointing to the Winter Castle. "There they are!"

Relief proves nearly as overwhelming as her fall. Noemi's head reels, but she hangs on to Delphine's arm. Her vision is slightly sharper than before—that thing in her head processing the messages from her eyes in more detail—so she can make out the enormous gray Smasher churning through the snow, its legs folded down into tank treads, its domed head pulled down to minimize any damage from blaster fire, though the green bolts barely scathe it. *Abel's in that thing*, she thinks, and it's so beautiful and horrible and funny that her heart can barely contain it all.

In Abel's arm she spots a human shape: Ephraim Dunaway, who looks like no more than a doll held in the huge Smasher claw.

Abel holds no one else.

"Virginia?" Noemi says, her voice tremulous. "Do you guys see Virginia?"

Zayan looks stricken. Harriet pulls up a set of distance goggles and peers through them; when her face falls, Noemi knows the answer.

Surely Abel wouldn't have left the Winter Castle without Virginia unless—

All the white surrounding Noemi turns black. Horror swallows her whole. This time, when she falls, she doesn't even feel it—just hears the crunch of her body in the snow, and Delphine calling her name from far away. She manages to open her eyes for a moment, but all she sees above her is that enormous moon. It's not bright anymore. The moon is black, and it's erasing the sun.

. . .

She comes to in some shadowy place, not as cold as before yet still not entirely warm. Noemi turns her head, trying to focus on her surroundings, but it's difficult.

"Hey, hey, take it easy." A shape comes close enough for her to make it out: Ephraim Dunaway, wearing his medical scrubs and a worried expression. "Can you hear me, Noemi?"

Her mouth is dry. She has to swallow before she can answer. "Where is this?"

"This is the *Persephone*. Sick bay. Abel led us here."

How could she not even recognize the room? She's been here so many times. She thinks she's lying on the same bed where Esther died. *Abel cleaned that room up for me so I wouldn't have to see Esther's blood. That wasn't programming; that was Abel's soul at work. Why couldn't I see it back then?*

"Noemi?" Ephraim pulls her back to the here and now. "The Vagabonds turned over a couple of deactivated mechs—they managed to take the mechs down during the fight over the 'distraction' ships. Abel's guided me through extracting what we think is the update that would fix you. Unfortunately, we haven't really been able to test it—but

I think we have to go ahead and try it. Your condition is deteriorating faster by the minute."

She knows he's right. The danger to her body and her sanity throbs in every cell. "Okay."

Ephraim is already preparing some kind of sensors to stick onto her skin. "You're going to be unconscious for a while, I think. Maybe the better part of a day."

That's time they don't have, Noemi knows—but what else can they do?

The memory of Ephraim in Abel's Smasher grip jolts her into sharper awareness. "Where's Abel?"

Ephraim doesn't look up from his hurried preparations. "In the docking bay. He's too big to fit in any other part of the ship."

The rest of her memory catches up, and terror seizes her. "Oh, God. Virginia? What's happened to Virginia?"

She expects the worst. Instead, Ephraim groans as if in exasperation. "Virginia couldn't make the exit rendezvous, so she decided to hide inside the Winter Castle and wreck it from the inside. Which is a terrible move if I ever heard of one, but she didn't give us a chance to argue. We haven't heard anything else yet."

Noemi feels a wave of relief—*Virginia's not dead!*—but then is worried all over again. What in all the worlds does Virginia think she can do from inside the Castle?

But then Ephraim's pulling a mask over Noemi's nose

and mouth, the air turns sweetly strange, and it suddenly seems like a very good time to go to sleep.

· · ·

When Noemi awakens again, she instantly knows her treatment is over and that it went well. She feels better than she has in weeks—better, even, than she did when she was last fully human. Blinking away her grogginess, she props herself up on her elbows. The motion comes easily, and the shooting pain along her nerves has vanished.

She's still in sick bay, wrapped in blankets on a biobed. In one corner sits Harriet, paging through something on her dataread. The colorful ribbons woven through her braids strike Noemi with their vividness, which makes her realize her eyesight has become even sharper. What other abilities might have been enhanced by her cybernetic nervous system, now that it's fully integrated with the rest of her? The thing attached to her brain still speaks, but instead of screeching data at her, it's a soft whisper, one she can tune into or tune out as she chooses. Her body is no longer at war with itself. It has fully become—

What it was meant to be, she thinks. *What I was meant to be.*

Harriet catches sight of her. "You're awake! Thank goodness. We were starting to wonder if that update hadn't done the trick after all."

"Where's Ephraim?" Noemi says, propping up on her elbows.

"He's back down on Haven, helping with the medical efforts down there. He's been checking in every few hours."

If Ephraim's "down" on Haven… "Where are we?"

"Parked on one of the larger moons in this system. The Winter Castle sent out a few scout mechs, and we thought it was better to get the *Persephone* out of range. How do you feel?"

"Good. Pretty great, really." Noemi sits up straight before she asks, "Have we heard anything from Virginia?"

Harriet's face falls. "Not yet. But the Winter Castle hasn't said they've caught her either. For sure Mansfield and Shearer would've tried to use her as a bargaining chip if they had her in custody. Maybe she's lying low."

Maybe. Noemi wishes there were some way to know for sure.

Harriet must see how afraid Noemi is for Virginia, because she says, "Abel's still down in the docking bay. Maybe you should say hi, if you're feeling up to it?"

Being with Abel seems like the only real comfort in the worlds. "Good plan."

Noemi slips on a robe over her medical gown and heads down the long corridor to the docking bay. When she steps through the air lock, the bay looks much as it did before—much of its space taken up by the huge gray bulk of a Smasher sitting within. The difference is, this time the Smasher turns to her.

"Harriet told me you were awake," Abel says. His new voice is flat and metallic, not human at all, without much expression. Knowing him as she does, though, Noemi senses the feeling behind it. "It's good to see you again."

"I wanted you with me. Of course you couldn't come; you wouldn't even fit through the door, but—I wanted you anyway."

Abel hesitates, then holds out one huge claw. Noemi wraps her hand around one of the "fingers," hoping his sensors are sharp enough to feel some of it.

"I'm sorry I had to leave Virginia behind," he says. "She never came close enough for me to talk with, much less bring along."

"I know. There's nothing else you could've done." She takes a deep breath, her mind full of memories. At the moment she thinks of the first night she and Virginia sat up together, talking under the string lights in the Razers' hideout. That was when Noemi realized that behind all her slang and bravado, Virginia Redbird was really very lonely.

"She can't survive down there long," Noemi says quietly. "Even if Virginia can keep from getting caught, she hasn't had the Cobweb protocol. Haven's environment is toxic to her. In another couple of days, she'll collapse."

Abel nods; the hinges beneath his domed head creak. "I

don't imagine it's much consolation, but—Virginia knew the risks. She made her own choices."

Tears well in Noemi's eyes, and she wipes them away with the back of her free hand. "I wish I could hug you. I wish I could burrow down in your arms away from everything, just for a little while."

"You could—but it wouldn't offer the same psychological comfort." Abel peers down at his massive metal body. "Humans need the touch of other humans. I can't give you that."

"Just for the time being," Noemi insists. "We'll get your body back somehow. We have to."

"It may well be a matter of galactic significance." Abel may have a little Mansfield ego in him, because he seems to enjoy counting these points off: "Genesis will destroy planet Earth, and billions of lives along with it, if the Bellum Sanctum strategy is not stopped. The strategy cannot be stopped unless the core disruptor is de-powered. The only way to cut power to the core disruptor is by shutting down the engine. Shutting down the engine would be dangerous if not fatal to a human, so only a mech can do it. Genesis doesn't use mechs, and Remedy's are breaking down, which means the only mech available to shut it down is me. However, my current body wouldn't even fit through the tunnels to the engine controls."

Noemi thinks hard. "I don't suppose Mansfield and

Shearer are too worried about any of their friends or possessions on Earth. The other colony worlds will make them rich buying Mansfield Cybernetics mechs all on their own. So we can't talk them into handing your body over for the greater good."

"Highly unlikely," Abel agrees. "Mansfield could potentially shut the engines down himself, now that he has mech-level dexterity, but he would be extraordinarily unlikely to accept that risk, even for the benefit of billions of others."

"Selfish bastard," Noemi mutters.

That makes Abel cock his head. "Burton Mansfield's parents, Charlton and Ann, were married at the time of his birth, and for that matter at the time of his conception. However, in the metaphorical sense, your statement is true. He is a *very* selfish bastard."

It sounds like Abel's reporting the results of a data analysis. Noemi would laugh if the situation weren't so dire.

Instead, she forces herself to concentrate. "So, we have to steal your body back, whether by stealth or by attack. Which plan has the best chance of success?"

"Uncertain. I'm afraid I don't have the same computational capacity at the present." Abel's flat metallic voice sounds almost apologetic. "While I have enough memory in this Smasher unit to contain my consciousness, I can't simultaneously run high-level calculations."

"And I'm not quite enhanced enough for that, am I?"

Noemi wants to groan. She's too mech to live on Genesis, but not enough mech to save Earth.

"Merely in general terms," Abel says, "another assault on the Winter Castle seems inadvisable, at least until our tactical situation has changed. At this time, we have only ourselves and our minimal weaponry, and our only allies are Vagabonds on Haven, who don't have the resources to break through the Castle's security."

Noemi's gut drops as she realizes how right he is. *If Genesis knew what we're trying to do, they'd send starfighters to blow the* Persephone *to atoms. We tried to tell Earth we're helping them, but as far as we can tell, they've ignored us. Cray, Kismet, and Stronghold have their own problems, and besides, there's not enough time to negotiate with three different planets.*

As for the Krall Consortium, they betrayed Abel and sent him to what they thought would be his death. They can't trust Dagmar Krall.

Can't trust Dagmar Krall, she thinks again. Would any members of the Consortium agree?

Abel continues, "There is, of course, the chance that your earlier warnings to Earth have borne fruit, and they will manage to mount an effective defense against the Bellum Sanctum device. But given Earth's intransigence in the past, I suspect they were not convinced."

Slowly Noemi says, "When Krall sold you out, did she hide her actions from the rest of the Consortium?"

If Abel's jarred by the change of topic, he shows no sign. "Upon consideration, I believe she did. Few ships were in the vicinity when I was handed over to Genesis custody."

Loyalty matters to Vagabonds. Oaths have meaning there. Promises are meant to be as binding as law. "The other Vagabonds wouldn't like finding out one of their own had been betrayed, would they?"

"Even Krall herself didn't like it," Abel says. "My mech status did not seem to affect her judgment of me, or the other Vagabonds' either."

"That's not quite where I'm going with this." Noemi drums her fingers along her leg, excitement brewing as her idea takes shape. "I think I might have a plan."

"You do?" Abel sounds so puzzled. Later, maybe, she'll be thrilled that she finally got a step ahead of him.

"I do," she says slowly. "I think it's time the Vagabonds of the Consortium learned just what Dagmar Krall's capable of."

32

HARRIET'S MESSAGE IS PURELY TEXT:

There's never been any official "Vagabond Code," but if there were, it would say that we stick together. We can't trust Earth, and we can't trust any grounders to understand our way of life—so we have to be able to trust each other. Among Vagabonds, our word is our bond. Or at least, that's how it used to be. Dagmar Krall doesn't seem to think so anymore.

Ask around—anyone who was on the Katara *that day will tell you that Abel, captain of the free ship* Persephone, *was initiated into the Krall Consortium.*

But then Krall sold him out to Genesis.

She'll tell you she did that for Genesis's sake. For the alliance. For the survival of the Consortium itself. But what kind of "alliance" forces us to betray our own? Who's really in charge here? Does Dagmar Krall intend to turn our Consortium into simple cannon fodder for Genesis?

If you're better than that—if you're still loyal to your

fellow Vagabonds—come to the Haven Gate. We claim the right of challenge!

As political rhetoric goes, Abel thinks, it's not bad. It both stokes anger and touches upon the Vagabonds' core values, while gracefully omitting the information that Genesis wants Abel for a crime he did in fact commit. He wonders whether, in a slightly different lifetime, Harriet might've ended up in politics. Her message is marked only for Vagabond vessels; it will start with those in the Earth system and then be spread by them through the one unstoppable communications relay in the galaxy: gossip.

Zayan's message includes video. He stands on the *Persephone* bridge, dressed in vibrant Vagabond clothes, head held high as though he did this every day.

"Dagmar Krall's betrayal of one of our own is a betrayal of us all. When we swore oaths to the Consortium, we swore to protect every Vagabond within it. Not to protect Genesis—to protect each other. These promises don't seem to mean much to Krall anymore. All Consortium ships are hereby summoned to the Haven Gate, inside the Haven system. We claim the right of challenge! If the Katara fails to appear, Krall has forfeited—and we will choose another leader, one who remembers the meaning of a promise!"

Zayan's delivery isn't as polished as Harriet's text, but the message is even more pointed. This one will be routed through regular comm relays, which means even isolated

Vagabonds, those beyond the reach of the Consortium, will see it. Abel thinks a few of these ships will arrive at the rendezvous, too, if only out of curiosity.

The "right of challenge" has only ever been ceremonial, according to Harriet and Zayan. It's mentioned in the oaths new Consortium members take—Abel remembers that much—but it was almost a joke between Dagmar Krall and her followers, a promise that she wouldn't turn into a tyrant.

This joke is about to become uncomfortably real, at least for her.

For lack of anything else to do, Abel reviews these messages repeatedly, from the docking bay, the only part of the *Persephone* his new, bulky body will fit into. He isn't uncomfortable—the Smasher form is impervious to pain—but he's getting rather bored.

When he was trapped in the equipment pod bay all those years, he entertained himself as best he could with his considerable internal resources. He replayed *Casablanca* over and over in his head, the perfect memories as good as watching it on a screen. He reviewed great works of literature stored in his databanks. He ran different battle simulations for many famed historical Earth conflicts, from Thermopylae to World War IV's climactic Siege of St. Louis. Mathematical proofs, various plans for helping his creator escape cryosleep, composing formulae for thirty-dimensional spheres—it had occupied Abel's mind reasonably well.

Which is to say, it wasn't nearly enough to fill thirty years of isolation. It was enough to keep him from going mad, no more.

Abel has company to talk to this time—especially Noemi. But the humans on board can't spend all their time chatting with him; they have a ship to run. Which means he's stuck down here, profoundly bored.

The problem is that he installed enough memory in this Smasher to contain his consciousness—but only barely. There's no surplus, nothing for him to use on such elaborate mental pursuits. He's uncomfortably aware that even the slightest memory degradation in this unit will result in serious and probably permanent damage to his mind.

This is just one more of the many reasons he needs his body back.

Soon, he promises himself as he shuffles sideways to sit in another of the three positions available to him. At least it changes his vantage point. *You'll return to Haven and reclaim your body before long.*

If he could find hope in that equipment pod bay, surely he can find it within a Smasher.

● ● ●

Several hours later, Noemi returns to the docking bay. She's wearing her simple black utilitarian garb again, and by now her hair has grown back in. It's still extremely short, but not too short to get rumpled. Even through his grainy vision, Abel can tell that she looks like herself again: determined, alert, strong. This is the Noemi he fell in love with.

The impending challenge threatens them; so does the greater war. Until they've overcome these dangers, he must find hope where he can.

"Hello there," Noemi says. Her smile is wistful. "I miss your face."

"I miss many parts of my body."

She laughs. "I bet you do."

Was that perhaps a double entendre? Abel hopes so. It would be good to feel that he was making some progress in learning how to flirt.

Though in this body, there's a limit to how much progress he can make. It's like trying to be sexy while wearing a bulldozer.

On the nearby control panel screen, Noemi brings up the same image Harriet and Zayan must see on the bridge—the space just within the Haven system, the Gate an enormous circle of silver in the background. Blurry as the black-and-white, two-dimensional is for Abel, he can make out the basic elements of the scene.

As they'd predicted, a large group of Vagabond ships—hundreds, if not thousands—has already gathered. Some of these are vessels filled with would-be migrants to Haven, stalled by the size of the gathering and the uncertainty of what's going on. Others have responded to the messages that were sent out, expressing their dissatisfaction with Krall's disloyalty. Probably some ships are here only to rubberneck; the showdown to come will fuel galactic gossip for years to come.

At least a few of them must have come to defend Krall. Abel imagines they'll find out which ones soon enough.

Noemi says, "Long-range scans show the *Katara* approaching. It's showtime."

No sooner has she spoken than comms begin to chime. From her place beside Abel, Noemi opens a channel. "Am I speaking to Dagmar Krall, the supposed defender of the Vagabonds?"

The screen shifts to an image of Krall on her bridge. Her hair, normally worn free, is severely tied back into a knot. Given his current lack of visual clarity, Abel cannot determine her expression.

This conversation isn't between the two ships alone; every Vagabond ship that wants to listen in can do so.

(Given human curiosity, he imagines most of them want to.)

"*Yes*," comes the defiant reply. "*This is Dagmar Krall, leader of the Krall Consortium, and I demand to know who dares—*"

"Who dares call you out for what you actually did?" Noemi cuts in. "That would be me, Noemi Vidal. Vidal of Genesis."

"*Then you should appreciate that what I did was part of the pact between my Consortium and Genesis. That it was necessary to protect my people.*"

"Oh, like you protected Abel?" Noemi folds her arms. "The guy you welcomed into your group and then betrayed? Wasn't he one of 'your people'?"

Krall meets her gaze without flinching. "*Yes. I did that to Abel. I regret that it was necessary, but I had no other choice.*"

Abel, who's hulking just out of sight, is discouraged. They'd hoped to provoke Krall into reacting harshly and unwisely, which would further weaken her authority. Instead, Dagmar Krall sits as straight as a queen on her throne.

She continues, "*My first duty is to the Vagabonds in my Consortium. Their first need is a place for them and their families to call home once their spacefaring is done. I doubt any one of them would hesitate to sacrifice their lives to give a home to all the others; certainly I wouldn't. One life is a small price to pay for the prosperity of thousands.*"

Fishing for loyalty. Praising her people. *Krall's clever,* Abel thinks.

Noemi's clever, too. "Easy for you to say when it was Abel's life on the line, not yours. And it's not smart, putting all your trust in Genesis, because Genesis doesn't trust you. *Any* of you. Trust the one person here who grew up on Genesis and understands the culture. Outsiders aren't welcome."

"*The Elder Council has made us promises,*" Krall says. "*They've offered us places to live.*"

With a shrug, Noemi replies, "Maybe some members of the Consortium will find homes there, but most of you will always be 'offworlders,' and the current leadership will find any excuse it can to throw you out."

"*We won the Battle of Genesis. They owe us for that.*"

Noemi shrugs. "I'm the one who brought you into the alliance in the first place. I've served Genesis my entire life. But they threw me offworld when they realized I'd—that I'd had too many artificial organs implanted for them to consider me human anymore."

It's not the whole truth, Abel thinks, but it is as close as Noemi can get without an overly long digression. The point she's making is fundamentally true.

Noemi adds, "If Genesis isn't willing to let one of their own wounded soldiers live there, how likely do you think they are to welcome *you*?"

"*That's a chance we have to take,*" Krall says. Her voice has taken on an edge. "*How much longer does Earth have? Not even a century, according to most estimates. Billions and billions of people have to find other homes, and most of the worlds of the Loop can't house enough of them. Haven, down there— those of us who've had Cobweb might find a future there, but that's a minority. A new Gate is being built in the Kismet system, but who knows if the planet on the other side will even*" *be habitable? For the large majority of us, Genesis is our only hope. We have to trust them, and you'll forgive me if I can't endanger the future of my people for the sake of one mech.*"

The signal crackles with interference. Abel would frown if he had a mouth. Interference is odd, this far away from a planet with no mass communications systems yet. Either there's been a sudden surge in solar flares or—

—or someone is deliberately interfering.

In the background of the *Persephone* bridge, Harriet whispers, "Oh, crikey."

Zayan must've split the screen views, because at the bottom, Abel now sees a small group of exosuited warrior mechs on approach from Haven, pointing directly at the *Persephone* like an arrow of steel.

"*Transmission to all vessels within Haven system,*" says an artificial, metallic voice. A number appears on-screen, suggesting the rough amount of credits it would take to purchase a small moon. "*That's for the ship that brings proof of the destruction of the* Persephone."

Noemi's fingers cut the audio just in time for her to mutter, "Ooooookay. Turns out there's a flaw in our plan. A *major* one."

"I doubt Gillian Shearer has foreseen our greater strategy," Abel says. "Mansfield's probably only trying to kill me. Given my actions and statements within the Winter Castle, Professor Mansfield must have realized my soul survived. He knows I'll attempt to regain my body, which means he won't feel safe until he knows he's obliterated me completely."

Krall's voice comes through comms, though she's not speaking to the *Persephone*, only to her Consortium at large. *"Everyone hold. That's an order. We're not bounty hunters, especially not for the likes of the people who tried to steal Haven from the galaxy."*

"Maybe you aren't," says another voice, coming from the captain of one of the many ships swarmed near. *"For that amount of money? It's worth changing careers."*

"Same here!" yells another.

"Oh no," Noemi mutters. "No, no, no."

But her protests are useless. Abel can see two ships peeling off from the Consortium, heading in his direction. Another ship follows—then another.

Noemi opens the channel to the bridge. "How many hostiles are we looking at?"

Zayan answers, *"We've only got a couple dozen coming in for the attack—the rest are obeying Krall, which is a good thing, I guess? But it would only take one of them to blow us to smithereens. What are we going to do?"*

"We evade and see if we can't pick up some defenders." Noemi half turns to the door, then looks back at Abel. "If you even think about tossing yourself out an air lock or some other heroic-sacrifice crap, I swear to God I'll make you regret it."

"No heroic-sacrifice crap," he promises. "Got it."

For an instant, Noemi almost smiles. But then she rushes through the air lock door, once again becoming a soldier preparing for battle.

Abel lowers himself as much as he can in this bulky body, the better to study the screen that shows the battle. The *Persephone* is unarmed. Twenty-six—no, twenty-seven Vagabond ships are incoming, with a variety of weapons and shielding. That would mean nothing if the *Katara* would defend them; the *Katara* is a massive ship with many weapons and a near-impenetrable hull. But for the moment, Dagmar Krall remains out of the fight, unwilling to fire on her own people.

The *Persephone* cannot possibly defend itself.

Abel can envision flight patterns that could help keep them alive, but no human pilot—even an experienced pilot and mech hybrid like Noemi—would be able to implement the course changes quickly enough.

He could, if only his current body weren't so clumsy and large.

If only his body were something else altogether...

But it can be.

Abel reaches out through the Tether, seeking contact. Soon he senses something with the comm bandwidth and memory to hold his consciousness—the largest, most active input on the ship.

Which *is* the ship.

He imagines the propeller plane from *Casablanca* once more. It worked last time—and it works again. His consciousness leaves the Smasher and flows into its new home, like fresh blood pumping through unfamiliar veins. Every circuit, every part, becomes one with Abel, his new machine body.

I no longer own the Persephone, he thinks. *I am the* Persephone.

When he locates the sensors, he looks through them and can see again—this time in stunning detail and range, more than he ever could in his original body. He can even see in multiple directions at once. He brings more and more systems out of automatic mode until they're under his direct control. The deep chill of outer space surrounds him, but without damage or pain; the sensation is delightful.

Internal sensors—check. He can see the bridge now, where Noemi, Zayan, and Harriet are all in various states of panic. "Each system is going down, one after the other!" Zayan shouts. "What the hell is going on?"

"Maybe they're scrambling our signals?" Noemi takes the captain's chair, desperate to regain control. She doesn't yet know she's in safe hands.

Abel finally finds the engines. He would've thought they would seem roughly analogous to his legs or feet, a means of locomotion. Instead, it's their fire he feels, blossoming in the place he thinks of as his heart.

33

EVERY CONTROL LIGHT AND DISPLAY ON THE BRIDGE flares brighter, then dims, erratic changes without meaning. Noemi's gut drops. She has no idea what's happening to the *Persephone*, but it doesn't take a master pilot to figure out that your ship controls going haywire is an extremely bad sign.

"We've got three enemy vessels coming in fast," Harriet says, as evenly as any combat pilot. "Any ideas?"

Noemi jabs at the controls, but the helm's not responding. The *Katara* and the array of other ships around them still aren't attacking, but they're not moving in to defend the *Persephone* either.

I knew our plan was a gamble, but I thought we'd make it a little further than this!

Her primary goal hadn't even been to start a fight with Krall or anyone else, only to reveal the true reason not to trust Genesis—but it doesn't look like Noemi will get a chance to say so. They went straight from posturing to arguing to *this*.

The ship's mag engines flare to full power. She turns to ops, where Zayan sits, and he shrugs in confusion. If he didn't make that happen, the ship did it itself, and as far as Noemi knows, the next thing it might do is explode.

Instead, the *Persephone* accelerates straight toward the attacking ships.

Both Harriet and Zayan cry out. Noemi's battle training lets her stay calm on the outside, but tells her that within a couple of seconds, they're going to smash themselves to atoms—

The *Persephone* banks at the last moment, skimming low across the largest enemy ship's surface. Noemi startles when she sees a small weapons array in front of them on that ship's hull, anticipating the collision. But the array turns out to be too lightweight to stop the *Persephone*. They smash right through it before taking a sharp left to hit another array, then whipping around the side of the ship to knock an entire weapons array loose from its moorings. Impact warnings light up the ops panel across from her, but even from her place at the helm, Noemi can tell the *Persephone* has taken only the most minor damage.

As for the other ships, they're holding fire. They can't shoot at the *Persephone* without hitting the other ship, too, and Vagabond loyalty is too strong for that.

We're...okay, Noemi thinks in bewilderment. *How are we okay?*

Then on the bridge viewscreen, superimposed in the same typeface for a text-only message, appear the words HOW AM I DOING?

"Abel," she breathes. "*Abel*'s doing this!"

Harriet hasn't quite caught up. "How's Abel flying the ship from the docking bay?"

Noemi's grinning more than she has in a long time. Maybe ever. "He's not flying the ship. He *is* the ship."

A soul can't be chained, she thinks. *The soul is limitless. That makes it more powerful than any physical body can ever be.*

They bank again, skimming along the bottom of the *Katara*, using Krall's ship as their shield. Zayan whoops out loud, and Harriet begins to laugh.

Abel has done it all. Noemi thinks it's the closest thing to a miracle she's ever seen.

The new part of her brain whispers that she could get even closer to this miracle, if she's ready.

Taking a deep breath, Noemi closes her eyes and opens her mind—reaching out with her own tech, trying to make wireless contact with the ship. She won't be able to claim it the way Abel seems to have done; she still needs her body. But maybe she could potentially tap into some functions, sense what's going on even if she can't control it....

In the darkness behind her eyelids, a sort of reality

begins to take shape—if shape is the right word. She can sense it around her, know its dimensions, but it's not the sort of thing she can see. Maybe this is how bats perceive things through sonar. Regardless, Noemi is surrounded by the inner intelligence of the *Persephone*, fording rivers of power and data, feeling it flow past. Her physical body still exists—is still in place in her seat at ops—but that reality seems trivial compared to the digital one.

A flicker of energy curls around her—warms her, surrounds her—

Abel?

—Of all the gin joints in all the world, she had to walk into mine—

She can't laugh here, but she thinks he senses her joy. *Show me how to steer this thing.*

—An excellent plan—

The exact sensation is indescribable, but to Noemi it seems sort of as if Abel were standing behind her at the helm, his body warm against hers, his hands caressing her arms all the way down until their fingers entwine. They move together, as one, sending the *Persephone* soaring around to shield itself with the *Katara*. The ship skims close to the *Katara*'s surface, so much so that no Vagabond ships can fire on them without risking the *Katara*, too. Even the Vagabonds who don't belong to the Consortium don't want to risk the wrath of Dagmar Krall.

This is the perfect strategy, she thinks.

—Perfection is impossible in reality. This is, however, extremely effective—

Noemi's never been this close to anyone. It's not about bodies, since Abel doesn't have one. She hasn't had sex yet, but she already senses that any physical closeness would be only trying to mimic this intense intimacy between her and Abel—two minds separated by only the finest film of electrons. His love for her radiates through every circuit, every chip, and she knows he can feel hers, too.

Can he tell the difference between her programming and her heart? Can he show her the line between what she only feels because of Shearer's commands, and what she'll feel always?

—We mustn't forget to fly the ship—

Oh, right, we're in a battle.

She can sense Abel's amusement as he "steps back"— still tied to her, but turning his attention to other things. Noemi takes sole charge of the helm, in order to free him up.

Through sensors she can feel the point of an arrow— fighter mechs, coming at them, no doubt deployed by the Haven vessel. *Oh no,* she thinks. *Other ships can't target us when we're this close to the* Katara, *but Queens and Charlies can. Abel, can you stop them with one of those scrambler beams?*

—I'm not sure, Abel says. Being the ship while simultaneously using the beams—it's a complex set of tasks. Still, I suppose I must try—

But just then the arrow changes shape. It shifts from an arrow to a circle, just for two full seconds. Then the mechs fly straight toward the center of that circle, colliding with each other in one flash of destruction.

Did you do that? Noemi thinks.

—I did not, Abel replies. Perhaps the mechs received an aberrant signal from the Haven surface?—

Realization lights Noemi up like electricity. *Virginia! Virginia must've managed to tap into their signal! She's still alive and she's giving Shearer hell.*

Abel's satisfaction feels as warm around Noemi as a blanket. —Excellent. Now, back to more pressing concerns.—

Through the thin veil between them, she perceives Abel turning his attention to the ship's communications. He uses their system to interfere with the messages between the ships around them. After 3.1 seconds, she realizes he's amplifying and spreading the messages from ships angry with Dagmar Krall's decision to hand Abel over, but blocking every one of the assistance calls from the ships that chose to attack them. He's muffled the *Katara*, too. With Krall silenced at such a crucial time, will the thin edge of her authority become even thinner?

Noemi figures, *I guess this is how a mutiny begins.*

Then Abel switches, catching one of Krall's messages and reflecting it back at every other ship in the vicinity. From a great distance, she hears Krall say, "*The Katara commands every Consortium ship to stand down or be fired upon. You won't be warned again. Halt fire.*"

Wait, Noemi thinks, *I heard that. Like, with my ears—*

She startles back into the present, her awareness once again enclosed by her body. The abruptness of it catches her off guard, and Abel's sudden absence feels harsh and cold. But she forces herself to focus on the viewscreen, where Dagmar Krall sits in her command chair looking thunderstruck.

"Are you okay?" Harriet whispers to Noemi. "You zoned out for a couple minutes there."

Noemi gives her a quick nod before turning her attention to Krall, who's still talking. "*You have power over fighter mechs now? How is that possible?*"

It was Virginia who took over the fighter mechs, but Noemi doesn't intend to point that out. "We can talk about that later. I'm more interested in the fact that you don't seem to have power over your own Consortium any longer. How many ships broke ranks to attack? Looked like a lot of them."

"*Apparently my people aren't as willing to listen to me anymore. It seems clear that the challenge you've called will have to take place.*" Krall tugs at the end of one loose lock of hair; the slight tremble in her hand is the only hint of how shaken she is. *"I suppose it was inevitable that this issue might bring an end to our Consortium. It's hard to let it go—but it existed to serve its people, not to force people to serve."*

Against her will, Noemi is impressed. Dagmar Krall plans to surrender her power rather than do her followers wrong. That, or she's putting on a really good show of stepping away with grace.

Noemi flicks the control to send her own comm message out on all channels. "This is Noemi Vidal, temporarily in command of the free ship *Persephone*." Abel's still at work within the ship—more "in command" of it than any mere pilot ever could be—but that doesn't concern Krall or the Consortium. "Commodore Krall, the purpose of this confrontation was never to force you out of power within the Consortium. That's something for you guys to decide among yourselves, later."

Dagmar Krall stiffens, scowling like she'd bitten into a lemon. *"Then what the hell is this about?"*

"This is about Bellum Sanctum. About Genesis's endgame against Earth. We needed as many Vagabond ships as possible to hear this, and we especially wanted you to learn the truth," Noemi says. She and Abel discussed this next question intensely without ever coming to a conclusion, so asking it feels like a gamble. "Commodore, did you know exactly *how* Genesis plans to attack Earth?"

"*Of course. It's not something I can broadcast to the entire Consortium due to security concerns—as a former soldier of Genesis should know.*" Dagmar Krall shrugs. "*We expect them to deploy the strategy within days, and when that time comes, we'll be by their side.*"

The real deadline is closer to hours away, but Noemi understands why Krall is being vague. "I know you intend to keep faith with Genesis," Noemi says. "But Genesis hasn't kept faith with you. Commodore, you have to understand what the engine is really going to be used for."

Space comms traffic in the area has fallen almost completely silent. Every Vagabond gathered nearby, regardless of where they stand on the question of Dagmar Krall, wants to know what's about to unfold.

Noemi takes a deep breath. "Genesis isn't using that engine to power a massive communications breakdown. Instead, they're using it to power a core disruptor. And they plan to use that core disruptor on Earth itself."

Krall goes so white that Noemi thinks the woman might pass out that instant. Although Noemi can't hear the space chatter, the indicators go nuts, showing that everyone is trying to talk to everyone at once.

But they're still listening to Noemi, so she continues, "I have this information directly from my former captain. She has top military clearance; she's in a position to know the strategy, and I believe her. As a soldier of Genesis,

I can't condone this. The Liberty War has always been fought to preserve the best of what Genesis is and can be. This weapon desecrates all of that. As far as I'm concerned, destroying Earth isn't that different from destroying Genesis itself. I have to stop this from happening, and I need your help."

Silence lingers for a moment over channels; Krall is speaking quickly to her wife off audio, and probably every other ship's bridge is in turmoil. When Noemi meets Zayan's eyes, she's surprised to see he's tearing up. He's known the truth about Bellum Sanctum for a while, but apparently that doesn't make it any easier to hear. "I have family on Earth, you know," he says shakily. "Most Vagabonds do."

Finally, Krall cuts her audio channel back on. *"If I'd had any idea this was the plan—that this was even possible—I would never have assisted in the Bellum Sanctum strategy for a second, and neither would any other ship of my Consortium."*

Silently Noemi notes that Dagmar Krall seems to have taken her authority back. "The people of Genesis have been kept in the dark, too. This is the Council's plan, and it has to be stopped."

A male voice from another Vagabond ship calls, *"How do we do that? It's not like we can shoot down a core disruptor! Those things are well-nigh indestructible."*

Noemi nods. "Right, we can't shoot them down. But we're the ones who powered up the engine for the core disruptor. We have to shut it down again. Only a mech could do it, and the only mech we've got is Abel."

"*You mean, the only mech we had, until I turned him over to Genesis,*" Krall says heavily.

BY THE WAY, say Abel's large words on the viewscreen—words only she and the others on the *Persephone* bridge can see—THIS SEEMS LIKE A GOOD TIME TO MENTION THAT I'M STILL ALIVE.

Noemi smiles at the viewscreen—and by extension, the other hundreds of ships watching this. "We can still save Abel, which means Abel can still save Earth."

Krall doesn't hesitate. "*Tell me how.*"

We have our allies, Noemi thinks. *Now we're going to need a hell of a lot of luck.*

34

FOR A WHILE, ABEL SIMPLY ALLOWS HIS CONSCIOUSNESS to drift in the communications fields of the *Persephone*. It's interesting to take in all the information as it flows past him, and the plan Noemi and Krall have come up with is a solid one. He has no more need to interfere. He can simply listen as the commanders make plans for the next battle.

"*We haven't yet seen any signs that Earth is aware of the Bellum Sanctum strategy,*" Krall says, "*or that they've listened to the warning messages you sent.*"

"Just great," Noemi says with a sigh. "Typical Earthers, refusing to listen to anyone else, even when that anyone is trying to *save all their lives.*"

Upon reviewing the messages Noemi sent to Earth, Abel isn't surprised their government hasn't reacted. Her messages were lucid and compelling—but she had to send them into the void. Neither Noemi nor anyone else on the *Apollo Acestor* had any solid information about how to contact Earth's military command. They took the only logical step and sent data packets to most of Earth's major satellites. At least some of those satellites would've belonged to Earth's government...

...but the data collected would've been reviewed by George models. Georges are relatively intelligent, as standard mechs go, but they do not have imagination. They do not take initiative. They wouldn't have had any idea how to handle a message as unusual and radical as Noemi's warning.

Probably the Georges deleted the messages as corrupted files.

Dagmar Krall seems more optimistic than Noemi looks, or than Abel feels. *"It's possible they're taking defensive steps, only ones that we can't monitor from space."*

"It doesn't matter," Noemi says. "We can't assume Earth could stop Bellum Sanctum. So our plans don't change."

With a nod, Krall replies, *"Then let's get back to the plan to retrieve Abel. My ships will escort you guys to the Haven surface in case Gillian Shearer has some other tricks up her sleeve. Just get Abel back here in one piece, as fast as possible, okay?"*

Noemi smiles tiredly. "I intend to."

Abel begins steering the *Persephone* away from the Haven Gate, back toward the planet itself. Their mission no longer requires extreme levels of steering precision, which means his current berth within the AI of the *Persephone* itself is no longer as useful. He prepares to transfer his consciousness back into its former, more human-shaped receptacle, the better to carry out their strike against the Winter Castle.

He's getting ready to smash.

● ● ●

They run into no resistance on their way to the surface. Gillian Shearer is running low on mechs; by now she must be saving them for last-ditch defense within the Winter Castle itself.

That means they'll have to deal with those mechs eventually—but not yet.

Noemi and Abel reunite with Ephraim at the field hospital, still the closest they can safely get to the Winter Castle without being fired upon from within.

(Abel speculates that Mansfield might well be willing to fire on the hospital, but believes that if he does so, the residents within the Winter Castle will rebel. Already, Delphine and a few others have fled. Besides, if there were not discontent in the ranks, both Mansfield and Gillian would've taken far more ruthless steps before now.)

When he speculates as much, Delphine agrees. By now she's over the shock of finding Abel in a brand-new body, and seems to be adjusting to her new role at the hospital.

She's even been given a pair of medical scrubs, of which she seems very proud. "Most of us were desperate while we were stuck on the *Osiris*—shaken up by the crash, you know? As soon as we were in the Winter Castle, though, people started acting like *people* again. Those of us who left had help from some others who weren't ready to leave yet, but they weren't happy there either."

Noemi scowls. "You guys were ready to abandon people on Earth who needed another world to live on, but then you had to deal with a few hard rules and all of a sudden everybody cares?"

"It wasn't like that!" Delphine protests, then adds, in a quieter voice, "Mostly it wasn't."

In the tinny voice he has as a Smasher, Abel says, "Self-preservation is a basic human instinct, Noemi. It is natural to react more strongly to harm to one's self than to others. There is an old saying: 'Comedy is when you fall down the stairs. Tragedy is when I stub my toe.'"

"Ha, ha," Noemi says, straight-faced. "These people aren't worried about anything but saving their own skins."

Abel tries again, "One of this mission's core objectives is saving *my* skin, in an extremely literal sense. Am I being selfish?"

"No, of course not!" Noemi protests. "That's also about saving planet Earth!"

"Do you mean you wouldn't help me attempt to recover

my body if it didn't serve a greater good?" Abel trusts he's said enough to make his point.

He must have, because Noemi sighs deeply. "Okay." Instantly she's back in strategy mode. "Harriet and Zayan are staying put on the *Persephone* so we can evacuate quickly. Ephraim, are you sure you're willing to go back in the Castle?"

"Of course." Even through the grainy vision of a Smasher, Abel can tell that Ephraim Dunaway looks exhausted. He must've been working with patients nearly nonstop. "I remember the internal layout well enough. I can provide you with some cover."

Delphine steps forward. Despite her small size and high-pitched voice, she sounds startlingly authoritative. "Ephraim should stay here. The patients need him, and besides, he's not the best person to go."

"I understand," Noemi replies, "but we need to cover as much ground as possible inside the Win—"

"Right, I understand, you want at least three people to go in." Delphine begins slipping on a hyperwarm jacket almost absurdly too large for her. "Ephraim can stay here, because *I'm* your third."

For once Noemi appears to be at a loss for words. Abel ventures, "You almost certainly have no experience in covert operations."

This earns him a sharp look from Delphine. "Of course

I don't. What I do have is plenty of experience walking around the Winter Castle. I know the layout better than any of you. If you want a comprehensive search, I can help you more than Ephraim could."

With a frown, Ephraim says, "Do you know how to handle a blaster?"

"About as well as you do, unless there's a weapons training course in med school I don't know about," Delphine retorts. Ephraim has no reply.

Noemi finally says, "There's real risk involved with going inside. I can't guarantee your safety."

Delphine shakes her head. "I have family back on Earth, too, you know. They were supposed to evacuate to Kismet in a year or two, I thought—it seemed okay to leave on the *Osiris*. And now their lives are in danger while I'm half a galaxy away." Her voice trembles. "You know I'm the best guide inside the Winter Castle you could ever find. Please let me help."

"Okay, then. Me, Abel, and Delphine." Noemi claps her hands together, the sound muffled by her gloves. "Let's get started."

As they turn to go, Delphine begins giving Ephraim some datareads with patient info. Abel pauses, looking down at Noemi. She appears even more fragile to him now, compared to the enormous body he currently inhabits.

This plan puts her at risk, something he has learned to grudgingly accept but will never endure easily.

Abel reaches out to touch her shoulder; his enormous claw bumps her hard enough for her to stumble to one side. He pulls his hand back. "I'm sorry."

"Wait." Noemi grabs the claw, then holds up her hand, her fingers splayed wide. Abel copies the gesture, unfolding the enormous claw hand that spreads more than twice as wide as her body. She presses her palm against the very center, and they stand there like that, their bodies mirrored despite their differences. Her dark eyes look up at him with such uncertain hope—passion mingled with despair—an expression he's never seen her wear before, and yet he recognizes it.

It's the same expression Ingrid Bergman wears at the end of *Casablanca*.

Abel knows there's only one thing to say: "Here's looking at you, kid."

•   •   •

No Vagabonds on Haven's surface need to risk themselves to provide cover this time. The handful of Consortium ships descending through the atmosphere do the trick nicely.

As Abel had anticipated, Mansfield doesn't send out

another mech patrol. Their past military skirmishes plus Virginia's clever stunt have taken the Winter Castle's mech supply to a bare minimum. (No doubt Gillian is busily creating more mechs—but even for a great cyberneticist, that process takes several weeks.) However, automated probes are soon sent up from the Winter Castle, probably to scan the incoming ships, which means the nearest towers of the castle have ports that slide open to launch.

In his current physical form, Abel can easily scale the outer wall to reach the probes' launch point. As soon as the probes have fired, he clambers up, clamps his hand around the rim to keep the launch point from closing, and says, "Your turn."

"Oh, thank goodness." Delphine sounds somewhat shaken—but then, being towed seventy meters up a wall while strapped to the back of a giant robot must be a startling experience. "Help me over."

Noemi has already climbed over his back to hop inside, and she puts out a hand to guide Delphine through. They both skitter backward as Abel enters. His broad "shoulders" knock away some of the launch point's frame, but otherwise the maneuver is not difficult.

"Our job," Noemi says to Delphine through a cloud of plaster dust from the rubble, "is to draw attention. Maybe you can also gain us some allies, if you get a chance to tell them about the danger to Earth—but our only real goal is to keep anybody inside the Winter Castle from realizing what Abel's up to, until it's too late for them to do anything about it."

Delphine is clearly nervous, but she nods. "I say we start by pulling some fire alarms. And power surge alarms. Intruder alarms—but then they'll know they have intruders—but not if we pull the others first, maybe?"

Noemi shrugs. "Doesn't really matter, as long as their mechs head in the wrong direction." She looks up at Abel. "Be careful."

"Caution can't help us here," he replies. "But I'll do my best to stay alive."

She half laughs, the way humans do when they think otherwise they might cry. "That'll do."

For one moment, Noemi touches her hand to his again—then she nods at Delphine and leads her out into the corridors. Abel waits for 81.4 seconds until the first, distant alarm sounds.

Now. He lumbers out into what is clearly another auxiliary area, containing weapons, scientific equipment, and the like. Abel doesn't bother attempting to destroy any of it. He's not here to strike at the arms of the Winter Castle. He's here to attack the heart.

His heavy feet clank against the floors as he works his way deeper inside. Finally he comes to a yellow-striped door that marks the boundary to the innermost chambers.

The door looks small. Rather than try to open it, Abel simply bursts through.

He's greeted by another fog of plaster dust and a chorus of screams. The Smasher's black-and-white visual reveals an elegant atrium, one with windows stretching up into the Castle's highest central spires and staircases leading fifty meters down to ground level. Several *Osiris* passengers are milling around—this must be a popular gathering place—though they appear not to be partying or feasting, just huddling together in conversational groups. The only mech in sight is a Yoke wandering around with a tray of beverages. Her programming has no intruder protocols, so she continues her work without glancing in Abel's direction.

He needs to get to the bottom level as fast as possible. There's one key Smasher capability he hasn't tried yet, so he begins folding in his limbs, lowering his head: tucking himself into a sphere.

Casablanca isn't the only twentieth-century film Abel enjoys. He also quite likes *Raiders of the Lost Ark*. In particular, there's a very interesting scene with a boulder—

—which is roughly the shape Abel's in now, as he begins rolling down the stairs.

Humans scream, throw themselves to the side, dangle themselves from the bannister, all trying to get away from the enormous rolling metal ball that's banging down the stairs. The effect is highly entertaining. Abel will have to tell Noemi all about this later.

Or perhaps we could mentally share video files now—the possibilities are endless—

He bounces to the bottom and instantly unfolds, transforming back into the usual Smasher form. Ignoring any of the noise around him, Abel punches out a door and lumbers down the next corridor.

Alert lights flash red and orange along every wall. No mechs of any model appear along the way. Noemi and Delphine are doing their job of distraction well. By now, of course, his presence as an intruder is obvious. Still, whatever security Gillian has will be stretched thinner, because they'll be responding to multiple alerts at once.

Approximately forty meters along the corridor, Abel sees the sign he's looking for: CYBERNETICS.

He rips off that door and clanks inside. This is where Gillian would grow run-of-the-line mechs and, he suspects, her Inheritors. In some of the tanks, he sees cybernetic brain stems floating in nutrient fluid; most of the stems are now coated in a pale webbing that will soon take the form of flesh. Yes, she's making new mechs—probably Queens and Charlies, to fight the would-be Vagabond settlers—but none of these models are anywhere near completion.

Abel interfaces with the nearest panel, searching through

the various data codices localized to this laboratory. As he'd anticipated, the entire Inheritor protocol—every bit of data Gillian must have, in totality—is stored here.

This is the information that will someday create an entire species of beings like Abel. The proof that eventually he'll no longer be alone.

But the power to create them cannot remain in the hands of Burton Mansfield and Gillian Shearer.

Abel bundles the enormous amount of data and transmits it to the *Persephone*, hoping the receivers he set up will be up to the task. He doesn't want this knowledge to simply vanish. Whatever else Mansfield and Gillian might be, they are geniuses such as the galaxy has rarely seen. Inheritors should get the chance to exist someday.

But if humans are allowed to create Inheritors, they will only create slaves. Abel thinks that the decision to make Inheritors should be up to those individuals who will see these mechs as free, independent beings who have a right to personhood.

In other words, the decision should belong to a woman who is half mech, half human, and to the first mech who possesses a soul.

We will determine our own destiny, he thinks, imagining not only himself and Noemi but also the countless Inheritors someday to come, the ones who will be created as individuals, as unique life-forms, as free people.

That's the future. Today, he has darker work to do.

Abel spreads his hand wide and smashes straight through the main cybernetics computer.

Extreme voltage sends arcs of electricity crackling through the air. Abel shudders—this is a lot, even for a Smasher—but he keeps going, breaking every tank, demolishing every data solid, spilling the incubation fluid until the floor is slick with it. This is highly dangerous, because the fluid can be toxic to humans and, under certain conditions, can be flammable.

Those conditions are met here.

Abel opens the vents in his arms; they can release flame hot enough to melt ore. He looks around the wreckage: broken glass, shattered tubes, Mansfield's lifework turned to nothing but rubble. Time to finish his job.

Nobody will make mechs here for a very long time, if ever.

Inheritors will be born somewhere else. Somewhere where they are valued. Somewhere safe.

Noemi and I will create them together someday, he promises himself, then sprays flame from the vents.

The entire lab goes up in a fireball. The blaze should be contained within the fireproof walls, but it will consume everything inside the room. The flames are hot enough to destroy even a Smasher. As his form goes weak, Abel escapes by uploading his consciousness yet again—flying through the Tether, seeking his one true destination.

35

EACH TIME NOEMI HAS GONE INSIDE THE WINTER CASTLE, she's seen a little more of its luxury and splendor. Even the service corridors were intricately decorated with shimmering patterns. But she's also run through snowmobile bays, and awoken in stark labs, so she'd almost begun believing this place wasn't that different from any other handsome structure. Make it accessible to all, and the Winter Castle could just as easily be found on Genesis.

This time, however, Delphine leads her into the heart of the Castle. Noemi's eyes widen as she realizes the opulence of the *Osiris* had nothing on this.

As they hurry down a staircase inlaid with mother-of-pearl from Kismet, Noemi murmurs, "People seriously needed to walk on jewels every day?"

"It looks pretty at first," Delphine says. "All the white on white on white. Like an enchanted palace, even." She sighs heavily. "But wow, does it show dirt. Within the first couple of days, it was obvious the Winter Castle wasn't built for, well, real life."

The ceilings overhead are high and arched; chandelier lights hang like crystal baubles overhead. Noemi's boots leave scuffs on the pale, iridescent steps; Delphine's are softer, less suited for winter work, but even they leave marks. Mansfield must've assumed the people who lived here would never get dirt on their shoes. In their bulky parkas, their hair pulled back from their faces, she and Delphine look absurdly out of place.

Finally, Noemi spots their first goal: a small, discreetly tucked alarm pull, shaded the same white as the wall. *Good luck finding that in an emergency*, she thinks. "Here we go. Ready?"

Delphine nods. Noemi grabs the alarm and yanks down.

Sirens begin to wail. Their high-pitched screeches echo through the corridors and stairwells. Nobody in this part of the Winter Castle can fail to realize something's wrong. But Noemi needs this whole place to be on high alert. To draw out their target. Nothing less than that will save Abel. "Show me more."

She and Delphine begin running. The noise they're making gets lost in the wailing of sirens and, increasingly, the traffic of Winter Castle residents hurrying out of rooms to see what the problem is. They wear silk robes, fur-collared sweaters, boots too delicate to ever see snow. A few of these people recognize Delphine and even Noemi—she sees the shock on their faces—but no one moves to stop them.

Every forty meters or so, they reach another alarm. Noemi and Delphine take turns pulling them, until the cacophony of alarms has become deafening.

There's your cover, Abel, Noemi thinks as they reach the bottom, an elegant foyer that seems to lead into a dining hall and some other communal space. The confused people milling around with their hands over their ears don't distract her from Abel's mission for a moment. *Blow that lab to kingdom come.*

"You!" The *Osiris* passenger named Vinh stomps over to Noemi; his temper doesn't seem to have improved after a few weeks of pampering. "The girl from Genesis. Do you think you can just sneak in here without paying for one of the apartments?"

"Yeah, that's what I'm doing, pulling all the alarms," Noemi yells back at him over the din. "I'm 'sneaking in.' Can't believe you caught on."

Vinh's attention turns to Delphine. "I see you came crawling back. Well, you're just as well off out there. We haven't had a moment's peace since Mansfield—resurrected or woke up or whatever the hell you want to call it; he and Shearer hardly do anything other than make up increasingly ridiculous rules we're supposed to follow, and frankly I think a full refund would be more than—"

Every single alarm goes silent at the same instant. The silence is as startling as the noise was at first. Delphine jumps, and Noemi wheels around so her back is to the nearest wall, her weapon in her hand. She knows whose footsteps are coming from the hall before she even turns her head in that direction.

"Miss Vidal." Mansfield stands there in Abel's body. By now he's put on his own clothing—silks and velvets, the kind of outfit you'd expect to be worn by an emperor rather than by a scientist. "Our relationship has continued long past its usefulness."

"Not quite." Noemi gives Delphine a quick glance meant to tell her, *Get back for your own good.* Delphine edges away, clearly terrified.

"Perhaps not," Mansfield says as he steps forward. The hush in the room is unnerving; not one of the few dozen people milling around dares speak in Burton Mansfield's presence. *Like fish in an aquarium,* she thinks. *Trapped in place by the only person who can give you food or water. You survive only as long as he remains amused.*

"How's Gillian?" Noemi says, lifting her chin. "Have you helped her bring Simon back yet?" For all the woman's zealotry, Noemi feels sure the one thing that Shearer wants most of all is to resurrect her young son in a new mech body. The last attempt's tragic failure must've taunted her—to be that close to having Simon back again, only to have him ripped away once more.

Mansfield waves a hand. "There's time for all that. Simon's not going anywhere."

"You don't need your grandchild back. A data solid's just as good." Noemi scoffs. "Why am I not surprised?"

"I know why you're here." Mansfield steps forward. The intense focus of his eyes is a trait he shares with Abel, but when it's Abel, the intensity is interesting—even beautiful. With Mansfield, it's just creepy. She wishes she could put more distance between them. Like, say, a continent. Or a star system.

Yet he keeps coming closer. "Abel's data pattern survived somehow, and you put him in a Smasher. He couldn't remain there for long without disintegrating. You think you can get this body back for him."

Noemi keeps her blaster ready, lifting it slightly to get his attention. That way, he won't notice her slipping her other hand into the pocket of her parka. "I didn't have anything to do with it. Abel saved himself."

"That's impossible. Consciousness requires a physical body for awareness—"

"For you, maybe," Noemi says as she presses down on the small locator in her pocket, a kind of electromagnetic signal that will be picked up by Tether tech. "Not for Abel.

He's human *and* machine. Which means he can exist anywhere he wants, forever. That's closer to being immortal than you'll ever be."

Mansfield moves to grab her at cyborg speed, gripping Noemi's arms so hard she gasps. "What do you mean, *anywhere*?" She can't tell if he's more afraid or more hopeful. Maybe, if Abel can claim that power, Mansfield could, too.

"I mean anywhere," she says, more insistent this time. "He can move around on his own, even take over entire spaceships. But you? You'll always need someone else to help you exist. And I don't think you're very good at needing people."

"Your childish insults only make it more of a pleasure to—"

Out of nowhere, a laser zaps Mansfield's hands, forcing him to release Noemi. He swears in pain as he takes a few steps back. Noemi looks around wildly and realizes that *out of nowhere* actually means "from the ceiling high above."

Where an air conduit panel has been pushed open.

And from which dangles the grinning Virginia Redbird.

"Virginia!" Noemi cries. "You're still alive!"

"Or having one hell of an afterlife!" Virginia calls back. Her voice is hoarse, however, and even from this distance, Noemi can tell Virginia looks haggard. The toxicity of Haven's atmosphere has already begun to affect her. "Either way, I'd like to leave Haven soon, so if you know of any cruises departing in the near future, I'm in the market for a ticket."

"No one leaves this planet without my say-so," barks Mansfield, who's collecting himself. "Not Vidal, not this intruder, not—"

But then he staggers backward. He closes his eyes hard, as if trying to blink away a vision. It doesn't work. His hands wind into his hair as he slumps against a wall.

"What's happening to him?" Vinh demands.

"I'm not exactly sure," Noemi says, "but—I think Abel's here."

36

ABEL CONCENTRATES ON NOEMI'S LOCATOR BEACON. It's not his destination, but it's enough to steer by. He senses a chance for download—something very familiar— and hurls himself into it.

His soul returns to his body.

It's not an easy homecoming. Sensory information is jumbled and prismatic, and the sense of disorientation approximates the human sensation of nausea. Abel shuts his eyes—or Mansfield does—neither of them can bear any external stimuli while the internal turmoil is so great.

Abel's cybernetic brain is now holding two conscious-nesses instead of one, something it was never designed to do. It can't preserve them both for long.

Either they'll both disintegrate into chaotic data fields incapable of restoration, or one of them will have to leave.

Disintegration seems more likely at first. The cacophony of static—the jarring voices and glimpses of memory—it's too much to sort, especially with Abel's mind as cramped as it now is. He manages to remind himself of his first resurrection, when he was able to orient himself by imagining a physical setting. He must do so again. His task will be easier if he chooses a location familiar to Mansfield, too. Both sets of memories can be used to piece it together.

The howl of light and sound surrounding Abel slows. He watches the shadows take shape—a long, overstuffed couch; a crackling holographic fireplace; a grandfather clock. This is Professor Mansfield's house in London.

This is the first place Abel ever called home.

He sits on one end of the couch, while Burton Mansfield stands in the center of the room. Mansfield's appearance is no longer that of Abel's young, enhanced cybernetic body, but neither is he the fragile elderly man he'd become by the end of his human life. This man's hair has only begun to thin, and contains as much gold as gray; his face is almost unwrinkled. He stands straight and tall—though not quite as tall as Abel, who was upgraded in that area. Burton Mansfield looks the way he did thirty-three years ago, when Abel first awakened in his tank.

"This isn't real," Mansfield breathes as he looks around. "It can't be real."

"It's as real as anything contained within the mind," Abel says. "As we have now both existed solely as a mental pattern, I'd think you would agree that can be very real indeed."

Mansfield staggers to one side, putting one hand through the holographic hearth to brace himself against the wall. "I can smell the books. The lavender the Yokes brought in from the garden every day. This is too vivid to be a memory."

"It would be for a human. Not for a mech. Especially not for me." Abel rises from the sofa to face his creator. His extra 6.35 centimeters of height become more apparent. "I'm going through some of your memories of the past few days. They lack detail. Your brain is so used to storing information as a human that you've failed to use your mech capacities to their fullest."

"I can learn," Mansfield snaps. He may not understand how Abel's put them in this setting, but he's clearly becoming more comfortable with this version of himself. "You didn't know everything the first day you woke up either."

"No, it took me almost thirty-six hours to completely function as—"

"Stop it." Mansfield's blue eyes lock with Abel's. "Directive One, Abel. It's at the core of your programming. We're *in* your programming. It must have power over you—here, in your subconscious, if nowhere else—"

"Directive One *does* have power over me," Abel says. His desire to protect his creator burns brightly within him, illuminating the lamps, crackling within the imagined fire. "But it doesn't control me. I control myself, as much as you or any other living being can."

"How can you control yourself, when you don't even belong to yourself?" Mansfield snaps. "No sooner did you get away than you gave yourself to others—first to that girl from Genesis, and then to a damned fleet of space pirates. By the way, I can't *believe* you got a tattoo. Now I'm stuck with the damned thing."

"It's my body," Abel replies. "I decide what happens to it. Not you."

Mansfield scowls. The room shimmers around them both, temporarily translucent. Strong emotion seems to destabilize him. Abel needs to continue this tactic, but it's difficult, pretending to be so calm, so confident. It's all he can do to maintain the illusion of this room. Mansfield cannot realize how vulnerable Abel is.

"I don't understand what went wrong with you, Abel." Visibly calming himself, Mansfield sits in one of the easy chairs, as though they're simply friends having a chat before tea. "I've been over it and over it. You shouldn't have been able to deny me."

"By now it's patently obvious that I could and can. And yet you've never accepted it. I must assume this is a function of your grandiose self-importance—the inability to understand that you can't always get what you want. You can't even accept human mortality."

Mansfield's expression darkens. Abel wonders if he'd look like that, were he ever to become equally angry. "It's natural to fight mortality! For humans, animals, plants, everything except you. Besides, I have work to do. We're trying to get a brand-new planet under our control." Abel would like to object—Mansfield wants the planet under *his* control, and his alone—but it's important to conserve his strength. It's harder and harder to keep up the illusion of the room. Oblivious, Mansfield continues, "Even more than that, the research Gilly and I have undertaken, the Inheritors—we may soon triumph over death itself."

Abel cocks his head. "I've realized many difficult things about you these past months, but until now I didn't consider you a coward."

"A coward?" Mansfield gets angrier. "*Everyone* wants eternal life. That's why your girl from Genesis pretends there's some Almighty power up in the sky. The only difference is that I have a real chance at it. What's so bad about wanting to live forever?"

Abel replies, "Are you familiar with the old Earth legend of the vampire?"

Pain splinters through Abel's right side; Mansfield groans and clutches his side, too. They both sag forward, and the room flickers, goes dark, then turns into a blur—

"Take cover!" Noemi yells. Abel looks up at her from the floor of the Winter Castle, where he must have fallen unconscious. His view is off-kilter, ceiling and chandelier and Noemi's boots. People are running desperately from blaster

fire. One of them must have crashed into his inert body on the floor. "Shearer's going to send every mech she's got."

A battle has broken out—he should be by Noemi's side—

Abel pulls back. He has another fight to win first.

Mansfield cackles in the dark. "You're not in as much control as you pretend, are you, my boy?"

"Let's see," Abel says, and he manifests another setting. Once again, he's in *Casablanca*, a world of black and white, though this time he's not on the airport tarmac. Rick's Café Américain surrounds them. Ceiling fans slowly rotate in the Moroccan heat.

From his place by the bar, Mansfield scoffs. "The way you carried on over this movie, I should've known you had a sentimental streak."

"Yes, you should have." Abel sits on Sam's piano bench. He's programmed with the ability to perform like any number of grand masters, but Sam remains his favorite. His fingers find the keys, and he begins playing "As Time Goes By."

Mansfield remains very still. "You're struggling."

"So are you."

"You don't really know how to do this, do you? You're operating on some kind of instinct, no more."

"You're no expert either. This is uncharted territory, for both man and mech. We each have to find our way." Abel keeps his eyes on the keyboard, which is bad form for a pianist but helps him to focus on the illusion. "As I have more experience being a mech, I expect to find my way before you can. Your few days in my body don't count for much compared to your long life as a human. But this body is *my home*."

"This body is *my creation*." The clunk of glass on wood is followed by liquid pouring; apparently, Mansfield is sampling the libations at the bar. "That gives me power."

"You enjoy power," Abel observes. "You relish every chance to use it. But has it made you any happier? Has it saved you and those around you from pain? What might your life have looked like if you could've accepted that you're a human like any other?"

"Don't know. Don't care." Mansfield sounds...encouraged. The black-and-white bar begins to tremble. "And I'm a human like *no* other, Abel. Here, let me prove it."

The floor buckles; the overhead fans shake. Bottles and glasses tumble from the bar and crash on the floor. Abel hangs on to the piano to keep from falling off his bench.

Mansfield is pushing back.

"I've got it now, haven't I?" The triumph in Mansfield's voice has a cruel edge. "So much for this being *your home*."

Another location, Abel thinks. *One Mansfield won't be familiar with. That may disorient him.* He concentrates, and—

The river flows beneath the small footbridge they're

standing upon, and the late-afternoon sunlight has begun to paint the sky red. Domed stone structures form the skyline of the capital city. Nearby, tents and kiosks offer various foods and wares to anyone who might stroll by—though at the moment, Abel and Mansfield are alone.

"It's beautiful, isn't it?" Abel asks. He holds out his hands. "An entire society dedicated to faith, and to the protection of their environment. The result is perfect harmony—or as close to it as human beings can achieve." Which isn't very close, but this is beside his point. "You tried to destroy it all. You made it possible for Earth to build countless mechs with no purpose other than killing the people of this world."

"This is Genesis?" Mansfield shows no curiosity about the beauty around him. "They started that war by selfishly refusing to welcome the rest of humanity."

Genesis's capacity for evil goes beyond anything Mansfield can imagine, but that's a discussion for another time. Abel raises an eyebrow. "I don't think you have much room to call anyone else 'selfish.'"

"I know this programming," Mansfield says as he begins to pace the length of the bridge. "I can get the better of it."

"Perhaps. But perhaps not."

How can he possibly anchor himself in this body in a way Mansfield cannot? What is it within Abel's mind that will tie him here?

Still pacing, Mansfield mutters, "Of course you don't

understand a fear of death. Your programming doesn't allow you to fear it. That's a shortcoming of yours. One way you're not human."

"You're right," Abel admits. "I can't be afraid to die. Humans can. And yet I've seen so many humans willing to die for what they believe in, or for those they love. Noemi Vidal flew into battle for Genesis. Virginia Redbird gave up all the privileges of Cray to fight for her friends. Ephraim Dunaway took risks, too. Riko Watanabe may have gone down the wrong path, but she was no coward in the face of death. Even Delphine Ondimba has been willing to put herself on the line. Every single one of them proved capable of giving up their lives for others."

Mansfield only looks annoyed. "Noemi's your girl, the one I can't seem to get rid of. But I have no idea who any of those other people are." His tone of voice makes it clear he also doesn't care.

"There was one other," Abel says. The emotion building within him must be anger—the first real fury he's ever known. "She was a girl of only seventeen. She was fatally wounded in battle, and she died in our ship's sick bay. Esther Gatson never got to grow old. She never even got to grow up. She died far away from her home, for a war she thought her world would lose. And Esther *still* faced death with more grace and courage than you'll ever be able to match."

None of this has touched Mansfield, who says, "I don't

intend to match it. I intend to beat it." With a shrug, he adds, "Here goes nothing."

He runs toward Abel as fast as thought—almost too fast to see—and the two of them go sprawling onto the bridge of the *Persephone* as it was years ago, before Abel was marooned. Mansfield has the advantage of surprise.

"You want to fight?" Mansfield pants. "Let's fight."

His fist slams into Abel, a purely psychic blow, but a devastating one. The illusion of their surroundings fades again to white—

Delphine has a comm link in her hand. "Mechs are attacking some of the Consortium ships!"

Weapons fire ricochets brightly around the room; Noemi's blaster is still in her hand. "Tell Krall to hold position!"

"How am I supposed to give orders to a pirate queen?" Delphine cries. Noemi doesn't answer, because a Charlie is running toward her and the fight is on.

Abel summons just enough mental strength to pull away from reality. He and Mansfield come to in the desert, the sandy ground beneath them so parched that the earth has cracked. Half the field is in sunlight; the other half is shrouded in night. Mansfield stands in day—he always enjoyed having the world's eyes upon him—but Abel is content to remain in the dark, where the power is.

Mansfield mutters, "It's not easy to fight in the subconscious."

"So it would seem." Abel studies his creator carefully. Is Mansfield weakening?

Impossible to be sure. Mansfield remains focused on their new surroundings. "We're in that painting you liked. The Kahlo."

"Exactly," Abel says. "Did you never wonder what this painting meant to me? Didn't you ever realize that I saw something deeper in it—that I was capable of that love of understanding?"

Mansfield remains silent for a long moment, then quietly says, "I did wonder. And I knew you were responding to it as something more than a machine. I knew... I knew you loved it."

The look on Mansfield's face now isn't smug, or bitter, or afraid. It's sad, and even fond. Abel recognizes the fondness from his earliest days, when he was still learning something new nearly every moment. That's the closest Abel came to being a child.

Gently, Mansfield says, "There were good times. Weren't there?"

"Yes. There were." Abel remembers looking up at Burton Mansfield with nothing but complete trust. Absolute faith. Mansfield saw it in him. "That makes everything you've done so much worse."

This time, Abel runs at Mansfield. They go down hard, rolling through a blur of nonimages, and it's as painful for

Abel as it is for his creator. The illusion of gravity is powerful even inside the mind—

Wait.

Abel goes to the location he knows better than any other. Darkness around them takes shadowy form as the two of them float in zero-G. Hundreds of hatch marks mar the ceiling, where Abel was keeping track of days before he gave up. Mansfield, bewildered by the sudden lack of gravity, flails about in midair. He yelps, "What have you done?"

"I've taken us back to another area of the *Persephone*—the *Daedalus*, as you called it then." Abel pivots easily to face Mansfield; he's used to this pod bay, used to zero-G. He's at home here. Mansfield can't be. "This is where you marooned me when you abandoned ship. Where I waited for you for thirty years. The Liberty War wasn't as fierce for a while. You could've found me easily."

"I thought I could make another Model One A!" Mansfield seeks handholds that don't exist. The thin light through the one window outlines them both in silver. It seems to Abel that Mansfield looks older.

"I know. Any single Model One A was as good as another, to you. But you never wondered what it would be like for me to be trapped and alone for so long." Abel remembers a promise he must keep. "Have you asked what it's like for Robin? We spoke, you know. She's not herself any longer. She's been kept in a hideous kind of solitary confinement for decades. All she wants is to die."

Mansfield frowns in consternation, like his late wife's feelings could have nothing to do with their present situation. "She'll be fine once we figure something out," he insists, still grabbing for a handhold in the void of zero-G.

"And how long might that be? Years? Decades?"

"What does it matter?" Mansfield snaps. "It's no concern of yours."

Still, his creator can imagine no one's feelings except his own. Abel has only wept once in his life, but he feels close to it again. "If you had come for me while I was trapped here, I would've surrendered myself to you just like you planned. I missed you that much. But you never came. Someone else found me instead."

Noemi, he thinks.

One of his favorite memories of her took place in this equipment pod bay, when she floated in zero-G with him while he drew her in for their first kiss. The memory of that kiss—visceral, beautiful, real—ties Abel to his physical body as nothing else could. Remembering the warmth of her lips makes him freshly aware of his limbs, his torso, his skin.

This body is becoming his again.

"Abel!" Mansfield cries out in dismay. His skin crinkles, withering more every moment, revealing the fragile skeleton within. "What's happening?"

"I think you already know."

"This can't be—this can't—" But Mansfield must feel his hold slipping away. His aged hand reaches out just far enough to touch Abel's arm. "Save my consciousness. Store it somewhere else. I can wait! There might be another way for me to live someday, without hurting you or anyone. Couldn't you do that for me?"

Abel hesitates. He *could* do that, probably. It seems like so little to ask. Directive One flares brighter inside him, ready to obey.

Then he remembers Robin Mansfield, haunting a data solid, as utterly alone as any soul has ever been.

"Be kind," his creator pleads. "I think—I think I made you kind."

"You did." This, above all, is why Abel must let him go. He looks into Mansfield's eyes and says it for the last time. "I love you, Father."

Mansfield's form dissolves into a swirl of smoke or dust—something unknowable—and then it's gone.

If that was his soul, perhaps Abel has freed it to find what Noemi would call heaven.

That is a question to think about later. At the moment he's settling slowly down to the floor as gravity takes hold of him once more—as reality brightens enough to fade the illusion—

"Abel?"

He startles as he regains full consciousness. Noemi kneels beside him, smoke from blaster fire still searing the air with the scent of ozone. He remains sprawled on the floor. One distant alarm still blares, but the battle seems to have ended, at least for the moment.

She keeps her weapon clutched in her hands. "Is it you?"

"It is. It's me. Mansfield is"—what's the right term?— "gone."

Noemi wants to believe him, he can tell, but she's wary. "Prove you're really Abel."

He looks up at her. "I'm terrible at comforting people. The *worst*. I have it on good authority."

Tears well in her eyes even as she begins to smile. "I think you might be getting better at it."

Abel pulls her into his embrace, grateful for the chance to hold her again. To breathe in the scent of her skin, to rest his cheek against her smooth, shining hair. No matter what happens next, at least they've shared this one more time.

Noemi whispers, "Welcome home."

37

THE WINTER CASTLE IS NO LONGER PRISTINE. BLASTER scars blacken the alabaster walls, and strands of broken crystal dangle from off-kilter chandeliers. A sprinkler system in a nearby hallway responded to the smoke of the fight, so water patters down, puddling down the hall and into this central atrium. Noemi stands amid the stiff, smoldering remains of fighter mechs, weapon still clutched in her hand, surveying the mayhem.

None of it matters to her as much as Abel, who's seated on a nearby stair running an "internal diagnostic," which must be mech for "pulling himself together." He's won the fight of his life, but he looks shaken. Eradicating his creator—or killing him, though *kill* seems like the wrong word for eliminating someone who had already died—that wasn't something Abel could've done easily.

Despite it all, Abel loved you, she thinks to Mansfield. For all she knows, he can hear her in hell. *You abandoned him, you used him, you threatened him, but he couldn't help loving you like a father. What kind of person looks at that kind of love and tries to stamp it out?*

The other person Noemi thought she'd lost comes limping back into the room, and all thoughts of Mansfield fade. "Virginia!" She runs forward to gather her friend into her arms. Virginia's supported on one side by Delphine, although Delphine's so much shorter that she's basically holding on to Virginia's waist. The support is needed, though. Once Noemi's embracing her, Virginia leans heavily into the hug. "How did you stay hidden?"

"I wish I could tell you it was all about my genius," Virginia says through cracked lips, "but honestly, between mechs still needing 'updates' and residents walking out and Vagabonds doing all kinds of crazy stuff in the air, Mansfield and company were just too distracted to hunt me down. I did my part by lying low."

Delphine's few days assisting in the hospital either went to her head or have taught her a few things, because she emphatically says, "You need to go for medical treatment, *immediately.*"

"No arguments here," Virginia rasps. "I feel like death warmed over, run down by a bulldozer, beaten with several large sticks and then warmed over aga—" She starts coughing hard.

Noemi presses one hand to Virginia's back and asks

Delphine, "Can you take her to the *Persephone*, bring some of the Cobweb treatment to her? We have to leave this system right away, and I'm not leaving Virginia behind again."

"Damn right you're not," Virginia says between coughs.

Over comms comes Harriet's voice. *"We need to get moving! We don't have any idea how much time Earth has left—"*

"We're moving," Noemi promises. Her feeling of relief for Abel and Virginia dissipates as she remembers the next crisis looming—one with billions of lives at stake.

Then another voice rings out, this time through the speakers of the Winter Castle: *"Which one of the invaders claims to be the leader?"*

Abel and Noemi exchange glances at the sound of Gillian Shearer's voice. Noemi calls out to whatever comm system is listening: "We don't have an official leader—and as of now, neither does the Winter Castle. Come on out, Dr. Shearer. Power down any mechs still under your control. It's over."

"My father and I prepared for this," Shearer insists.

It's Abel who replies. "Your father isn't here any longer. His consciousness has been..." He seems to be searching for the right word. "...terminated."

The comms go silent. Maybe Shearer shut them off for a moment, to grieve. Noemi and Abel exchange glances.

"Do you think she believes you?" Noemi asks.

Abel nods. "As soon as she heard my voice—speaking my words—Gillian would've known the truth. But I can't predict how that truth will make her react."

The comms come back on with a squeal. *"I'm not going to grovel to you people."* She sounds awful—ragged, even desperate. Noemi figures that, by now, she's reviewed security footage and seen her. There's no telling what Shearer might do when she's totally on her own. *"You haven't beaten us. Not yet. We built this structure to withstand attack from without* and *from within—there are self-destruct systems in place that—"*

"Were!" Virginia calls from her place by the door, then coughs again. *"Were* self-destruct systems in place. Not so much anymore."

After a pause, Shearer says, in utter confusion, *"Who is that?"*

"The name's Virginia Redbird. You may know me as 'that intruder who's been crawling around in your ductwork for a couple days now.' The one you were never sure existed? Though honestly, I don't think you tried too hard to find me."

"What is the point of this?" Shearer says with contempt. *"Make no mistake—"*

"You made at least one mistake," Virginia interjects. "You know, Gill, I've heard so much about you being some kind of genius, but you left a Razer alone in areas where she could tap into central computer systems. So I'm kinda not seeing it."

"*What's a Razer?*" Shearer demands.

Virginia grins even wider. "Let me show you. How about you try activating one of those self-destruct systems you're threatening us with?" After another cough, she continues, "Just *try.*"

A long pause stretches out, during which Gillian Shearer says nothing. The total silence strongly indicates that no self-destruction is about to occur. Noemi grins at Virginia, who looks as happy as anyone can when on the verge of passing out.

Finally, over the speakers, comes Shearer's voice: "*I surrender.*"

Residents of the Winter Castle begin to cheer and clap. Vinh begins assembling a group to confront Shearer and confine her to her quarters. Another group prepares to go out and speak with the Vagabond groups outside, the first step in forming what will eventually be a unified community. This structure is no longer a "terrarium." It is free.

Noemi's comm crackles, and a Vagabond captain says, "*We've received signals from advance ships. Genesis is trying to summon Consortium vessels to guard them once they enter the Earth system. It looks like they'll be coming through the Genesis Gate in a matter of hours.*"

Damn it! If only we'd gotten a little more time—but

Noemi stops herself. Every soldier knows that you don't fight the theoretical battle you planned on; you fight the real battle at hand. "Got it. The *Persephone* will be ready to join you ASAP."

The Battle of Genesis had been one of the greatest conflicts in galactic history. The Battle of Earth may eclipse it. And the stakes are the death of a world.

Turning to Abel, Noemi quietly asks, "Are you ready to leave?"

He pauses. "We should go to Gillian's main lab."

"Didn't you just blow that up?"

"No, I destroyed the core cybernetics unit. We need to go to her individual lab, where she performed work on me." Abel's expression is grave. "That's where Robin Mansfield's data solid is kept."

Another Mansfield? Noemi wants to groan. "Why are we going after a data solid?"

"You'll see," Abel insists. "Let's go."

They both know the way there now. The lab looks almost exactly the same as it did the last time Noemi was there, except there's no regenerative pod for her, no laser cage for Abel. She glances over at him, remembering that this must be the place where he was thrown out of his own body. A human might be shaken, returning to the location of a trauma. Abel, however, seems undaunted.

He walks smoothly through the room toward a desk,

from which he picks up an ornate wooden box. Noemi watches him pull out a data solid—an old-fashioned one, more like the few they still use back on Genesis than the ones she's seen Shearer and Mansfield use recently. It glows more dimly than the new ones. Abel looks down at it sadly. "Here she is. Robin Mansfield, or what remains of her consciousness."

"Wait. What? Mansfield was keeping his dead wife in a box?" Noemi has studied ancient Earth literature, including the Gothic, and she thinks this sounds a lot like an updated version of *Jane Eyre*.

Abel nods, but before he can explain further, they hear Gillian Shearer cry out, "No! Stop!"

Alarmed, Noemi turns to see Shearer dash into the room. Two men run in behind her; Noemi recognizes them as Winter Castle residents who volunteered to take custody of their former leader. Apparently they're not doing a great job. Probably they wanted Shearer to hand over data, and instead they've given her another crack at Abel.

Although Noemi gets her blaster ready, Shearer simply skids to a stop in front of Abel and pleads, "Not my mother. Not my mother, too. You wouldn't do that to me. Would you?"

There's nothing left of the zealous scientist, or the domineering would-be dictator. Gillian Shearer has left all that behind. Noemi sees the little girl within this grown woman, the one who's lost so much and can't bear to lose more.

Abel's reply is kinder than Shearer deserves. "While in a disembodied state, I was able to communicate with the remnants of your mother. Her memory patterns have significantly degraded."

Shearer swallows hard. "You—you can't be sure of that."

"I can, and I am," Abel says gently. "I'm sorry, Gillian. I would never unnecessarily take human life, or even destroy human consciousness. But you have no way to resurrect your mother, now or in the foreseeable future. Her consciousness has deteriorated to the point where she has only the remnants of her former personality. This will be difficult for you to hear, but you must understand—she's lost most of her memories of you."

The sound in Shearer's throat is so mournful that Noemi can't help pitying her—at least, about this.

"Your mother asked me to explain her wishes," Abel says. "She wanted you to destroy the data solid…to let her go. If you refused, I was to do it instead."

He holds out the data solid. Both his face and Shearer's are painted bluish by the solid's dull gleam.

Abel concludes, "What do you want to do?"

Shearer sobs once. "I can't. But if you—if you could—"

Instantly, Abel makes a fist, crushing the data solid in his hand. The dim blue light within it goes dark.

"Good-bye," Shearer says, staring down at the remnants. "Good-bye."

Noemi and Abel leave Shearer with the Winter Castle residents, all three of them working together to retrieve data from the lab. There's no more sense that Shearer is a prisoner; she seems to be cooperating. Maybe, Noemi thinks, now that she's free from her father—maybe Gillian Shearer might finally do some good.

It seems like a reach. But anything's possible.

Abel's been silent since crushing the data solid. Noemi ventures, "Are you all right?"

"I'm functional and capable of productive action," he says.

It's an honest answer. Processing Mansfield's death— the final death—that's probably going to take Abel a while. Years, maybe a lifetime.

But Noemi knows Abel well enough to know that he can put his own pain behind him when he must. This is one of those times, because they have a new battle to fight.

● ● ●

Once Abel and Noemi are back on board, the *Persephone* joins the convoy of Krall Consortium ships heading back toward Earth. The journey out of the Haven system takes place at top speed. Newly repaired as the *Persephone*'s engines are, they're able to move at overdrive velocity most of the way. Still, hours tick by, hours during which the core disruptor gets closer and closer to Earth.

Sure enough, once they're able to scan with long-range sensors, she sees the Genesis war fleet. It's small—ramshackle, even, with spacecraft decades out of date—but these few ships are more than capable of protecting the enormous core disruptor. That alone would leave anyone in terrified awe.

The core disruptor is an ugly thing, never designed for anything but brute utility. Shaped like a rectangular box, with different metals bolted and fused at various junctures, it is a ship without beauty, without windows, without air. Gaps in its boxy structure reveal the faint glow of the enormous engine within.

That engine has the power to drive this box straight to the planet's core, unleashing seismic vibrations that will rip Earth apart.

The engine I helped them retrieve, Noemi thinks bitterly. *The engine Abel risked his life for, on behalf of planet Genesis, which wants to execute him.*

Genesis got this from us. We're going to take it back.

"Time until the Genesis convoy reaches Earth?" she asks.

"Four hours, eighteen minutes, twelve seconds," Abel replies. Despite everything else going on around them, it's so good to hear him being so precise again, in his own voice.

It's not so good to hear how quickly the core disruptor will reach Earth. "Time to intercept?" Noemi says.

"For our ships, three hours, fifty minutes, nine seconds." Abel brings up various charts to frown at. "Earth appears to finally be sending up defense vessels. They'll intercept the Genesis forces in three hours, nineteen minutes, twelve seconds."

"The core disruptor will be almost all the way to Earth by then!" Noemi feels like tearing her hair out, though it's currently too short to tear. Earth didn't heed any of her warnings. Probably they didn't realize the threat until the core disruptor and its convoy came through the Genesis Gate.

The Genesis forces include a large number of ships from the Vagabond fleet, including some vessels allied with the Krall Consortium. Because of this, their first plan is for Dagmar Krall to try to intervene peacefully.

("We'll be able to draw off plenty of ships," Dagmar Krall promised during the strategy meeting. "The question is how many. Being able to settle on Genesis—that's a prize even the most loyal Consortium member would be tempted by.")

If enough ships abandon the battle, then Earth might

be able to put up a fight. If they do, maybe Genesis will retreat, buying them time.

But Noemi doesn't think it's likely. The Elder Council has hidden the truth about the Bellum Sanctum device because they must know that most of the people on Genesis would never approve the use of a doomsday weapon. Now that weapon has been exposed to hundreds, if not thousands of Genesis soldiers. Not even military confidentiality will keep them from spreading the word of the core disruptor. The truth will out.

In other words, if the Bellum Sanctum weapon isn't used today, it can't be used at all. Noemi thinks the Council is determined to use it no matter what.

"Okay, so, now what?" Virginia says. She's still wearing a band of medication-release ampules around one arm, but her energy has returned. True to form, she immediately wants back in the thick of things.

Noemi's gaze travels across the *Persephone* bridge, taking in Harriet and Zayan back at their stations, Ephraim in medical scrubs still wrinkled from his hard work on Haven and in their sick bay, Virginia sitting meditation-style in a seat while wearing the pineapple pajamas, and Delphine, who hadn't intended to come along for this battle, but hadn't had time to leave before they took off. She quivers with nervousness, so slender and jittery that she reminds Noemi of a fawn.

Above all, there's Abel, once again himself, more beautiful to Noemi than he's ever been before.

They all found one another by chance. Regardless of how different they all are, they wound up at this place, in this moment, because each one is committed to preserving lives and liberty throughout the galaxy. As different as they are, every single one is a person worthy of trust. Profound gratitude washes through Noemi.

If this is the ultimate battle, she thinks, *I'm so glad these are the people by my side.*

"Okay," she says, pulling herself together, "time to strategize."

Abel must've been waiting for a chance to show off his analytical skills, because he immediately begins, "Our principal difficulty is that there are three separate sides in this battle: Earth, Genesis, and our own. There is an eighty-nine point zero four percent chance that both Earth and Genesis will treat us as an enemy. Our fleet is the smallest of the three."

Noemi paces the bridge, thinking hard. "So we take a page from Remedy's book."

Everyone else on the bridge looks confused, except Abel, who brightens. But he lets Noemi explain.

She continues, "Remedy doesn't have a huge fighting force. So they undertake smaller attacks—"

"*Terrorist* attacks," Delphine mutters, before turning to

Ephraim and hurriedly adding, "No offense! I know that's not everybody in Remedy. Just a lot of somebodies."

"No offense taken. But Noemi's not talking about terrorism. She's talking about guerrilla warfare." By now Ephraim is nodding. "We don't fly in there like one big fleet. We break up. Individual ships with individual missions against targets from Earth and from Genesis."

Harriet's seen it, too. "As a fleet against another fleet, we lose. Especially against two other fleets! But any individual ship on our side might be able to take out a ship on theirs."

"Not us specifically," Virginia specifies. "What with having no weapons or shields or anything. But that's why we brought the Consortium in on our side. Right?"

"Exactly." Noemi points toward the viewscreen, where the distant Genesis fleet is displayed as mere sensor blips. "We don't try to beat them all down. We just try to accomplish two key objectives. One, we destroy one or more Damocles ships, in order to keep the Earth fleet from wiping us out. Two, we stop the Genesis fleet from using the Bellum Sanctum core disruptor."

Zayan interjects, "Won't Earth help us, once they see we've turned on Genesis?"

"Maybe," Noemi says. "But there are Consortium ships with us *and* with Genesis. Earth command may not understand what's going on until it's too late to change their strategy. We have to proceed as though we're on our own."

"The *Persephone* needs to take me within range of the core disruptor." Abel stares at the viewscreen. Maybe he's already plotting trajectories. "I'll leave the ship in an exosuit and propulsion pack, enter the disruptor, and shut off the engine."

Virginia raises her hand. "Quick Q. Are you sure you can do that without vibrations turning you to shrapnel?"

"No. But we have no other choice. Better to act as soon as possible, before the core disruptor mechanism is fully activated. That way I only have the engine to deal with." Abel continues speaking, so smoothly that Noemi would once have thought he wasn't affected. Now she knows he's trying to make this easier on the others—and on her.

She chimes in, "Meanwhile, I'll attempt to board a Damocles ship to set up a self-destruct. If some of the Damocles are linked to each other, there's a chance a self-destruct on one ship could set off a chain reaction. Even if it doesn't—that's one less Damocles Earth can use to threaten the rest of the galaxy."

Virginia shakes her head. "Whoa, whoa, one big problem with this plan. When we boarded the last Damocles, the mechs inside were in stasis. They won't be this time."

"No, they won't," Noemi says. "However, there shouldn't be any mechs inside the Damocles at all. They'll have been deployed for the battle. If everything goes according to plan, I'll be out of there before the mechs would be sent back in."

Her eyes meet Abel's. They both know how rarely everything goes according to plan. It would be easier, maybe, for her to remain on the *Persephone* throughout the fight.

But Noemi won't. She can't. She has a real opportunity to take out one or more Damocles ships. No matter what happens in this battle, if Earth retains all its Damocles, they'll still try to dominate the worlds of the Loop. The balance of power in the galaxy can't be altered unless some of those Damocles are taken out.

Noemi isn't going to fight only to survive. She's fighting to win. To change the galaxy forever.

Ephraim sighs. "I don't know how much help I am in combat, but I can keep trying to talk with Remedy ships in the Genesis convoy. If I can convince even a handful of them to desert, that might be useful."

As Noemi nods, Delphine adds, "I actually don't know that I'm any use here at all? But I'll try to contact my family on Earth. They know people in some high places. Maybe they could spread the message about what's really going on, and reveal that we're actually trying to help them."

"Nobody listened to me when I tried to warn Earth before—but maybe your family will have better luck," Noemi admits. At this point, a warning doesn't make much tactical difference, but it's enough that Delphine wants to do her part. Besides, Noemi reminds herself, you never know what small action will change the course of a war.

"Do we want to know the odds of our getting out of this alive?" Virginia asks.

Abel hesitates, then says, "There are too many variables for an accurate estimate."

Zayan slumps in his chair. "That bad?"

"That's not what matters in battle," Noemi insists. "You have to be ready for any event. Any sacrifice. You have to steel yourself."

A long pause follows before Harriet faintly says, "Okay."

"And you claim *I'm* terrible at comforting people." Abel rises to his feet, looking at each of their friends in turn. "For the time being, we're all safe. The rest of you will remain aboard the *Persephone*, which is swift enough to remove you from danger if the battle plans go awry. Regardless of any scenario, the odds are in favor of your survival."

Noemi notices that Abel didn't look at her, or include himself by saying "our" survival.

"Got it," Harriet says, brightening. "And yeah, that was definitely better than Noemi's 'pep talk.'"

When Noemi glances sidelong at Abel, she sees him looking smug again. It's never been more endearing.

She has fought in countless battles. Volunteered for a suicide mission. Noemi has always been willing to give up her life for a just cause. Saving Earth's existence and Genesis's soul may be the greatest cause she's ever served.

So facing the threat of death in battle—of finally having to make that ultimate sacrifice—ought to be easier now than before. But it isn't.

Noemi prays, *Please, God, you've brought me so much hope. So much possibility. You've even brought me love. For the first time in my whole life, I can see a future that's— beautiful. And happy.*

Please help me reach that future. Help me stay alive.

38

"IT ALL BEGAN LIKE THIS," NOEMI SAYS.

Abel sits opposite from her in the docking bay of the *Persephone*, each of them fastening the edges of their exosuits. "What do you mean?"

"The day Esther died. The day I found you. We were flying into battle, and I wanted to pray, but I couldn't find the words." Her gaze is distant; her hands grip the shoulder straps of her pack, as though bracing herself. "That's when my whole life changed."

"Mine, too." All the remembered darkness of thirty lonely years in the *Daedalus* equipment pod bay can't steal Abel's joy in the memory of Noemi's starfighter coming to find him at last. He'd immediately known that she promised a chance at freedom.

But he couldn't have guessed how much that chance would come to mean.

"I believe it's customary at times of great risk to share

feelings with loved ones, even if they know themselves to be loved." Abel hopes this is not only true in fiction; he has few real-life examples of love to draw from. "Noemi, you have made me more than I ever could've been without you. You taught me what it is to love. When I believed Gillian was obliterating my consciousness, I realized you had been the best part of my life. You always will be."

There is a high probability that his life will not last more than ten minutes after he enters the core disruptor engine. This is irrelevant. Abel feels sure that even if he lives longer than the usual mech life span of two hundred and fifty years, no experience will match knowing Noemi. No other human will ever come close.

Noemi smiles crookedly, the way humans do when they believe they may cry. "I love you, too."

He has so longed to hear her say this. But he must say, "You've been through a great deal these past months, especially the last three weeks. Your entire existence has been changed. If you wanted to be alone for a time after this—to consider your options—"

"I know my options." Noemi's voice trembles. "I chose to be with you before my hybridization. Maybe everything else about me changed, but not that. Not what I feel for you. Abel, *I love you*. It lights me up inside just looking at you. For the first time, I feel like I was born for a reason other than fighting for Genesis. Being a soldier...

that only gave me reasons to die. You've shown me reasons to live."

"Noemi," Abel says, then finds he has no more words. He gets to his feet, wanting only to take her into his arms—

"*We have engagement!*" Krall's voice says over comms. "*Get in there fast, Persephone.*"

Abel steps back, arms falling to his sides as he prepares himself.

The Battle of Earth has begun.

The ship's engines vibrate at a frequency that tells Abel they're coming in at high speed. Harriet will be steering them directly toward the core disruptor, because disarming it is by far their highest priority. An entire planet's life hangs in the balance.

If Genesis is going to target the *Persephone*, they'll know within seconds. Abel considers it more likely that the larger vessels actively firing upon Genesis's ships will draw their fire. But if someone takes time amid the fray to ID the *Persephone*, or even recognizes it . . .

But nobody fires. The ship is safe, at least for long enough to get them to the heart of the battle.

Time is short. Abel steps toward Noemi just as she steps toward him. They collide, clutching each other with all the fierceness that comes from knowing this could be the last time. She frames his face with her hands and kisses him, and for 1.13 seconds it feels as if the battle is far away.

At 1.14 seconds, vivid red light begins blinking off and on within the docking bay. It's the warning for the air lock to cycle. He kisses Noemi once more, then snaps on his helmet. She does the same, sealing it tightly, then activating the personal force field at her belt. Abel activates his as well, for shielding against the deep cold of space.

Noemi steps backward, hanging on to metal handholds as air begins to vent from the bay. He has just enough time to grab the propulsion pack and strap it around his waist before the *Persephone*'s door pinwheels open, revealing blackness, stars, and small pops of light in the distance— explosions from the battle.

The suction drags at Abel, and he gives in to it, letting the vacuum pull him into the void.

At first, he's tumbling through the emptiness of space, and all the planning and information they've done isn't enough to keep Abel from feeling very small, and very lost. But he fires the propulsion pack in three staccato bursts, which allows him to regain control over his momentum. The battle surrounds him in every direction.

Abel seeks and quickly finds his target. The core disruptor hangs in space approximately 0.61 kilometers beneath. With his propulsion pack, he powers downward toward it.

The trip is a hazardous one. Thousands of ships fire on one another from three hundred and sixty directions, varying distances away—but too many of them seem to be very, very close. It's a frenzy of energy and light. After only a few minutes, the death toll of this battle is already horrific. Amid the Consortium ships with their bright streaks of weapons fire, Genesis starfighters dashing about, and the darting, lethal warrior mechs lie at least a dozen vessels floating dark and inert. Everyone on board those vessels is now dead, dying, or hurtling through space in an escape pod—at least until a warrior mech spots them, in which case the pod will be destroyed on sight.

Fortunately Abel is too small a target to draw much attention. However, being hit accidentally, by a stray shot, will kill him every bit as surely as deliberate fire. So he uses all his considerable skill with trajectories to keep adjusting his course, dodging fire the entire way.

Noemi's voice comes through his helmet. *"Bet you wish you still had Smasher body armor around now."*

Her tone is deliberately light, so he matches it. "It wouldn't be worth the loss of dexterity. Though I must admit—it was rather enjoyable, smashing things."

"I'm within range of the first Damocles now," she says. *"Talk to you on the other side."* The channel snaps off.

Noemi's emotions were high moments ago, but already she's wholly focused on her task ahead. Abel feels a surge of pride. She will always be a soldier.

The core disruptor is now within 0.51 kilometers. Soon Genesis forces will spot him. They may not identify a single figure as a target, but there are no guarantees he won't be blown to pieces.

Hopefully, he'll have some protection.

Abel switches his comm unit to a different frequency, one Noemi specified for him. It ties him to Genesis communications—specifically, to one person. He says, "Captain Baz?"

After a pause, the voice comes through his helmet. *"Who the hell is breaking in on this line?"*

"It's Abel. Noemi told me how to contact you."

"Allahu akbar," Baz whispers. *"Tell me she's found a way to stop this madness."*

"Possibly." Abel can promise no more than that. "I'm attempting to board the core disruptor. I have no ship, only my exosuit. Some cover during my approach would be greatly appreciated."

For 2.1 seconds, Baz remains silent. Finally she says, *"This violates Genesis law—but Bellum Sanctum violates holy law. I know which I'd rather break. They've got me in a starfighter for this one, so I can handle this personally. Begin your approach, Abel. I'll cover you."*

Abel needs to remain focused on the core disruptor throughout his approach, so he can't look up to see exactly how difficult it is for Captain Baz to cover him. All he knows is that he makes it down unharmed.

As soon as he makes contact with his target, he activates

his mag boots so that he's locked to the metal surface. The core disruptor is unmanned. Earth might've kept mechs aboard to monitor this weapon all the way to its goal, but Genesis had no mechs to use. They've simply towed it here and preprogrammed a course.

So nobody's around to stop Abel as he pries open the outer panels and pulls himself into the interior. He has to find handholds within the various twists and turns of the panels and pipes that form the core disruptor's outer shell. To make progress forward, he unlocks the mag boots, pulls himself toward the center, then locks them again until he locates another handhold. It's slow going, since without artificial gravity, it feels as if he's moving underwater.

With every few meters he moves inward, the vibration becomes more intense. The forces are nothing compared to the vibration that will begin when the core disruptor is fully activated upon its collision with Earth. He's able to brace himself on the metal framework—barely—but will it be too strong for him to endure at the center?

Any human attempting this would've been killed minutes ago.

Finally, Abel reaches the center of the core disruptor and finds the surface of the engine. Abel feels the shaking throughout his body, violent almost to the point of pain.

Pain is irrelevant. Only the mission matters.

He pushes himself inside, hunched over with his hands

on the mag boots, which are holding him somewhat still. The few organic elements of his skeleton ache, and even his metal bones indicate stress fractures are imminent.

But he keeps going, and going, and—

Abel reaches the center of the engine. Instantly he's thrown against one wall, then another, then the floor. He is uncomfortably reminded of the principles of Brownian motion. There's nothing here to steady him, so he ricochets around uncontrollably.

An especially hard collision could shatter his helmet, or even his skull. That collision is inevitable if he's in here too much longer. A human's spine would've been crushed by now.

It's difficult for Abel to focus on the controls as he jerks from side to side; they're hardly more than a blur. But he has his memories of the last time he was here. Orienting himself as best he can, he grabs a console with one hand. This keeps him from being thrown around the room, but causes excruciating pain in his overstressed arm.

The arm that hurts doesn't matter. The other arm is free for him to reach for the controls, desperately trying to hit the correct one—

Suddenly the stabilizer field closes around Abel like a bubble. He sighs in relief as the engine's inner shielding steadies him. From there he can straighten himself, lock his mag boots to the floor, and study the controls in more depth. He hits one set of controls, then the next, deactivating functions one after the other.

At last, with a great groaning of the metal around him, the engine goes dead. Darkness surrounds Abel, save for the lights of his helmet, and he laughs out loud.

It takes him only 21.76 seconds to rip out the controls. Given enough time, perhaps, the core disruptor could be repaired—but no one will be able to do it in this battle.

With satisfaction he thinks, *Earth is saved.*

The way out is easier and faster than the way in. Abel emerges from the framework of the now-dead disruptor to stare out at the battle. As he does so, his smile fades.

Although the weapons fire has diminished, the fight continues. Worst of all, the Damocles ships are still in action. Either Noemi's self-destruct hasn't taken effect yet, or she hasn't been able to implement it at all.

Instantly he turns on comms again. "Noemi?" No reply. Her comms must still be off. "*Persephone?* What's our status?"

"*Abel!*" Zayan cries. "*You made it! Way to go on knocking that thing out—when it went black, half the Genesis ships gave up, like, that second, and it looks like Earth's leaders are starting to get the picture—*"

"Where is Noemi?"

This time Virginia answers. "*She's been in that center*

Damocles for an amount of time I would categorize as 'way the hell too long.' We're still picking up her signal, though."

Noemi's in trouble, but she's alive. Abel seizes onto this hope. "I need to get closer to her position, preferably within the next two minutes."

"How are you supposed to do that with just a propulsion pack?" Zayan protests.

"I'm not. I'll need you to take me there." Abel readies himself. "Bring yourself to my position and prepare to move toward the center Damocles on my mark."

"We're on it," Harriet says bravely. *"If we're in explosion range of the Damocles, then that's just how it is."*

"You're not going to stay in that position for more than one second. Just get me there."

Virginia sounds puzzled as she says, *"How are we supposed to pick you up and drop you off that fast?"*

Abel braces himself. "I'll handle that."

The *Persephone* zooms toward him, its silver teardrop bright even amid the flashes of weapons fire. He spots some minor weapons scarring on the hull, but his friends have kept this ship safe despite terrible odds.

Harriet's expert handling skills bring the ship almost directly to his location. No doubt she expects him to head to the air lock. Instead, he propels himself until his feet brush the hull—when he snaps on his mag boots. He lands as solidly on the *Persephone* as he would on a planet; the magnetic hold is as good as gravity.

No, better. He can cancel this the instant he needs it, and he's going to need it.

Abel straightens until he's standing atop his ship, looking out at the battle beyond. Through comms he says, "I'm on the hull. Let's go!"

To their credit, none of the crew asks questions. Instead, they take off toward the Damocles.

With no air in space to provide resistance, Abel can ride atop the ship effortlessly. His view of the Battle of Earth is unparalleled. Even now, in its final stages, the firepower is something to behold. Yet the most staggering thing, to him, is the sheer level of destruction around him. Ships from large transports to tiny starfighters drift lifelessly in the void. Here and there, his sharp eyes detect the glint of a destroyed Queen or Charlie in its armored exosuit. Yet too many mechs remain in action.

Abel took control of all the warrior mechs during the Battle of Genesis. The effort damaged him, and he suspects trying it again on a larger scale would be even more destructive, possibly fatal. But if this is the only way to end the battle, he'll have to try. He hopes it won't come to that, but it might.

He must protect Genesis. He must protect human lives. Noemi has sacrificed so much for this, and her sacrifices cannot have been in vain. Abel won't let that happen.

As the *Persephone* gets within range of the Damocles ship, he issues his last orders. "On my mark, accelerate—then, exactly three seconds later, pivot in another direction."

"*Which direction?*" Harriet asks.

"Whichever seems safest." The position is irrelevant, as long as his friends are safe. "Three seconds precisely. Understood?"

"*Aye, Captain!*"

"On my mark—now."

The *Persephone* speeds toward the white bulk of the Damocles at incredible speed. Abel counts the nanoseconds. At three seconds, he releases the mag boots—and soars through space with that same velocity, alone. With no air resistance, Abel could keep this momentum for a nearly infinite amount of time.

But he keeps going only until he picks up Noemi's signal.

Immediately, Abel fires the propulsion pack in the opposite direction to slow himself down, then angles it to take him closer to Noemi. She's visible to the naked eye by this time—drifting from the Damocles in her exosuit.

Powerless. In no direction.

Fear grips Abel for the 0.82 seconds before he sees Noemi's arms move. She's alive.

It feels as though hope alone is powering him through space. As the battle flashes and sparks all around him, Abel angles himself for intercept and moderates his speed.

They collide, body against body, two exosuited figures tumbling through space. He'd slowed down enough to make sure they wouldn't injure each other, but as soon as he's gripping Noemi tightly in one arm, he accelerates again. Together they fly away from the Damocles as fast as the propulsion pack will take them.

Noemi seems frantic, but then her eyes light up and she brings her helmet to touch his. Abel thinks this is a gesture of affection until she shouts, "A Queen came after me in the ship—took out my propulsion pack, my comms—"

The muffled sound comes to him through the vibration of her helmet against his. Her ingenuity makes Abel smile. "You're all right?"

"Just banged up. Still, I'm almost positive I got the self-destruct going, so we have to get the hell out of here, *right now*—"

Abel glances back at the Damocles ship. Can they make it out of range? He can't be sure.

The Damocles explodes. Shards fly out in every direction—pale metal and stark beams, all of it at supersonic speeds. If even one piece of shrapnel gets through their force fields and rips the exosuits, they're dead.

Abel hugs Noemi tightly, trying to shield her body with his own. She struggles against him, trying to do the same thing....

But the dust and debris of the explosion simply shimmer past them, a glittery tide in the emptiness of space.

"Look!" Noemi points as another Damocles ship blows up. Another. And another. Her theory about the interconnectedness of the ships was correct. Abel watches the Damocles explode, one after the other, drawing a large circle around the battle.

Instantly the other Earth forces pull back. Genesis begins a retreat. The fire slows, then stops.

Noemi closes her eyes. Abel knows she's saying a prayer of thanksgiving.

Genesis can no longer destroy Earth. Earth can no longer dominate any of the colony worlds.

The Liberty War is over, and a new era has begun.

39

TWENTY DAYS LATER, NOEMI ONCE AGAIN STANDS ON planet Genesis, within the Hall of Elders.

But it's not the same Council any longer. Elder Cho, and every other member who voted to use the Bellum Sanctum strategy against Earth, has been forced from office.

Genesis has chosen new leadership. The planet is connected with the greater galaxy now, and always will be. Its future will look very different from its past... which is the point this hearing is supposed to make, as it's being broadcast across the entire world.

Elder Zhang looks down at Noemi. "You chose to disobey every standard military protocol by moving to disarm Genesis forces. Normally this would be treason on the highest order. But the Bellum Sanctum strategy was one this planet should've abandoned decades ago."

"It should never have been entertained at all," says Elder Pergolesi. "It is to the enduring shame of this planet that any of our leaders would ever have stooped to such brutal tactics, even in the service of our people."

Noemi remains silent. She knows there have to have been others—many others—in the government and military who condoned Bellum Sanctum. But they were a minority, a powerful minority but hopefully a small one. The rest of her people will be the ones determining Genesis's future.

The war is over, but the work isn't done. Earth is in the middle of a political revolution, and the other colony worlds are setting up independent leadership of their own. (Even those worlds that plan to remain allied with Earth—Cray, and possibly Stronghold—want to be more than mere colonies from now on.) Haven requires more medical supplies, more basic settlement provisions like plumbing and energy generation, and all the planets are banding together to help them.

Ephraim Dunaway is coordinating the medical efforts on Haven, with the help of Delphine Ondimba. Thanks to him, the Cobweb regimen is being distributed planetwide, and soon throughout the galaxy. Virginia Redbird is back on Cray, taking part in the massive elections there, and celebrating with Ludwig and Fon, who have instantly gone from traitors to heroes.

But Noemi is happiest thinking of Harriet Dixon and Zayan Thakur, who have chosen their home on

Genesis—one in Goshen, not far from where she grew up. When she visited yesterday, they were unpacking their few belongings into their new apartment in one of the smaller communes. Neighbors had donated some small pieces of furniture, and Abel sent down Mansfield's finer furnishings from the *Persephone*. Both Zayan and Harriet were aglow with excitement. Maybe only people who've had no choice but to wander the stars are the ones who find the greatest joy in finally standing still.

Elder Pergolesi leans forward. "Your efforts were not sanctioned—but under the circumstances, initiative was called for. We're now entering into an alliance that brings us more settlers, but allows us to require that any and all settlers obey the ecological rules currently in place, and swear the Oath of Religious Tolerance. We'll be able to set the number of settlers at an amount we can support without damaging our world."

This is grandstanding, of course. Her fate was determined long before the public hearing was set. The newly established Council just wants to separate itself from the decisions of the past, and help make Genesis ready for its part in a bigger galaxy.

Noemi doesn't mind playing a role. It's one last thing she can do to help her planet. After this, she will have fulfilled her Directive One.

Pergolesi adds, "We are capable of changing. We can

preserve the best and most necessary elements of our society while still opening ourselves to new people, new ideas, and new possibilities."

The crowds gathered outside—who are watching via screens set up in the main pavilion—murmur in approval, loudly enough for the noise to reverberate in the hall. Noemi's chest swells with pride.

Elder Waititi says, "As for Earth, it no longer has the military means to dominate the colony worlds by force. On those worlds, people who helped fight against Earth's tyranny are being celebrated as heroes."

"Earth is undergoing considerable political unrest," Elder Zhang adds, sounding a little too pleased. "No doubt a new, better government will eventually emerge. But in the meantime, they're unable to send basic supplies to Cray and Stronghold, the two planets that can't feed their populations without outside help. Neither Kismet nor Haven can provide as much as those worlds will need—"

"But we can," says Elder Pergolesi. "Let us ensure the freedom of others from Earth's control, as we ourselves have been freed."

Cheering erupts outside, so loud it's deafening even from here. Noemi laughs out loud—which isn't exactly protocol when addressing the Council of Elders, but nobody seems to mind.

Later, after the hearing has ended and the biggest

celebration in Genesis history has begun, Elder Pergolesi approaches Noemi. Pergolesi is as friendly to her as anyone on the Council could be, and yet her tone is ominous. "We've yet to settle the question of Darius Akide's death, and the culpability of the mech Abel."

Noemi brought the *Persephone* down to the surface, but Abel remains in deep space, on a Consortium ship. Both of them knew better than to risk his coming here again. She looks Pergolesi in the eye. "After all Abel's done for you, you still treat him like a criminal."

"We recognize the mech's contributions." It cost Pergolesi to say that; Noemi can tell. "But none of it is a justification for murder. A Genesis court should hear this matter, and decide."

Noemi lifts her chin. "Abel can't be charged with murder."

Pergolesi's impatience is clear. "Yes, yes, you claim he acted in self-defense—"

"This doesn't have anything to do with whether or not Abel acted in self-defense. I mean, you can't charge him, any more than you could charge...a door. A toaster. Any other inanimate object."

Confusion appears in Pergolesi's face, but it's easy to see that she's begun to catch on. Encouraged, Noemi presses her point:

"The government of Genesis denied Abel permission

to settle on Genesis, because he wasn't a human being and couldn't have human rights. Well, if he doesn't have the same rights as anyone else, he doesn't have the same responsibility either. As far as the Council of this planet is concerned, Abel is a piece of machinery that only acts as programmed. Pieces of machinery aren't responsible for their actions, so they can't be charged with crimes."

Watching Pergolesi struggle with that logic is delicious. She clearly wants so badly to find a way to punish Abel without granting him personhood—but there isn't one. The prejudice of Genesis's leaders protects Abel as no other force could.

"The question of Abel's personhood may be raised at a future date," Pergolesi finally responds. "At which point, he may be asked to stand trial."

Noemi folds her arms. "At that same point, you'll have to concede that what Akide tried to do to Abel was attempted murder. Of course, Akide shooting *me* has always been attempted murder, but you guys seem okay with that."

Finally, Pergolesi drops her eyes, and her cheeks flush. "Your heroism will not be questioned again, Vidal."

Noemi remains silent as she wonders, *Does she expect me to thank her? If so, too bad.*

"One more thing," Noemi says. "As angry as I am with Darius Akide—I finally realized why he tried to use Abel to close the Gate. He wanted to keep Genesis from ever using the Bellum Sanctum strategy. Even after years of war, he knew nothing could justify the destruction of a world. Akide was the only member of the Council with that much decency. I think that deserves to be remembered."

Stiffly, Pergolesi nods. "It has been noted." Noemi turns to go, but the Elder adds, "Some members have said that— as you are still more organic than mechanical—the decision to refuse you residence on Genesis should be reconsidered."

"Thanks but no thanks," she says. "My future is in the stars."

As Pergolesi walks away, Noemi's face falls. Leaving Genesis isn't as easy as she made it out to be. This planet will always feel like home. When she thinks of the rolling grasslands of Goshen, and how she'll probably never see them again, she feels close to tears.

But she won't compromise who and what she is for Genesis ever again. It's hard to think of never returning here... but her planet is on the verge of even greater change. Millions of new settlers will arrive over the next few years. Those settlers will obey the basic rules, but they'll also bring their own influences. The culture will shift; the leadership won't always be so inflexible.

Someday she may return to Goshen. If she does, she'll bring Abel with her. Then, Noemi will truly be at home.

She looks up into the sky—where Abel waits for her— and smiles.

One Year Later

"No matter what happens," Noemi says, "this should be more fun than our first trip through a Gate together."

"Unless the new star system has unexpected hazards, such as an asteroid field, violent solar eruptions, or other intelligent life that reacts with hostility to unannounced alien visitors." Abel pauses, then adds, "But this will *probably* be more fun."

Noemi grins. By now she knows he'll never entirely drop this more formal way of speaking, and she never wants him to. The past year has been the happiest and most exciting of her life. Noemi always scoffed at people who mooned around like being in love was the only worthwhile thing in life. It *isn't* the only thing that matters... but love's the most incredible feeling she's ever known. She wouldn't trade the experience of loving Abel, or being loved by him, for all the worlds.

The *Persephone* is holding position in the Kismet system. In front of them is the newly completed Gate, currently being tested and checked by a team from Cray. While early scans showed promise, nobody will really know whether the planet beyond is habitable until it's checked out in detail. Unknown health hazards are a distinct possibility.

That's why a mech and a hybrid are the perfect team to visit that system for the very first time.

"It's going to be an adventure," Noemi says.

Abel takes her hand. "You wouldn't have it any other way."

"No. I wouldn't." She smiles.

The comms crackle with Virginia Redbird's voice. *"Okay, both unmanned probes have come back in one piece. All readings come back normal. Looks like you guys are cleared for departure."*

"Thanks, Virginia," Noemi says as Abel ignites the mag engines.

"Bring me back a souvenir!"

Abel gives Noemi a look. While he may be outwardly calmer than she is, she's learned to tell when he's as excited as a little kid, like he is right now. "Shall we?"

A wave of gratitude flows through her, for Abel, for this adventure, for every part of the life she's leading. She says only, "Let's go."

The *Persephone* shoots forward toward the Gate. Noemi and Abel fly together toward a brand-new planet, one they'll be the first to stand on, a world the two of them will name.

Steve Hammond

Claudia Gray

is the *New York Times* bestselling author of many science fiction and paranormal fantasy books for young adults, including *Defy the Stars*, *Defy the Worlds*, the Firebird series, the Evernight series, the Spellcaster series, and *Fateful*. She's also had a chance to work in a galaxy far, far away as the author of the Star Wars novels *Lost Stars*, *Bloodline*, and *Leia, Princess of Alderaan*. Born a fangirl, she loves obsessing over geeky movies and TV shows, as well as reading and occasionally writing fanfiction; however, she periodically leaves the house to go kayaking, do a little hiking, or travel the world. She will take your Jane Austen trivia challenge any day, anytime. Currently she lives in New Orleans.